Jack Vance was born in 1920 and educated at the University of California, first as a mining engineer, then majoring in physics and finally in journalism. He has since had a varied career: his first story was written while he was serving in the US Merchant Marine during the Second World War. During the late 1940s and early 1950s, he contributed a variety of short stories to the science fiction and fantasy magazines of the time. His first published book was THE DYING EARTH (1950). Since then he has produced several series of novels – for example, the *Planet of Adventure*, *Durdane* and *Demon Princes* series – as well as various individual novels.

Jack Vance has won the two most coveted trophies of the science fiction world, the Hugo Award and the Nebula Award. He has also won the Edgar Award of the Mystery Writers of America for his novel THE MAN IN THE CAGE (1960). In addition, he has written scripts for television science fiction series.

Jack Vance's non–literary interests include blue-water sailing and early jazz. He lives in Oakland, California.

D1147536

By the same author

The Five Gold Bands
Son of the Tree
Vandals of the Void
To Live Forever
Big Planet
The Languages of Pao
The Man in the Cage
The Dragon Masters
The Houses of Iszm
Future Tense
The Moon Moth
The Blue World
The Last Castle
Emphyrio
Fantasms and Magics
Trullion: Alastor 2262
Marune: Alastor 993
Wyst: Alastor 1716
Showboat World
The Best of Jack Vance
Lyonesse I

Demon Princes series
Star King
The Killing Machine
The Palace of Love
The Face
The Book of Dreams

Planet of Adventure series
City of the Chasch
Servants of the Wankh
The Dirdir
The Pnume

The Durdane series
The Anome
The Brave Free Man
The Asutra

The Dying Earth series
The Dying Earth
The Eyes of the Overworld
Cugel's Saga
Rhialto the Marvellous

JACK VANCE

Lyonesse II

The Green Pearl

GRAFTON BOOKS

A Division of the Collins Publishing Group

LONDON GLASGOW
TORONTO SYDNEY AUCKLAND

Grafton Books
A Division of the Collins Publishing Group
8 Grafton Street, London W1X 3LA

Published by Grafton Books 1986

ISBN 0-586-06751-5

Printed and bound in Great Britain by
Collins, Glasgow

Set in Clarendon

For David Alexander
Tim Underwood and Chuck Miller
Kirby, Kay and Ralph
John II and Norma

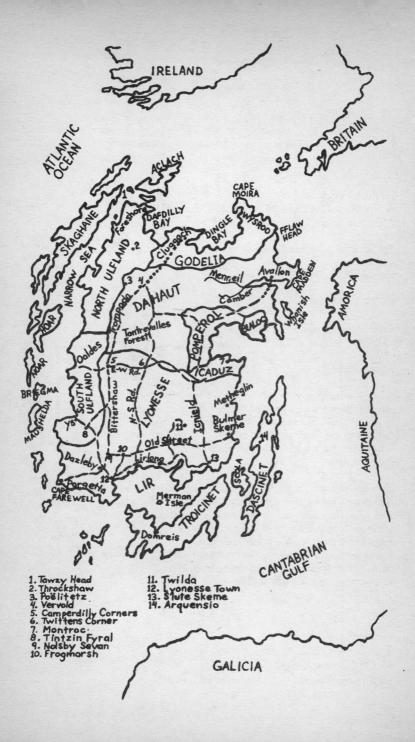

IRELAND

ATLANTIC OCEAN

BRITAIN

ACLACH

CAPE MOIRA

1

SKAGHANE

NARROW SEA

Foreshore

DAFDILLY BAY

DINGLE BAY

WYSROD

FFLAW HEAD

2

Cloggach

GODELIA

NORTH ULFLAND

3 4

Mennreil

Avallon

CAPE RADDEM

XNAR

DAHAUT

Camber

Timpoda

Winnish Isle

AMORICA

Tantrevalles Forest

POMPEROL

BALOC

Oaldes

5   6

CADUZ

7

BREGMA

E-W Rd.

SOUTH ULFLAND

MAUDELIA

Bittershaw

N-S Rd.

LYONESSE

Metheglin

Ichield

Bulmer Skeme

5 8

11

Dazleby

10   Old Street

Lirlong

13

AQUITAINE

Fergetta

CAPE FAREWELL

12

LIR

Merman Isle

SCOLA

14

DASCINET

TROICINET

Domreis

CANTABRIAN GULF

1. Tawzy Head
2. Throckshaw
3. Poëlitetz
4. Vervold
5. Camperdilly Corners
6. Twittens Corner
7. Montroc
8. Tintzin Fyral
9. Nolsby Sevan
10. Frogmarsh

11. Twilda
12. Lyonesse Town
13. Slute Skeme
14. Arquensio

GALICIA

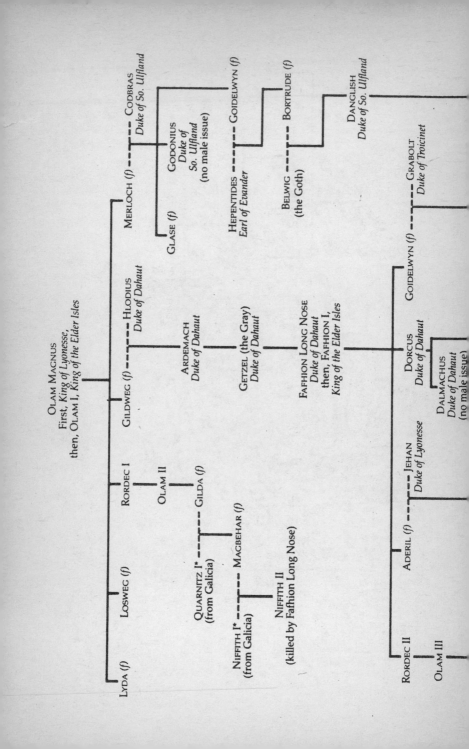

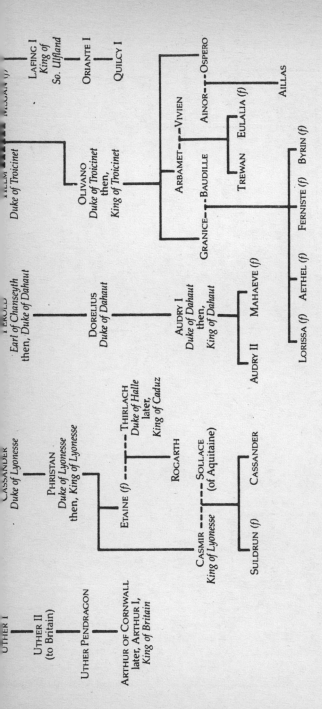

Female Issue = (f)

*The Galician Cuckoos

Siblings away from chain of descent,
collateral lines, and grass-marriages are not
indicated to avoid over-complexity.

Chapter 1

I

VISBHUME, apprentice to the recently dead Hippolito, applied to the sorcerer Tamurello for a similar post, but was denied. Visbhume then offered for sale a box containing articles which he had carried away from Hippolito's house. Tamurello, glancing into the box, saw enough to warrant his interest and paid over Visbhume's price.

Among the objects in the box were fragments of an old manuscript. When news of the transaction came by chance to the ears of the witch Desmëi, she wondered if the fragments might not fill out the gaps in a manuscript which she had long been trying to restore. Without delay she took herself to Tamurello's manse Faroli in the Forest of Tantrevalles, and there applied for permission to inspect the fragments.

With all courtesy Tamurello displayed the fragments. "Are these the missing pieces?"

Desmëi looked through the fragments. "They are indeed!"

"In that case they are now yours," said Tamurello. "Accept them with my compliments."

"I will do so most gratefully!" said Desmëi. As she packed the fragments into a portfolio, she studied Tamurello from the corner of her eye. She said: "It is somewhat odd that we have not met before."

Tamurello smilingly agreed. "The world is long and wide. New experiences await us always, for the most part to our pleasure." He inclined his head with unmistakable gallantry toward his guest.

"Nicely spoken, Tamurello!" said Desmëi. "Truly, you are most gracious!"

"Only when circumstances warrant. Will you take refreshment? Here is a soft wine pressed from the Alhadra grape."

For a time the two sat discussing themselves and their concepts.

Desmëi, finding Tamurello both stimulating and large with vitality, decided to take him for her lover.

Tamurello, who was keen for novelty, made no difficulties and matched her energy with his own, and for a season all was well. However, in due course Tamurello came to feel that Desmëi, to an enervating degree, lacked both lightness and grace. He began to blow hot and cold, to Desmëi's deep concern. At first she chose to interpret his waning ardor as a lover's teasing: the naughtiness, so to speak, of a pampered darling. She thrust herself upon his attention, tempting him with first one coy trick, then another.

Tamurello became ever more unresponsive. Desmëi sat long hours with him, analyzing their relationship in all its phases, while Tamurello drank wine and looked moodily off through the trees.

Neither sighs nor sentiment, Desmëi discovered, affected Tamurello. She learned that he was equally proof against cajolery, while reproaches seemed only to bore him. At last, in a facetious manner, Desmëi spoke of a former lover who had caused her pain and hinted of the misfortunes which thereafter had dogged his life. Finally she saw that she had captured Tamurello's attention, and veered to more cheerful topics.

Tamurello let prudence guide his conduct, and once again Desmëi had no complaints.

After a hectic month Tamurello found that he could no longer maintain his glassy-eyed zest. Once again he began to avoid Desmëi, but now that she understood the forces which guided his conduct, she brought him smartly to heel.

Desperate at last, Tamurello invoked a spell of ennui upon Desmëi: an influence so quiet, gradual and unobtrusive that she never noticed its coming. She grew weary of the world, its sordid vanities, futile ambitions and pointless pleasures, but so strong was her disposition that she never thought to suspect a change in herself. From Tamurello's point of view, the spell was a success.

For a period Desmëi moved in gloomy contemplation through the windy halls of her palace on the beach near Ys, then at last decided to abandon the world to its own melancholy devices. She made herself ready for death, and from her terrace watched the sun set for the last time.

At midnight she sent a bubble of significance over the mountains to Faroli, but when dawn arrived, no message had returned.

Desmëi pondered a long hour, and at last thought to wonder at the dejection which had brought her to such straits.

Her decision was irrevocable. In her final hour, however, she bestirred herself to work a set of wonderful formulations, the like of which had never been known before.

The motives for these final acts were then and thereafter beyond calculation, for her thinking had become vague and eerie. She surely felt betrayal and rancor, and no doubt a measure of spite, and seemed also urged by forces of sheer creativity. In any event she produced a pair of superlative objects, which perhaps she hoped might be accepted as the projection of her own ideal self, and that the beauty of these objects and their symbolism might be impinged upon Tamurello.

In the light of further circumstances* her success in this regard was flawed, and the triumph, if the word could so be used, went rather to Tamurello.

In achieving her aims, Desmëi used a variety of stuff: salt from the sea, soil from the summit of Mount Khambaste in Ethiopia, exudations and pastes, as well as elements of her personal substance. So she created a pair of wonderful beings: exemplars of all the graces and beauties. The woman was Melancthe; the man was Faude Carfilhiot.

Still all was not done. As the two stood naked and mindless in the workroom, the dross remaining in the vat yielded a rank green vapor. After a startled breath, Melancthe shrank back and spat the taste from her mouth. Carfilhiot, however, found the reek to his liking and inhaled it with all avidity.

Some years later, the castle Tintzin Fyral fell to the armies of Troicinet. Carfilhiot was captured and hanged from a grotesquely high gibbet, in order to send an unmistakably significant image toward both Tamurello at Faroli to the east and to King Casmir of Lyonesse, to the south.

In due course Carfilhiot's corpse was lowered to the ground, placed on a pyre, and burned to the music of bagpipes and flutes. In the midst of the rejoicing the flames gave off a gout of foul green vapor, which, caught by the wind, blew out over the sea. Swirling low and mingling with spume from the waves, the fume condensed to become a green pearl which sank to the ocean floor, where eventually it was ingested by a large flounder.

II

SOUTH ULFLAND FACED ON THE SEA from Ys in the south to Suarach in the north: a succession of shingle beaches and rocky headlands along a coast for the most part barren and bleak. The three best harbours were at Ys and Suarach and at Oäldes, between the two. Elsewhere harbours, good or bad, were infrequent, and often no more than coves enclosed by the hook of a headland.

---

*The details are chronicled in *LYONESSE I: Suldrun's Garden.*

Twenty miles south of Oäldes, a line of crags entered the ocean and with the help of a stone breakwater, gave shelter to several dozen fishing boats. Around the harbour huddled the village Mynault: a clutch of narrow stone houses, two taverns and a market-place.

In one of the houses lived the fisherman Sarles, a man black-haired and stocky, with heavy hips and a small round paunch. His face, which was round, pale and moony, showed a constant frown of puzzlement, as if he found life and logic always at odds.

The bloom of Sarles' youth was gone forever, but Sarles had little to show for his years of more or less diligent toil. Sarles blamed bad luck, although if his spouse Liba were to be believed, indolence was by far the larger factor.

Sarles kept his boat the *Preval* drawn up on the shingle directly in front of his house, which made for convenience. He had inherited the *Preval* from his father, and the craft was now old and worn, with every seam leaking and every joint working. Sarles well knew the deficiencies of the *Preval* and sailed it out upon the sea only when the weather was fine.

Liba, like Sarles, was somewhat portly. Though older than Sarles, she commanded far more energy and often asked him: "Why are you not out fishing today, like the other men?"

Sarles' reply might be: "The wind is sure to pipe up later this afternoon; the dead-eyes on the port shrouds simply cannot take so much strain."

"Then why not replace the dead-eyes? You have nothing better to do."

"Bah, woman, you understand nothing of boats. The weakest part always breaks first. If I fixed the dead-eyes, then the shrouds might part, or a real blow might push the mast-step right through the bottom of the boat."

"In that case, replace the shrouds, then repair the strakes."

"Easier said than done! It would be a waste of time and I would be throwing good money after bad."

"But you waste much time at the tavern where you also throw away good money, and by the handfuls."

"Woman, enough! Would you deny me my single relaxation?"

"Indeed I would! Everyone else is out on the water while you sit in the sun catching flies. Your cousin Junt left the harbour before dawn to make sure of his mackerel! Why did you not do the same?"

"Junt does not suffer miseries of the back as I do," muttered Sarles. "Also he sails the *Lirlou*, which is a fine new boat."

"It is the fisherman who catches fish, not the boat. Junt brings in six times the catch you do."

"Only because his son Tamas fishes beside him."

"Which means that each out-fishes you three times over."

Sarles cried out in anger: "Woman, when will you learn to curb your tongue? I would be off to the tavern this instant had I one coin to rub against another."

"Why not use the leisure to repair the *Preval*?"

Sarles threw his hands in the air and went down to the beach where he assessed the deficiences of his craft. With nothing better to do, he carved a new dead-eye for his shrouds. Cordage was too dear for his pocket, so he performed a set of make-shift splices, which strengthened the shrouds but made an unsightly display.

And so it went. Sarles gave the *Preval* only what maintenance was needed to keep it afloat, and sallied out among the reefs and rocks only when conditions were optimum, which was not often.

One day even Sarles became alarmed. With a soft breeze blowing on-shore, he rowed from the harbour, hoisted his sprit-sail, set up the back-stay, adjusted the sheets and bowled nicely across the swells and out toward the reefs, where the fish were most plentiful. . . . Peculiar! thought Sarles. Why did his back-stay sag when he had only just set it up taut? Making an investigation, he discovered a daunting fact: the stern-post to which the stay was attached had become so rotten from age and attacks of the worm that it was about to break loose to the tension of the back-stay, thereby causing a great disaster.

Sarles rolled up his eyes and gritted his teeth in annoyance. Now, without fail or delay, he must make a whole set of tedious repairs, and he could expect neither leisure nor wine-bibbing until the repairs were done. To finance the repairs he might even be forced to beg a place aboard the *Lirlou*, which again was most tiresome, since it meant that he would be forced to work Junt's hours.

For the nonce, he shifted the back-stay to one of the stern-cleats, which, in mild weather such as that of today, would suffice.

Sarles fished for two hours, during which time he caught a single flounder. When he cleaned the fish, its belly fell open and out rolled a magnificent green pearl, of a quality far beyond Sarles' experience. Marvelling at his good fortune, he again threw out his lines but now the breeze began to freshen, and concerned with the state of his make-shift back-stay, Sarles hoisted anchor, raised his sail and turned his bow toward Mynault, and as he sailed he gloated upon the beautiful green pearl, the very touch of which sent shivers of delight along his nerves.

Once more in the harbour, Sarles beached his boat and set out for home, only to meet his cousin Junt.

"What?" cried Junt. "Back so soon from your work? It is not yet noon! What have you caught? A single flounder? Sarles, you will die in penury if you do not take yourself in hand! Truly you should give the *Preval* a good work-over and then fish with zeal, so that you may do something for yourself and your old age."

Nettled by the criticism, Sarles retorted: "What of you? Why are you not out in your fine *Lirlou*? Do you fear a bit of wind?"

"Not at all! I would fish and gladly, wind or no wind, but for caulking and fresh pitch done to *Lirlou's* seams."

As a rule Sarles was neither clever, spiteful, nor mischievous, his worst vice being sloth and a surly obstinacy in the face of chiding from his spouse. But now, impelled by a sudden tingle of crafty malice, he said: "Well then, if zeal rives you so urgently, there is the *Preval*; sail out to the reef and fish until you have had enough."

Junt gave a derisive grunt. "It is a sad comedown for me after working my fine *Lirlou*! Still, I believe that I will take you at your word. It is odd, but I cannot sleep well unless I have rousted up a good catch of fish from the deep."

"I wish you good luck," said Sarles and continued along the jetty. The wind, so he noted, had shifted and now blew from the north.

At the market Sarles sold his flounder for a decent price, then paused to reflect. He pulled the pearl from his pocket and considered it anew: a beautiful thing, though the green luster was unusual and even — it must be admitted — a trifle unsettling.

Sarles grinned a curious mindless grin and tucked the pearl back into his pocket. He marched across the square to the tavern, where he poured a good half-pint of wine down his throat. The first called for another, and as Sarles started on his second half-pint he was accosted by one of his cronies, a certain Juliam, who asked: "How goes the world? No fishing today?"

"I am not up to it today, owing to my sore back. Also, Junt decided that he wished to borrow *Preval* and I told him 'Go to it; fish all night, if you are so frantic in your zeal!' So off went Junt in my good old *Preval*."

"Ah well, that was generous of you!"

"Why not? After all, he is my cousin and blood is thicker than water."

"True."

Sarles finished his wine and strolled out to the end of the jetty. He scanned the sea with care but neither to the north, the west, nor the south could he glimpse the patched yellow sail of the *Preval*.

He turned away and went back along the jetty. Down on the shingle other fishermen were beaching their boats. Sarles went down and made inquiries in regard to Junt. "From the kindness of my heart I let him take out my *Preval*, though I warned him that the wind was rising and seemed to be veering to the north."

"He was out by Scratch Bottom an hour ago," said one of the fishermen. "Junt will fish while honest men drink wine!"

Sarles scanned the sea. "Possibly true, but I do not see him now. The wind is swinging about and he will be in trouble if he does not head for the harbour soon."

"Never fear for an old sea-dog like Junt, in a stout boat such as the *Lirlou*," said a fisherman who had just come up.

The first fisherman gave a raucous laugh. "But he is aboard the *Preval*!"

"Aha. That is something else again. Sarles, you would be wise to make repairs."

"Yes, yes," muttered Sarles. "In due course. I can neither walk on water nor blow gold coins out of my nose."

Sunset came and still Junt failed to return to Mynault harbour. Sarles finally reported the circumstances to Liba. "Today my back was poorly, and I could not fish over-long. From motives of generosity I allowed Junt the use of my boat. He has not yet returned and I fear that he has been blown off down the coast, or even has wrecked the *Preval*. I suppose this should be a lesson for me."

Liba stared. "For you? What of Junt and his family?"

"I am concerned on both counts. That goes without saying. However, I have not told you yet of my amazing good luck."

"Indeed? Your back is well so that finally you can work? Or you have lost your taste for wine?"

"Woman, control your tongue or you will feel the weight of my hand! I am bored with acrid jokes."

"Well then, what is your luck?"

Sarles displayed the pearl. "What do you think of that?"

Liba looked down at the gem. "Hmm. Curious. I have never heard of a green pearl. Are you sure it is genuine?"

"Of course! Do you take me for a fool? It is worth a goodly sum."

Liba turned away. "It gives me the chills."

"Is not that just like a woman? Where is my supper? What! Gruel? Why cannot you cook a tasty pot of soup, like other women?"

"I should work miracles, when the cupboard is bare? If you caught more fish and drank less wine we would eat better."

"Bah! From now on all will be different."

During the night Sarles was troubled by unsettling dreams. Faces peered at him through swirls of mist, then spoke gravely aside to each other. Try as he might he could understand none of the comments. A few of the faces seemed familiar, but Sarles could put no names to them.

In the morning Junt still had not returned in the *Preval*. By virtue of established custom, Sarles therefore became privileged to fish from the fine new *Lirlou*. Tamas, Junt's son, wished also to go out aboard the *Lirlou* but this Sarles would not allow. "I prefer to fish by myself."

Tamas made a hot protest. "That is not reasonable! I must protect my family's interests!"

Sarles raised his finger high. "Not so fast! Are you forgetting that I also have interests? The *Lirlou* becomes my own until Junt returns me my *Preval* safe and sound. If you want to fish, you must make other arrangements."

Sarles sailed the *Lirlou* out to the fishing grounds, rejoicing in the strength of the craft and the convenience of the gear. Today his luck was unusually good; fish fairly seized at his lines and the baskets in the hold became filled to the brim, and Sarles sailed back to Mynault congratulating himself. Tonight he would eat good soup or even a roast fowl.

Two months passed, during which Sarles profited from fine catches, while nothing seemed to go right for Tamas. One evening Tamas went to the house of Sarles, hoping to make some sort of adjustment in a situation which no one in Mynault considered totally fair, though all agreed that Sarles had acted only within his rights.

Tamas found Liba alone, sitting by the hearth spinning thread. Tamas came to the middle of the room and looked all around. "Where is Sarles?"

"At the tavern, or so I would expect, pouring his gut full of wine." Liba spoke in a flat voice which held a metallic overtone. She glanced at Tamas over her shoulder, then returned to her spindle. "Whatever you want you will not get. He is suddenly a man of property, and struts around like a grandee."

"Still, we must have an understanding!" declared Tamas. "He lost his rotten hulk and gained the *Lirlou*, at the expense of myself, my mother and my sisters. We have lost everything through no fault of our own. We ask only that Sarles deal fairly with us, and give us our share."

Liba moved her shoulders in a stony shrug. "It is useless to talk to me. I can do nothing with him. He is a different man since he brought home his green pearl." She raised her eyes to the mantel, where the pearl rested in a saucer.

Tamas went to look at the gem. He took it up and hefted it in his fingers, then whistled through his teeth. "This is a valuable object! It would buy another *Lirlou*! It would make me rich!"

Liba glanced at him in surprise. Was this the voice of Tamas, everywhere considered the very soul of rectitude? The green pearl seemed to corrupt with greed and selfishness all those who touched it! She turned back to her spinning. "Tell me nothing; what I do not know I can not prevent. I abhor the thing; it gazes at me like an evil eye."

Tamas uttered a queer high-pitched chuckle: so odd that Liba glanced at him sidelong in surprise.

"Just so!" said Tamas. "It is a time for a righting of wrongs! If Sarles complains, let him come to me!" With the pearl in his hand, he ran from the house. Liba sighed and returned to her spinning, with a heavy lump of apprehension in her chest.

An hour passed with no sound but the sough of the wind in the chimney and an occasional sputter of the fire. Then came the lurching thud of Sarles' steps as he staggered home from the tavern. He thrust the door wide, stood a moment in the opening, his face round as a plate under the untidy ledges of his black hair. His eyes darted here and there and halted on the saucer; he went to look and found the saucer empty. He uttered a cry of anguish. "Where is the pearl, the lovely green pearl?"

Liba spoke in her even voice. "Tamas came to talk with you. Since you were not here he took the pearl."

Sarles gave a howl of rage. "Why did you not stop him?"

"It is none of my affair. You must settle the matter with Tamas."

Sarles moaned in fury. "You could have stayed him; you gave him the pearl!" He lurched at her with clubbed fists; she raised the spindle and thrust it into his left eye.

Sarles clapped his hand to the bloody socket, while Liba stood back, awed by the magnitude of her deed.

Sarles looked at her with his right eye, and stepped slowly forward. Liba, groping behind her, found a broom of tied withes which she lifted and held ready. Sarles came forward one step at a time. Never taking his eye from Liba, he bent and picked up a short-handled axe. Liba screamed and thrust the broom into Sarles' face, then ran for the door. Sarles seized her hair and, pulling her back, did gruesome work with the axe.

Neighbors had been attracted by the screams. Men seized Sarles and took him to the square. The town elders were summoned from their beds and came blinking out to do justice by the light of lanterns.

The crime was manifest; the murderer was known, and there was nothing to be gained by delay. Sentence was passed; Sarles was marched to the hostler's barn and hanged from the hay derrick, while the village population stared in wonder to see their neighbor kick and jerk by lantern light.

III

OALDES, TWENTY MILES NORTH OF MYNAULT, had long served the South Ulfish kings as their seat, though it lacked the grace and historical presence of Ys, and showed to poor advantage when compared to

Avallon and Lyonesse Town. To Tamas, however, Oäldes with its market square and busy harbour seemed the very definition of urbanity.

He stabled his horse and made a breakfast of fish stew at a dockside tavern, all the while wondering where best to sell his wonderful pearl, that he might realize a maximum gain.

Tamas made a guarded inquiry of the landlord: "I put you this question: if someone wished to sell a pearl of value, where would he find the best price?"

"Pearls, eh? You will find small clamor for pearls at Oäldes. Here we spend our miserable few coins on bread and codfish. An onion in the stew is all the pearl most of us will ever see. Still, show me your wares."

Somewhat reluctantly Tamas allowed the landlord a glimpse of the green pearl.

"A prodigy!" declared the landlord. "Or is it a cunning puddle of green glass?"

"It is a pearl," said Tamas shortly.

"Perhaps so. I have seen a pink pearl from Hadramaut, and a white pearl from India, both adorning the ears of sea-captains. Let me look once more on your green jewel. . . . Ah! It glows with a virulent light! There, yonder, is the booth of a Sephard goldsmith; perhaps he will offer you a price."

Tamas took the pearl to the goldsmith's booth and laid it upon the counter. "How much gold and how much silver will you pay out for this fine gem?"

The goldsmith pushed a long nose close to the pearl and rolled it with a bronze pick. He looked up. "What is your price?"

Tamas, ordinarily equable, found himself infuriated by the goldsmith's bland voice. He responded roughly: "I want the full value, and I will not be cheated!"

The goldsmith shrugged narrow shoulders. "The worth of an article is what someone will pay. I have no market for such a fine trinket. I will give a single gold piece, no more."

Tamas snatched the pearl and strode angrily away. And so it went all day. Tamas offered the pearl to every one whom he thought might pay a good price, but met no success.

Late in the afternoon, tired, hungry and seething with repressed anger, he returned to the Red Lobster Inn, where he ate a pork pasty and drank a mug of beer. At a nearby table four men gambled at dice. Tamas went to watch the play and when one of the men departed, the others invited him to join their game. "You seem a prosperous lad; here's your chance to enrich yourself even further at our expense!"

Tamas hesitated, since he knew little of dice or gaming. He thrust his hands into his pockets and touched the green pearl, which sent a pulse of reckless confidence coursing along his nerves.

"Certainly!" Tamas cried out. "Why not?" He slid into the vacant seat. "You must explain your game to me, since I lack experience at such sport."

The other men at the table laughed jovially. "All the better for you!" said one. "Beginner's luck is the rule!"

Another said: "The first thing to remember is that if you win your count, you must not forget to collect your wager. Secondly, and even more important from our point of view, if you lose, you must pay! Is that clear?"

"Absolutely!" said Tamas.

"Then, just as a gentlemanly courtesy, show us the colour of your money."

Tamas brought the green pearl from his pocket. "Here is a gem worth twenty gold pieces; this is my surety! I have no smaller moneys."

The other players looked at the pearl in perplexity. One of them said: "It may be worth exactly as you claim, but how do you expect to gamble on that basis?"

"Very simply. If I win, I win and nothing more need be said. If I lose, I lose until I am in debt to the amount of twenty gold pieces, whereupon I give up my pearl and depart in poverty."

"All very well," said another of the gamblers. "Still, twenty gold pieces is a goodly sum. Suppose I were to win a single gold piece and thereupon had enough of the game; what then?"

"Is it not absolutely clear?" demanded Tamas peevishly. "You then give me nineteen gold pieces, take the pearl and depart with your gains."

"But I lack the nineteen gold pieces!"

The third gambler cried out: "Come, let us play the game! No doubt matters will sort themselves out!"

"Not yet!" cried the cautious gambler. He turned to Tamas. "The pearl is useless in this game; have you no smaller coins?"

A red-haired red-bearded man wearing the varnished hat and striped trousers of a seaman came forward. He picked up the green pearl and scrutinized it with care. "A rare gem, of perfect luster and remarkable colour! Where did you find this marvel?"

Tamas had no intention of telling everything he knew. "I am a fisherman from Mynault, and we bring ashore all manner of marine treasure, especially after a storm."

"It is a fine jewel," said the cautious gambler. "Still, in this game you must play with coins."

"Come then!" cried the others. "Put out your stakes; let the game begin!"

Tamas grudgingly laid down ten coppers, which he had been reserving for the night's supper and lodging.

The game proceeded and Tamas's luck was good. First copper, then silver coins rose before him in stacks of gratifying height; he began to play for ever higher stakes, deriving assurance from the green pearl which rested among his winnings.

One of the gamblers abandoned the game in disgust. "Never have I seen such turns of the dice! I cannot defeat both Tamas and the goddess Fortunato!"

The red-bearded seaman, who named himself Flary, decided to join the game. "It is probably a lost cause, but I too will challenge this wild fisherman from Mynault."

The game proceeded once again. Flary, an expert gambler, secretly introduced a pair of weighted dice into the game, and seizing an appropriate opportunity, placed a wager of ten gold pieces on the board. He called out: "Fisherman, can you meet such a wager?"

"My pearl is security!" responded Tamas. "Start the game!"

Flary cast down the dice and once more, to Flary's great perplexity, Tamas had won the stakes.

Tamas laughed at Flary's discomfiture. "That is all for tonight. I have gambled long and hard, and my winnings will buy me a fine new boat. My thanks to you all for a profitable evening."

Flary pulled at his beard and squinted sidelong as Tamas counted his money. As if on sudden inspiration Flary swooped down upon the table and pretended to inspect the dice. "As I suspected! Such luck is unnatural! These are weighted dice! We have been robbed!"

There was sudden silence, then an outburst of fury. Tamas was seized, dragged out to the yard behind the tavern and there beaten black and blue. Flary meanwhile retrieved his dice, his gold pieces and also possessed himself of the green pearl.

Well pleased with the night's work, he departed the tavern and went his way.

IV

THE SKYRE, A LONG BIGHT OF PROTECTED WATER, separated North Ulfland from the ancient Duchy of Fer Aquila, now Godelia, realm of the Celts.* Two towns of very different character looked at each other across the Skyre: Xounges, at the tip of a stony peninsula, and Dun Cruighre, Godelia's principal port.

---

*See Glossary I

In Xounges, behind impregnable defenses, Gax, the aged king of North Ulfland, maintained the semblance of a court. The Ska, who effectively controlled Gax's kingdom, tolerated his shadowy pretensions only because an attempt to storm the town would cost far more Ska blood than they were willing to spend. When old Gax died, the Ska would take the town through intrigue or bribery: whichever best served practicality.

Viewed from the Skyre, Xounges showed an intricate pattern of gray stone and black shadow, under roofs of mouldering brown tile. In total contrast, Dun Cruighre spread back from the docks in an untidy clutter of warehouses, hostleries, barns, shipwright's shops, taverns and inns, thatched cottages and an occasional two-story stone manse. The heart of Dun Cruighre was its noisy and sometimes raucous square, often the scene of impromptu horse-races, for the Celts were great ones at contention of any sort.

Dun Cruighre was enlivened by much coming and going, with constant sea-traffic to and from Ireland and Britain. A Christian monastery, the Brotherhood of Saint Bac, boasted a dozen famous relics and attracted pilgrims by the hundreds. Ships from far lands lay alongside the docks, and traders set up booths to display their imports: silk and cotton from Persia; jade, cinnabar and malachite from various lands; perfumed waxes and palm-oil soap from Egypt; Byzantine glass and Rimini faience — all to be exchanged for Celtic gold, silver or tin.

The inns of Dun Cruighre ranged in quality from fair to good: somewhat better, in fact, than might have been expected, for which the itinerant priests and monks could be thanked, since their tastes were demanding and their pouches tended to chink loud with coin. The most reputable tavern of Dun Cruighre was the Blue Ox, which offered private chambers to the wealthy and straw pallets in a loft to the penurious. In the common room, fowl constantly turned on a spit, and bread came fresh from the oven; travellers often declared that a plump roast pullet, stuffed with onions and parsley, with fresh bread and butter, and a pint or two of the Blue Ox ale made as good a meal as could be had anywhere in the Elder Isles. On fine days service was provided at tables in front of the inn, where patrons could eat and drink and watch the events of the square, which in this boisterous town never lacked for interest.

Halfway through one such fine morning a person of portly habit, wearing a brown cassock, came to sit at one of the Blue Ox's outside tables. His face was confident and clever, with round alert eyes, a short nose, and an expression of genial optimism. With nimble white fingers and an earnest snapping of small white teeth he devoured first a roast pullet, then a dozen honey-cakes, meanwhile drinking grandly of mead from a pewter mug. His cassock, if judged by its cut and the excellence of its weave, suggested a clerical connection, but the gentleman had thrown back his hood and where once his pate had been shaved clean, a crop of brown hair now once again was evident.

From the common room of the tavern came a young man of aristocratic demeanour. He was tall and strong, clean-shaven and clear of eye, with an expression of tranquil good humor, as if he found the world a congenial place in which to be alive. His garments were casual: a loose shirt of white linen, trousers of gray twill and an embroidered blue vest. He looked right and left, then approached the table where sat the gentleman in the brown cassack. He asked: "Sir, may I join you? The other tables are occupied and, if possible, I would enjoy the air of this fine morning."

The gentleman in the cassock made an expansive gesture: "Be seated at your pleasure! Allow me to recommend the mead; today it is both sweet and strong, and the honey-cakes are flawless. Indeed, I plan an immediate second acquaintance with both."

The newcomer settled himself into a chair. "The rules of your order are evidently both tolerant and liberal."

"Ha ha, not so! The restrictions are austere and the penalties are harsh. My transgressions, in fact, have brought me expulsion from the order."

"Hmm! It seems an exaggerated response. A sip or two of mead, a taste of honey-cake: where is the harm in this?"

"None whatever!" declared the ex-priest. "I must admit that the issues possibly went a trifle deeper, and I may even found a new brotherhood, devoid of those stringencies which too often make religion a bore. I am restrained only because I do not wish to be branded a heretic. Are you yourself a Christian?"

The young man made a negative sign. "The concepts of religion baffle me."

"This inscrutability is perhaps not unintentional," said the ex-priest. "It gives endless employment to dialecticians who otherwise might become public charges or, at very worst, swindlers and tricksters. May I ask whom I have the pleasure of addressing?"

"Of course. I am Sir Tristano of Castle Mythric in Troicinet. And yourself?"

"I also am of noble blood, or so it seems to me. For the nonce, I use the name my father gave me, which is Orlo."

Sir Tristano, signaling the servant girl, ordered mead and honey-cakes for both himself and Orlo. "I assume, then, that you have definitely resigned from the church?"

"Quite so. It makes for a sordid tale. I was called before the abbot that I might answer to charges of drunkenness and wenching. I put forward my views in a manner to enlighten and convince any reasonable person. I assured the abbot that our merciful Lord God would never have created succulent pasties nor smacking ale, not to mention the charms of merry-hearted women, had he not wished these commodities to be enjoyed to the fullest."

"The abbot no doubt fell back upon dogma for his rebuttal?"

"Precisely! He cited passage after passage from the scriptures to justify his position. I suggested that errors might well have crept into the translation, and that, until we were absolutely sure that self-starvation and tormented glands were the will of our glorious Lord, I proposed that we give ourselves the benefit of the doubt. The abbot nevertheless cast me out."

"Self-interest also guided him; of this I have no doubt!" said Sir Tristano. "If every one worshipped in the manner he found most congenial, the abbot, and the pope as well, would find themselves with no one to instruct."

At this moment Sir Tristano's attention was attracted by a scene of activity across the square. "What is the commotion yonder? Everyone is dancing and skipping as if they were on their way to a festival."

"It is indeed a celebration of sorts," said Orlo. "For close on a year a bloody-handed pirate has been terrorizing the sea. Have you heard the name 'Flary the Red'?"

"I have indeed! Mothers use the name to frighten their children."

"Flary is a none-such!" said Orlo. "He has elevated cutthroat daring to a pinnacle of virtuosity, and always he has worn a lucky green pearl in his ear. One day he misplaced his pearl, but nevertheless launched an attack. This was his great mistake. What seemed a fat merchantman was a trap, and fifty Godelian fire-eaters swarmed aboard the pirate ship. Red Flary was captured and today he will lose his head. Shall we observe the ceremony?"

"Why not? Such spectacles assert the inevitable triumph of virtue, and we will be better men for the instruction."

"Well spoken! I could wish that all men were so rational!"

The two made their way to the executioner's platform, and here Orlo was prompted to chide a gray-faced little man who sought to rifle his pouch. "Fellow, your conduct is leading you directly up to the executioner's block! Have you no foresight? I now must turn you over to the guard!"

"Pest take you!" The pick-pocket jerked free fron Orlo's grasp. "There were no witnesses!"

"Wrong!" spoke Sir Tristano. "I saw the whole thing! I myself will summon the guard!"

The pick-pocket uttered another epithet and, dodging away, was lost in the press.

"A thoroughly unpleasant incident," said Orlo. "The more so since all hearts should now be gay and all faces radiant with joy."

Sir Tristano felt impelled to add a qualification: "Save only the heart and face of Flary the Red."

"That goes without saying."

From the crowd came muted cries of anticipation as a pair of black-masked jailers pulled Flary up to the platform. Behind came a massive man, also masked in black, moving with a stately, even pompous, tread. He carried an enormous axe on his shoulder, and in his wake ambled a priest, smiling first to one side, then the other.

A crier, dressed parti-colour in green and red, jumped to the platform. He bowed toward a construction of raised benches where sat Emmence, Earl of Dun Cruighre, with his friends and family. The crier addressed the throng: "Hear, all ye gracious gentlefolk, as well as all other classes of the region: low, high and ordinary. Hear, I say, and all will learn of the justice imposed by Lord Emmence upon the clapperclaw Flary the Red! His guilty acts are many and not in dispute; his death is perhaps too merciful. Flary, speak your final words on this world which you have so misused!"

"I sorely regret my capture," said Flary. "The green pearl betrayed me; it harms all who touch it! I knew that someday it would bring me to the block, and so it has."

The crier demanded: "Are you not awed as you stand here facing your doom? Is it not time to come to terms with yourself and the world?"

Flary blinked and touched the green pearl which he wore in his ear. He spoke in a halting voice: "To both questions, I reply in the affirmative, especially to the last. It is time and more than time that I think hard and deep upon such matters, and since there are many incidents and events to review, I hereby request a stay of execution."

The crier looked toward Lord Emmence. "Sir, is this request allowed or denied?"

"It is denied."

"Ah well, perhaps I have thought long enough," said Flary. "The priest has put a choice to me. I may either repent my sins and be shriven, and thereby ascend to the glories of Paradise; or I may refuse to repent, and not be shriven, and thereby suffer forever the torments of Hell." Flary paused and looked around the crowd. "Lord Emmence, gentle-folk, persons of all degrees! Know then; I have made my decision!" He paused again, and held his clenched fists dramatically high, and all the folk present leaned forward to learn what Flary's decision might be.

Flary cried out: "I repent! I sorely regret those crimes which have brought me to my present shame! To each man, woman and child within my hearing I utter this advice: stray never an inch from the path of rectitude! Bear true faith to your earl, your father and mother and to the great Lord God, who I hope will now pardon my mistakes! Priest, come now! Shrive me my sins, and send me flying clean and pure heavenward where I may take my place among the angels of the sky and rejoice forever in transcendent bliss!"

The priest stepped forward; Red Flary knelt and the priest performed those rites requested of him.

The priest retreated from the platform. The crowd began to mutter and stir and everywhere there was a craning of necks.

Lord Emmence raised his baton and let it fall. The jailers thrust Flary to the block; the executioner raised his axe on high, held it poised, then struck. Flary's head dropped into a basket. A small green object bounced free, rolled to the edge of the platform, and fell almost at Sir Tristano's feet.

Sir Tristano jerked back in distaste. "Look, there is Flary's pearl, red with his blood." He bent his head. "Almost it seems alive. See how the blood seethes and crawls along the surface!"

"Stand back!" cried Orlo. "Do not touch it! Remember Flary's words!"

From under the platform reached a long thin arm; thin fingers clutched the pearl. Sir Tristano stamped smartly down upon the bony wrist, and from under the platform came a shrill scream of pain and anger.

A nearby guard came to look. "What is this disturbance?"

Sir Tristano pointed under the platform; the guard seized the arm and pulled out a small gray-faced man with a long broken nose. "What have we here?"

"A thief and pickpocket, unless I am very much mistaken," said Sir Tristano. "Examine his pouch and discover what sort of loot he carries."

The pickpocket was dragged to the platform; his pouch was turned out, yielding coins, brooches, golden chains, clasps and buttons, which folk from the crowd came forward in all excitement to claim.

Lord Emmence rose to his feet. "I discover here an exercise in sheer impudence! While we rid ourselves of one thief, another circulates among us, stealing those valuables and ornaments which we have worn for the occasion. Hangman, your axe is sharp! The block is ready! Your muscles are in good tone! Today you shall earn a double fee. Priest, shrive this man and ease his soul for the journey he is about to take."

Sir Tristano told Orlo: "I am sated with head-loppings; let us return to our mead and honey-cakes. . . . Still, what shall we do with the pearl? We cannot leave it lying in the dirt."

"One moment." Orlo found a twig, which he split with his knife, then cleverly caught the pearl in the cleft. "In such matters, one cannot be too cautious. Already today we have seen the fate of two who have avidly seized the pearl."

"I do not want it," said Sir Tristano. "It is yours."

"Impossible! Remember, if you will, that I am vowed to poverty! Or, better to state, I am reconciled to the condition."

Sir Tristano gingerly picked up the twig and the two returned to the Blue Ox, where once more they sat down to their refreshment. "It is only just noon," said Sir Tristano. "Today I had planned to set out along the road to Avallon."

I am of the same inclination," said Orlo. "Shall we ride together?"

"Your company is most welcome, but what of the pearl?"

Orlo scratched his cheek. "Now that I think of it, nothing could be simpler. We will walk to the pier, and drop the pearl into the harbour, and that will be the end of it."

"Sound thinking! Bring it along, then."

Orlo squinted down at the pearl in distaste. "Like yourself, I am made queasy by the sultry gleam of the thing. Still, we are in this affair together, and fairness must be observed." He pointed to a fly which had settled on the table. "Put down your hand beside mine. I will move first, then you must move, as much or as little as you wish, but you must always go at least beyond my hand. When the fly at last departs in fright, whoever moved his hand last shall carry the pearl."

"Agreed."

The trial was made, and each man moved his hand according to his best reading of the fly's emotion, but eventually, the fly took alarm at Sir Tristano's sudden move and flew away.

Sir Tristano groaned. "Alas! I must carry the pearl!"

"But not for long, and only so far as the dock."

Sir Tristano gingerly lifted the end of the twig and the two crossed the square to a vacant place on the dock, with all the Skyre before them.

Orlo spoke: "Pearl, farewell! We hereby return you to that salt green element from which you originated. Sir Tristano, cast away, and with a will!"

Tristano tossed twig and pearl into the sea. The two watched as the gem sank from view, then returned to their table. Here, clean and wet, they discovered the pearl, directly in front of Sir Tristano's place, causing the hairs to rise at the back of his neck.

"Ha ha!" said Orlo. "So the thing has decided to play us tricks! Let it beware! We are not without resource! In any event, sir knight, time has not come to a halt and our way is long. Take up the pearl and let us be on our way. Perhaps we shall meet the arch-bishop, who will be grateful for a gift."

Sir Tristano dubiously looked down at the pearl. "You then advise that I should carry this object upon my person?"

Orlo held out his hands. "Would you leave it here for some poor wight of a serving boy?"

Sir Tristano grimly split another twig and took up the pearl in the cleft. "Let us be on our way."

The two men procured their horses from the stables and departed Dun Cruighre. The road led first along the shore: past sandy beaches pounded by surf and, at intervals, a fisherman's hut. As they rode they spoke of the pearl.

Orlo said: "When I reflect upon this strange object, I seem to detect a pattern. The pearl fell to the ground, where it belonged to no one. The pick-pocket seized upon it and so it became his. You stamped on the pick-pocket's wrist, and in effect wrested away the pearl and took it into your own custody. But since you have not touched the pearl, it cannot work its magic upon you."

"You feel, then, that it can cause me no harm unless I touch it?"

"That is my guess, inasmuch as such an act would represent your intent to partake of the pearl's evil."

"I expressly deny any such intent and I hereby state that any contact, should it occur, must be considered accidental by all parties to the incident." Sir Tristano looked at Orlo. "What is your opinion of that?"

Orlo shrugged. "Who knows? Such a disclaimer may — or may not — dampen the evil ardor of the pearl."

The road turned inland and presently Sir Tristano pointed ahead. "Mark the the bell-tower which rises so high above the trees! It surely signifies the church of a village."

"Undoubtedly so. They are great ones for churches, these Celts; nevertheless they are still more pagan than Christian. In every forest you will find a druid's grove and when the moon shines full they leap through fires with antlers tied to their heads. How does it go in Troicinet?"

"We do not lack for Druids," said Sir Tristano. "They hide in the forests and are seldom seen. Most folk, however, revere the Earth-goddess Gaea, but in an easy fashion, without blood, nor fire, nor guilt. We celebrate only four festivals: to Life in the spring; to the Sun and Sky in the summer; to the Earth and Sea in the Autumn; to the Moon and Stars in the winter. On our birthdays, we place gifts of bread and wine on the votive stone at the temple. There are neither priests nor creed, which makes for a simple and honest worship, and it seems to suit the nature of our people very well. . . . And there is the village with its grand church, where, unless my eyes deceive me, an important ceremony is in progress."

"You are observing the panoplies of a Christian funeral," said Orlo. He drew up his horse and slapped his leg. "A notable scheme has occurred to me. Let us look in on this funeral."

Dismounting, the two men tied their horses to a tree and entered the church. Three priests chanted above an open coffin as mourners filed past to pay their last respects.

Sir Tristano asked in a somewhat anxious voice: "Exactly what do you have in mind?"

"I conceive that the holy rites of a Christian burial must effectively stifle the evil force of the pearl. The priests are uttering benedictions by the score and Christian virtue hangs thick in the air. The pearl must surely be confounded, absolutely and forever, when surrounded by such a power."

"Possibly true," said Tristano dubiously. "But practical difficulties stand in the way. We cannot possibly intrude upon this mournful rite."

"No need whatever," said Orlo in a jaunty fashion. "Let us join the mourners. When we reach the coffin I will distract the priests while you drop the pearl among the cerements."

"It is at least worth a try," said Sir Tristano and so the deed was done.

The two stood back to see the coffin lid closed down on corpse and pearl together. Pall-bearers carried the coffin to a grave dug deep into the mold of the churchyard; four sextons lowered the coffin into the grave and, amid the wailing of the bereaved, the coffin was covered with sod.

"A good funeral!" declared Orlo with satisfaction. "I also notice a sign yonder which betokens the presence of an inn, where perhaps you may wish to take lodging for the night."

"What of yourself?" asked Sir Tristano. "Do you not intend to sleep under a roof?"

"I do indeed, but here, sadly enough, our paths diverge. At the crossroad you will bear to the right, along the road to Avallon. I, however, will turn to the left and an hour's ride will bring me to the manor of a certain widowed lady whose lonely hours I hope to console or even enliven. So then, Sir Tristano, I bid you farewell!"

"Orlo, farewell, and I regret parting with so good a companion. Remember, at Castle Mythric you will always be welcome."

"I will not forget!" Orlo rode off down the street. At the crossroad he turned, looked back, raised his arm in farewell and was gone.

Sir Tristano, now somewhat melancholy, rode into the village. At the Sign of the Four Owls he applied for lodging and was conducted up a flight of stairs to a loft under the thatch. His chamber was furnished with a straw pallet, a table, a chair, an old commode and a carpet of fresh reeds.

For his supper Sir Tristano ate boiled beef, served in its own broth with carrots and turnips, with bread and a relish of minced horseradish in cream. He drank two tall mugs of ale and, fatigued by the exertions of the day, went early to his chamber.

Quiet held the village, and a near-absolute darkness, with an overcast cloaking the sky, until close on midnight, when the clouds broke open to reveal a sad quartering moon.

Sir Tristano slept well until this time, when he was awakened by the sound of slow footsteps in the hall. The door to his chamber squeaked ajar, and footsteps told of a presence slowly entering the room, and approaching the pallet. Sir Tristano lay rigid. He felt the touch of cold fingers, and an object dropped upon the cloak which covered his chest.

The steps shuffled back across the room. The door eased shut. The steps moved away down the corridor and soon could be heard no more.

Sir Tristano gave a sudden hoarse outcry and jerked up his cloak. A luminous green object fell to the floor and came to rest among the reeds.

Sir Tristano at last fell into a troubled sleep. The cool red rays of dawn, entering the window, awakened him. He lay staring up at the thatch. The events of last night: were they a nightmare? What a boon, if so! Raising on an elbow, he scrutinized the floor, and almost at once discovered the green pearl.

Sir Tristano arose from his bed. He washed his face, dressed in his clothes and buckled his boots, at all times keeping the green pearl under close surveillance.

In the commode he found a torn old apron which he folded and used to pick up the pearl. With pad and pearl secure in his pouch he left the chamber. After a breakfast of porridge with fried cabbage, he paid his score and went his way.

At the cross-roads he turned right along the road toward the Kingdom of Dahaut, which at last would take him to Avallon.

As he rode, he cogitated. The pearl had not been content with a Christian burial, and it was his until it was taken from him, by force or subterfuge.

During the early afternoon he came into the village Timbaugh. A pack of cur dogs, barking and snapping, raced out to warn him off, and only desisted when he alighted from his horse and pelted them with stones. At the inn he paused for a meal of bread and sausages, and as he drank ale an idea entered his mind.

With great care he inserted the pearl into one of the sausages, which he took out into the street. The dogs came out again to chide him, snarling and snapping and ordering him out of town. Sir Tristano cast down the sausage. "There it is: my good sausage which belongs to me and no other! I seem to have misplaced it. Whoever takes that sausage and its contents is a thief!"

A gaunt yellow cur darted close and devoured the sausage at a gulp. "So be it," said Sir Tristano. "The act was yours and none of my own."

Returning to the inn, he drank more ale, while turning over the logic of his act. All seemed sound. And yet. . . . Nonsense. The dog had exercised a thieving volition. To the dog must now fall the problem of disposing of the pearl. And yet . . .

The longer Sir Tristano pondered, the weaker seemed the rationale which had guided his act. A persuasive point could be made that the dog had thought of the sausage as a gift. In this case, the transfer of the pearl must be considered Tristano's rather crude subterfuge, and not in any way a *bona fide* theft.

Recalling his previous attempts to be rid of the pearl, Sir Tristano became ever more uneasy, and he began to wonder in what style the pearl might be returned to him.

A tumult in the street attracted his attention: a horrid howling, wavering between shrill and hoarse, which caused his stomach to knot. From along the road came the cry: "Mad dog! Mad dog!"

Sir Tristano hastily threw coins on the table and ran out to his horse, that he might depart the village Timbaugh in haste. He took note of the yellow dog, at a distance of a hundred yards, where it bounded back and forth, foaming at the mouth, meanwhile roaring its opinion of the world. It launched itself at a peasant lad who trudged beside a hay-cart; the boy leapt up on the hay and, seizing a pitch-fork, thrust down to pierce the dog through the neck. The dog fell over backward, and shaking furiously as if it were wet, bounded away, still trailing the pitch-fork.

An old man trimming the thatch of his cottage, ran inside and emerged with a long-bow; he nocked, drew and let fly an arrow; it drove through the dog's chest, so that the point protruded from one side and feathers from the other; the dog paid no heed.

Glaring up the road, the dog took note of Sir Tristano, and fixed on him as the source of its travail. Moving at first with sinister deliberation, head low, one leg carefully placed before the other, it approached, then, halting and moaning, it lunged to the attack.

Sir Tristano jumped on his horse and galloped away down the road with the dog, baying and groaning deep hoarse tones, coming in hot pursuit. The pitch-fork fell from its neck; it closed in on the horse, and began to leap at its flanks. With sword on high, Sir Tristano leaned low, and slashed down, to split the dog's skull. The dog turned a somersault into the ditch, quivered and lay watching Sir Tristano through glazing yellow eyes. Slowly it crawled up from the ditch, sliding on its belly, inch after inch.

Sir Tristano watched fascinated, sword at the ready.

Ten feet from Sir Tristano the dog went into a convulsion, vomited into the road, then lay back and became still. In the puddle it had brought from its belly the green pearl gleamed.

Sir Tristano considered the situation with vast distaste. At last he dismounted, and going to a thicket, cut a twig and split the end. Using the same technique as before, he clamped on the pearl and lifted it from the road.

In the near distance a bridge of a single arch spanned a small river. Leading his horse and carrying the pearl as far from his body as the length of the twig allowed, Sir Tristano marched to the bridge, where he tied his horse to a bush. Clambering down to the stream, he washed the pearl with care, then washed his sword and wiped it dry on a clump of coarse sedge.

A sound attracted his attention. Looking up, he discovered on the bridge a tall thin man with a narrow face, long bony jaw, high broken nose, and long sharp chin. The tall crown of his hat, wound with red and white ribbons, advertised the profession of barber and blood-letter.

Sir Tristano, ignoring the keen scrutiny from above, rolled the pearl in a pad of cloth and tucked it into his pouch, then climbed back to the road.

The barber, now standing by his cart, doffed his hat and performed a somewhat obsequious salute. "Sir, allow me to state that I sell elixirs against your infirmities; I will barber your hair, shave your face, cut the most stubborn toenails, lance boils, clean ears, and draw blood. My fees are fair, but not mean; you will nevertheless consider the money well-spent."

Sir Tristano mounted his horse. "I need none of your goods nor services; good day to you."

"One moment, sir. May I ask where you are bound?"

"To Avallon in Dahaut."

"You ride a long road. There is an inn at the village Toomish but I suggest that you ride on to Phaidig, where the Crown and Unicorn is justly famous for its mutton pies."

"Thank you. I will bear your advice in mind."

Three miles along the road Sir Tristano came to Toomish, and as Long Liam the Barber had suggested, the inn seemed to offer no great comfort. Although the afternoon was drawing to its close, Sir Tristano continued onward toward Phaidig.

The sun sank into a bank of clouds, and at the same time the road entered a heavy forest. Sir Tristano looked frowningly into the gloom. His choices were two: he could either ride on through the ominously dark woods or return to Toomish and its uninviting inn.

Sir Tristano made his choice. Touching up his horse to a canter, Sir Tristano entered the wood. After a half mile the horse stopped short and Sir Tristano saw that a barricade of poles had been placed across the road.

A voice spoke to his back: "Arms on high! Lest you wish an arrow in the back!"

Sir Tristano raised his arms in the air.

The voice said: "Do not turn, do not glance aside, and offer no tricks! My associate will approach you while I watch down the length of my arrow! Now then, Padraig, about your work! If he so much as quivers, cut him deep with your razor, I mean your knife."

A rustle of careful steps sounded in the road; hands pulled at the thongs which tied the wallet to Sir Tristano's belt.

Sir Tristano spoke: "Stop! You are taking the great green pearl!"

"Naturally!" said the voice from a point close behind. "That is the whole point of robbery: to acquire the victim's valuables!"

"You now have all my wealth; may I depart?"

"By no means! We want your horse and saddle-bags too!"

Sir Tristano, assured that a single footpad had waylaid him, clapped spurs to his horse, bent low, and rode pell-mell around the barricade. He looked over his shoulder to see a very tall man shrouded in a black cloak, with a hood concealing his face. A bow hung at his shoulder; he snatched it free and let fly an arrow, but the light was poor, the target fugitive and the range long; the arrow sang harmlessly away through the foliage.

Sir Tristano galloped his horse until he had won free of the woods, and the threat of pursuit was past. He rode with a light heart; in his wallet he had carried, along with the green pearl, only two or three small silver coins and half a dozen copper groats. For protection against just such events, he carried his gold in his slotted belt.

Full dusk drowned the landscape with purple-gray shadow before Sir Tristano came to Phaidig, and there he took lodging at the Crown and Unicorn, where he was nicely accommodated in a clean private chamber.

As Long Liam the Barber had attested, the mutton pie was of excellent quality, and Sir Tristano felt that he had dined well. Casually he inquired of the landlord: "What of robbers in these parts? Do they often molest travellers?"

The landlord looked over his shoulder, then said: "We hear reports of one who calls himself 'Tall Toby' and his favorite resort appears to be the woods between here and Toomish."

"I will offer you a hint," said Sir Tristano. "Are you acquainted with Long Liam the Barber?"

"Of course! He plies his trade everywhere about these parts. He also is a very tall man."

"I will say no more," said Sir Tristano. "Save only this: the correspondence goes somewhat deeper than mere stature, and the King's Warden might well be interested in the news."

V

LONG LIAM THE BARBER wended his way by lane and by-road south into Dahaut, that he might ply his trade at the harvest festivals of the late summer. Arriving at the town Mildenberry, he did brisk trade and one afternoon was summoned to Fotes Sachant, the country house of Lord Imbold. A footman took him into a drawing room, where he learned that, owing to the illness of the valet, he would be required to shave Lord Imbold's face and trim his mustache.

Long Liam performed his duties with adequate proficiency, and was duly complimented by Lord Imbold, who also admired the green pearl in the ring worn by Long Liam. So distinctive and remarkable did Lord Imbold think the gem that he asked Long Liam to put a price on the piece.

Long Liam thought to take advantage of the situation and quoted a large sum: "Your Lordship, this confection was given to me by my dying grandfather, who had it from the Sultan of Egypt. I could not bear to part with it for less than fifty gold crowns."

Lord Imbold became indignant. "Do you take me for a fool?" He turned away and called to the footman. "Taube! Pay this fellow his fee and show him out."

Long Liam was left alone while Taube went to fetch the coins. Exploring the room, he opened a cupboard and discovered a pair of gold candlesticks which inflamed his avarice to such an extent that he tucked them into his bag and closed up the cupboard.

Taube returned in time to notice Long Liam's suspicious conduct, and went to look into the bag. In a panic Long Liam slashed out with his razor, and cut a deep gash into Taube's neck, so that his head fell back over his shoulders.

Long Liam fled from the chamber but was taken, adjudged and led to the gallows.

A crippled ex-soldier named Manting for ten years had served the county as executioner. He did his work efficiently and expunged Long Liam's life definitely enough, but in a style quite devoid of that extra element of surprise and poignancy, which distinguished the notable executioner from his staid colleague.

The perquisites of Manting's position included the garments and ornaments found on the corpse, and Manting came into possession of a valuable green pearl ring which he was pleased to wear for his own.

Thereafter, all who watched Manting declared that they had never seen the executioner's work done with more grace and attention to detail, so at times Manting and the condemned man seemed participants in a tragic drama which set every heart to throbbing; and at last, when the latch had been sprung, or the blow struck, or the torch tossed into the faggots, there was seldom a dry eye among the spectators.

Manting's duties occasionally included a stint of torture, where again he proved himself not only the adept at classical techniques, but deft and clever with his innovations.

Manting, however, while pursuing some theoretical concept, tended to over-reach himself. One day his schedule included the execution of a young witch named Zanice, accused of drying the udders of her neighbor's cow. Since an element of uncertainty entered the case, it was ordained that Zanice die by the garrote rather than by fire. Manting, however, wished to test a new and rather involved idea, and he used this opportunity to do so, and thereby aroused the fury of the sorcerer Qualmes, the lover of Zanice.

Qualmes took Manting deep into the Forest of Tantrevalles, along an obscure trail known as Ganion's Way, and led him a few yards off the trail into a little glade.

Qualmes asked: "Manting, how do you like this place?"

Manting, still wondering as to the reason for the expedition, looked all about. "The air is fresh. The verdure is a welcome change from the dungeons. The flowers yonder add to the charm of the scene."

Qualmes said: "It is fortunate that you are happy here, inasmuch as you will never leave this place."

Manting smilingly shook his head. "Impossible! Today I find myself at leisure, and this little outing is truly pleasant, but tomorrow I must conduct two hangings, a strappado and a flogging."

"You are relieved of all such duties, now and forever. Your treatment of Zanice has aroused my deep emotion, and you must pay the penalty of your cruelty. Find yourself a pleasant place to recline, and choose a comfortable position, for I am imposing a spell of stasis upon you, and you will never move again."

Manting protested for several minutes, and Qualmes listened with a smile on his face. "Tell me, Manting, have any of your victims made similar protests to you?"

"Now that I think of it: yes."

"And what would be your response?"

"I always replied that, by the very nature of things, I was the instrument, not of mercy, but of doom. Here, of course, the situation is different. You are at once the adjudicator, as well as the executioner of the judgement, and so you are both able and qualified to consider my petition for mercy, or even outright pardon."

"The petition is denied. Recline, if you will; I cannot chop logic with you all day."

Manting at last was forced to recline on the turf, after which Qualmes worked his spell of paralysis and went his way.

Manting lay helpless day and night, week after week, month after month, while weasels and rats gnawed at his hands and feet, and hornets made their lodges in his flesh, until nothing remained but bones and the glowing green pearl, and even these were gradually covered under the mold.

Chapter 2

I

EIGHT KINGS RULED the realms of the Elder Isles. The least of these was Gax, nominal King of North Ulfland, whose decrees were heeded only within the walls of Xounges. In contrast, King Casmir of Lyonesse and King Audry of Dahaut both ruled wide lands and commanded strong armies. King Aillas, whose possessions included three islands: Troicinet, Dascinet and Scola, as well as South Ulfland, guarded his communications through the power of a strong navy.

The other four kings varied as greatly. Mad King Deul of Pomperol had been succeeded by his son, the eminently sane King Kestrel. The ancient Kingdom of Caduz had been absorbed by Lyonesse, but Blaloc, under the rule of bibulous King Milo, retained its independence. Milo had contrived a wonderful ruse, which never failed in its purpose. When envoys from Lyonesse or Dahaut came to enlist Milo's support, he seated them at his table and poured them full of wine, while musicians played jigs and quicksteps, so that the envoys presently forgot their business and cavorted in drunken abandon alongside King Milo.

Godelia and its boisterous population were in some degree controlled by King Dartweg. The Ska elected their 'First Among the First' at ten-year intervals; the current 'First' was the strong and able Sarquin.

The eight kings differed in almost every characteristic. King Kestrel of Pomperol and King Aillas of Troicinet, were both earnest young men, brave and honorable, but where Kestrel was humorless and diffident, Aillas showed an imaginative flair which sometimes perturbed more settled personalities.

The courts of the eight kings were no less disparate. King Audry spent lavishly upon vanity and pleasure, and the splendor of his court at Falu-Ffail was the stuff of legend. King Aillas used his revenues to build ships for his navy, while King Casmir spent large sums upon espionage and intrigue. His spies were active everywhere, and especially in Dahaut, where they monitored King Audry's every sneeze.

Casmir found information from Troicinet more difficult to secure. He had managed to suborn certain high officials, who transmitted their reports by carrier pigeon, but he relied most heavily upon the master spy 'Valdez', whose information was uncannily accurate.

Valdez reported at intervals of about six weeks. Casmir, shrouded under a hooded gray cloak, went to a storeroom at the back of a wine-merchant's shop, where presently he was joined by a man who might well have been the wine merchant: a person of no great distinction, stocky of physique, clean-shaven, economical of speech, with neat regular features and cold gray eyes.

From Valdez, Casmir learned of four new warships on the ways at the Tumbling River shipyard, two miles north of Domreis. Despite strict security, Valdez was able to report that these ships were light fast feluccas, with catapults hurling iron arrows a hundred yards with sufficient force to open up the hull of any ordinary vessel. These new ships were intended specifically to defeat the long-boats of the Ska and thus hold open the sea-lanes between Troicinet and South Ulfland. *

Valdez, before his departure, remarked that he had recently recruited new and highly placed sources of information.

"Well done!" said Casmir. "This is the efficient work which we have come to expect from you."

Valdez turned toward the door, where he paused and seemed about to speak, but once again turned away.

Casmir had noticed the hesitation. "Wait! What troubles your mind?"

"No great problem, though I can conceive of possible inconvenience."

"How so?"

"I am aware that you have informants in Troicinet other than myself, and I suspect that at least one of these is highly placed. From your point of view, this is a happy situation. Still, as mentioned, I have made contact with a person of high degree who may well cooperate with me, although at the moment he is as timid as a bird. I can work less

---

*At the moment Troicinet and Lyonesse kept an uneasy peace, but only after an accommodation whereby Casmir undertook to build no warships which might challenge Troice control of the sea. Aillas had put his case to Casmir in these terms: "Your armies, with your four hundred knights and multitude of soldiers, protect you well against our attack. If Lyonesse could bring these troops to Dascinet or Troicinet, we would know mortal danger! Lyonesse cannot be allowed the means to land armies on our soil."

Casmir yielded the point without display of emotion, though inwardly he seethed with rage, and the violent dislike he felt for Aillas exacerbated the situation.

tentatively and with less chance of cross-purposes if I know the identities of your other informants."

"The point is well taken," said Casmir. He reflected a moment, then uttered a small harsh chuckle. "You would be surprised to learn the elevation at which my ears listen! But it is probably better to keep you and these other sources separate. My reasons are not abstract. In case one is discovered and put to the question, the other is safe."

"True enough." Valdez took his leave.

II

SIR TRISTANO, after yielding his green pearl to the robber, traveled through the pleasant countryside of Dahaut, and in due course arrived at Avallon. He found accomodation, changed into suitable garments and presented himself at Audry's palace Falu Ffail.

A haughty footman in blue velvet livery stood by the door. He surveyed Sir Tristano head to toe with a hooded stare, listened with a face of stone as Sir Tristano identified himself, then grudgingly led the way to a foyer, where Sir Tristano enlivened the wait of an hour by watching the fountain where sunlight, refracting through a dome of crystal prisms, sparkled against the spray.

The High Chamberlain at last appeared. He listened to Sir Tristano's request for an audience with King Audry, and shook his head dubiously. "His Majesty seldom sees anyone without prior arrangements."

"You may announce me as an envoy from King Aillas of Troicinet."

"Very well. Come this way, if you will." He conducted Sir Tristano to a small parlour and left him sitting alone.

Sir Tristano waited an hour, then another, until finally, having nothing better to do, King Audry condescended to receive him.

The High Chamberlain led Sir Tristano through the galleries of the palace and out into the formal gardens. King Audry lounged at a marble table with three of his cronies, watching a bevy of maidens play at bowls.

King Audry, engrossed in making wagers on the game with his friends, could not immediately attend Sir Tristano, who stood quietly appraising the frivolous King of Dahaut. He saw a man large and handsome, somewhat loose of jowl, moist and round of eye, and heavy in the buttocks. Black curls clustered beside his cheeks; black eyebrows almost met above his long straight nose. His expression was rich and easy; his disposition would seem to be petulant, rather than vicious.

At last, with eyebrows raised, King Audry listened as the chamberlain introduced Sir Tristano: "Your Majesty, this is the emissary from Troicinet: Sir Tristano of Castle Mythric and cousin to King Aillas."

Sir Tristano performed a conventional bow. "Your Majesty, I am pleased to offer my best respects and the regards of King Aillas."

Audry, leaning back, surveyed Sir Tristano through half-closed eyes. "Sir, I must say that for a mission of this importance I would have expected a person of somewhat more august wisdom and experience."

Sir Tristano smiled. "Sir, I admit that I am only three years older than King Aillas, who perhaps for this reason regards me in the light you mention. Still, if you are dissatisfied, I will instantly withdraw to Troicinet and there express your views to King Aillas. I am sure that he can find a qualified emissary: sage, elderly, of your own generation. May I have your leave to depart?"

Audry gave a peevish grunt and straightened in his seat. "Are all Troice so high-handed in their dignity? Before you rush off in a fury, perhaps you will at least explain the regrettable Troice sortie into South Ulfland."

"Sir, with pleasure." Sir Tristano glanced at the three courtiers, who sat listening with unabashed interest. "You might prefer to delay our conference until you are alone, since we will touch upon sensitive matters."

Audry uttered an impatient ejaculation. "Stealth, whispers, intrigue: how I despise them, one and all! Sir Tristano, be acquainted with my philosophy: I have no secrets! Still and however . . ." Audry signaled to his cronies who departed with poor grace.

Audry pointed to a chair. "Sit, if you will. . . . Now then: I continue to wonder as to this madcap Troice expedition."

Tristano smiled. "I am surprised by your surprise! Two excellent and obvious reasons prompted us into South Ulfland. The first is self-explanatory: the crown devolved upon Aillas through legitimate and ordinary succession, and he went to claim his due. He found the realm in deplorable order and now works to set things right.

"The second reason is as starkly simple as the first. If Aillas had failed to secure both Kaul Bocach and Tintzin Fyral, which are forts along the way between Lyonesse and South Ulfland, King Casmir would now rule in South Ulfland. Nothing could prevent him from invading your Western March while at the same time attacking you from the south. Then, after you had been safely clapped into a dungeon, he could overwhelm Troicinet at his leisure. We preceded him into South Ulfland and he is now thwarted. So there you have it."

King Audry gave a cynical snort. "I also perceive an extension of Troice ambition. It adds new dimensions to the charade! I already have problems enough from Godelia and Wysrod, not to mention the Ska who occupy my strong fortress Poëlitetz. . . . Aha there! Well bowled, Artwen! Now then, Mnione, to the attack! Smite your oppressor hip and thigh!" So called King Audry to the maidens playing at bowls. He lifted a goblet of wine to his lips, drank, then poured out a goblet for Sir Tristano. "Be at your ease; this is a careless occasion. Still, I could wish that Aillas had sent a full-fledged plenipotentiary, or even had come himself."

Sir Tristano shrugged. "I can only repeat what I have said before. King Aillas has imparted to me the full details of his program. When I speak, you listen to his voice."

"I will be blunt," said Audry. "Our common enemy is Casmir. I am at all times ready to unite our forces and end, once and for all, the danger he represents."

"Sir, this idea naturally comes as no surprise to King Aillas — nor to Casmir, for that matter. Aillas responds in these words. At the moment Troicinet is at peace with Lyonesse, a condition which may or may not endure. We are putting the time to good use. We consolidate our position in South Ulfland; we augment our navy, and if the peace persists a hundred years, so much the better.

"In the meantime the most urgent situation confronting us is the Ska. If we joined you to defeat Lyonesse, the Ska problem would not go away; and we would then confront a new aggressive Dahaut without the counterbalance of Lyonesse. We cannot tolerate a preponderance in either direction, and always must throw our weight behind the weaker antagonist. For the immediate future, this would seem to be you."

Audry frowned. "Your statement is almost insultingly crass."

Sir Tristano refused to be daunted. "Sir, I am not here to please you, but to present facts and listen to your remarks."

"Hmmf. These, you say, are the words of King Aillas."

"Precisely so."

"I gather that you have no high opinion of my military might."

"Would you care to hear the appraisal we have received at Domreis?"

"Speak on."

"I will quote the report more or less as it reached us: 'Above all else, the knights of Dahaut are required to appear on parade with armour shining and all caparisons resplendent, and indeed they make a brave show. In battle, they may not fare so well, since they have been enervated by luxury and are disinclined to the rigors of the campaign. If forced to confront an enemy, no doubt they could wheel their horses in gallant caracoles and defy the foe with insouciant gestures, but all from a safe distance.

" 'Archers and pike-men march with full precision, and at the parade are the marvel of all who see them. The compliments have befuddled poor Audry; he reckons them to be invincible. Again, they are trained to the parade ground, but barely know which end of their weapons is hurtful. They are all overweight and clearly have little stomach for fighting.'"

Audry said indignantly: "That is a graceless canard! Are you here only to mock me?"

"Not at all. I came to deliver a message, part of which you have just heard. The second part is this: King Casmir well understands your military deficiencies. He has been denied his easy passage through South Ulfland, and now must think of direct attack. King Aillas urges that you take command of your army away from your favorites and put it into the hands of a qualified professional soldier. He recommends that you abandon your dress parades for field exercises, and spare no one his necessary effort, including yourself."

Audry drew himself up. "This kind of message verges upon sheer insolence."

"This is not our intent. We see dangers of which you may not be aware, and we so warn you, if only from motives of self-interest."

Audry drummed his white fingers on the table. "I am unacquainted with King Aillas. Tell me something of his nature. Is he cautious or is he bold?"

Sir Tristano reflected. "In truth, I find him a hard man to describe. He is cautiously bold, if that answers your question. His disposition is easy; still he never stands back from a harsh duty. I suspect that often he forces himself, because his nature is mild, like that of a philosopher. He has no taste for war but he recognizes that force and intimidation are the way of the world; hence he studies military tactics and few can match him at sword-play. He abominates torture; the dungeons below Miraldra are empty, yet few criminals or footpads are at work in Troicinet because Aillas has given them all to the noose. Still, in my opinion, he would abandon the kingship tomorrow to a man he could trust."

"That should be no problem! Many would gladly take over his post."

"Those are precisely the ones he would not trust!"

Audry shrugged and drank wine. "I did not ask to be born king, or — for that matter — to be born at all. Still, I am king, and I might as well enjoy my luck to the hilt. Your Aillas, on the other hand, seems victimized by guilt."

"I hardly think so."

Audry filled his own and Sir Tristano's goblets. "Let me send back with you a message for King Aillas."

"I listen, sir, with both ears."

Audry leaned forward and spoke in sententious tones: "It is time that Aillas should marry! What better match could be made than that between Aillas and my eldest daughter Thaubin, thus uniting two great houses? Look, see her yonder where she watches the game!"

Sir Tristano followed the direction of Audry's gesture. "The comely lass in white beside the plain little creature so uncomfortably pregnant? She is indeed charming!"

Audry spoke with dignity. "The maiden wearing white is Thaubin's friend Netta. Thaubin stands beside her."

"I see. . . . Well, I doubt if Aillas plans an early marriage. He might well be surprised if I were to affiance him to the Princess Thaubin."

"In that case—"

"One more matter before I depart. May I speak with candor?"

Audry grumbled: "You have done little else! Speak!"

"I must warn you that traitors report your every act to King Casmir. You are surrounded by spies; they masquerade as your intimates; they might include one or more of the gentlemen who just now sat here with you."

Audry stared at Sir Tristano, then threw back his head and laughed hugely. He turned and called to his friends: "Sir Huynemer! Sir Rudo! Sir Swanish! Join us, if you will!"

The three gentlemen, somewhat puzzled and resentful, returned to the table.

King Audry, among chuckles, told them: "Sir Tristano insists that traitors are rife at Falu Ffail; indeed he suspects that one among you spies for King Casmir!"

The courtiers jumped to their feet, roaring in anger. "This fellow insults us!" "Give us leave to show our steel; we will teach him the etiquette he has failed to learn elsewhere!" "Poppycock and hysteria! The gabble of geese and old women!"

Sir Tristano smilingly sat back in his chair. "It appears that I have touched a sore nerve! Well, I will say no more."

"It is all absurdity!" declared King Audry. "What are my secrets that spies should seek them out? I have none! The worst is known!"

Sir Tristano rose to his feet. "Your Majesty, I have brought you my messages; give me leave to depart."

King Audry waved his fingers. "You may go."

Sir Tristano bowed, turned away and departed Falu Ffail.

III

SIR TRISTANO, RETURNING TO DOMREIS, went directly to Miraldra, a dour old castle of fourteen towers overlooking the harbor. Aillas greeted his cousin with affection. The resemblance between them, as they faced each other, was noticeable. Where Tristano was tall and loosely muscular, Aillas, less tall by an inch, seemed spare and taut. Their hair alike was light golden brown and cut square at ear-level; Tristano's features were blunt where those of Aillas were crisp. Standing together and smiling in the pleasure of each other's company, they seemed like boys.

At Aillas' suggestion they seated themselves on a couch. Aillas said: "Before all else, let me mention that I am on my way to Watershade; why not join me?"

"I will be happy to do so."

"We shall leave in two hours. Have you had your breakfast?"

"Only a dish of bread and curds."

"We shall repair that." Aillas called the footman and presently they were served a pan of fried hake, with new loaves and butter, stewed cherries and bitter ale. Meanwhile Aillas had asked: "How went your expedition?"

"Certainly it has included interesting episodes," said Sir Tristano. "I debarked from the ship at Dun Cruighre, and rode to Cluggach where I was granted an audience with King Dartweg. Dartweg is a Celt, true, but not all Celts are red-faced louts smelling of cheese. Dartweg, for instance, smells of ale, mead, and bacon. I learned nothing of profit from King Dartweg; the Celts think only of drinking mead and stealing each other's cattle: this is the basis of their economy. I firmly believe that they place higher value upon a brindle cow with large udders than upon an equally buxom woman. Still, I cannot fault King Dartweg's hospitality; in fact, you can insult a Celt only by calling him mean. They are too excitable to make truly good warriors, and, while obstreperous, they are as unpredictable as virgins. At a moot-place near Cluggach I saw fifty men at loggerheads, shouting each other down, and often laying hands to their swords. I thought that they must be debating between peace and war, but, so I found, the dispute concerned the largest salmon caught during a season three years back, and Dartweg was in the midst, bawling the loudest of all. Then a druid appeared in a brown robe with a sprig of mistletoe pinned to his hood. He uttered a single word; all fell silent, then slunk away and hid in the shadows.

"Later I spoke of the incident to Dartweg and commended the druid's counsel of moderation. Dartweg told me that the druid cared not a fig for moderation, and objected only because the noise offended a flock of sacred crows in a nearby grove.

"Despite the Christian churches which are now appearing everywhere, the druids still hold power."

"Very well!" said Aillas. "You have told me enough of Godelia. To gain influence I must either ride down from the sky on a white bull holding the disk of Lug, or catch the largest salmon of the season. What next?"

"I crossed the Skyre by ferry and entered Xounges. This is the only access, since the Ska control the approaches by land. Gax lives in a monstrous stone palace named Jehaundel, under ceilings lost in the high shadows. The halls are like caverns, and afford little comfort to visitors, courtiers or Gax himself."

"But you were able to meet with Gax?"

"Only with difficulty. Gax is now something of an invalid, and his nephew, a certain Sir Kreim, apparently tries to insulate Gax from visitors, claiming that Gax's health can not suffer excitement. I paid a gold crown to ensure that Gax knew of my presence, and was called to an audience despite the disapproval of Sir Kreim.

"Gax in his prime must have been a most impressive man. Even now he overlooks me by two inches. He is lean and spare, and talks in a voice like the north wind. His sons and daughters are dead; he does not know his own age but reckons it to exceed seventy years. No one brings him news; he thought that Oriante still reigned in South Ulfland. I assured him that Aillas, the new king of South Ulfland, was a sworn enemy of the Ska, and already had sunk their ships and barred them from South Ulfland.

At this news King Gax clapped his hands in joy. Sir Kreim, who stood at Gax's elbow, declared that Aillas' rule was transitory, and why? The reason, according to Sir Kreim, was well-known: Aillas' sexual perversions had made him sickly and limp. This caused Gax to spit on the floor. I declared this 'well-known fact' to be a slanderous lie, untrue in every detail. I stated that whoever had imparted such news to Sir Kreim was a debased and dastardly liar, and I advised Kreim never to repeat the allegation lest he be accused of perpetuating the lie.

"I pointed out that Sir Kreim was otherwise mistaken: that Aillas even now energetically worked to curb the highland barons, and would soon rebuff the Ska."

Aillas gave a sour chuckle. "Why did you not also promise that I would reverse the course of the rivers and cause the sun to rise in the west?"

Sir Tristano shrugged. "You have not previously so much as hinted of these ambitions."

"All in good time," said Aillas. "First I have fleas of my own to scratch. But tell me more of King Gax and the sinister Sir Kreim."

"Kreim is somehat older than myself, with a purple mouth and a black beard. He is surly and suspicious, and almost certainly a creature of the Ska.

"I mentioned other events of the last year and King Gax had known none of them. The old rascal seems well aware of Kreim's ambitions, and apparently from sheer mischief kept turning to him and crying out: 'Kreim, fancy that!' And: 'Kreim, these are the men we must count on if ever we are to escape the toils of the Ska!' And: 'Kreim, were I once again young, I would do as Aillas does!'

"Finally King Gax sent Sir Kreim away on one pretext or another. Sir Kreim went reluctantly, looking back over his shoulder all the way. King Gax then told me: 'As you see, my life and my reign together are dwindling into oblivion.'

"Here King Gax looked all around, as if to assure himself against eavesdroppers. 'I have made many mistakes in my life. There is one last mistake I wish not to make.'

" 'And that is?'

"Gax only waved a finger at me. 'You are a subtle young man, despite your easy mask. Can you not guess?'

" 'I can guess of a dozen mistakes you might make. You hope to avoid dying before your time, and so perhaps you walk a narrow line.' "

" 'That is one of the right guesses. I am dying, but only in the sense that every man of my age is dying. The Ska are patient; they will wait. But I must be prudent, because I fear poison or a knife in the dark, and it would be a cold death here in Jehaundel, with no son to avenge my murder.'

" 'Let me ask this, from simple curiosity. How do the laws of North Ulfland regulate the succession of kings?'

" 'By the ordinary lines of descent, if I die and am dead, which means Kreim. But see this circlet on my head? Were you fool enough to accept it, I could transfer the kingship to you at this moment, and then, like mine, your life would be in pawn to the Ska and you would wonder at every mouthful of food.'

" 'Keep your kingship,' I told him. 'My ambitions fly much lower.'

"At this moment Sir Kreim returned, and I took my leave of King Gax."

Aillas went to look out the window, across the harbour where the wind blew up white-caps. "How do you judge his health?"

"For a man of seventy, he seems sound, though his eyes are not so keen as before. His mind is agile and his voice is steady."

"And after you left Xounges?"

"I had a most curious adventure involving an evil green pearl, which I joyfully relinquished to a robber, then proceeded across Dahaut to Avallon.

"I had an audience with King Audry in his palace. He is pompous and foolish and vain, but he shows a sense of humor, which is a trifle ponderous; still it exists.

"I warned him that spies infested his household, and he laughed in my face. Since he had no secrets of any kind, Casmir wasted his money, which suited Audry perfectly well. There is nothing much more to tell, except that Audry is willing that you should marry his pregnant daughter Thaubin."

"This I am not ready for."

A footman entered and muttered into Aillas' ear.

Aillas screwed up his face and turned to Tristano. "Wait for me in the yard; for this business I am committed to privacy."

Tristano departed and a moment later Yane came into the room, so quietly that the air seemed not to stir behind him.

Aillas jumped to his feet. "Once more you are back and once more I can breathe again!"

"You over-estimate the danger," said Yane.

"If you were taken, you would sing a different song."

"No doubt. Sing I would, loudly and quickly, and hope to avoid Casmir's persuasions. There are few men I fear. He is one of them."

Aillas again went to look out the window. "He must have other spies beside yourself."

"He does indeed, and one of them is a traitor among your close advisors. Casmir almost named me his name, then thought better of it. But this man sits in a high place."

Aillas pondered. "I wonder how close and how high."

"Very high and very close."

Aillas shook his head pensively. "I find it hard to believe."

"You confer often with your ministers?"

"Every week, at least."

"These ministers are the same, from week to week?"

"There is no great change."

"What are their names?"

"They are six, all lords of the realm: Maloof. Pirmence. Foirry. Sion-Tansifer. Langlark. Witherwood. None could gain by Casmir's victory."

"Which have cause for resentment?"

Aillas shrugged. "Perhaps I am reckoned too young or too reckless or too headstrong. The South Ulfland expedition is not everywhere popular."

"Which of the six is the most zealous?"

"Probably Maloof, who is Chancellor of the Exchequer. All are apt to their work. Langlark at times seems listless, but I have reason to exempt him from suspicion."

"What reason is this?"

"I have tried to put the event out of my mind — now, it seems, wrongly. In Blaloc, as you know, shipyards build fishing boats and coastal traders. Recently a certain Duke Geronius of Armorica contracted for the construction of four heavy war-galleasses, of a class which could easily give us trouble on a calm day. Upon inquiry I discovered that Duke Geronius of Armorica is non-existent. He is Casmir, trying to create a navy on the sly. As soon as the ships are launched and Casmir has paid over his gold, I will send a force and burn them to the water-line, and there will be a great gnashing of teeth in Haidion Palace."

"So then?"

"During a conference, with four ministers present, I mentioned rumors of ship-building at Port Posedel in Blaloc. I mentioned that I had asked a merchant dealing in glass bottles, now on his way to Port Posedel, to look into the matter.

"The merchant never returned. I made inquiries at his factory and discovered that he had been murdered in Blaloc."

Yane nodded in slow rumination. "And the ministers who listened to your remarks?"

"Maloof, Sion-Tansifer, Pirmence and Foirry. Langlark and Wither-wood were not present."

"The incident would seem significant."

"Exactly so. But enough for now. I am off to Watershade with Tristano and Shimrod, where, if you will believe it, there is a vexing problem to be solved. With Shimrod's help, the problem may dissolve and we will have a few days of simple peace. Would you care to join the company?"

Yane excused himself. "I must go to my place Skave, and make sure of kegs for the new wine. What troubles the placid ways of Water-shade?"

"The druids. They have settled the island Inisfadhe, where they put a fine fright into Glyneth, and I must set things to rights."

"Send Shimrod out to throw a gloom on them, or, better, transform them all into crayfish."

Aillas looked over his shoulder as if to make sure that Shimrod was not within earshot. "Shimrod already wonders at my sudden invitation. When dealing with druids, magic is a comforting convenience. I will let Glyneth tell her story; she can twist Shimrod around her finger, and any other man she chooses to wheedle."

"Including a certain Aillas, so I have noticed."

"Yes. A certain Aillas very much so."

Chapter 3

I

WATERSHADE HAD BEEN BUILT during a long-past time of troubles, to guard the traffic on Janglin Water and to over-awe the warrior knights of the Ceald, and never had it so much as come under assault.

The castle stood at the very edge of the lake, with part of the barrel-shaped keep rising from the water itself. Low conical roofs capped both the keep and the four squat towers adjoining. Trees overshadowed both towers and keep, and softened the castle's mass, while the quaint conical roofs seemed almost comically inadequate to the task of sheltering the heavy structures below.

Aillas' father Ospero had built a terrace around the base of the keep, where it shouldered into the lake. On many a summer evening, while sunset faded into dusk, Aillas and Ospero, perhaps with guests, took supper on the terrace, and often, if the company was good, sat long over nuts and wine and watched the stars come out.

On the shore grew several large fig trees, which during the heat of summer exhaled a pervasive sweetness attracting countless droning insects; the boy Aillas was not infrequently stung as he clambered among the smooth gray boughs after fruit.

The keep encompassed a great round hall containing a dining table in the shape of a C thirty feet in diameter at which fifty persons could sit in comfort, or sixty with somewhat less elbow-room. Ospero's library occupied the floor above, along with a gallery, several parlours and retiring rooms. The towers housed airy bed-chambers and pleasant sitting-rooms for the lord of the castle, his family and guests.

When the court moved to Domreis the moat was neglected and at last became a quagmire choked with reeds, blackberry thicket and scrub willow. Fetid odors rose from the slime and at last Aillas ordained restoration. Work-gangs were employed three months; then finally the gates were opened and fresh water rushed once again into the channel, though the moat now served only domestic purposes. During storms boats were brought in from the lake and moored in the moat. Ducks and geese paddled among the reeds, and the calm waters were fished for carp, eels and pike.

For Aillas, Watershade was the scene of his most pleasant memories, and across the years changes were few. Weare and Flora now used the titles 'Seneschal' and 'Chatelaine of the House'. Cern, once a stable-boy and Aillas' playmate, had become 'Under-Master of the Royal Stable'. Tauncy, the one-time bailiff, had gone lame. As 'Master Vintner to the Royal Estates', he controlled the work of Aillas' winery.

After long delay, and only at the behest of Weare, Aillas agreed to move into his father's old chambers, while Dhrun took over those rooms once used by Aillas.

"So it must be," Weare told Aillas. "There is no stopping the fall of the autumn leaves, nor the coming of new leaves in the spring. As I have often remarked to Dame Flora, you are perhaps over-inclined to sentimentality. Now, all has changed! How can you hope to rule a kingdom if you are too timid to venture from your childhood nursery?"

"Weare, dear fellow, you have put a hard question! If truth be known, I am not anxious to rule a kingdom, much less three. When I am here at Watershade, it all seems a joke!"

"Nevertheless, things are as they are, and I have heard good reports of you. Now it is only proper that you occupy the High Chambers."

Aillas gave an uncomfortable grimace. "No doubt but what you are right, and you shall have your way. Still I feel my father's presence everywhere! If you must have the truth, sometimes I think to see his ghost standing on the balcony, or looking into the embers when the fire burns low."

Weare made a scornful sound. "What of that? I see good Sir Ospero often. On moonlight nights, should I step into the library, he will be sitting in his chair. He turns to look at me, and his face is placid. I suspect that he loved Watershade so dearly that even in death he can not bear to depart."

"Very well," said Aillas. "I hope that Sir Ospero will forgive my intrusion. I will change none of his arrangements."

Again Weare found cause for protest. "Now then, lad! That is not as he would want it, since he loved you as well! The chambers are now yours and you must arrange them to your own taste, not to those of a ghost."

"So it shall be! Well then, what would you suggest?"

"First, a good scraping, scouring and re-waxing of the woodwork. Then a careful over-wash of the plaster. The green, so I have noticed, tends to go dingy with time; why not try a nice pale blue with yellow for the moldings?"

"Perfect! Exactly what is needed! Weare, you have a rare talent for such matters!"

"Also, while we are on the subject, perhaps we should renovate the Lady Glyneth's chambers. I will of course consult with her, but I suggest that we plaster over the stone and use washes of pink and white and yellow, for good cheer and happy awakenings!"

"Just so! Look to it, Weare, if you will!"

In the case of Glyneth, Aillas had fixed upon her a pretty little estate in a valley not far from Domreis, but she showed no great interest in the property and much preferred Watershade. Now fifteen years old, Glyneth, for the grace and charm of her own life, and the enlivenment of her friends', used a mingling of limpid simplicity and sunny optimism, together with a joyous awareness of the world's absurdities. During the previous year she had grown taller by an inch, and though she liked to wear a boy's trousers and blouse, only a person blind to beauty could mistake her for a boy.

Dame Flora, however, considered not only her garments but her conduct unconventional. "My dear, what will folk think? When does a princess sail out on the lake in a cock-boat? When does one find her climbing trees and perching among the owls? Or wandering the Wild Woods alone like a hoyden?"

"I wish I might meet such a princess," said Glyneth. "She would make me a fine companion; our tastes would be exactly alike!"

"I doubt if two like her exist!" declared Dame Flora. "It is time that this present princess learns the uses of propriety, so that she will not disgrace herself at court."

"Dame Flora, have pity! Would you cast me out, perhaps into the cold and rain, merely because I cannot sew a fine seam?"

"Never, my darling! But we must observe, we must learn, and we must practice the dictates of etiquette! You have reached the age and come into certain attributes of the body which make trousers altogether unsuitable, and we must plan for you a wardrobe of pretty frocks."

"Still, we must be practical! How can I jump a fence in a pretty frock? Ask yourself that!"

"It is not necessary that you jump fences! I jump no fences. Lady Vaudris of Hanch Hall jumps no fences. Before long suitors of high degree will be trooping out here by the score to ask your hand in marriage. When they arrive and wish to pay their respects, and when they ask, I must say: 'You will find her somewhere about the estate, either here or there.' So off they go to look, and what will they think when they find you dangling in a tree, or catching frogs in the moat?"

"They will think that they do not want to marry me, which is exactly to my taste."

At this, Dame Flora aimed a spank at Glyneth's bottom, but Glyneth dodged nimbly aside. "That is the art of agility."

"Shameless little hussy, you will come to a bad end!" Flora spoke without heat, and indeed she was grinning to herself. A moment later, for a special treat, she gave Glyneth a dish of lemon cakes.

Glyneth wore her curling golden hair loose, or tied with a black ribbon. While apparently artless, she sometimes indulged in games of mild flirtation, which she played as a kitten pretends the predacity of the jungle. Often she used Aillas as the subject of her experiments, until Aillas, gritting his teeth and turning his eyes to the sky, by main force of will drew back lest he take the game into an area where relationships might forever be altered.

Sometimes, lying abed of nights, he wondered what went on in Glyneth's mind, and how serious she was in her play. Always at these times other images came to disturb him.

These were no longer dreary recollections of the secret garden at Haidion. Suldrun had long become a misty shape lost and gone across the gulfs of time. Another more vital figure marched through Aillas' mind. Her name was Tatzel; she was Ska, and she lived at Castle Sank in North Ulfland. Tatzel's style was unique. She was slim as a wand, with dark hair hanging loose past her ears; her complexion, like that of all the Ska, was pale olive; her eyes glowed with intelligence. Aillas had seen her most usually striding along the main gallery of the castle, looking neither right nor left. She took no notice of Aillas; as a slave, he was of less concern to her than a chair.

Aillas could not easily define his feelings toward Tatzel. There was resentment and challenge, generated by his abraded self-esteem, but other more subtle yearnings had brought him queer little pangs whenever she walked past unseeing; he wanted to step forward to where she must stop to notice him, to look into his eyes and take heed of his own prideful being. Never could he have dared to touch her; she would have instantly cried out for the guards and Aillas would have been dragged away in disgrace, perhaps even to the gelding-board and a future too awful to contemplate, with both his manhood and all hope of Tatzel's good opinion forever lost and gone.

When finally Aillas had escaped Castle Sank in company with Cargus and Yane, he had turned at one point, and, looking back, had muttered: "Tatzel, take heed! Someday we shall meet again, and on different terms, so it may be!" And such was the phantom haunting Aillas' mind.

II

AFTER PASSING THE NIGHT AT HAG HARBOR, and at noon crossing over
Green Man's Gap, Aillas and Tristano late in the afternoon rode clat-
tering across the drawbridge and into the stable-yard at Watershade.
Dhrun and Glyneth ran out to greet them, followed by Weare, Flora
and others of the household, while Shimrod* waited in the shadow of
the arched passage leading out upon the terrace.

The travelers retired to their chambers to refresh themselves, then
came down to the terrace, where Weare served the best supper his
larders could afford, and the company sat long while the afterglow faded
and dusk became night.

Tristano told of the green pearl and its sinister infection. "I am baffled
by the power of the object! It seemed a true pearl, except for its colour,
which was the green of sea-water! Shimrod, what do you make of it?"

"I am ashamed to admit that, for me, in the realm of magic there
is far more unknown than known. The green pearl is beyond my conjecture."

"It might have been the brain-stone of a demon," mused Glyneth.
"Or perhaps a goblin's egg."

"Or a basilisk's eye," suggested Dhrun.

Glyneth said thoughtfully: "There is a valuable lesson here, say, for
a youth in his formative years, like Dhrun. Never steal or rob objects
of value, especially if they are green!"

"Good advice!" declared Tristano. "In cases of this sort, honesty is
the best policy."

"You have frightened and daunted me," said Dhrun. "I will stop
stealing at once."

"Unless, of course, it is something nice for me," said Glyneth. Tonight,
perhaps to please Dame Flora, she wore a white frock and a silver fillet
enameled with white daisies to contain her hair; she made a charming
picture, to which Tristano was by no means oblivious.

Tristano said modestly: "My conduct at least was exemplary. I took

---

*Shimrod, while wandering the Daut countryside as 'Doctor Fidelius, Charlatan
and Mender of Sore Knees', had befriended a pair of vagabond children named
Dhrun and Glyneth, and thereafter the three had traveled together. Across the
years Shimrod had changed little. A long nose, crooked mouth and gaunt cheeks
gave his face a droll cast; he retained his spare physique, pale gray eyes under
half-closed lids, and as ever wore his light brown hair cut short in the peasant
style. See *LYONESSE I: Suldrun's Garden*.

the pearl only as a public service and I gave it up willingly to one less fortunate in his birth than myself."

Dhrun said: "Here, evidently, you refer to the dog, since we have no knowledge of the robber's lineage."

Glyneth spoke severely: "Your treatment of the dog was truly rather heartless! You should have brought the pearl to Shimrod."

"So that he might feed it to me in a sausage?" demanded Shimrod. "I prefer it otherwise."

"Poor Shimrod!" murmured Aillas. "Foaming at the mouth, running down the road at full speed, halting only to bite passers-by!'

Glyneth said with dignity: "Shimrod could properly dispose of the thing, whatever its nature. The dog lacks this competence."

"I now understand my mistake," said Tristano. "When this dog came to snap at my horse's heels, I admit that I lacked kindly feeling for the beast. I therefore acted on an impulse which almost instantly I regretted, and more when I saw the disreputable quality of the beast."

"I do not quite understand," said Glyneth. "You almost instantly regretted your cruelty?"

"Well, not altogether. Remember that I indemnified the dog with a sausage for his risk."

"Why, then?"

Tristano gave a fastidious flutter of the fingers. "Since you press me, I will explain, and as delicately as possible. On the previous midnight the pearl was returned to me in an uncanny fashion. As I considered the dead dog, I thought at first to depart at full speed and to leave the dog behind. Then I began to ponder on the night ahead: specifically, on the hour of midnight while I lay asleep. At this time the pearl would have progressed well on its way along the dog's digestive tract—"

Glyneth clapped her hands over her ears. "That is enough. Already you have told me more than I want to hear."

"The subject would seem to lack any further interest," said Aillas.

"Just so," said Tristano. "I only wanted to excite Glyneth's compassion for the travail to which I was subjected."

"You have done so," said Glyneth.

There was a moment of quiet, and Glyneth looked up the table to Aillas. "Tonight you are quiet! "What troubles you? Affairs of state?"

Aillas looked off across the dark water. "Miraldra seems a thousand miles away. I wish that I need never go back."

"Perhaps you take too much responsibility upon yourself."

"With my counselors and ministers all older men, watching to catch me out in mistakes, I have no choice except to go carefully. There is a chaos in South Ulfland which I must organize, and perhaps come to grips with the Ska, unless they mend their ways. And all the while, even as we sit here, Casmir hatches new plots."

"Then why not work plots upon Casmir, until he desists?"

"If only it were so easy! Clever plots are Casmir's specialty; I can never beat him at intrigue. His spies are everywhere; they would know my clever plots before I know them myself!"

Dhrun made a sound of outrage. "Can we not identify the spies and drown them all in the Lir?"

"Nothing is ever simple. Naturally, I want to identify them, but thereafter I prefer to make their life easy and befuddle them with false information. If I drowned them all, Casmir would merely send over a group of strangers. So I make do with the lot I have and try not to cause them anxiety."

"This 'befuddling' seems a clever plot in itself," said Glyneth. "Is it effective?"

"I will know better after I identify the spies."

Glyneth asked: "Certainly our own spies keep watch on Casmir?"

"Not as carefully as he watches us. Still, we are not utterly overmatched."

"In some ways, it seems an interesting business," said Glyneth. "I wonder if I would do well as a spy."

"Beyond a doubt," said Aillas. "Beautiful girls make excellent spies! Still, they must be dedicated to their work, and take the good with the bad, since the choicest items are usually told to them in the dark."

Glyneth made a scornful sound. "And these are the spies you befuddle all night long, and make their lives easy, rather than hanging them on the gibbet!"

"Ha! No such luck! Casmir is not so considerate! He subverts one of my close counselors instead. Needless to say, impart this knowledge to no one!"

Dhrun said: "It must be a a strange feeling to look from face to face and wonder which conceals the spy."

"It is just that, indeed."

Tristano asked: "How many are the suspects?"

"They are my six august and irreproachable ministers: Maloof, Langlark, Sion-Tansifer, Pirmence, Foirry and Witherwood. Each is a lord of the realm! In all logic each should be as faithful to me as the moon to the sun. Nevertheless, one of the lot is a traitor. I say this with embarrassment, since it grinds at my self-esteem."

"And how will you find him out?"

"I wish I knew."

For a period, while the stars moved across the sky, the party discussed schemes for exposing the traitor. At last, when candles guttered low, they rose yawning to their feet and took themselves off to bed.

III

THE VISITORS MADE READY to return to Domreis. Glyneth and Dhrun, as they watched the preparations, became ever more restless; Watershade would seem quiet and lonely when the company had gone. Also, both had become intrigued by the mystery of the highly-placed spy. At the last minute, the two decided to join the group returning to Domreis, and hastily made their own preparations.

Across the Ceald rode the party, now five: up to Green Man's Gap where, as was the custom, all turned for a final glimpse of Watershade, then down Rundle River Valley to Hag Harbour and a night at the Sea Coral Inn. Then: an early departure, with harness jingling loud in the pre-dawn chill and up over Cape Haze with the first red rays of day shining wan on their backs, and, early in the afternoon, arrival at Domreis.

Aillas was not deceived as to the purposes of Dhrun and Glyneth. He took them aside and cautioned them to the most extreme discretion. "This is far from a game of quick wits and good-fellowship! There are lives at stake and Casmir cares nothing of how he spends them!"

"He must be a strange harsh man!" said Dhrun.

"He is indeed, and one of his spies watches us at close range, as we might watch chickens going about their affairs in the barnyard."

Glyneth asked in perplexity: "This spy of course is a traitor, but what could be his purpose? Where is his gain?"

Aillas shrugged. "Perhaps he spies from caprice, from the thrill of playing a dangerous game. Certainly he will be the most suspicious of men, alert to every glance and whisper, so be subtle!"

"I think that you can trust us," said Dhrun with dignity. "We are not absolute fools; we do not intend to glance and nudge each other, or peek quickly, then whisper together."

"I know this very well," said Aillas. "In fact, I am curious to learn your opinions!" And Aillas thought to himself: who knows? One or the other might perceive discords or inconsistencies overlooked by others.

For such reasons Aillas arranged a banquet to which he invited his ministers and a few others. The event took place on a cheerless afternoon, with the wind veering down from a hard blue sky. With garments flapping and hands to hats, the dignitaries rode out along the causeway to Miraldra. In the foyer they were met by Sir Este the Seneschal, who conducted them to the smallest of the banquet halls. Here, Aillas with Dhrun and Glyneth awaited the company.

On this informal occasion the six ministers were seated in order of their arrival, three to each side of the table, without reference to precedence. Beyond were placed Sir Tristano and two noblemen of foreign parts. The first of these was a gentleman tall and spare, with a wry long-jawed face, who called himself Sir Catraul of Catalonia. He wore strange and lavish garments and powdered his face in the style of the Aquitanian court. Dhrun and Glyneth could barely restrain their merriment to see Shimrod bedizened in such gorgeous fashion.

Across from Shimrod sat Yane, who had darkened his skin, concealed his chin behind a black beard and his hair under a turban. He called himself Sir Hassifa from Tingitana, and spoke almost no words whatever.

When his guests were seated, Aillas rose to his feet. "Today I give welcome to my cousin, two grandees from far lands, and six gentlemen who are not only my advisers but also my friends, trusted and true! I wish to introduce you to my son, Prince Dhrun, and to my ward, Princess Glyneth! First, from Dascinet, Lord Maloof of Maul House."

Maloof, who was robust, of no great stature, with black curling hair and a short thick beard framing a round pale face, rose to his feet. He bowed with a flourish of the hand toward Glyneth and sat once again.

Aillas spoke: "Lord Pirmence of Castle Lutez!"

Pirmence rose and bowed: a gentleman somewhat older than Maloof, slim and handsome, with silver-gray hair, disdainfully arched eyebrows, a short silver-gray beard, and features of fastidious distinction.

"Lord Sion-Tansifer of Porthouse Faming!"

Sion-Tansifer, oldest of the ministers, and easily the most brusque and truculent, stood stiffly erect. His field of knowledge was military strategy, in its most conservative and orthodox phases, and Aillas found his views interesting more often than useful. Sion-Tansifer was valuable for a different reason: his opinions, often couched in the form of dogmatic truism, annoyed the others and diverted their criticism from Aillas himself. Sion-Tansifer subscribed to the chivalric ideal and on this informal occasion bowed first to Princess Glyneth, then to Prince Dhrun, allowing gallantry to over-rule the dictates of precedence.

"Lord Witherwood of Witherwood House!"

Lord Witherwood, a gentleman of middle years, was pallid and thin, with haggard cheeks, eyes of intense black and a mouth clenched as if to control great inner energies. He was passionate in his convictions and impatient with orthodoxy, a trait which endeared him not at all to either Sion-Tansifer or Maloof, the first of whom Witherwood considered a narrow-minded martinet and the second a niggling and fussy mother hen. He acknowledged the introduction with a pair of cursory nods and subsided in his seat.

"Lord Langlark of Black Chine Castle!"

Langlark, as if gently to admonish Witherwood for his brusque behavior, rose ponderously and bowed right and left in grand style. A
portly gentleman of undistinguished appearance, Langlark nevertheless
contributed humour, moderation and practicality to the deliberations
of the council. Aillas tended to find him the most supportive of all his
ministers.

"Lord Foirry of Suanetta."

Foirry performed a pair of polite, if perfunctory, bows. He was slight
and somewhat hunched at the shoulders, and, though not so old as
Maloof, he had gone bald save for a fringe of black curls. Quick movements of the head, darting brown eyes, with a lean hooking nose and
a cynically curling mouth, gave him a look of minatory vigilance.
Foirry's moods were mercurial, and sometimes his points of view as
well, since he liked to consider an issue from every side, and tended
to argue with its proponents in order to test the strength of their concepts.

"Sir Tristano is of course well known to you. Beyond sit Sir Catraul
of Catalonia and Sir Hassifa of Tingitana."

The banquet proceeded: at first sedate and guarded, with Lord Sion-
Tansifer stonily silent. Lord Pirmence attempted conversation first with
Sir Catraul, then Sir Hassifa, but receiving only blank looks and shrugs
of incomprehension, turned his attention elsewhere.

Meanwhile Glyneth and Dhrun studied the six ministers in minute
detail. They discovered that each was in some degree a specialist, with
his own area of expertise. Maloof controlled the exchequer, advised in
regard to the imposition of taxes, fees, rents and imposts. Witherwood
worked to codify the judicial systems of the land, reconciling regional
differences and making the laws universally responsive, to persons of
high and low degree alike. Sion-Tansifer, a relict from the reign of King
Granice, advised as to military organization and strategy. Foirry was
an expert in the field of naval architecture. Pirmence, who had traveled
widely, from Ireland to Byzantium, was in effect the Minister of Foreign
Affairs, while Langlark had been commissioned by Aillas to establish
at Domreis a university of letters, mathematics, geography and the
several sciences.

Aillas, also studying the six ministers, felt a peculiar chilly emotion
compounded of mystery and awe, and even something of terror. One
of the six who sat so placidly at his table, eating his food and drinking
his wine, was a traitor: a creature working to his defeat and doom.

Which of the six?

What might be his reasons?

Aillas looked sideways to Dhrun, and felt a swelling of pride for his handsome young son. He looked to Glyneth, and felt a surge of different emotion. She sensed his attention and, turning to meet his eyes, smiled and gave her head a shake to indicate her bafflement; the mystery was beyond her understanding.

The banquet proceeded. The first course, a mince of olives, shrimp and onions baked in oyster shells with cheese and parsley was followed by a soup of tunny, cockles and winkles simmered in white wine with leeks and dill. Then, in order, came a service of broiled quail stuffed with morels, served on slices of good white bread, with side dishes of green peas; artichokes cooked in wine and butter, with a salad of garden greens; then tripes and sausages with pickled cabbage; then a noble saddle of venison glazed with cherry sauce and served with barley first simmered in broth, then fried with garlic and sage; then honey-cakes, nuts and oranges; and all the while the goblets flowed full with noble Voluspa and San Sue from Watershade, along with the tart green muscat wine of Dascinet.

Despite long association the ministers were not easy with each other and, as the banquet progressed, each tended to assert his views with ever more vehemence, so that each came to seem a caricature of himself, and evidence of discord began to appear.

The most severe of the group was Sion-Tansifer, veteran of a dozen campaigns; his grizzled hair twisted and grew askew where scars marred his scalp. His statements were couched in biting, crisp accents, as if each yielded an unassailable truth; those who disagreed earned side-glances of contempt.

Maloof, sitting opposite, tended to qualify all his opinions, so that, compared to Sion-Tansifer, he seemed somewhat vague and indecisive.

In contrast to both was Pirmence, a person suave and handsome, of grand address, easy wit and an unshakable vanity. Pirmence had traveled far and Castle Lutez was said to be a treasure-house of beautiful objects.

Langlark, plump, florid, and modest, used a tactic of half-rueful, half-perplexed self-deprecation which by some devious means made the arguments of others seem foolish and over-heated. Often he pointed out simplicities which everyone else had overlooked, and Pirmence took great care not to run afoul of Langlark, who was perhaps the single minister more subtle than himself.

Witherwood, neat and precise, attacked views which he considered illogical with vicious fervor regardless of person; Aillas had often felt the sting of his criticism, and Maloof despised him utterly. Foirry spoke little and listened to others with an air of sardonic amusement, but when aroused he could be almost as acerb as Witherwood.

During the venison course, the conversation veered toward the South Ulfland involvement*, and few optimistic opinions were heard.

Maloof spoke in measured detachment: "It is an uncomfortable land, all rocks and moors, with here and there a bog, or a ruined hut. It may at some time yield a bare sustenance to its folk, but only if they till their soil with the same zeal they use toward killing each other. The Ulfs are a brutal people!"

"A moment!" cried Glyneth, speaking for the first time. "I was born at Throckshaw, in North Ulfland, and my parents were by no means brutal. They were kind and good and brave, and they were killed by the Ska!"

Maloof blinked in embarrassment. "My apologies! I overspoke, of course! I should have said that the South Ulfish barons are a warlike folk, and that prosperity will come only with a cessation of their feuds and raids."

Sion-Tansifer gave a disparaging grunt. "This on the day gold coins fall from the sky in the place of hail. The Ulfs cherish vendettas as a dog his fleas."

Pirmence said: "Ten years ago I had occasion to visit Ys. I then traveled the overland road to Oäldes. I saw very few folk: herdsmen and crofters, and fishermen along the shore. The land is windy, open and generally empty, and here is its single advantage: it will provide holdings for all our younger sons, if King Aillas so dispenses."

"The country is empty for good reason," stated Foirry. "If the mountain barons released all those immured in their dungeons or stretched out on their racks, the land might even be over-populated."

The literal-minded Maloof raised his eyebrows in consternation. "Why have we ventured into this unhappy land? We waste toil, blood and gold on warlike sorties! The Ulfs are nothing to us!"

"I am their king," said Aillas in a mild and reasonable voice. "They are my subjects. I owe them justice and security."

"Bah!" snapped Witherwood. "The argument fails. Suppose suddenly you were acclaimed King of Cathay; must we then send a flotilla of ships and regiments of Troice soldiers to guard their security and see to their justice?"

---

*Upon the death of South Ulfland's King Oriante, the crown devolved by a torturous line of descent to King Aillas of Troicinet. King Casmir was taken by surprise; while he paced fuming back and forth in the Green Parlour at Haidion, Troice ships brought an expeditionary force to the jetties of Old Ys. This force reduced the terrible castle Tintzin Fyral, garrisoned the fort Kaul Bocach and so guarded South Ulfland from the ambitions of King Casmir.

Aillas laughed. "Cathay is far away, South Ulfland is near at hand."

"Nevertheless," said Maloof stubbornly, "I feel that the proper use of your revenues is here, among your own people!"

Sion-Tansifer issued a surly pronouncement: "I confess that I am not happy with this expedition. The rogue barons guard their glens like wolves and eagles! If we killed them all, as many more would hop from the gorse to take their places, and all would be as before."

Langlark looked across the table with brows knitted, in his customary expression of perplexity. "Do you suggest that we abandon this wide land! Is such a surrender to our advantage? Pirmence definitely exaggerates the case; the land is not without resources, and was once considered a rich kingdom. The mines yield tin, copper, gold and silver, and there are wide deposits of bog iron. In other times, cattle and sheep grazed the moors and the fields were planted to oats, corn and barley."

Sion-Tansifer gave a grim chuckle. "The Ulfs can keep their 'wide land' and enjoy their splendid wealth, with my compliments and indeed my gratitude, if they will strike back the Ska and spill their own blood in the process. Why should we pull their chestnuts from the fire? For wealth? There is none at hand. For glory? Where the glory in chasing bog-trotters over the moors?"

"Hm ha!" Pirmence patted his silver-gray beard with a napkin. "You are mordant in your views!" He looked up the table toward Aillas. "Sir, what do you say to these carkers and pessimists?"

Aillas leaned back in his chair. "I have spoken at length on this topic; are your memories all so short? I will repeat myself. We have occupied South Ulfland in search of neither wealth nor glory nor fallow land, but for one reason only: survival."

Sion-Tansifer gave a skeptical shake of the head. "Either I am stupid, or the concept is at flaw."

"This is a judgment which perhaps only King Aillas will care to make," suggested Pirmence delicately.

Aillas laughed. "Obviously Lord Sion-Tansifer's alternatives are not exclusive." He looked around the table. "Who else would wish to withdraw from South Ulfland? Maloof?"

"The venture is a serious drain upon the exchequer. I feel competent to say no more."

"Pirmence?"

Pirmence pursed his lips. "We are there! Difficult if not impossible to disengage now with honour."

"Langlark?"

"Your arguments are compelling."

"Witherwood?"

"I feel that we have cast our dice on a very long roll. I hope that good luck goes with us."

"Foirry?"

"Our ships own the sea. So long as this is the case, Troicinet need not fear."

"Sir Tristano, what is your opinion?"

Tristano hesitated a moment, then: "Let me ask this: what might be the consequences if indeed we relinquished Kaul Bocach and Tintzin Fyral and departed South Ulfland?"

Aillas said: "The hour in which we abandoned South Ulfland, King Casmir, after pinching himself to make sure that he was awake and then dancing a brief jig of sheer joy, would march his troops north on the double-quick. Later, at leisure, with all his armies at the ready, he would attack Dahaut from two directions, and in a month King Audry must flee to Aquitania or die. Casmir would then bring Cairbra an Meadhan the Table and Evandig the Throne to Lyonesse Town, and name himself King of the Elder Isles. In the Mermeil estuary he could and would build a flotilla adequate to land his troops on Dascinet, and we would be lost. By moving into South Ulfland we have thwarted Casmir's plan, and have forced him to a more difficult program."

"You have quite convinced me," said Sir Tristano. "Lord Sion-Tansifer, what of you?"

"In all due respect, the premises are at fault. At this moment Casmir can march north up the Trompada and never set foot into South Ulfland."

"Not so," said Aillas. "He would find himself immediately at war with us, and his logistics would be impossible. So long as we held South Ulfland and the Teach tac Teach, Casmir would never dare the Trompada. Using only local troops, we could interdict him with ease."

Maloof spoke almost querulously: "Why all this talk of menace and hostility? Have we not ratified treaties of peace with Lyonesse? Why presume the worst case? If we show Casmir that we truly want peace, then he will reciprocate in kind, and there need be no more bluster, or clanking and clashing of weapons, which can only exacerbate the case."

"Cast your mind back a few years," said Aillas. "Granice was king of Troicinet. Ivar Excelsus of Dascinet thought to punish us by a war and called on Casmir for help. Casmir was only too anxious to bring his armies across the Lir, and if our ships had not smashed his armada, none of us would be dining here today at Miraldra. Has Casmir changed his spots? Obviously not."

Maloof was not convinced. "Still, South Ulfland is not Dascinet."

Witherwood asked him drily: "You believe, then, that if we are polite to Casmir, he will cause us no trouble?"

"We have nothing to lose," said Maloof with dignity. "Anything is preferable to war."

"Not anything," said Langlark.

Aillas said: "None of us wants war, not even Casmir, who would prefer to build his triumph upon our weakness and folly. While I am king this will not be; still, I will work to keep the peace. You may be interested to learn that King Casmir and Queen Sollace are coming to Domreis for a state visit."

"I consider that good news!" declared Maloof. "When will this be?"

"In about a month."

Foirry gave a hoot of sardonic laughter. "What a farce is diplomacy!"

Aillas smiled. "As king I must be the very model of propriety, no matter how my guts roil inside me. . . . I have said more than I chose to say."

The banquet came to an end. Aillas and Yane, with Glyneth and Dhrun, went to sit before a fire in one of the small parlours.

Aillas asked, "So then: what is the general consensus?"

Yane looked long into the flames. "It is hard to judge. Langlark and Foirry are unlikely because of the glass-merchant episode. Sion-Tansifer is no doubt brave, if perhaps a trifle single-minded. A traitor? Unlikely. Maloof? Witherwood? Pirmence? My intuition settles upon Maloof. He is anxious for peace and so is ready to make concessions. Many such folk are known to history; Maloof might even consider himself a great hero of secret diplomacy, appeasing Casmir and so fostering some far-fetched concept of goodwill.

"Then there is Pirmence. He seems flexible and might be induced to spy — for gold or from sheer boredom. He is one of that deceptively dangerous sort who, in the name of tolerance, will condone any sort of strange behavior — especially in himself.

"Witherwood? If he is a spy, his motives are hard to guess."

IV

AT NOON OF THE DAY after the banquet, Lord Maloof reported to King Aillas upon the condition of the royal exchequer. Maloof's demeanor was somber and he brought bad news: "By reason of the incursion into South Ulfland, together with the costs of naval construction at the Tumbling River yards, our financial reserves have been reduced to a critical level."

"Hmm," said Aillas. "This does not make for good hearing."

"I have long given warnings in this direction." Maloof spoke with gloomy satisfaction. "Now the crows have come home to roost."

"So it may be. . . . What of our Dascinet revenues: have they arrived?"

"Not yet, sir, nor the Scola moneys. Neither are due until next week."

"For a week, then, we must live on the cheap. Before long, or so I hope, South Ulfland will be paying its own way. I have sent mining engineers to examine the old mines, which, so I am told, were never worked out, but simply abandoned because of bandits and robbers. Also, there may be alluvial gold in the rivers. They have never been worked and may eventually yield a large return: enough to pay all our expenses. What do you say to that?"

"So far, this flood of wealth is all hypothetical, and no doubt will require a substantial investment before we can so much as prove its existence."

Aillas grinned. "Maloof, you have a most dampening habit of practicality! If worse comes to worst we shall rely for funds on that method known far and wide as 'Old Infallible': taxes! Squeeze them till their shoes squeak! Kings alone should be allowed the use of money! It is far too good for the common people."

Maloof said sadly: "Sir, I suspect that you jest."

"Not altogether. I intend to impose port taxes at Ys; so far they have gone unscathed. Also, we must start to collect those revenues from the Evander Valley which were formerly paid to Carfilhiot. So there is profit in sight! And sooner or later we will shake the barons loose from the hoarded gold they have gained by robbing from each other."

Maloof frowned at what he considered flaws in the idea, but again decided that Aillas was indulging his humour. "A formidable program!" said Maloof.

Aillas laughed. "But in practice very simple. I shall dictate laws which I know they will break; then I will fine them large sums, which they must pay or be turned out upon the moors. I only wish I could do the same for King Casmir and his illicit warship, but I fear he would not pay his fines."

Maloof raised his eyebrows in wonder. "You are not entitled to levy fines upon King Casmir!"

"Sadly true. Therefore I must use stronger measures."

Again Maloof frowned in puzzlement. "How so?"

"Exactly two weeks from tonight a party of raiders will descend upon the shipyard at Sardilla and burn Casmir's illicit hulk to the ground. In times to come Casmir will take his commitments more seriously."

Maloof shook his head. "Risky business!"

"Less risky than allowing Casmir a fleet of warships."

Maloof had no more to say and took his leave. Later in the day Aillas spoke with Lord Pirmence to whom he imparted the same information. Still later, toward the end of the afternoon, Aillas let slip to Lord

Witherwood and Lord Sion-Tansifer together that the raid at Sardilla would occur in precisely ten days.

Meanwhile, Sir Tristano assured Foirry and Langlark that the raid would take place in twenty days, even though these two were not considered prime suspects.

Early the next day Sir Tristano set off at speed to Sardilla in Caduz, that he might discover which of the three reports prompted countermeasures.

In due course Sir Tristano returned, bone-weary from hard riding and a rough passage across the Lir. Aillas and Yane heard his report with great interest. On the tenth night, no unusual precautions were put into force. On the night of the two-week interval, a hundred heavily armed warriors had lain in ambush, and through a long dismal night awaited an assault which never came.

For full verification, Tristano had delayed until the twentieth night had passed, without event, and then had returned homeward.

"Three facts are now clear," said Aillas. "First, the ship has definitely been commissioned by Casmir. Second, a traitor sits on my Council of Ministers. Third, he is either Maloof or Pirmence."

"Either one fits the role," said Yane. "What now?"

"For the moment, stealth. Let us identify our man without causing him alarm."

V

REPORTS HAD REACHED AILLAS as to rich deposits of bog-iron in South Ulfland, not far from Oäldes, and he had requested that Maloof discover the costs involved in the construction of a foundry.

The figures, as submitted by Maloof, seemed remarkably high. Aillas considered them a moment without comment, then put the document aside. "The project clearly demands a closer scrutiny. At the moment my mind wanders; I could not sleep last night for dreaming."

Maloof showed polite concern. "Indeed, sir! Dreams are prodromes of future truth! They provide bodes which we ignore to our risk!"

"The dreams of last night were remarkably vivid," said Aillas. "They concerned the forthcoming visit of King Casmir. As his ship entered the harbor, I saw Casmir on the deck bare-headed, as clearly as I now see you. He turned away, and a voice spoke into my ear: 'Watch with care! If his hat shows two plumes, blue and green in color, he proves himself friend and faithful ally! If he wears a single yellow plume, he is a treacherous enemy who must be destroyed at any cost!' Three times the voice spoke these words! But when I turned to watch as Casmir donned his hat, I was called aside and never could see."

"A remarkable dream!" said Maloof.

Later, Aillas recounted his remarkable dream to Pirmence: " — the voice spoke in the tones of an oracle. 'Heed the hat which Casmir puts to his head! If it shows a silver medal in the shape of a bird, he is friend and ally! If he displays a golden lion, he signals his treachery!' So spoke the voice, and I am in a quandary. I cannot rule a kingdom on the basis of dreams, yet I might be ignoring true portents to our general danger! What is your opinion?"

Pirmence stroked his silver-gray beard. "I am a practical man; as such I accept anything of value, whatever its source. What sort was the hat?"

"A simple turret of crushed black velvet, lacking brim or standing crown."

"Let me suggest this: observe how closely Casmir's hat matches the hat of your dreams; then be guided by the nature of the emblem."

VI

FROM THE TERRACE of Miraldra's north tower, Aillas and others watched the approach of the carrack *Star Regulus* from Lyonesse: a heavy vessel, blunt of bow and high of poop, and a brave sight with both foresail and mainsail bellied and straining and with red and yellow banderoles streaming from the mast-heads.

The carrack entered the harbor and the crew smartly brailed up the sails. Work-boats brought out lines and the *Star Regulus* was warped to the dock beside Miraldra, and there moored to bollards.

King Aillas now waited on the jetty, along with twenty grandees of the realm and their ladies. A gangplank was raised to the carrack's well-deck, where the stir of splendid personages could be glimpsed. A crew of liveried footmen rolled a strip of rose plush carpet across the dock from gangplank to the three high-backed chairs of state, where King Aillas waited with Prince Dhrun at his right and Princess Glyneth to his left*.

---

*An arrangement decidedly at odds with the dictates of rigorous etiquette, inasmuch as the title 'Princess' which King Aillas had fixed upon Glyneth was honourific only. Aillas, partly from frivolity and partly from motives less easily defined, had in this case over-ruled his Chief Herald, and Glyneth, somewhat self-consciously wearing the diadem of a royal princess, and quite aware of the gossip being promulgated, sat beside Aillas, and presently began to enjoy herself.

On the deck of the *Star Regulus* a stately gentleman stepped forward: King Casmir. At the head of the gangway he paused and was joined by a lady of noble proportions with blonde hair coiled at her ears and netted under white pearls: Queen Sollace. Looking neither right nor left the two descended the gangway to the dock.

Aillas came forward. His gaze went to Casmir's hat: a turret of black velvet, lacking both crown and brim. A silver medal in the shape of a bird adorned the front of the hat; a pair of plumes, blue and green, rose to the side.

Behind Queen Sollace came Prince Cassander and the Princess Madouc. Cassander, a sturdy youth of fifteen, wore a smart green cap over his brass-yellow curls. He was clearly the son of his father and had already adopted certain kingly mannerisms. His round blue eyes, as he surveyed the company, were a trifle minatory, as if to warn all against the slightest disrespect.

In contrast, the Princess Madouc, a long-legged urchin with russet curls, clearly cared nothing either for dignity or the company's approval; after a single brief glance she dismissed them all from her consciousness, and came hopping and jumping down the gangplank like an active young kitten. She wore a long gown of orange-russet velvet tied at the waist with a black sash; her hair, approximately the colour of her gown, hung in loose ringlets. Madouc's mind was clearly as active as her conduct; her snub-nosed little face registered each trifling shift of mood with total transparency. Aillas, who well knew her antecedents, watched her with amusement. Evidently the rumors of Madouc's precocity and exuberant wilfulness had not been exaggerated.

King Casmir, as he offered his arm to Queen Sollace at the foot of the gangplank, gave Madouc a cold glance of admonition, then turned to greet King Aillas.

A half dozen other notables of Lyonesse, in careful order of precedence, descended the gangplank with their ladies, to be announced with appropriate gusto by Miraldra's Chief Herald.

Last to leave the ship were a pair of the queen's personal attendants and, finally, the Christian priest Father Umphred, a portly figure in a plum-colored cassock.

After the formal welcomes, Casmir and Sollace were escorted to their chambers, where they might rest and refresh themselves after the inconveniences of their voyage.

Later in the evening King Aillas sat as host at a casual supper; the full state banquet would be served on the following day. Both Aillas and Casmir dealt austerely with plate and goblet, and both rose sober from the table. They repaired to a private parlour, and, sitting before the fire, sipped a heavy golden Olorosa and discussed those matters which interested them. Neither, however, saw fit to mention the ship being built to Casmir's order in Caduz.

Casmir somewhat quizzically spoke of the fortifications at Kaul Bocach, the gorge which contained the road between Lyonesse and South Ulfland. "Even without fortications, twenty determined men can guard the way against an army. But I am told that now fortress frowns over fortress, that every approach is protected by traps, walls and barbicans, so that impregnability is reinforced a dozen times over. Similarly with Tintzin Fyral, where now the mountain Tac Tor is crowned with a fort as harsh as Tintzin Fyral itself. I cannot understand these feverish preparations, since we have ratified between us treaties which make such works redundant."

"Your information is correct," said Aillas. "The fortifications have been augmented, and certainly they guard against invasion from Lyonesse. But is not the rationale clear? You are not immmortal; imagine, if you will, that a monarch cruel, treacherous and warlike came to rule Lyonesse! Let us suppose that this monarch, for reasons beyond conjecture, decided to attack Ulfland — well then! We are prepared for him and if he is sane he will be dissuaded."

Casmir showed a wintry smile. "I grant a theoretical basis for this line of thought, but is it not, in practice, somewhat far-fetched?"

"I certainly hope so," said Aillas. "May I pour you more of this wine? It is produced on my own estate."

"Thank you; it is very fine indeed. The wines of Troicinet are not as well known at Haidion as they should be."

"That, of course, is a lack easy to overcome, and I shall see to it."

Casmir thoughtfully lifted the goblet, swirled the wine and watched the golden ripples. "It is hard to recall the harsh old times when bad blood existed between our peoples."

"All things change," said Aillas.

"Exactly! Our treaty, signed in the heat of ruffled feelings, stipulated that Lyonesse should build no warships, on an outmoded presumption. Now that amity has returned — "

"Just so!" declared Aillas. "The present equilibrium has served us well! It is a balance which encourages peace across all the Elder Isles. This balance and this peace are vital to us and form the basis of our foreign policy."

"Oh?" King Casmir frowned. "And how can you implement so broad a policy?"

"The principle is simple enough. We can allow neither Lyonesse nor Dahaut to gain ascendancy over the other, because then our own security would disappear. Should King Audry attack Lyonesse and by some miracle gain advantage, then we must join the war on the side of Lyonesse until the stasis returns; and vice versa."

Casmir managed an easy laugh and, draining his goblet, set down the empty vessel with a thump. "I wish that my own goals could be so easily defined. Alas! They depend on such ineffable considerations as justice, the redressment of old wrongs, and the thrust of history."

Aillas poured wine into Casmir's goblet. "I do not envy you your maze of uncertainties. Still, you need be at no doubt in regard to Troicinet. Should either Lyonesse or Dahaut grow strong enough to menace the other, then we must throw our strength behind the weaker. In effect, you are protected by a strong navy without incurring any of the expense."

King Casmir rose to his feet. He spoke somewhat curtly. "I am tired after the voyage, and I will now bid you good evening."

Aillas, rising, said: "I hope that your rest will be comfortable."

The two went to the drawing room where Queen Sollace sat with ladies of both courts. King Casmir went only to the doorway and bowed stiffly to the occupants of the room. Queen Sollace rose to her feet, bade the company goodnight and the two were escorted to their chambers by footmen bearing flamboys.

Aillas returned along the great gallery toward his parlour. From the shadows stepped a stout person in a plum-red cassock. "King Aillas! A moment of your time, if you please!"

Aillas stopped and surveyed the rubicund face of Father Umphred, as he now called himself. Aillas pretended no cordiality. "What do you want?"

Umphred chuckled. "I thought, first of all, to renew our old acquaintance."

Aillas, from sheer distaste, moved back a step. Nothing daunted, Umphred spoke on. "As you may know, I have successfully brought the Holy Message to Lyonesse Town. King Casmir almost certainly will sponsor the construction of a noble cathedral, to glorify the name of God within the precincts of his happy city. If so much transpires, I may well wear the mitre."

"This is nothing to me," said Aillas. "In fact, I am surprised that you dare show your face in my presence."

With a jovial smile and a flourish of the hand, Father Umphred erased every vestige of ill-feeling which might have existed between the two. "I bring to Troicinet the joyous message of the Gospels! Pagan pomp still holds sway in Troicinet, Dascinet and South Ulfland. Nightly I pray that I may bring King Aillas and all his people into the glory of the true faith!"

"I have neither time nor inclination for such matters," said Aillas. "My people believe or disbelieve as they see fit, and that is the way of it." He started to turn away, but Father Umphred put a soft white hand on his arm. "Wait!"

Aillas turned. "Well then, what now?"

Father Umphred smiled a rich and tender smile. "I pray for your personal salvation, and also that, like King Casmir, you will encourage the construction of a cathedral at Domreis the better to disseminate the Truth of God! And, if you like, to rival in splendor the cathedral at Lyonesse Town, and I might hope for the arch-bishopric itself!"

"I will sponsor no Christian church, in Domreis or elsewhere."

Umphred thoughtfully pursed his lips. "Such are your present views but perhaps you may be induced to change them."

"I think not."

Again Aillas turned away, and again Father Umphred detained him. "A great pleasure to see you again, though my mind reverts with sadness to the unhappy events of our first acquaintance. To this day King Casmir is not aware of your old identity! I am assured that you do not wish him to know; otherwise you would have informed him yourself. Am I right in this?" And Father Umphred, standing back, surveyed Aillas with kindly interest.

Aillas reflected a moment, then said in a neutral voice: "Come with me, if you will."

A few steps along the gallery, Aillas paused beside a uniformed footman. "Ask Sir Hassifa the Moor to join me in the small parlour." Aillas beckoned to Umphred. "Come."

His smile now somewhat less fulsome, Umphred followed. Aillas ushered him into the small parlour, shut the door, then went to stand by the fire, to look silently down into the flames.

Father Umphred attempted a pleasantry. "Yes indeed! Your present condition far exceeds your old! Poor little Suldrun: a sad end indeed! The world is a vale of woe, and we are sent here that we may be tested and purified for the halcyon times to come!"

Aillas made no comment. Encouraged by what he thought to be Aillas' deep concern, Umphred continued. "My fondest hope is to lead the King of Troicinet and his noble folk into salvation, and a grand cathedral would cause the angels themselves to sing! And then, naturally, since you seem to prefer it, the facts of your old identity shall remain as secure as the secrets of the confessional."

Aillas darted him a single bright glance, then continued to brood into the flames.

The door opened. Yane, still in the guise of Sir Hassifa the Moor, came quietly into the parlour. Aillas straightened up and swung around. "Ah, Sir Hassifa! May I ask, are you a Christian?"

"By no means."

"Good: a simplification. Take note of this fellow here: what do you see?"

"A priest, fat, white and sleek as a beaver, and no doubt unctuous of tongue. He arrived today from Lyonesse."

"Just so. I want you to examine him with care, so that you will never mistake him for any other."

"Sir, he could pull the hood tight around his face, name himself Beelzebub and hide in the deepest catacomb of Rome and still I would know him."

"You will find this amazing! He claims old acquaintance with me."

Sir Hassifa turned to examine Umphred with wonder. "What could be his motives?"

"He wants me to build him a fine church at Domreis. If I refuse, he threatens to betray my identity to King Casmir."

Sir Hassifa inspected Umphred anew. "Is he addled? King Casmir already knows your identity. You are Aillas of Troicinet."

Umphred began to dislike the tone of the conversation. He licked his lips. "Yes, yes, of course. I merely ventured a pleasantry, as might pass between old friends!"

Aillas spoke to Sir Hassifa: "He persists in his claim! I am becoming annoyed. If he were not here as a guest, I might well clap him into a dungeon. I may do so in any case."

"Do not soil your hospitality on his account!" Sir Hassifa advised. "Wait until he returns to Lyonesse. I can have his throat cut at any hour of day or night, with a sharp or dull knife."

Aillas said: "It might be best to drag him before Casmir at this very moment and hear what he has to say. Then, if he utters some malicious tale—"

"Wait!" cried Umphred desperately. "I now understand my error! I was mistaken, in whole and in part! I have never seen you before in my life!"

Sir Hassifa said: "I fear that he might yet blurt out some tumble of dirty nonsense, to the detriment of your dignity." He produced a gleaming dagger. "Let me cut out his tongue, at least. We will cauterize the wound with a hot poker."

"No, no!" cried Umphred, now sweating. "I will say nothing to anyone! My lips are sealed! I know a thousand secrets; all are immured forever!"

Aillas said to Yane: "Since he is a guest, I can take the matter no farther. But if ever a rumor or hint of his folly be heard—"

"No need to threaten!" declared Umphred. "I have made a sad mistake, which will never be repeated!"

"That is good news," said Aillas. "Especially for you. Remember that the person for whom you mistook me has reason to take a savage revenge upon you."

"The episode is forgotten," said Umphred. "Pray excuse me now; I am fatigued and I still have my devotions to perform."

"Go."

VII

FROM MIRALDRA'S MAIN GALLERY a portal opened into the great hall. To either side of the opening stood a heroic marble statue, the pair brought from the Mediterranean five centuries before. The statues represented warriors of ancient Hellas, naked save for helmets, with short swords and shields held in attitudes of attack.

King Casmir and Queen Sollace, after taking breakfast in their chambers, strolled along the gallery, pausing now and again to examine those objects of craft and virtue which across the years had been collected by the kings of Troicinet.

Beside one of the marble statues stood a footman in the livery of Miraldra, armed with a ceremonial halberd. As King Casmir and Queen Sollace paused to examine the heroic figures, the footman made a signal to King Casmir, who, turning his head, recognized that person whom he knew as 'Valdez'.

King Casmir looked up and down the gallery, then stepped apart from Queen Sollace and approached the footman. "So this is your vantage-point!" he muttered. "I have often wondered!"

"You would not see me here today, had I not wished to speak with you. I will no longer be coming to Lyonesse Town; my movements are attracting notice among the fishermen."

"Oh?" King Casmir's voice was flat. "What will you do now?"

"I intend a quiet life in the country."

King Casmir, pretending interest in the statue, reflected a moment. "You must come to Lyonesse Town one last time, that I may reward you properly for your service. Perhaps we might arrange a new system, from which you would derive profit but know no risk."

"I think not," said Valdez drily. "Still, if someone speaks my name at Haidion, give him attention; he will bring news. . . . Someone approaches."

King Casmir turned away, and with Queen Sollace strolled down the gallery.

After a moment Sollace asked: "Why do you frown so?"

King Casmir forced a laugh. "Perhaps I envy King Aillas his fine statues! We must see to something similar at Haidion."

"I would rather have a set of authentic relics for my church," mused Queen Sollace.

King Casmir, lost in thought, spoke absent-mindedly: "Yes, yes, my dear; so it shall be, just as you wish."

Events, in fact, were not going to King Casmir's satisfaction. When spies left his employ, he liked to terminate the relationship in a definite manner, so that they might never sell their services elsewhere, and perhaps apply what they had learned to his detriment. . . . Slowly he became aware of Queen Sollace's voice: " — so Father Umphred assures me, is to buy before the need is recognized. He knows of three authentic splinters from the Holy Cross that we could acquire at this moment for a hundred crowns apiece. The Holy Grail itself is known to be somewhere about the Elder Isles, and Father Umphred has had the opportunity to buy maps providing exact — "

Casmir demanded: "Woman, what are you talking about?"

"The relics for the cathedral, of course!"

"How can you talk of relics when the cathedral itself is no more than a hallucination?"

Queen Sollace spoke with dignity. "Father Umphred declares that in time the Holy Lord will surely bring you to grace."

"Ha. If the Holy Lord wants a cathedral so badly, let him build it himself."

"I shall so pray!"

Half an hour later King Casmir and Queen Sollace again passed by the statues, but now Valdez was nowhere to be seen.

Chapter 4

THE *STAR REGULUS* EASED AWAY from the jetty and with yards braced hard on the port tack, gathered way and departed Miraldra. King Casmir climbed to the poop deck and went to stand by the taff-rail. He raised his arm high toward the notables on the dock; his expression, placid and benign, indicated only satisfaction with his visit.

The carrack, leaving the harbour, rose and fell to long swells from the west. Casmir descended the companionway and retired to the main saloon. He settled into the great chair and, gazing out the stern casements, mulled over the events of the past few days.

Apparently, and for all to see, the visit had gone exactly to the precepts of courtly etiquette. Still, despite the exchange of public compliments, antipathy hung dark and heavy between the two kings.

The scope of this mutual dislike puzzled King Casmir: where was its source? Casmir's memory for faces was exact; almost certainly he had known King Aillas in other less amiable circumstances. Long years before, Granice, then King of Troicinet, had visited Haidion at Lyonesse Town. His company had included Aillas, then an obscure little princeling not even reckoned in the line of royal succession. Casmir had barely noticed him. Could this child have created so mordant an impression? Most unlikely; Casmir, a practical man, wasted no emotion on trivial causes.

The mystery weighed on Casmir's mind, especially since he felt that somewhere a significant portent awaited his knowing. Aillas' face slipped in and out of mental focus, always pinched into an expression of cold hatred. The background remained indistinct. A dream? A magic spell? Or simple discord between the rulers of competing states?

The problem chafed at Casmir's nerves until finally he thrust it aside. Still he gained no peace of mind. Everywhere obstacles worked to thwart his ambition. . . . Ultimately, so Casmir told himself, these barriers must break apart if only before the sheer brutal force of his will, but meanwhile they carked at his patience and troubled the ease of his existence.

As King Casmir sat drumming his fingers along the arms of the chair and reflecting upon the circumstances of his life, a quandary five years old surfaced into his mind. This was the augury spoken by Persilian the Magic Mirror, on his own initiative: an occasion unique in itself. Persilian, without prompting of any sort, had called out a rasping, chanting fragment of doggerel. Casmir remembered only the gist of the words, something like: "Casmir, Casmir! Your daughter is Suldrun the Fair, and she is fey! Her first-born son before his death shall sit properly at Cairbra an Meadhan, nor shall you sit there nor on Evandig before him!"*

Casmir had uttered a poignant question: "But shall I sit at these places afterwards?"

Persilian spoke no more. The mirror, with almost palpable malice, reflected only Casmir's face, distorted and congested with annoyance.

Casmir had pondered the augury at length, especially when Suldrun died after yielding a single child to the royal household: the unpredictable and less than tractable Princess Madouc.

The *Star Regulus* arrived at Lyonesse Town. King Casmir and the royal family, disembarking, stepped into a white double-sprung carriage drawn by four unicorns with gilded horns. Father Umphred thought to jump nimbly into the carriage, but was deterred by King Casmir's wordless glare. Smiling a bland smile, Umphred hopped back to the ground.

The carriage rolled up the Sfer Arct to the portals of Haidion, where the palace staff waited in ranks of formal welcome. King Casmir gave them perfunctory nods and, entering the palace, repaired to his chambers and immediately immersed himself in the business of his kingdom.

Two days later Casmir was approached by Doutain, his chief falconer. Doutain tendered a small capsule. "My lord, a pigeon in lading has returned to the west cote."

King Casmir, instantly interested, said: "Reward the little creature well, with corn and millet!"

Doutain replied: "It has already been done, your Majesty, and done well!"

"Good work, Doutain," murmured King Casmir, his attention already fixed upon the message. He unfolded the wisp of paper and read:

---

*See Glossary III

Your Highness:

To my sorrow J have been posted to South Ulfland, to service of a most dreary and objectionable sort. J can no longer maintain communication, certainly not in the immediate future.

The message was signed with a code symbol.

"Hmf," said Casmir, and tossed the message into the fire.

Later in the day Doutain appeared once again. "A pigeon has come down to the east cote, my lord."

"Thank you, Doutain."

The message, signed with a different symbol, read:

Your Highness:

For reasons beyond understanding J have been despatched to South Ulfland, where my duties are unlikely to accord either with my disposition or my inclination. This must, therefore, for the nonce, be my last communication.

"Bah!" said King Casmir, and cast the message into the flames. He threw himself down into his chair, and tugged at his beard. The two messages: coincidence? Unlikely, though not impossible. Might Valdez have betrayed the two? But Valdez had been denied knowledge of their names.

Still, it was interesting that Valdez had retired at this particular juncture. If he could be induced to return to Lyonesse, the truth might well be ascertained.

Casmir grunted. Valdez was far too sly a fox to risk such a visit; though the sheer fact of his visit would almost certainly prove his faith.

II

QUEEN SOLLACE HAD LONG BEEN CONVERTED to Christianity and Father Umphred saw to it that her fervor remained fresh. Of late she had become beguiled by the concept of sanctity; twenty times a day she murmured to herself: "Holy Saint Sollace of Lyonesse!" And: "How fine it sounds! The Cathedral of the Blessed Saint Sollace!"

Father Umphred, whose ambitions had never precluded the bishop's mitre, nor would he have scorned an arch-bishopric over all the Lyonesse Diocese, encouraged Sollace in her hopes for beatitude. "Dear queen, indeed! Of the seven holy acts, a noble house of prayer where none before existed affords our Lord God the most exalted refinement of bliss, and his joy consecrates those responsible! Ah, what glory gleams

across the future! What singing in the choirs of heaven as they contemplate the cathedral soon to grace Lyonesse Town!"

"I will so dedicate myself in every phase of my being!" declared
Sollace. "Might we truly name this cathedral with my name?"

"That decision must be affirmed by higher authority, but my influence
carries weight! When the bells ring loud across the land and paternosters
enrich the air, and King Casmir himself kneels before the altar to receive
my benediction, who would deny the style 'Sanctissima' to your name?"

"'Sollace Sanctissima!' Yes! That is good! On this very day I will again
bring our business to the attention of the king!"

"What a victory when Casmir accepts the Gospel and comes to Jesus!
The whole kingdom must then follow his lead!"

Sollace pursed her lips. "We shall see, but let us try one victory at
a time. If I am truly sanctified, the world will rejoice at the news, and
his Majesty will be impressed!"

"Precisely so! One step must follow on another!"

During the evening, while Casmir stood with his back to the fire,
Sollace entered the chamber. Father Umphred came behind but modestly slipped aside to stand in the shadows.

Queen Sollace, aglow with hope, swept across the chamber and after
exchanging civilities with the king, broached her concept of the noble
cathedral, with towers on high and bells tolling the message of salvation
far across the countryside. In her fervor she neglected to notice the
narrowing of Casmir's round blue eyes and the constriction of his mouth.
She described grandeur on a scale to amaze all Christendom: an edifice
so majestic and rich that Lyonesse Town must surely become a destination of pilgrimage.

King Casmir, hearing nothing to please him, at last spoke out: "What
kind of wild talk is this? Has that fat priest been spewing nonsense again?
I always know when you have seen him; he brings to your face something of his own look, which is that of a dying sheep!"

Queen Sollace cried out indignantly: "My lord, you mistake the transports of holy rapture for the facial expression you so unkindly describe!"

"No matter! He connives and lurks with crafty skill; I find him loiter-
ing wherever I look; indeed, I am much of a mind to send him packing."

"Sir, reflect on this! The Cathedral of Saint Sollace would bear my
name!"

"Woman, have mercy! Can you imagine the cost of such an edifice?
Enough to bankrupt the kingdom, while the priest trots here and there,
smirking as he thinks how he has befuddled the King and Queen of
Lyonesse!"

"Not so, my lord! Father Umphred is known and respected in Rome
itself! His single goal is the advancement of Christendom!"

Casmir turned to kick the fire into a more active blaze. "I have heard of these cathedrals: treasure-houses of gold and jewels wrung from the folk of the land, who then cannot pay their taxes to the king."

Queen Sollace said wistfully: "Our land is wealthy! It could support such a fine cathedral."

Casmir chuckled. "Tell the priest to bring me gold from Rome, some of which I will spend on a fine church."

Sollace said with dignity: "Good night, my lord. I am retiring to my chambers."

King Casmir bowed and turned back to the fire, and so failed to notice the departure of Father Umphred from the room.

III

KING CASMIR'S FIRST URGENCY was to repair the damage done to his intelligence network. One afternoon he went to a chamber in the old wing of Haidion, in the squat Tower of Owls above the armoury. This room, furnished sparsely, had much experience of harsh judgments and quick justice.

King Casmir, seating himself at the bare wooden table, poured wine from a white beechwood flagon into a white beech-wood cup, and waited in stony calm.

Minutes passed. King Casmir showed no impatience.

In the corridor sounded a shuffle of feet and muttering voices. Oldebor, a functionary of no definite title*, looked through the door. "Your Majesty, will you see the prisoner?"

"Bring him in."

Oldebor stepped forward into the room and gestured over his shoulder. Two jailers, in black leather aprons and conical leather hats, jerked on a chain and brought their prisoner stumbling into the room: a tall spare man in his early maturity, wearing a soiled shirt and ragged pantaloons. Despite his disheveled condition, the captive showed a notably good address; his posture, indeed, seemed incongruously easy, under the circumstances, and even a trifle contemptuous. In person, he was broad of shoulder, narrow at the hip, with long strong legs and the hands of an aristocrat. His hair, matted and dirty, was a thick black thatch; his eyes were clear hazel under a low forehead. Wide cheekbones converged to a narrow jaw; a high-bridged nose hooked over a bony chin. His skin, dark sallow-olive, seemed to show a curious

---

*Oldebor liked to style himself: 'Chief Under-chamberlain in Charge of Special Duties'.

plum-colored undertone, as if from the close flow of rich dark blood.

One of the jailers, annoyed by the captive's composure, jerked again at the chain. "Show proper respect! You stand in the presence of the king!"

The captive nodded toward King Casmir. "Good day to you, sir."

King Casmir responded in an even voice: "Good day to you, Torqual. How have you found your confinement?"

"Tolerable only, sir, and not for the fastidious."

Another person came quietly into the room: a gentleman somewhat past his first youth, stocky, brisk as a robin, with good features, neat brown hair and clever brown eyes. He bowed. "Good day, my lord."

"Good day, Shalles. Do you know Torqual?"

Shalles inspected the prisoner. "To this moment, I have had no contact with the gentleman."

"That is to our general advantage," said King Casmir. "You will therefore have no prejudicial emotions in his direction. Jailers, remove the chains so that Torqual may sit in comfort; then you may wait in the corridor. Oldebor, you may wait outside as well."

Oldebor protested. "Your Majesty, this is a desperate man, with neither hopes nor qualms!"

King Casmir showed a faint chilly smile. "That is why he is here. Abide in the corridor. Shalles is well able to protect me."

While Shalles turned the prisoner a dubious side-glance, the jailers removed the chains, then, with Oldebor, withdrew to the corridor.

King Casmir pointed to benches. "Gentlemen, be seated. May I offer you wine?"

Both Torqual and Shalles accepted cups of wine, and seated themselves.

Casmir looked back and forth between the two, then said: "You are men of different sorts; so much is clear. Shalles is the fourth son of the honourable knight Sir Pellent-Overtree, whose estate includes three farms of sixty-three acres in total. Shalles has learned the niceties of noble behavior together with a taste for good food and wine, but so far has found no means to indulge his yearnings. Torqual, of you I know little, but I would learn more. Perhaps you will tell us something of yourself."

"With pleasure," said Torqual. "To begin with, I am the member of a class which may well include a single individual: myself. My father is a duke of Skaghane; my lineage is longer than the history of the Elder Isles. My tastes, like those of Sir Shalles, are nice; I prefer the best of everything. While I am a Ska, I care not a fig for the Ska mystique.*

---

*See Glossary II

I have cohabited freely and often with Underfolk women and bred a dozen hybrids; therefore they call me a renegade.

"The epithet is inaccurate and undeserved. I cannot be faithless to a cause which I never have endorsed. Indeed, I am absolutely faithful to the only cause I espouse, which is my own welfare. I take pride in this unswerving loyalty!

"I came away from Skaghane early, with several advantages: the strength, vigor and intelligence of the typical Ska, which was my birthright, and the expert use of weapons, for which I must take credit upon myself, since there are few, if any, who can excel me, especially with the sword.

"In order to maintain a gentlemanly style, and lacking sympathy for working up the Ska hierarchies, I became a brigand; I robbed and murdered with the best. However, there is little wealth to be had in the Ulflands, and so I came to Lyonesse.

"My plans were simple and innocent. As soon as I took enough gold and silver to fill a wagon, I intended to become a robber baron of the Teach tac Teach, and live out my life in relative seclusion.

"Through a freak of luck, I was trapped by your thief-takers. I now await drawing and quartering, though I will be glad to consider any other program your Majesty may see fit to propose."

"Hm," said King Casmir. "Your execution is scheduled for tomorrow?"

"That is my understanding."

Casmir nodded and turned to Shalles. "What do you think of this fellow?"

Shalles considered Torqual sidelong. "Obviously, he is a blackguard of the deepest dye, with the conscience of a shark. At this moment he has nothing to lose and so feels free to exercise his insouciance."

"What faith would you put in his word?"

Shalles dubiously cocked his head to the side. "It would depend upon how far his self-esteem rides with his faith. I am sure the word 'honour' means something different to him than it does to me or to you. I would trust him better on a system of rewards after stipulated service. Still, if only from caprice, Torqual might serve you well. He is clearly intelligent, energetic, forthright, and despite his present condition, I would guess him to be resourceful."

King Casmir turned to Torqual. "You have heard Shalles' opinions. What is your comment?"

"He is a person of discernment. I cannot argue with his remarks."

King Casmir nodded, and poured wine into the three mugs. "The circumstances are these. King Aillas of Troicinet has extended his power into South Ulfland, where it impedes my own ambitions. I therefore wish to make South Ulfland ungovernable for the Troice. I intend that you two should serve me to this end, both singly, or, when occasion arises, in tandem. Shalles, what do you say to this?"

Shalles considered. "Your Majesty, may I be frank?"

"Naturally."

"The task is dangerous. I am willing to serve you in this regard, at least for a limited period, if the rewards are commensurate to the danger."

"What do you have in mind?"

"Full knighthood and a prosperous estate of at least two hundred acres."

King Casmir grunted. "You value yourself highly."

"Sir, my life, drab and insipid though it may seem to others, is the only life given me to live."

"Very well; so it shall be. Torqual, what of you?"

Torqual laughed. "I accept, regardless of risk or your distrust, or whatever the nature of the task, or whatever the reward."

King Casmir said drily: "Essentially, I want you to establish yourself in the highlands of South Ulfland and there wreak as much disorder as possible, but only upon the forces cooperating with the Troice. You are to make contact with other high-country barons and counsel disobedience, insurrection and banditry similar to your own. Do you understand my needs?"

"Perfectly! I accept your proposal with enthusiasm."

"I thought as much. Shalles, you shall, like Torqual, visit among such of the barons you suspect of disaffection, and give them counsel and coordinate their efforts. If necessary, you may offer bribes, though this will be your last resort. You will also work closely with Torqual, and at intervals you will report to me, by methods which we will arrange."

"Sir, I will do my best in this regard, for a period which perhaps we now should define for our exact understanding."

Casmir drummed a quick tattoo on the table-top, but when he spoke, his voice was even. "Much depends upon circumstances."

"Exactly so, sir, which is why I wish to define an upper limit upon my service. The danger is very great in this game which you want me to play. In short, I do not care to roam the moors until finally I am killed."

"Hm. How long a term do you suggest?"

"In view of the danger, a year seems long enough."

Casmir grunted. "In a year you will hardly learn the lay of the land."

"Sir, I can only do my best, and, remember, King Aillas will send out his own spies. Once I am identified, then my usefulness decreases."

"Hmf. I will think on it. Come before me tomorrow afternoon."

Shalles rose to his feet, bowed and departed. Casmir turned to Torqual. "Shalles may be somewhat too scrupulous for this sort of work. Still, he is avaricious, which is a good sign. As for you, I am under no illusions. You are a wolf's-head, a crafty murderer and a blackguard."

Torqual grinned. "I also ravish women. Usually they cry and hold out their arms when I leave them."

King Casmir, who was something of a prig in such matters, turned him a cold stare. "I will provide you weapons and, at your option, a small company of cutthroats. If you succeed well, and, like Shalles, desire a life of rustic gentility, I will also find for you a suitable estate. So I hope to guarantee your faith. You have reason to serve me well."

Torqual smiled. "Why not? As scoundrels go, we are a pair."

The remark, in King Casmir's view, verged close upon insolence, and he gave Torqual another cold stare. "I will confer with you again in two days. Meanwhile, you will continue to be my guest."

"I would prefer Haidion to the Peinhador."

"No doubt. Oldebor!"

Oldebor entered from the corridor. "Your Majesty?"

"Take Torqual back to the Peinhador. Let him bathe, provide him decent garments, house him in a clean cell and give him food to his choice—within reason, of course."

The jailers came into the room. "Are we not to see the colour of his guts? He is the worst of the worst!"

"And a Ska, to boot!" declared the other. "I hoped to work the knife myself!"

"Another time," said King Casmir. "Torqual has been assigned to dangerous work in the service of the state."

"Very well, your Majesty. Come along, dog-dirt."

Torqual fixed the jailer with a cool stare. "Jailer, take care! I am soon to be free and in the king's service. On a whim I might seek you out; then we shall see who does good work with the knife!"

King Casmir made an impatient gesture. "Enough of this!" He looked to the jailers, now subdued and uneasy: "You have heard Torqual's remarks; if I were you, I would henceforth use him with courtesy."

"Sire, it shall be as you command. Torqual, come; we spoke in jest. Tonight you shall drink wine and eat roast fowl."

King Casmir smiled his wintry smile. "Oldebor, in two days I will again see Torqual."

Chapter 5

I

THREE DAYS AFTER THE DEPARTURE of King Casmir and his retinue aboard the carrack *Star Regulus*, Aillas himself set sail for South Ulfland with a flotilla of seventeen ships.

The company included Lord Maloof and Lord Pirmence, both seething with resentment. Dhrun and Glyneth remained at Domreis, to be educated in a style befitting their rank. Both would learn Latin and Greek, geography, the natural sciences, calligraphy, the mathematics of Pythagoras, Euclid and Aristarchus, as well as the new style of Moorish numeration. Through readings in Herodotus, Tacitus, Xenophon, Clavetz of Avallon, Dioscuros of Alexandria, the Chronicles of Ys, and Khersom's *War of the Goths and the Huns*, they would gain an overview of history. They would learn to name stars, planets and constellations, and ponder a variety of cosmological theories. Dhrun would attend a school of military science, where he would learn the skill of weapons, and the strategies of warfare. Glyneth and Dhrun both would attend classes in the courtly arts, which included dancing, declamation, music and the proprieties.

Both Glyneth and Dhrun, had their preferences been heeded, would have accompanied Aillas to South Ulfland. Not so with Lords Maloof and Pirmence, each of whom had advanced a dozen reasons why he should not be plucked so rudely from his familiar routines.

To Maloof's protests Aillas made the response: "I appreciate your concern for the work which will be interrupted, but your talents are more urgently needed in South Ulfland; this is where you may best serve king and country."

"My skills are complex and sophisticated," grumbled Maloof. "Any clerk can weigh up broad-beans and count out onions."

"You still do not understand the scope of our project! I will want an inventory of every estate in the land, so that we know its extent and resources, and — no less important — the acreage unoccupied, unclaimed, wild or in dispute. You will direct a staff of surveyors, cartographers and clerks to research the existing records."

Lord Maloof stood limp. "That is a monumental task!"

"Naturally the work will not be accomplished in a day, but it is only the beginning. I will expect you to establish and regulate an exchequer for South Ulfland. Third —"

" 'Third'?" groaned Maloof. "Already you have laid out a whole life-time of work! Your confidence in me is flattering but unreal; I can work only by day and by night: no other periods of time exist. Meanwhile my work here at Domreis will be muddled by bunglers and hacks!"

"Here, so I suppose, you refer to your work with the exchequer?"

Lord Maloof flushed and looked askance toward Aillas. "Naturally: just so!"

"I have made inquiries and I am assured that we leave the work, and again I refer to the exchequer, in capable hands. It is time for a change! A clever man such as yourself needs challenge to develop his full potential, and also to keep him out of mischief. South Ulfland with its intransigent barons and threatening Ska offers a hundred such challenges!"

"But I know nothing, and want to know nothing, of troubles and conflicts and war! I am a man of peace!"

"And I no less! But even men of peace must learn to fight. The world is often brutal, and not everyone shares our ideals. Therefore, you must be prepared to defend yourself and your loved ones, or reconcile yourself to slavery."

"I prefer to reason, to proffer kind counsel, to ameliorate and to compromise!"

"As a preliminary and tentative policy, these activities are useful!" said Aillas. "If we behave reasonably, our conscience is clear! Then, should decency fail and the tyrants attack, we can lop off their heads with righteous zest."

"I have few skills along these lines," said Maloof in a bleak voice.

"Now then, Maloof: do not underestimate yourself! You are sturdy and deft, if a trifle overweight. After a few brisk campaigns, you will gallop your horse and brandish your battle-axe with as much fury as any!"

"Bah!" grumbled Maloof. "I am not the hell-for-leather bravo you take me for. I will waste my life in this dour wilderness."

"Never! You may use well this life of yours in South Ulfland, but we will find scope for all your skills: perhaps in the suppression of espionage. You might — or might not — be startled to learn that I have discovered treachery in the most exalted circles!"

Maloof blinked and responded in a subdued voice: "Your Majesty, it shall be as you command."

Lord Pirmence used different tactics when it came his turn. "Your Majesty, I deem this appointment in the nature of an accolade! I shall always cherish this evidence of your high esteem! But I am a modest man, and I must resolutely decline the honour. No, sir! Do not press it upon me! My withdrawal is definite and irrevocable! I have gained distinction enough for a single lifetime; let the eager young bloods take their turn!" Lord Pirmence performed a courtly bow, and would have considered the matter closed had not Aillas called him back.

"Lord Pirmence, your abnegation does you credit. However, I assure you that honour sufficient for all will be won on the moors of South Ulfland!"

"That is good to hear!" declared Lord Pirmence. "But alas! You forget my advancing years! I have enemies, yes: pangs and aches, failing vision, asthma, toothlessness and senile cachexis; but they are no longer cruel knights, ogres, Goths and Moors. I intimately know the ague, gout, rheumatism and palsy. If truth be known, I am almost ready to creep away to Castle Lutez, to wrap myself in eiderdowns and quiet my roaring digestion with a diet of curds and gruel."

Aillas said soberly: "Lord Pirmence, I am greatly distressed to hear of your decrepitude."

"Alas! It is an end to which we all must come!"

"So I am led to believe. Incidentally, are you aware that a person who bears a striking resemblance to yourself roams the coarser districts of Domreis? No? He does your reputation no credit! Recently, close on midnight, I happened to look into the Green Star Inn and there I saw this person with one foot on a bench, the other on a table, brandishing high a tankard of ale and trolling a mighty stave; meanwhile he clasped one of the tavern wenches with an iron grip. His whiskers were exactly like your own and he seemed to enjoy almost an excess of exuberant good health."

"How I envy the man!" murmured Lord Pirmence. "I wonder at his secret!"

"Perhaps you will learn it in South Ulfland. I consider your presence indispensable. After all, when one hunts important game, he calls out the old hound. I rely upon you to impose order upon the barons of the moors."

Lord Pirmence gave a delicate cough. "I would survive not a single windy day on those desolate fells!"

"To the contrary! You will thrive in the fresh climate! 'An Ulf lives forever — unless he is cut with steel, or chokes on his meat, or falls drunk into the mire!' So say the Ulfs. You will soon be as hearty as ever!"

Lord Pirmence shook his head. "Truly, I am not your man! I have little tact with boors and bog-trotters. With the best will in the world I will surely do our cause a disservice."

"Odd," mused Aillas. "I was told that you have recently become expert in the field of secret diplomacy!"

Lord Pirmence pursed his lips, pulled at his mustache, and looked toward the ceiling. "Hum, ha! Not quite true! Still — when duty calls I must ignore all else and leap into the breach."

"That is the response I expected from you," said Aillas.

An hour before the flotilla's departure, Aillas came down to the jetty to find Shimrod lounging against a stack of bales. Aillas stopped short. "What are you doing here?"

"I have been waiting for you to appear."

"Why did you not show yourself in Miraldra? I sail on the tide for South Ulfland!"

"No difficulty there. I will accompany you, if I may."

"Aboard the ship? To Ys?"

"That is my hope."

"Naturally you may come." Aillas scrutinized Shimrod keenly. "I sense a mystery here. Why your sudden yearning for the hinterlands?"

"The city Ys? Hardly a hinterland."

"I see that you plan to tell me nothing of consequence."

"There is nothing to tell. I have a few items of business at a place not far from Ys, and during the voyage I shall enjoy myself in your company."

"Come aboard, then. But you must be prepared to sleep in the bilge."

"Any little cranny, such as the captain's saloon, will suit me well."

"I am happy to find you so flexible. Let us see what we can do."

II

PROPELLED BY FAIR WINDS and riding sunny blue seas, the ships from Troicinet made a pleasant voyage along the Lir. On the second day they rounded Cape Farewell, then discovered three days of calms and fickle winds, while only a mile to the east rose the tall Cliffs of Kegan, bearded with white foam.

Mile by mile the flotilla made its northing until finally the shape of Cape Kellas appeared on the horizon.

Rounding the cape, past the colonnaded Temple of Atlante, the fleet entered the estuary of the Evander and dropped anchor beside the docks of the city Ys.

One by one the ships approached the docks, discharged troops and cargo, took aboard fresh water and contingents on their way home, and put out to sea again.

Aillas, conferring with his commanders, heard both good and bad news. His strictures against raids, pillaging and the prosecution of feuds had, for the most part, been heeded. Some of the barons wholeheartedly endorsed the call for public order; others seemed to be watching and waiting before committing acts which could bring them to ruin: each, in effect, waiting for someone to test the mettle of the new king. This peace, no matter how fragile and tentative, was good news.

On the other hand, the barons had not fulfilled the total scope of Aillas' commands. Few, if any, had disbanded their companies of armed retainers that they might return to more productive work, in field, quarry and forest, and so bring some small measure of prosperity to the land.

Aillas immediately sent messengers to every castle, fortress and mountain keep, requiring that the barons, or knights, or earls, however they styled themselves, should meet with him at Stronson, the castle of Sir Helwig, high in the heart of the moors.

Aillas rode to the meeting in company with Sir Tristano, Lord Maloof, who was glum, and Lord Pirmence, who showed an airy detachment, together with an escort of thirty knights and a hundred men-at-arms. The day of the meeting was blessed with fine warm weather; the moors smelled fresh of heather, gorse and fern, with the elemental reek of the dank turf rising heavy below.

The company, assembled on the meadow to the side of Stronson Castle, made a fine spectacle, with metal gleaming and colours ablaze in the sunlight. The barons for the most part wore mail shirts and metal caps; their jupons, capes and trousers were of rich colour and fine fabric, and many wore sleeveless aprons embroidered with personal emblems or the arms of their houses. Almost all had brought heralds who held high gonfalons displaying the baronial arms.

Thirty-six of the forty-five barons commanded to the conclave were on hand. Sir Helwig called out a summons and those present came to sit at a semi-circular table, each with his herald and gonfalon at his back. To one side Aillas' escort rested at ease. Not so those retainers and clansmen who had come to Stronson in company with the barons; they stood in knots and groups, with those parties at feud darting lambent glances toward each other.

For several minutes Aillas considered the thirty-six more or less amicable faces. Privately he felt the turn-out to be satisfactory, but to ignore the nine cases of contumacy would instantly make a mockery of his authority. Here, in fact, was his test, and the barons watched him with curiosity as he stood to the side with Tristano and Sir Helwig's herald, conning the list of those not on hand.

Aillas went to confront the company; standing clean-shaven and crisply handsome before the grizzled and hard-bitten barons of the moors, he seemed almost ludicrously inexperienced and untried; certain of the barons took no pains to conceal their opinions.

Amused rather than nettled, Aillas spoke a polite greeting and expressed his pleasure for the fine weather which favored the occasion. He took up his list and called out the names of the missing nine barons. Receiving no response, he turned to Sir Tristano: "Despatch a knight with five soldiers to the home-places of each of these truants. Let the knights express my displeasure. Let them announce to each that since he would not meet me here at Stronson, or send a message of courteous explanation, he is therefore commanded to my camp at Ys. Let each understand with the utmost clarity that if he fails to appear within the week, he shall be disenfranchised from his lands and reduced to the rank of commoner, and all his property shall immediately revert to the king. These truants must also be told that their punishment, should they fail to appear, will be my first order of business, and that, one by one, I will strike them low. Let the knights and their escorts depart at once."

Aillas turned back to the now grimly attentive barons. "Gentlemen, as you have heard before, the Kingdom of South Ulfland is no longer a land of lawlessness. My remarks today will be brief but most important. First: I command that each of you dissolve his company of armed soldiery, that these men, so released, may devote their efforts either to tilling the soil and enriching the land, or enlisting in the King's Army. You may retain your household servants, gardeners and stable-men; but you will no longer need garrisons nor an armed guard.

"Through these economies and the increase of your rents you will yourself prosper, even after paying into the exchequer those taxes which Lord Maloof will presently fix upon you. These monies will not be spent upon vanity or proud display, but will go to improve the land. I intend to re-open the old mines, forge iron and in due course build ships. Everywhere in South Ulfland are the ruins of old villages; each is a stark sight, and each shall be rebuilt or replaced to house the population. In this new prosperity you all must certainly share.

"So that an Ulf army may protect Ulfland, and so that the soldiers you see here may return to Troicinet, I now announce that Lord Pirmence will recruit a force of strong and able men. For your younger sons and landless brothers the army will offer means to advancement, with promotion and rewards based upon merit rather than birth. The men-at-arms released from your personal services may also find careers in the Ulfish Army.

"Initially I intend a force of a thousand men. They will be trained until they are equal or superior to any other troops in the world, including the Ska. They will wear proper uniforms, eat good food, and will be paid in accordance with the schedule of the Troice army. At the end of their service they will be granted a freehold acreage of arable land.

"These first thousand troops will become an elite cadre, and assist in the training of future recruits. They will learn a strict discipline and they will learn to defeat the Ska, who until now have marched through South Ulfland as they chose, looting and taking slaves. Those days are now in the past.

"I have said all I wish to say. You must abide by the new law of the land or face the consequences. If you wish to ask questions of me, or bring important matters to my attention, here I sit, and I will be pleased to listen and respond as well as I can. For those who thirst, I notice that a cask of ale has been broached."

The barons rose somewhat uncertainly to their feet and looked around the area. Presently they separated into small knots and groups. One of the barons, a person close to middle-age, tall and massive, with a great bush of black beard, approached Aillas and stared at him intently. "Lord King, do you know me?"

By sheer chance, Aillas had heard the man's name mentioned. "You are Sir Hune of Three Pines House."

Sir Hune nodded. "I look at you, a boy almost, and I marvel!"

"How so, Sir Hune?"

"See me! I am the very substance of the moor! One of my arms would make both your legs! Were we to drink from yonder cask I would put down four pints to your one and still be merry and clear of eye when you were snoring head-down on the table! I can hurl a lance through an oak plank; I can kill a bull with a blow. I know every trail and rock and rill of the fells; I know where the grouse nest and the pools where the trout hide. But now you arrive from Troicinet and wave a piece of paper at us to declare yourself our king. All very well, and this is the way such things are done, but what do you know of how life is lived along the moors? Have you tasted our cruel days and bitter nights, or crept up to cut the throat of the enemy who would have preferred to cut your throat? Still your orders must be obeyed. Is there not an absurdity in all this? And I ask it in all kindliness."

"Sir Hune, it is a fair emotion which you feel and a fair question. You are indeed a doughty man, and I would not wish to wrestle you. Would you care to try me in a foot-race, the loser to carry the winner back on his shoulders?"

Sir Hune laughed and slapped the table. "I know little of running. Is this what you will teach your soldiers?"

"They will run certainly, though not in battle. And as for life along these moors, I know more of it than you might think. Someday, if you are of a mind, I will tell you the story."

Sir Hune indicated the barons in their groups. "Hear my words! If you hope to stop the bickers and ambushes, if you would halt the midnight sallies and escapades — well then, young king, you will discover a thankless task." Sir Hune turned and, looking across the meadow, jerked his thumb. "See them now, each clan to itself! Each man gives off hate through his back for those who have done him wrong across the ages! And tell me, lad: what else have we to live for, if it is not the hunt and the chase, the raid and the rape, and the glad slaughter of one's foe? Here is our life; it is our way and we have no other amusement."

Aillas leaned back in his chair. "It is the life of an animal. Have you no sons and daughters?"

"I have four of both, and already two sons are dead, and yonder stands their murderer. Soon I will take him and nail him to my gate, and have my dinner as he dies."

Aillas rose to his feet. "Sir Hune, I like you, and if you commit this deed I will hang you with great regret. I would much prefer to use your strength and that of your sons in my army."

"You would hang me? What then of Dostoy yonder, who killed my sons with his black arrows?"

"And when was this deed done?"

"Last summer, before the rut."

"And before I issued my general orders. Herald, convene the group once more to attention."

Once again Aillas spoke to the barons, and now he stood leaning on the pommel of his sword. "I have spoken with Sir Hune, who has launched a complaint against Sir Dostoy."

From among the barons came a guffaw and a cry: "How dares that black-hearted villain complain in any wise whatever, him whose hand drips red with innocent blood?"

Aillas said: "At some specified time the murders must stop. I have already defined that time. I will do so once more, in terms you all can understand. Whoever commits murder, whoever kills except in self-defense — he shall be hanged. I will bring law to South Ulfland, and the sooner you realize that I am in earnest, the easier for all of us. I need fighting men in my army; I do not want them killing each other and I do not want to waste my time hanging all the barons of the moorlands. Still, if I must I must! Go now to your homes and think well on my words."

III

AILLAS, RETURNING TO Ys, sought about the camp for Shimrod, without success. He sent an aide to look through the dock-side taverns, but Shimrod was nowhere to be found, to Aillas' annoyance. Several matters hung heavy in his mind. First, he had cultivated a hope that Shimrod might provide some trifle of magic — a spell of temporary meekness, to be used against such as Sir Hune; or a glossic to make Sir Hune's weapons shrivel and droop and all his arrows fly awry. Such assistance, so Aillas assured himself, would rest comfortably with Murgen's edict*, since it could be justified on humanitarian principles.

Aillas also had hoped for the weight of Shimrod's presence during a meeting with the factors of Ys, which events had now made necessary. With Shimrod off about his affairs, Aillas was cast upon his own resources and must confront the cryptic oligarchs alone.

First he must identify the responsible authorities, which he knew to be no simple process. Upon reflection, Aillas decided that Lord Pirmence was precisely qualified to the task, and sent him out to arrange the conference.

Late in the afternoon Pirmence made his report to Aillas.

"Unusual and bizarre!" declared Pirmence in response to Aillas' question as to how the day had gone. "These folk are as subtle as eels! I can well believe them to be derived from the Minoans of Crete!"

"How does this follow?"

"I have no clear evidence," said Pirmence. "It is a matter of intuition. These people of Ys move in that ambience of mingled innocence and mystery which is so appealing an attribute of the Minoans. Today they have bewildered me to the verge of apoplexy. I inquired everywhere for their magnates, or a council of elders, or even an influential clique, but in response received only smiling shrugs and blank looks. When pressed, the folk, after frowning and pondering and dubiously shaking their heads and staring in all directions, deny that such authority exists. When I turn away, I suspect that they are laughing at my back, but when I swing about to surprise the insolence, they have already gone off about their business, and this is the larger indignity: they are too bored with me even to laugh.

"Finally I discovered an old man sunning himself on a bench. When I put my questions to him, he at least had the grace to make me an elucidation.

---

*Murgen's edict prohibited magicians from taking sides in secular conflicts. With minor exceptions, the magicians were pleased to obey the rule.

"Ys, so I discover, is controlled by an unspoken consensus. Custom and convenience take the place of coercive law; at Ys the concept of central authority is felt to be both repugnant and faintly ridiculous. I asked the old fellow: 'Who then is qualified to represent the city in a consultation with King Aillas upon important business?' He gave me a typical shrug, and said: 'I know of no important business and do not see fit to so consult.'

"At this moment a kindly lady came by. She helped the gentleman to his feet and they went off together. From the solicitude of her manner, I gathered that the old fellow suffers from some advanced form of senile dementia, and so perhaps his analysis is not totally accurate."

Pirmence paused to chuckle and to preen his neat beard. Aillas reflected that the decision not to hang Pirmence outright, but rather to exploit his devious skills, had so far worked to advantage. "What next?"

Pirmence continued with his report. "I refused to be thwarted either by evasions, vagaries or the ravings of a madman, if such they were. I told myself that natural law operated at Ys as rigorously as elsewhere, and that, inevitably, the most influential factors would tend to inhabit the oldest and finest of the palaces. I visited several of these and informed the resident factors that, since everyone in Ys denied the existence of a governing counsel, I now took it upon myself to appoint such a body, of which these gentlemen were now full and fast members. Further, I notified them that they were stringently required to meet with you at mid-morning tomorrow."

"Clever and ingenious! Well done, Pirmence! Would it not be a great joke if I came to find you indispensable?"

Pirmence dourly shook his head. "I have transcended that phase in my intellectual growth where I discover humour in simple freakishness. What exists is real; therefore it is tragic, since whatever lives must die. Only fantasy, the vapors rising from sheer nonsense, can now excite my laughter."

"Ah, Pirmence, your philosophy lies beyond my understanding."

"Just as yours does mine," said Pirmence with courtly grace.

Next day at mid-morning six factors strolled down from the city and made their way to the blue silk pavilion where Aillas waited in company with Lord Maloof and Lord Pirmence. The factors seemed much alike: slight of physique, almost pallid of complexion, with fine features, dark eyes and black hair cut short and clasped with golden fillets. Their dress was modest: white linen kirtles and sandals, and none bore arms.

Aillas came forward to meet them. "Gentlemen, I am pleased to welcome you. Be seated. These are my aides Lord Maloof and Lord Pirmence, both men of cultivated experience and totally dedicated to our common goals. Will you take refreshment?" Without waiting for response, Aillas signaled to his stewards, who served out goblets of wine, which the factors ignored.

"Our business today is of considerable importance," said Aillas. "I hope that we can conduct it efficiently and with decision.

"The background is this: by reason of weak rulers, Ska attacks, and general demoralization, South Ulfland, save for the Vale of Evander, has become a wilderness. I intend to restore order and law, beat back the Ska, and eventually restore South Ulfland to its former prosperity. In pursuing these purposes, I cannot for long rely upon Troice blood or Troice gold: the resources must come from South Ulfland.

"My first concern is an army to enforce the law and to repel the Ska. In this regard no one is exempt from service. That is the thrust of our business for today."

The factors rose to their feet and, bowing, turned to depart. "Wait!" called Aillas. "Where are you going?"

"Are you not finished with your remarks?" inquired one of the factors. "You said that they would be brief."

"Not that brief! I also said that we must make decisions. Will you act as spokesman, or will each speak his mind as occasion dictates?" Aillas looked from face to face, but discovered only empty expressions.

"I am unaccustomed to such modesty," said Aillas. "You, sir, what is your name?"

"I am styled Hydelos."

"I now appoint you the Honourable Hydelos, Chairman of the Council. The six of you, naturally, comprise the council. You, sir: your name?"

"I too am styled Hydelos."

"Indeed! How are you distinguished from this other Hydelos?"

"By our intimate names."

"What, then, is your intimate name? We must be practical."

"It is Olave."

"Olave, you are appointed overseer of military conscription. The two gentlemen sitting next to you will be your assistants. You will recruit for the Ulf army up and down the Vale of Evander. Maloof, record their names, both intimate and otherwise. You, sir, how are you styled?"

"I am Eukanor."

"Eukanor, you are now tax collector for the Vale of Evander. The gentleman at your left hand will assist you. Maloof, record their names. Hydelos, I hope that the conference is moving briskly enough to please you. Your duties will be, first, supervision, and I need not spell out the details at this moment; and also you will serve as liaison officer between the others of the council and myself, or my representative. You must render a daily report."

Hydelos said gently: "Sir, your requirements are impossible and cannot be effected."

Aillas laughed. "Hydelos, I urge you to face facts, no matter how reluctantly. You must alter your style of life, at least until South Ulfland is once again whole. You have no choice and I will hear no arguments. If the six of you will not work with me, I must exile you to the Isle of Terns, and try six other folk of Ys, until either I find proper cooperation, or until all Ys has been transported to the dismal crags of the isle.

"My requirements, in the context of today, are not oppressive and can easily be effected. I am your king and I so command."

Hydelos spoke in a voice wherein the petulance was carefully restrained: "We have existed many years with neither king, nor army nor taxes; the Ska have never threatened us, nor are we in danger from the barons. Why should we now be hasty to obey a Troice invader?"

"You tolerated Faude Carfilhiot at Tintzin Fyral; you ignored the Ska on their slave-raids; you bought peace for yourselves with the pain of others! These carefree days are gone, and you must share the costs of justice! Gentlemen, this very instant, choose; I will argue not another word."

"No need," said Hydelos softly. "We are persuaded."

"Very well. Maloof will furnish details of what must be done." Aillas rose to his feet, bowed to the disconsolate factors and turned away. He stopped short at the sight of a tall figure approaching across the compound. With the conference at an end, and all issues resolved, Shimrod at last had elected to show himself at the camp.

Chapter 6

I

DURING A PERIOD IN THE PAST, not long after Shimrod had taken up residence at Trilda, in the Forest of Tantrevalles, his sleep had been disturbed by a series of dreams. They came night after night, in a sequence which obsessed Shimrod's attention, despite a cadence to the events which suggested that their resolution might be fateful, and perhaps even tragic.

The dreams were extraordinary for several reasons. The locale, a white beach with the ocean to one side and a white villa to the other, never altered. There were neither illogical nor grotesque elements to the events; indeed, their most startling quality was the haunting beauty of a woman who, alone with Shimrod, inhabited the dreams.

In the first of the sequence, Shimrod found himself standing by the balustrade in front of the villa. The sunlight was warm; the sound of low surf came with languid regularity. Shimrod waited in a mood of expectation. Presently, looking up the beach, he saw approaching a dark-haired woman of middle height, slender, almost slight. She walked barefoot and wore a white gown, knee-length and sleeveless. Without haste she approached, and passed in front of Shimrod. With a single side-glance, she continued on her way and Shimrod was left to look after her with pangs of wonder and yearning.

The dream faded and went its way, to whatever place dreams go when their time has passed, and Shimrod awoke, to lie staring into the dark.

On the next night the dream returned, and again on the next, and so it went. On each occasion the woman deigned a trifle more warmth, and at last she paused and listened as he spoke. He tried to learn her identity and why she came this way; and finally she specified a time and place outside the confines of the dream where they might meet.

A pulse of exultation surged through Shimrod, even though he knew that the occasion must almost definitely be intended for his misfortune. He therefore took counsel with Murgen, at the castle Swer Smod, on the flanks of the Teach tac Teach.

Murgen laid the plot bare. The woman was Melancthe, and she worked at the command of Tamurello. What was their purpose? No mystery here. Tamurello intended to confuse and weaken Murgen by destroying his scion Shimrod.

A single question remained, the age-old cry of anguish: "How could one so beautiful be so base?"

In this regard Murgen could offer no explanation.

Shimrod kept the rendezvous, but the plot had been vitiated and Shimrod retained his life. Later, when he first visited Ys, he discovered the beach on which Melancthe had walked, and, half a mile to the north, the white villa where in his dreams he had awaited the coming of Melancthe.

Shimrod could now remember the episode with dispassion and even a flicker of curiosity. There was another matter: an obligation which had never been fulfilled. How Melancthe might deal with this obligation was a question which, in due course, prompted Shimrod to slip quietly away from Ys and saunter up the beach.

He arrived at the front of the villa and halted beside the balustrade; déjà vu hung heavy in the air. Looking up the beach, as if in a reprise of his dreams, he observed the approach of Melancthe.

As before, she wore a knee-length white gown and walked barefoot. If she felt surprise at the sight of Shimrod, she gave no such indication and her pace neither slowed nor quickened.

Melancthe arrived at the gate. Her eyes flickered a single instant toward Shimrod; then, ignoring his presence, she climbed the steps to the terrace and disappeared into the shadows of the colonnade.

Shimrod followed behind her and so entered the villa, which he had never before visited.

Melancthe crossed the hall and went into a chamber with an arcade of windows overlooking the ocean. She seated herself on a couch beside a low table, and leaning back stared out toward the horizon.

Shimrod quietly drew up a chair and sat at the end of the table, where he could watch her without turning his head.

A maid entered with a tall silver ewer, and poured for Melancthe a goblet of wine punch, fragrant with the juice of oranges and lemons. Melancthe, paying no heed to Shimrod, sipped from her goblet, and again looked out over the sea.

Shimrod watched with head cocked at a quizzical angle. He considered lifting the ewer in both his hands and drinking from the side, but concluded that such an act, with its hint of vulgarity, might compromise his already fragile acceptance. Instead he worked a small spell. Into the room flew a blue and red bird, to circle Melancthe's head and settle on the rim of her goblet. It chirped a time or two, committed a nuisance into the goblet and flew away.

With studied deliberation Melancthe leaned forward and placed the goblet on the table.

Shimrod spoke another quiet spell. A small Moorish slave-boy wearing an enormous blue turban, a red and blue striped shirt and pale blue puff-breeches, appeared in the doorway. He carried a tray with a pair of silver goblets. He proffered the tray to Melancthe, and stood waiting.

With a still face Melancthe took one of the goblets and set it on the table. The boy approached Shimrod, who graciously accepted the other goblet and drank of its contents with satisfaction. The slave-boy departed the room.

With lips thrust forward at the center and drooping dolefully at the corners, Melancthe continued to study the sea.

Shimrod thought: 'How she schemes! In her mind she formulates plan after plan, then discards each in turn as ineffective, or crass, or not in accord with her dignity. She can discover no words which will not leave her vulnerable to whatever reproaches or demands I choose to make. So long as she is silent, she commits herself to nothing and thinks to hold me at bay! But pressure builds inside her; at some point she must undertake an initiative.'

Shimrod noticed a twitch at the corners of Melancthe's mouth. 'She has come to a decision,' he told himself. 'Her least graceful but most effective course is to rise to her feet and leave the room; naturally, I can not follow her into the lavatory and still retain my reputation for gallantry. Well, then, let us see! Her conduct will reveal much in regard to her mood.'

Melancthe tilted her head back and seemed to go to sleep. Shimrod rose and went to look about the room. There was little furniture and an odd lack of personal belongings: neither articles of skill and craftsmanship nor curios, nor yet scrolls, books, librams or portfolios. On a side-table a green faience bowl held a dozen oranges; nearby a group of water-washed pebbles which had given Melancthe pleasure were spread at random. Three Mauretanian rugs lay on the floor, woven in bold patterns of blue, black and red on a buff background. A heavy candelabra of black iron hung from the ceiling. On the table in front of Melancthe a bronze bowl displayed a bouquet of orange marigolds, no doubt arranged by the maid. Essentially, thought Shimrod, the room was neutral and reflected nothing of Melancthe.

Melancthe spoke at last: "How long do you intend to stay here?"

Shimrod returned to his chair. "I am free for the rest of the day, and the night as well, if it comes to that."

"You have a most casual attitude toward time."

"'Casual?' I think not. It is a subject of great interest. According to the Esqs of Galicia, time is a pyramid of thirteen sides. They believe that we stand at the apex and overlook days, months and years in all directions. This is the first premise of Thudhic Perdurics, as enunciated by Thudh, the Galician god of time, whose thirteen eyes ring his head so that he may perceive in all directions at once. The visual capability, of course, is symbolic."

"Has this doctrine any immediate effect?"

"I would think so. Novel ideas exercise our minds and enliven our conversation. For instance, while we are still discussing Thudh, you might be interested to learn that each year the Esq magicians alter a hundred human foetuses, hoping that one may be born with thirteen eyes in a circlet around its forehead, and thus would they know Thudh's avatar! So far, nine eyes is their limit of capability, and these become priests of the cult."

"I find no great interest in such things, nor in the conversation as a whole," said Melancthe. "You may leave as soon as you feel that courtesy makes this demand upon you."

"At that time I will do so," said Shimrod. "As for now, if you permit, I will call your servant that she may bring us more wine, and perhaps prepare a pot of mussels cooked with oil and garlic. Served with new bread, this is a hearty dish, consumed by folk of good conscience."

Melancthe turned away from the table. "I am not hungry."

"Are you tired?" asked Shimrod solicitously. "I will come rest with you on your bed."

Melancthe turned him a slow golden glance from the side of her eye. She said presently: "Whatever I do, I prefer to be alone."

"Really? It was not so in the old days. You sought me out with regularity."

"I have changed completely since that time. I am in no way the same person."

"Why this metamorphosis?"

Melancthe rose to her feet. "By living quietly alone, I had hoped to avoid intrusions into my privacy. To some extent I have succeeded."

"And now you have no friends?"

Melancthe shrugged and, turning away, went to the window. Shimrod came to stand close behind her. The odor of violets came to his nostrils. "Your response is ambiguous."

"I have no friends."

"What of Tamurello?"

"He is not a friend."

"I hope he is not your lover."

"Such relationships are of no interest to me."

"What sort of relationship is of interest?"

Melancthe, glancing over her shoulder and finding Shimrod uncomfortably close, moved a step to the side. "I have given the matter no thought."

"Do you wish to learn magic?"

"I do not care to be a witch."

Shimrod returned to his chair. "You are something of a puzzle." He clapped his hands, and the servant appeared. "Melancthe, will you ask for the wine to be served?"

Melancthe sighed and gave a signal to the servant, and went back to the couch in a manner of strained resignation. The maid returned with wine and a pair of goblets, and served both Shimrod and Melancthe.

Shimrod said: "Once I thought of you as a child in a woman's body."

Melancthe smiled a cool smile. "And now?"

"The child seems to have wandered away."

Melancthe's smile became a trifle wistful.

"The woman is as beautiful as the dawn," said Shimrod. "I wonder if she realizes this. She seems to be clean; she uses a certain degree of effort to tend her hair. She carries herself like a woman who is well aware of her charm."

Melancthe spoke in a colorless voice: "You insist upon boring me."

Shimrod paid her no heed. "It would seem that you are content with your life and yourself. Still, when I try to enter your mind I am lost as if in a jungle."

Melancthe responded flatly: "That is because I am not truly a human being."

"Who taught you this? Tamurello?"

Melancthe gave an indifferent nod. "These are dull topics. When will you leave?"

"Soon. But tell me this: why did Tamurello teach you such extraordinary folly?"

"He taught me nothing. I know nothing. My mind is empty, like the dark places behind the stars."

Shimrod asked: "Do you consider me human?"

"So I would guess."

"I am Murgen's scion."

"This is something I do not understand."

"At a time now far in the past, Murgen went abroad in this guise, that he might act and do and see as someone other than the fabulous Murgen. I know nothing of those times; Murgen controlled my deeds and the memories are his. Eventually, through usage, Shimrod took on substance and became real, and no longer was he connected with Murgen.

"Now I am Shimrod. Should I not think myself a man? I look like a man. I hunger and thirst; I eat and drink and in due course void the dross. I am gladdened by joy and I weep tears for grief. When I see your beauty I feel a wistful longing which is both sweet and hurtful. In short, I am all too human, and if not, I notice nothing of the lack."

Melancthe looked back to the sea. "My shape is human; my body like yours performs its functions; I see, I hear, I taste. But I am empty. I have no emotion. I do nothing but walk the beach."

Shimrod moved to sit on the couch beside her. He put his arm around her shoulders. "Let me fill the emptiness."

Melancthe showed him a sardonic side-glance. "I am well enough as I am."

"You will be better when you are different. Far better."

Melancthe pulled away and went to stand by the window.

Shimrod, with nothing more to say, chose this moment to depart, and did so without words of farewell.

On the following day Shimrod went back to the white villa, calculatedly at the same time. If Melancthe followed her routine of yesterday, he would learn something of her mood. He waited beside the terrace for an hour but Melancthe failed to appear. At last he went thoughtfully back to Ys.

During the late afternoon the fine weather failed before a fresh breeze from the west; a high mesh of cirrus flew at speed across the sky, and the sun sank into a purple bank of nimbus.

In the morning brightness and gloom struggled to control the landscape. Shafts of sunlight burst down through rents in the clouds, only to be constricted and shut off. So it went until afternoon, when black walls of rain swept in from the sea.

Late in the day Shimrod, on impulse, threw a cloak around his shoulders and, after making a purchase at the market, strode down the beach to the white villa. He climbed the steps, crossed the terrace and made his presence known by rapping upon the carved wooden door.

He discovered no response and rapped again. At last the door opened a crack and the serving maid looked out. "Lady Melancthe is receiving no guests."

Shimrod pushed through the door. "Excellent; we will not be disturbed by intruders. I will be staying for supper; here are some excellent cutlets. Broil them properly with herbs and serve a good red wine. Where is Melancthe?"

"In the parlour with the fire."

"I will find my way."

The maid went dubiously to her kitchen. Shimrod, looking from room to room, presently discovered the parlour: a chamber with white walls and an oak-beamed ceiling. Melancthe stood warming herself by the fire. As Shimrod came into the room, she looked over her shoulder, then turned moodily back to look down into the flames.

Shimrod approached. Without looking at him she said: "I knew that you would come tonight."

Shimrod put his arm around her waist and drawing her close, kissed her. He found no response; he might as well have kissed the back of his hand. "Well then — are you pleased to see me?"

"No."

"But neither are you trembling with anger?"

"No."

"I kissed you once before; do you remember?"

Melancthe turned to face him. Shimrod understood that he was about to hear a well-rehearsed statement. "I remember almost nothing of that occasion. Tamurello instructed me exactly. I was to promise you anything and, if need be, accede to any demand you might make of me. It proved not to be necessary."

"And the promises: are they to be broken?"

"They were spoken through my mouth, but they were Tamurello's promises. You must look to him for their satisfaction." And Melancthe smiled down into the fire.

Shimrod, still with his arm around her waist, pulled her close and put his face to her hair, but she detached herself and went to sit on the couch.

Shimrod came to sit beside her. "I am not the world's wisest man, as well you know. Still, there is much which I can teach you."

"You pursue an illusion," said Melancthe, almost contemptuously. "How so?"

"You are affected by the look of my body. If you looked at me and saw a wrinkled yellow skin and a crooked nose with warts, you would not be here tonight, and even if you were you would not kiss me."

"There is no denying any of this," said Shimrod. "Still, I am hardly unique. Would you choose to live in such a body?"

"I am accustomed to this one; and I know it is beautiful. Still, what lives inside the body is I — something which is probably not at all beautiful."

The serving maid entered the room. "Shall I lay supper in here by the fire?"

Melancthe looked around in puzzlement. "I ordered no supper."

"This gentleman brought out some fine cutlets and commanded that they be properly cooked, and so they are: broiled over vine cuttings, with garlic and lemon and a whiff of thyme, and there is a new loaf, some nice fresh peas and the good red wine is ready to drink."

"Serve us in here, then."

During the meal Shimrod worked to achieve an atmosphere of warmth and ease, with little encouragement from Melancthe. Immediately after the supper, she announced that she was tired and intended to retire to her bed.

"There is rain," Shimrod observed. "I will stay tonight."

"The rain has stopped," said Melancthe. "Go now, Shimrod; I want no one in my bed save myself."

Shimrod rose to his feet. "I can depart as graciously as the next man. Melancthe, I wish you good night."

II

A STEADY GRAY RAIN DISCOURAGED SHIMROD from new ventures up the beach. Tactical considerations also gave him pause: an excess of zeal might do his cause more harm than good. For the moment enough had been done. He had brought the unique flavor of his personality to Melancthe's attention; he had shown himself to be gentle, steadfast, entertaining and considerate; he had demonstrated a reassuring degree of ordinary human lust: more might have been considered coarse; less would have demeaned Melancthe's charm and caused her to wonder about both herself and him.

Shimrod sat in the common room of the Rope and Anchor, his favorite of the dockside taverns, drinking ale, watching the rain, and musing upon Melancthe.

She was, beyond question, a fascinating case. Her beauty was a vast treasure; her body seemed too slight to support so urgent a weight. Shimrod wondered: could this beauty alone be the source of her attraction? Where else was her charm?

Looking out across the rain-swept water, Shimrod listed those endearing traits common to all lovable and beloved women. Melancthe lacked them all, including the mysterious and indefinable quality of femininity itself.

Melancthe had asserted the emptiness of her mind; Shimrod saw that he had no choice but to believe her. Conspicuously absent were curiosity, humour, warmth and sympathy. She used that total candor which was not truly honesty so much as indifference to the sensibilities of those who heard her. He could remember no trace of emotion other than boredom and the mild repugnance she seemed to feel for him.

Shimrod ruefully drank his ale and looked up the beach, but the white villa could not be seen for the rain. . . . He nodded slowly to himself, awed by the profundity of a new concept. Melancthe represented the witch Desmëi's last act and her final revenge on Man. Melancthe in her present state was a blankness upon which every man might project his idealized version of ultimate beauty, but when he tried to possess this beauty and make it his own, he would discover a void, and so, according to his capacity, suffer as Desmëi had suffered!

Assuming these conjectures to be correct, mused Shimrod, how would they affect Melancthe, were she to learn of them? If she knew her condition, how ardently might she wish to change it? Could she change, even if she wished to do so?

Aillas came into the tavern. He went to dry himself by the fire, then he and Shimrod took their supper in an alcove to the side of the common room. Shimrod inquired as to the new Ulf army and Aillas declared himself not at all discouraged.

"Indeed, taking all with all, I could expect no better progress. Every day I get a new influx of recruits and the number grows. Today there were fifty-five: strong young lads down from the the moors and mountains, each as brave as a lion and each prepared to teach me the lore of warfare, which is hiding in the gorse until a sufficiently small group of the enemy happens to pass, after which throats are cut, purses are ransacked, and swift retreat is made; that is all there is to it."

"And what of your nine recalcitrant barons?"

"I am happy to report that all presented themselves before the appointed time. None were precisely humble, but the point has been made and I was not forced to march up into the moors — not yet, at any rate."

"They still watch and wait, and wonder how best to circumvent you."

"True, and sooner or later I will be forced to hang a number of incredulous Ulfs, when I would much prefer that they kill themselves fighting the Ska, and even these young Ulf firebrands talk in subdued voices when the Ska are mentioned."

"This should encourage them to learn Ska discipline."

"Unfortunately they are convinced that the Ska can eat them alive, and the battle is lost before the armies so much as face each other. I will have to bring them to it very gradually and rely upon my Troice troops until we win a few victories. Then their pride and manhood will be called into question, and they will be anxious to outdo the Troice outlanders."

"Assuming, of course, that you can beat them with your Troice army."

"I have few fears on that score. The Ska are military experts, no question as to this, but they are relatively few, and each man must fight like five. On the obverse, each Ska casualty is like five, and that is my plan: to bleed them white."

"You seem resigned to a war with the Ska."

"How can it be avoided? In the Ska program, South Ulfland must necessarily be next on the list. As soon as they feel strong enough they will try us out, but not before I am ready for them, or so I hope."

"And when hostilities occur?"

"I will not attack their strength, that is certain. If I had the full support of the barons, my way would be easier." Aillas drank from his goblet. "Today I heard a strange report, from Sir Kyr, who is second son to Sir Kaven, of Black Eagle Keep. Three days ago a knight, purportedly Daut from Dahaut's Western March, stopped by Black Eagle Keep. He named himself Sir Shalles and reported in all seriousness that soon there will be a war and that King Casmir will conquer Troicinet, so that all those who ally themselves with King Aillas now will be driven from their castles. Better, he says, to organize a secret cabal of resistance in the defense of Ulf liberties."

Shimrod chuckled. "I assume that you are looking for Sir Shalles."

"Most definitely. Sir Kyr himself rides at speed for the moors, that he may track down Sir Shalles, capture him and bring him here."

III

THE RAINS DEPARTED; dawn was clear and soft. In the square Shimrod noticed Melancthe's serving maid arriving at the market with a basket. Shimrod went to speak to her. "Good morning to you! It is I, Shimrod!"

"I remember you well, sir; you have a fine taste in cutlets."

"And you have a fine hand in their broiling!"

"That is true, if I myself must admit it. Part of the virtue lies in the vine cuttings; nothing does so well for pork."

"I could not agree more. Was your mistress appreciative?"

"Ah, she is a strange one; sometimes I doubt if she knows what she eats, and cares much less. I notice that she picked the bones of the cutlets, and I will buy some more today, and perhaps a pair of plump fowl. These I like to cut small and fry in olive oil with much garlic, and turn out the whole dish, oil and all, over bread."

"You have the soul of a poet. Perhaps I will—"

The maid interrupted him. "I am sorry to say that I am no longer allowed to admit you to the house. This is a pity, since the lady is in need of someone to admire her. She is so sad that I suspect an enchantment."

"Not impossible! Does Tamurello come to call?"

"In truth, I know of no one who visits her, save yourself and yesterday certain factors from the town, that they might mark her on their rolls."

"Surely a most solitary life!"

The maid hesitated. "Perhaps I should not say this, but tonight is the night of the half-moon waning, and when the weather is fine Lady Melancthe leaves the house an hour before midnight, and returns somewhat later, after moondown. Truly, I fear for her, since this is not altogether a kind coast."

"You are wise to tell me this." Shimrod gave the maid a gold crown. "This will help when you marry."

"Indeed it will, and my thanks to you! Please do not take it to heart if I say that you may not come again to the house."

"I wonder why."

"The lady evidently finds nothing in you to amuse her, and that is the truth of it."

"Most strange!" said Shimrod despondently. "I have succeeded with ladies of every degree, from high to low. A fairy damsel at one time became my lover; the Duchess Lydia of Loermel conferred significant favors upon me. Yet here, on this barren and almost forgotten coast a maiden living alone in a villa bars me from her sight. Is it not a farce?"

"Very strange, sir!" The maid dimpled. "Were you to come knocking on my door, I would not turn you away."

"Aha! We must look into that!" Shimrod seized the maid, kissed her soundly on both cheeks, and sent her smiling away to market.

IV

SHIMROD PREPARED WITH CARE for the night's adventure. He donned a black cloak and arranged the hood so as to cover his sandy-brown hair and to shadow his face. At the last minute, almost as an afterthought, he rubbed the soles of his sandals with water-spite, that he might be enabled to walk on water. Tonight he doubted if the facility would be needed, though at other times it had served him well, except in heavy surf when the charm tended to be a nuisance.

Afterglow gave way to dark night and the waning half-moon started down the sky. At last Shimrod set off up the beach. Approaching the villa, Shimrod climbed the shore dune and settled himself where he could watch in comfort.

From within the villa yellow lamplight outlined a row of high windows. One by one the lamps were snuffed and the villa went dark.

Shimrod waited while the moon descended the sky. From the villa came a shape, conspicuous only as a blot moving across the sand. The size of the blot and the rhythm of its motion identified Melancthe. Shimrod followed at a discreet distance.

Melancthe walked purposefully, but without haste; so far as Shimrod could determine, she showed no interest in the possibility of someone following.

She walked half a mile, just above the reach of the glimmering surf, and presently arrived at a ledge of dark stone which, thrusting into the sea, created a rough little peninsula something over a hundred feet long. In bad weather, waves would break over the ledge; in the calm of the dying moon, the waves merely flowed over the low areas with intermittent sucking and gurgling sounds.

Arriving at the ledge, Melancthe paused a moment and took stock of her surroundings. Shimrod halted, crouched and pulled the hood about his face.

Melancthe took no heed of him. She climbed up on the rock and picked her way out toward the end, where a smooth wave-washed shoulder of stone created a vantage a man's height above the water. Melancthe seated herself on the stone and looked out to sea.

Crouching low, Shimrod scuttled forward like a great black rat and crawled up on the ledge. With great care, testing each step for loose footing, he moved forward. . . . A sound behind him: the pad of slow steps!

Shimrod threw himself to the side and huddled into black shade under a jut of rock.

The steps shuffled close; peering up from under the hood Shimrod saw a creature half-lit by moonlight: a squat torso, massive legs, a distorted head with a low crest. The air disturbed by the creature's passage carried a reek which caused Shimrod to hold his breath, then exhale slowly.

The creature shuffled out the toward the end of the ledge. Shimrod heard a muffled conversation, then silence. He raised himself to a crouching position and went cautiously forward. Melancthe's silhouette blotted out the stars to the west. Nearby huddled the creature who had come after her. Both stared out to sea.

Minutes passed. A dark shape rising from below broke the surface with a hiss and a soft coughing sound. It floated to the end of the ledge and pulled itself up to squat beside Melancthe. Again there was a conversation, which Shimrod could not overhear, then the three sat in silence.

The half-moon settled low, into a long frail wisp of cloud. The three creatures moved somewhat closer together. The sea-thing produced a soft contralto tone. Melancthe uttered a sound somewhat higher in register; the land-thing sang a vibrant deep note. The chord, if such it might be called, persisted for ten seconds, then one after the other the singers changed their tones and the chord altered, then dwindled into silence.

Shivers ran along Shimrod's skin. The sound was of a strange desolate nature, of a sort unfamiliar to Shimrod.

Silence held at the end of the ledge as the three brooded upon the quality of their music. Then the land-thing produced its deep throbbing sound. Melancthe sang: "Ahhhh — ohhhhh" in a descending pitch across an octave. The sea-thing uttered a contralto tone like the chime of a far sea-bell. The sounds altered, in timbre and pitch; the chord dwindled into silence, and Shimrod, skulking low in the shadows, returned to the beach, where he felt less vulnerable to whatever magic might be latent in the sounds.

Fifteen minutes passed. The half-moon became yellow-green and sank into the sea. In the dim light the three at the end of the ledge were almost invisible. . . . Once again they sang their chords, and Shimrod wondered at the melancholy sweetness of the sounds and their ineffable loneliness.

Silence again. Time passed: ten minutes. The land-thing padded across the rock to the shore. Shimrod watched it mount the slope and disappear into a gully. . . . He waited. Melancthe came along the ledge of rock, jumped down to the sand and set off down the beach. As she came to the spot where Shimrod sat, she halted and peered through the dark.

Shimrod rose to his feet, and Melancthe turned to go her way. Shimrod fell in step beside her. She said nothing.

Finally Shimrod asked: "For whom are you singing?"

"No one."

"Why do you go there?"

"Because I choose to do so."

"Who are those creatures?"

"Outcasts like myself."

"Do you talk? Or do other than sing?"

Melancthe laughed, a strange low laugh. "Shimrod, you are ruled by your brain. You are as calm as a cow."

Shimrod decided that silence gave him better credence than hot denial, and so they returned to the villa.

Without a word or a backward glance Melancthe turned through the portal, crossed the terrace and was gone.

Shimrod continued back to Ys, dissatisfied and convinced that he had conducted himself incorrectly: in what fashion, he could not say. Also, what might have been gained by proper deportment? Perhaps a seat in the choir?

Melancthe: hauntingly, strangely, beautiful!

Melancthe: singing across the sea while the waning moon sank low!

Perhaps in sheer passion he should have seized her as they returned along the beach and taken her by force. At least she would not have criticized him for intellectuality!

Even in this program, so superficially attractive, definite flaws existed. Even while repugning the charges of intellectuality, Shimrod still comported himself by the precepts of gallantry, which were uncompromising in such cases. Shimrod decided to think no more of Melancthe: "She is not for me."

In the morning, the sun rose into another fine day. Shimrod sat brooding at a table in front of the Rope and Anchor. A falcon swerved down from the sky and dropped a willow twig upon the table before him, then flew away.

Shimrod looked at the twig with a grimace. But there was no help for it. He rose to his feet and sought out Aillas. "Murgen has summoned me and I must go."

Aillas was not pleased. "Where must you go and why? And when will you be back?"

"I have no answers for these questions; when Murgen calls, I must respond."

"Farewell then."

Shimrod tossed his few belongings into a sack, crushed the twig in his fingers and called out: "Willow, willow, take me now where I must go!"

Shimrod felt a rush of wind and the ground whirled beneath him. He glimpsed upland forests, the peaks of the Teach tac Teach ranked in a long line to north and south; then he slid down a long chute of air to the deck beside the entry to Murgen's stone manse Swer Smod.

A black iron door eleven feet tall barred his way. The central panel displayed an iron Tree of Life. Iron lizards clinging to the trunk hissed and, darting iron tongues, scuttled to new vantages; iron birds hopped from branch to branch, first peering down at Shimrod, then avidly inspecting the iron fruit which none dared taste and occasionally producing small chiming sounds.

Shimrod spoke a cantrap, to soothe the sandestin who controlled the door: "Door, open to me, and let me pass unscathed. Heed only my true wishes, without reference to the mischievous caprices of my dark under-minds."

The door whispered: "Shimrod, the way is clear, though you are over-fastidious in your stipulations."

Shimrod forebore argument and advanced upon the door, which swung aside and allowed him access to a foyer illuminated by a glass dome of green, golden-yellow and carmine-red panes.

Shimrod selected one of the passages leading away from the foyer and so entered Murgen's private hall.

At a heavy table sat Murgen, legs outstretched to the fire. Today he appeared in the semblance which so long before he had conferred upon Shimrod: a tall spare form with a gaunt bony face, dust-colored hair, a whimsical mouth and a set of casual mannerisms.

Shimrod stopped short. "Must you confront me as myself? It is distracting to be instructed or, worse, chided under these circumstances."

"An oversight," said Murgen. "Ordinarily I would not work this prank upon you, but now, as I think of it, the exercise of dealing with unfamiliar concepts from your own mouth may be of ultimate value."

"With due respect, I consider the point far-fetched." Shimrod advanced into the room. "Well then, if you will not change, I will sit with my back partially turned."

Murgen gave an indifferent wave of the hand. "It is all one. Will you take refreshment?" He snapped his fingers and flasks of both mead and beer appeared on the table, along with a platter of bread and cold meats.

Shimrod contented himself with a mug of beer, while Murgen elected to drink mead from a tall pewter tankard. Murgen asked: "Have the priests at the temple dealt courteously with you?"

"You refer to the Temple of Atlante? I never troubled to pay them my respects, nor have they sought me out. Is any gain to be had from their acquaintance?"

"They have long traditions which they are willing to recite. The steps leading down from the temple are impressive and perhaps merit a visit. On a calm day, when the sun is high, a keen eye can look down through the water and count thirty-four steps before they disappear into the murk. The priests claim that the number of steps above the surface is dwindling: either the land is sinking or the sea is rising: such is their reasoning."

Shimrod reflected. "Either case is hard to credit. I suspect that their first count was made at low tide; then later, when the tide was at flood, they made their second count, and so were misled."

"That is a practical explanation," said Murgen. "It seems plausible enough." He glanced toward Shimrod. "You drink only sparingly. Is the beer too thin?"

"Not at all. I merely wish to keep my wits about me. It would not do if both of us became addled, and later woke up in doubt as to who was who."

Murgen drank from his pewter tankard. "The risk is small."

"True. Still, I will keep my head clear until I learn why you have summoned me here to Swer Smod."

"Why else? I need your help."

"I cannot refuse you, nor would I if I could."

"Well spoken, Shimrod! I will come to the point. Essentially, I am irked with Tamurello. He resents my authority and obtrudes his force on my own; ultimately, of course, he hopes to destroy me. At the moment his work is ostensibly trivial or even playful, but, if left unchallenged, it could become dangerous, after this analogy: a man attacked by a single wasp has little to fear; if ten thousand wasps attack him, he is doomed. I cannot give Tamurello's activity the care it deserves; I would be diverted from other work of great importance. Hence, I assign this task to you. At the very least, your vigilance will distract him exactly as he hopes to distract me."

Shimrod frowned into the fire. "It might be wiser to destroy him, once and for all."

"That is easier said than done. I would be perceived as a tyrant, so that the other magicians might decide to form a concert of defense against me, with unpredictable consequences."

Shimrod asked: "How, then, shall I watch him? What must I look for?"

"I will instruct you in due course. Tell me how things go in South Ulfland."

"There is nothing much to report. Aillas trains an army of lummoxes, and has had signal success; now, when he cries out 'March right!', most of them do so. I have attempted a social relationship with Melancthe, to no avail. She feels that I over-intellectualize. No doubt I could win her approval if I chose to sing a fourth part with her choral group."

"Interesting! Melancthe then is musical?"

Shimrod related his experiences on the night of the waning moon. Murgen commented: "Melancthe is woefully confused as to her identity, which Desmëi purposely left empty, in derision and revenge against the masculine race."

Shimrod glowered into the fire. "I will think no more about her; she is as she is."

"A wise decision. Now, in connection with Tamurello . . ." Murgen issued his instructions, after which Shimrod was once again sent whirling through the sky, this time south and east to Trilda, his manse at the edge of Forest Tantrevalles.

V

THE ANCIENT ROAD KNOWN AS OLD STREET traversed Lyonesse from Cape Farewell in the west to Bulmer Skeme in the east. At a place halfway along its length, not far from the village Tawn Twillett, a lane branched off to the north. Up hill and down dale went the lane, by hawthorn hedges and old stone fences, past drowsy farmsteads and across the River Sipp by a low stone bridge. Entering the Forest of Tantrevalles, the lane wound through sun and shadow for another mile, then broke out into Lally Meadow, passed by Shimrod's manse Trilda, and ended at a wood-cutter's dock on Lally Water.

Trilda, a stone and timber cottage at the back of a flower garden, was notable for its six dormers in a high gabled roof: two to each of the upstairs front bedrooms. The ground floor included a foyer, two parlours, a dining saloon, four bed-chambers, a library and work-room, a kitchen with an attached pantry and buttery, and several rooms of convenience. Four bays with diamond-paned windows overlooked the front garden, and all the glass of all the windows had been enchanted by spells of low magic, so that they remained at all times sparkling and clear, with no trace of dirt, fly-speck, streak, nor the dimness of dust.

Trilda had been designed by Hilario, a minor magician of many quaint notions, and built overnight by a band of goblin carpenters who took their pay in cheeses. Some time later Trilda became the property of Murgen who eventually gave it to Shimrod. An old peasant couple tended the gardens and ordered the chambers during Shimrod's absences; they avoided the work-room as if demons stood waiting behind the doors, which was the conviction Shimrod had been at pains to fix into their minds. The creatures who in fact stood there, fangs glistening, black arms raised on high, while resembling demons, were merely harmless phantasms.

Arriving at Trilda, Shimrod found all in order. The house-keepers had maintained full cleanliness, with not so much as a dead fly on the window-sills. The furniture glowed to the use of bee's-wax and patient rubbing; in the chests and presses the linens lay crisp and smelled fragrant with lavender.

Shimrod's only complaint was over-tidiness. He threw open doors and casements so that air from the meadow might banish the fust of stagnant days and silent nights, then went from room to room shifting this and moving that, to disturb the unrelenting exactitude imposed by his house-keepers.

Arriving in the kitchen, Shimrod kindled a fire and brewed a pot of tea, using horehound for heart, penny-royal for savor and lemon verbena for zest, then took the tea into his day parlour.

Trilda seemed very quiet. From across the meadow came the *chirrup chi chi chi* of a lark. At the end of the song, the silence seemed more profound than ever.

Shimrod sipped the tea. At one time, so he remembered, solitude had been an adventure, to be enjoyed for its own sake. Since that time events had altered him; he had found within himself a capacity for love, and of late he had become accustomed to the merry company of Dhrun and Glyneth, and, more recently, to that of Aillas.

Melancthe? Shimrod made an ambiguous sound. In connection with Melancthe, the word 'love' would seem to have a most dubious application. Beauty compelled admiration and erotic yearning; such was its organic function. But never by itself could it command love: so Shimrod assured himself. Melancthe was a shell, empty inside. Melancthe was no more than a warm breathing symbol of great power, but no more than this. Over-intellectualization? Shimrod made a sound of disgust. Did she expect him not to think?

Shimrod continued to drink tea. The time had come when he must put aside his obsession and address himself to the program defined by Murgen: work which might embroil him in more excitement than he had bargained for, so that he would think back upon this placid interlude with longing.

Murgen had so warned him: "You will be impinging yourself upon Tamurello's notice! You will be rudely interrupting his work and arousing his anger! These are not trivial acts: make no mistake! He will find a means, crude or subtle, to retort, and you must be prepared for amazement!"

Shimrod put aside the tea, which no longer soothed him. He went to his work-room, dismissed the guardians and entered. The room was aptly named. Everywhere, work cried out for sympathetic attention. The center table supported stuffs and articles confiscated from Tintzin Fyral: thaumaturgical equipment, *materia magica*, books and paraphernalia — all to be inspected, classified, then either retained or discarded.

First and most urgently, Shimrod must set out monitors to scrutinize Tamurello and his conduct, as required by Murgen. These devices, when they came to Tamurello's notice, as they inevitably must, would dissuade him from other bold and arrogant mischiefs: so went Murgen's theory, and Shimrod had no reason to fault it, save that it put him in the position of a goat staked out in the jungle for the purpose of enticing a tiger.

Murgen had waved aside Shimrod's misgivings. "Tamurello's bravado must be curbed, and this will be the effect of our program."

Shimrod had proposed another objection: "When he feels the scurch,* he will merely use new tactics, or a clever subterfuge."

"Still, he will be inhibited from truly grandiose ventures, and these are the efforts I fear the most."

"And meanwhile he will take pleasure in wreaking a multitude of small harms in such a way that they cannot be imputed to him."

"We will estimate his crimes and punish him accordingly, and soon Tamurello will be acclaimed the meekest of the meek!"

"Tamurello is not one to turn the other cheek," grumbled Shimrod. "More likely he will send a sandestin** with a plague of stag-beetles for my bed."

"Anything is possible," Murgen agreed. "Were I you, I would maintain double vigilance. Dangers which can be imagined can be refuted!"

With Murgen's dictum in mind, Shimrod surrounded Trilda with a network of sensitive tendrils, to achieve at least a modicum of security. Then, once more in his work-room, he cleared the clutter from one of his work-tables and spread out a sheet of buff-colored parchment provided by Murgen.

The substance of the parchment merged into the oak, so that the table-top became a great map of the Elder Isles, with each of the domains tinted a different color. At Faroli, Tamurello's manse, a point of blue light glittered, to indicate Tamurello's presence. Should Tamurello travel near or far, the blue light would trace his movements. Shimrod had solicited other lights from Murgen, that he might know the movements of other folk; Murgen would hear nothing of this. "You must concentrate your attention upon Tamurello and nowhere else."

Shimrod continued to argue. "We should use the instrument to its full scope. Assume that a red light marked your whereabouts. Assume further that one of your lady-loves seduced you into a dungeon, I could find you easily and release you from the cell, to your minimum inconvenience."

"The contingency is remote."

In such a fashion the map was arranged, and, by the evidence of the blue light, Tamurello remained in residence at Faroli.

---

*Scurch: untranslatable into contemporary terms; generally: 'susurration along the nerves', 'psychic abrasion', 'half-unnoticed or sublimated uneasiness in a mind already wary'. 'Scurch' is the stuff of hunches and unreasoning fear.

**Sandestin: a class of halfling which wizards employ to work their purposes. Many magical spells are effected through the force of a sandestin.

Days passed. Shimrod refined the techniques of his surveillance, using unobtrusive methods which Tamurello, if he so chose, could ignore and still maintain his dignity.

Tamurello, however, refused to tolerate the inspection gracefully, and attempted several artful mischiefs upon Shimrod, which were vitiated by Shimrod's protective system. Meanwhile Tamurello worked to blind Shimrod's optical wisps and shatter his listening shells with concentrations of sound.

Shimrod, warming to his task, introduced a whole new order of sensitive devices, to cause Tamurello a new set of vexations. Murgen's strategy, to monopolize Tamurello's energies with trivial annoyances, seemed generally to be successful.

The lunar month approached the night of the waning half-moon, and Shimrod's thoughts irresistibly went to the white villa beside the ocean. For the briefest of moments he contemplated a second visit by midnight to the rocky ledge which thrust into the ocean; as quickly as the idea came it went, and once again Shimrod was left with unwelcome images and the haunting fragrance of violets.

Shimrod tried to exorcise the visions: "Go! Away! Depart! Dissolve into the void, and never return to disturb me! Were it not absurd, I might think you another of Tamurello's tricks, as he does to me what I try to do to him!"

On the night itself, Shimrod became restless, and went out to observe the moon. The meadow was quiet; nothing could be heard but crickets and a few far frogs. Shimrod wandered across the meadow to the old dock on Lally Water, where the moon already had started its decline down the sky. The water was calm and dark; when Shimrod threw a pebble, the expanding ripples gleamed silver. . . . A watch-wisp floating over his head issued a sudden warning: "Someone stands near; magic has come and gone!"

Shimrod turned and, not altogether to his surprise, discovered by the shore a slight figure in a white gown and a black cloak: Melancthe. She stood looking up at the moon and seemed not to see him.

Shimrod, turning away, paid her no heed.

She came down the dock and stood beside him. "You do not seem surprised to find me here?"

"I only wonder how Tamurello could induce you to come."

"He found no difficulty; in fact, I came of my own volition."

"Strange! Tonight you were to sing with your friends on the rocks."

"I decided to go there no more."

"How so?"

"It is simple enough. I had a choice: to live or to die. I chose to live, which brought me to new choices. Should I continue as an outcast and sing on the rocks, or should I simulate the ways of the human race? I decided to change."

"You do not regard yourself as human?"

Melancthe said softly: "Tamurello has informed me that I am a neutral intelligence of no great vigor in a female mask." She looked up into Shimrod's face. "What do you think?"

"I think that Tamurello listens and smiles. Wisp: look sharp, high and low: what listens and what watches?"

"I apprehend nothing."

Shimrod gave a dubious grunt. "And what were Tamurello's instructions to you?"

"He said that humanity in the main was crass, stupid, boorish and vulgar, and that I could learn at least this much from you."

"Some other time. Now, Melancthe, I will bid you good night."

"Wait, Shimrod! You told me that I was beautiful, and you took pains to kiss me. Tonight I have come to Trilda and you are the one who now backs away. That is a curious contradiction."

"Not at all. I am taken aback, and cautious. Tamurello's motives are clear enough, but yours are in doubt. I believe that you exaggerate my crassness and stupidity. And now, Melancthe, if you will excuse me — "

"Where are you going?"

"Back to Trilda; where else?"

"And you will leave me alone in the dark?"

"You have been alone in the dark before."

"We will go to Trilda together, since I have no other place to go. And, as I have already mentioned, I came here of my own volition."

"You show little overt warmth. It is more as if you had steeled yourself to a great challenge."

"It is a new experience for me."

With an effort Shimrod controlled his voice. "I might have welcomed you more gladly had you not told your maid to bar the door in my face. When one is judging the disposition of another, this sort of act would seem a significant straw in the wind."

"Possibly so, but the inference might be wrong. Remember, you had intruded into my life and had troubled my mind with your persuasions. At length I was swayed and now I am here, at your behest."

"At Tamurello's behest."

Melancthe smiled. "I am I and you are you. How does Tamurello concern us, one way or another?"

"Is your memory so short? I have reason for concern."

Melancthe looked off across the water. "He gave no orders. He said that you were here at Trilda making a nuisance of yourself. He said that if not for Murgen, he would have long since sent you riding to the far side of the moon on a saw-horse. He said he would be pleased if I beguiled and besotted you until your eyes looked like boiled eggs and you fell asleep at breakfast with your face in the porridge. He said that you had a low-order mind and could deal with no more than one thought at a time, and that if I were at Trilda you would completely forget your meddling, to his great satisfaction, and now you know all of it."

"Just as well." Shimrod looked moodily out over the water. "I wonder what calumnies another five minutes might have brought."

Melancthe moved a step back. "Well then, here I am. What is it to be? Shall I go away? Consult the factions of your brain, and perhaps you will find a consensus."

"I have already decided," said Shimrod. "You shall come to Trilda." And Shimrod, with grim emphasis, added: "There we shall discover who most notably distracts whom, and every morning Tamurello will receive a cheerful greeting. . . . Notice the waning moon; already it declines into the west. Time that we returned to Trilda."

The two went silently back along the lane, and as they walked a new and disturbing possibility entered Shimrod's mind: might this creature beside him which used the name Melancthe be a guise for another, of a different sort, which at some delicate moment might reveal itself in its true form, and so punish Shimrod for his impudent surveillance?

The concept was not on its face improbable. Luckily, the trick could readily be detected.

Once in the parlour at Trilda, Shimrod took Melancthe's cloak and poured two goblets of pomegranate wine. "The flavor like yourself, is at once sweet and tart, haunting, mysterious and by no means obvious. . . . Come! I will show you around Trilda."

Shimrod first took her into the dining saloon ("The oak is cut from a tree which grew on this very site."), across the formal parlour ("Notice the tapestries in the cartouches; they were woven in ancient Parthia."), then into the work-room. Shimrod immediately went to look at his map. The blue point of light glittered from the site of Faroli, far to the north in Dahaut: so much for one of his suspicions, that the woman at his side might even be a guise of the epicene Tamurello; this was clearly not the case.

Melancthe looked here and there without great interest. Shimrod described two or three pieces of his paraphernalia, then took her before a tall mirror, which reflected her image in clear detail, and another of Shimrod's misgivings was put to rest. Had she been a succuba or a harpy, the creature's true image would have reflected from the mirror.

Melancthe studied the glass with absorbed interest. Shimrod said: "The mirror is of magic. You see reflected the person you think yourself to be. Or you may say: 'Mirror, show me as I appear to Shimrod!' or,

'Mirror, show me as I appear to Tamurello!' and you will see these versions of yourself."

Melancthe moved away without undertaking the trials Shimrod had suggested. Shimrod surveyed the mirror from the side. "I could easily confront the mirror and say: 'Mirror, show me as I appear to Melancthe!' but, in all candor, I lack the courage."

"Let us leave this room," said Melancthe. "It reeks of the brain."

The two returned to the small parlour, where Shimrod brought fire to the hearth, then turned to inspect Melancthe.

She spoke in her soft voice: "You are pensive. Why is this?"

Shimrod stood looking down into the flames. "I find myself with a dilemma. Do you care to hear it?"

"I will listen, certainly."

"At Ys, only a few weeks ago, Shimrod visited Melancthe, to renew their acquaintance and perhaps to discover some mutuality of interest which might enhance their lives. In the end Melancthe scornfully barred the door to him.

"Tonight Shimrod strolls beside Lally Water, watching the moon-set. Melancthe appears, and now, instead of Shimrod pursuing Melancthe, it is Melancthe who pursues Shimrod, that she may beguile and befuddle him in his manse Trilda, that he may desist from molesting her friend Tamurello.

"With perhaps disingenuous frankness she reports Tamurello's unflattering opinion of Shimrod, so that now Shimrod must throw self-esteem to the winds if he obeys his impulses and succumbs to Melancthe's allurements. If he proves steadfast and expels Melancthe from Trilda with the rebuke she deserves, he shows himself to be pompous, inflexible and foolish.

"His dilemma, then, is not whether, or how, or if, to retain pride, dignity and self-respect, but in which direction to cast them aside."

Melancthe asked: "How long do you intend to ponder? I have no self-esteem whatever, and I can make up my mind instantly, according to my inclinations."

"Perhaps that is the best wisdom, after all," said Shimrod. "My character is intensely strong, and my will is like iron; still, I see no reason to demonstrate their strength needlessly."

Melancthe said: "The fire blazes hot, and the room is warm. Shimrod, help me from my cloak."

Shimrod stepped close, parted the clasp at her neck, and took her cloak; in some way her gown also fell to the floor, so that she stood nude in the firelight. Shimrod thought that never had he seen a sight so beautiful. He embraced her and her body first stiffened, then went flexible.

The fire had burned low. Melancthe said in a husky voice: "Shimrod, I am frightened."

"How so?"

"When I looked into the mirror, I saw nothing."

VI

THE DAYS GLIDED BY, easy and quiet, without untoward incident to mark one day from the next. Shimrod occasionally thought that Melancthe attempted to tease and provoke him, but he maintained at all times a manner of imperturbable composure, and in the main all went smoothly. Melancthe seemed at least passively content, and was at all times accessible, or even more than accessible, to Shimrod's erotic inclinations. With dour amusement Shimrod recalled events of the past: her distrait conduct as she walked through his dreams; her boredom during his visits to her villa; her barring of the door against him — and now! His most far-fetched amorous fantasies had become real!

Why? The question constantly came to perplex him. Somewhere there was mystery. Shimrod could not understand how Tamurello profited from the arrangement; according to the blue glint, he never strayed from Faroli.

Melancthe herself volunteered no information, and pride prevented Shimrod from putting aside his pose of urbane equanimity and placing sharp questions.

Now and then, during the course of conversation, Shimrod made an idle inquiry or two, but Melancthe commonly returned only a blank stare, or sometimes an evasion or at worst accused him of over-intellectualization. "When something needs to be done I do it! When my nose itches, I scratch it, without an agonizing analysis of the situation."

"Scratch at will, so long as it pleases you," said Shimrod in a voice of austere courtesy.

As time passed, the novelty of Melancthe's presence diminished, but not so her amorousness, which, perhaps through boredom, actually increased until it quite exceeded Shimrod's competence, causing him guilt and sheepishness. Remedies were available, had he chosen to use them: for instance, an elixir known as 'The Bear', in jocular reference to the constellation Ursa Major, always aloft by night and by day. Shimrod also knew of a magical spell which worked to the same effect, known popularly as 'The Phoenix'.

Shimrod refused to consider such adjuncts, for several reasons. First, Melancthe already took up more of his time than he cared to reckon, and absorbed a large fraction of his energies in the process, leaving him often in a state of lassitude, so that his surveillance over Tamurello was at times desultory. Secondly — and here was a contingency which Shimrod could never have anticipated — the unadorned copulations, lacking humour, sympathy and grace, gradually came to lose much of their charm. Finally, a suspicion occasionally seeped into Shimrod's mind that Melancthe found him wanting, in quality as well as quantity. Shimrod at all times pridefully dismissed the idea; what had sufficed for his other partners in dalliance must do equally well for Melancthe.

A month passed and another. Each morning, after one or more erotic episodes, Shimrod and Melancthe took a leisurely breakfast of porridge with cream and fresh red currants, or perhaps griddle-cakes, butter, cherry conserve or honey, with ham, water-cress and boiled eggs, and usually either a half-dozen broiled quail or a brace of fresh trout, or poached salmon in dill sauce, along with new bread, fresh milk and berries. A pair of pale falloys* prepared and served the meal, and cleared away the soiled plates, cups and trenchers.

After breakfast Shimrod might take himself to his workroom, though more often he dozed for an hour or two on the couch, while Melancthe wandered about the meadow. Sometimes she sat in the garden plucking the strings of a lute, contriving sounds in which Shimrod discovered no pattern but which nonetheless seemed to please Melancthe.

After two months Shimrod found her moods as enigmatic as on the day of her arrival. He fell into the habit of squinting at her sidelong, in wonder and speculation. The mannerism evidently vexed her, so that one morning she gave a sudden grimace and demanded: "You watch me as a bird watches an insect: why do you do so?"

Shimrod finally gathered his wits and said: "For the most part I watch you out of sheer pleasure! You are certainly the most beautiful creature alive!"

Melancthe muttered, as much to herself as to Shimrod: "Am I alive? I may not even be real."

Shimrod responded in that whimsical manner which also annoyed Melancthe, though not as much as an alternative style of logical exposition: "You are alive; otherwise you would be dead and I would be a necrophile. This is not so; hence you are alive. If you were not real, your clothes — " Melancthe now wore pale buff peasant breeches and a peasant smock " — would find no support and would fall into a heap on the ground. Are you satisfied?"

"Then why did not the mirror show my image?"

---

*falloy: a variety of halfling, much like a fairy, but larger and far more gentle of disposition.

"Have you looked into it recently?"

"No. I dread what I might see. Or might not see."

"The mirror gives you back your self-assessment. You have no personal image because Tamurello has denied it to you, to keep you subservient. That, at least, is my guess. Since you refuse to confide in me, I cannot help you."

Melancthe looked away across the meadow, and caught unawares, perhaps said more than she wanted: "The advice of a man would only weaken me."

Shimrod frowned. "Why should that be?"

"Because that is how things are."

Shimrod said nothing and presently Melancthe cried out: "You are looking at me again!"

"Yes. In wonder. But now at last I am beginning to guess what you will not tell me, and I wonder not so much any more; in fact I think I know."

"Do you ever do aught but think? You keep the whole world under your forehead: a queer dead Shimrod-shaped illusion! But what do you truly know?"

"For convenience, let us restrict our remarks to your presence at Trilda. Tamurello sent you here to distract me. This is so clear as to be rudimentary. Am I wrong?"

"You would never believe otherwise, no matter what I told you."

"You are clever. Of course I am wrong. You evade my question in order to fool me. Why should I be surprised? You have fooled me before; now I know you well."

"You know me by not so much as an inkling! By not even the inkling of an inkling! You think, you ponder, even while we lie engaged I hear your thoughts clicking together!"

Astonished by Melancthe's vehemence, Shimrod could only say: "Nevertheless, I understand you at last!"

"You are a prodigy of pure reason."

"Your ideas are absolutely wrong! It is proper that you should realize your error. I have not the heart to tell you the whole of it, especially now, while you are angry. You have won the erotic war; the Female Principle has defeated the Male! You are welcome to the victory; it is empty. I will say no more."

"No!" cried Melancthe. "You have gone too far; you must say more!"

Shimrod shrugged. "You decided to sing no longer with the outcasts; you chose to join the human society, but here, willy-nilly, you were forced to obey the function Desmëi imprinted upon you. I had come to your villa and there aroused your hostility. I suspect that it was a queer bitter-sweet emotion: you both liked and disliked me. In any event

I became your first antagonist. Did you defeat me? Think as you like. And now I will say no more, except only this: you can tolerate Tamurello because he is not truly masculine; hence he is not an antagonist." Shimrod rose to his feet. "Excuse me; I have neglected much of late, and I must see to my duties."

Shimrod went to his work-room. The tables had been ordered; again the room was a pleasant place in which to work, though Shimrod had done precious little of this during the last two months.

Today his first business concerned the wizard Baibalides, who lived in a house of black rock on Lamneth Isle, a hundred yards off the coast of Wysrod.

Shimrod opened a cabinet and extracted a case from which he took a mask representing Baibalides. Next he brought out a skull on a pedestal and arranged the mask in place over the skull. Instantly the mask seemed to come alive. The eyes blinked; the mouth opened to allow a tongue to moisten the lips. Shimrod called: "Baibalides, can you hear me? It is Shimrod who speaks."

The mouth of the mask responded using Baibalides' voice. "Shimrod, I hear you. What is your business with me?"

"I have here an article which I took from Tintzin Fyral. It is an ivory tube carved on one side with odd runes and on the other with characters spelling out your name. I wonder what might be the purpose of the tube, and whether you claim it as your property, or whether it might have been a gift, either to Tamurello or to Faude Carfilhiot."

Baibalides answered: "I know the tube well: it is Gantwin's Millenial Spectator; it depicts events of the last thousand years anywhere within its purview. I lost it at wager to Tamurello, who evidently gave it to Carfilhiot. If you have no need for it, I will gladly resume ownership. It is invaluable when one wishes to locate buried treasure or to learn the deeds of dead heroes, or, on a more practical basis, to determine paternity. As I recall, the activating spell is of three resonances and a quaver."

"The article is once more yours," said Shimrod. "If ever I require its use, perhaps you will allow me this favor."

"With pleasure!" said Baibalides heartily. "I celebrate the return of this article with special satisfaction since I believe that Tamurello cheated me during the course of the wager."

"Not impossible," said Shimrod. "Tamurello is a man of peculiar predilections. From sheer perversity, he prefers evil to good. Someday he will press Murgen too far."

"That is my own opinion. Only last week I attended a conclave on Mount Khambaste in Ethiopia, where Tamurello was already in residence. During the important business he offended a Circassian witch who began to corrode Tamurello with Blue Ruin, and Tamurello was forced to make concessions, though later he cursed the witch with foot-long toenails, so that now and forever she must wear special boots."

Shimrod's attention had been caught. "Last week, you say? And where did Tamurello go after leaving the conclave?"

"Perhaps he returned to Faroli; I am not sure."

"It is no great matter. I will see that you receive your tube in short order."

"Shimrod, I thank you!"

The mask lost its vitality. Shimrod replaced both mask and skull in the cabinet. He went to his map and inspected the blue point of light which so definitely had placed Tamurello in residence at Faroli over the previous two months.

Peering close, Shimrod discovered the source of the error. A small section of adhesive membrane had been applied to the map, immobilizing the blue glint in place.

Shimrod, turning slowly away from the map, examined each of the other instruments which, so he believed, kept a vigilant watch upon all phases of Tamurello's activities. Each, by one means or another, had been rendered useless, in such a way that a casual inspection might not reveal the failure.

Shimrod aroused Facque, the sandestin which, disguised as a gargoyle carved into the facing above the fireplace, guarded the workroom against intruders. "Facque, are you asleep?"

"Naturally not."

"Why have you not kept diligent watch?"

"If you please, I cannot properly answer negative questions. There are numberless acts which I have not performed; we could confer here forever while I detailed the deeds I have not done."

Patiently Shimrod asked: "Did you, then, keep vigilant watch over the workroom?"

"Yes, of course."

"Why did you not warn me of intruders?"

Facque made another peevish protest: "Must you again and again ask questions presuming non-existent facts?"

"Did you notice intruders, or better: who has during the past two months entered the workroom?"

"You, Murgen, and the female who has been sent here to bemuse and befuddle you."

"Has the woman come in alone, while I was not present?"

"On several occasions."

"Did she tamper with my map and my instruments?"

"She stilled the light in place, and interfered with other devices."

"Did she do anything else?"

"She made marks with a stylus in your Book of Logotypes."

Shimrod gave a startled exclamation. "Small wonder that my magic has lately been so flat! What more?"

"Nothing of consequence."

Shimrod removed the immobilizing film from the map; instantly the blue glint, as if to relieve pent pressures, darted in all directions back and forth, hither and yon, finally to settle once again upon the site of Faroli.

Shimrod addressed himself to his instruments, and after some difficulty restored their functions.

Once again he called out to Facque: "Awake!"

"I am awake. I never sleep."

"Has Tamurello, or anyone else, installed instruments of surveillance, or any other function, here at Trilda?"

"Yes. The woman may fairly be included into that category. Secondly, Tamurello has commissioned me to report upon your activities, and lacking instructions to the contrary, I have obliged him. Thirdly, Tamurello has attempted to use mayflies for purposes of espionage, but without any great success."

"Facque, I hereby instruct you, definitely and without qualification, to desist from reporting information of any sort to anyone save Murgen or myself: especially and specifically to Tamurello, or to any of his agents or instruments, or to the air at large, on the theory that it might by some means be collected and directed to the attention of Tamurello."

Facque said: "I am pleased that you have clarified this point. In short, Tamurello is not to receive information of any kind."

"Exactly so, and this includes both positive and negative information, or the use of coded silences, or the manipulation of any device, or signal, or musical selection from which Tamurello could elicit information. You must neither initiate, nor make response, in any wise whatever, and I include all types and permutations of communication I have overlooked."

"At last I understand your requirements," said Facque. "All is now in order."

"Not quite," said Shimrod. "I must decide how to deal with Melancthe."

"Spend no great effort in this regard," advised Facque. "It would be time wasted."

"How so?"

"You will find that the woman has left the premises."

Shimrod rushed from the workroom, and looked everywhere, but Melancthe was nowhere to be seen, and Shimrod somberly returned to his workroom.

VII

TAMURELLO SELDOM APPEARED in his natural semblance, preferring an exotic guise for a variety of reasons, not the least of the which was sheer caprice.

Today, stepping out on a balcony above the octagonal garden court at Faroli, he was a frail and ascetic youth, somewhat languid, pale as new milk, with a coriolus of orange-red hair, the strands so fine and luminous as to be invisible. A thin nose, thin lips and blazing blue eyes suggested spiritual exaltation, as Tamurello intended.

Tamurello came slowly down a curving sweep of black glass steps to the courtyard. At the foot of the staircase he halted, then came slowly forward and finally, turning his head, chose to take notice of Melancthe, who stood to the side in the shade of a flowering mimosa tree.

The boy-man approached Melancthe, and it was she who seemed the more earthly and dank. She watched him with a still face; his ethereal but definite masculinity was a posture with which she could feel no possible sympathy.

Tamurello, halting, looked her up and down, then raised an indolent finger and turned away. "Come."

Melancthe followed him into a parlour and seated herself stiffly at the center of a sofa. From her point of view, Tamurello's guises were little more than clues to his mood. This boy-man puzzled rather than annoyed Melancthe. On the whole she cared not a pin as to how he showed himself, and now she put Tamurello's peculiar guise and its possible significance to the side of her mind. Other affairs were more important.

Tamurello again looked her up and down. "You seem none the worse for wear."

"Your tasks have been fulfilled."

"Even over-fulfilled! Ha hum, be it so! Now it seems that in my turn I must address myself to your concerns.

"As I recall, you are troubled because you cannot mesh yourself comfortably into the ways of the world. This is a legitimate source of dissatisfaction. You therefore want me to make changes in the world or, failing this, in you." The boy-man's lips curved in a thin smile, and Melancthe thought that never before had Tamurello affected so acrid a guise.

Melancthe said, simply: "You told me that my mind works at discord to the minds of other persons."

"So I did. Notably with persons of the masculine gender. This is Desmëi's attempted revenge upon the cosmos, and particularly that segment with external genital organs. What a joke! It is only such innocents as poor Shimrod who must bear the brunt of Desmëi's rage."

"In that case, remove her curse from my soul."

The boy-man studied Melancthe with grave attention. He said at last: "I fear that you crave the impossible."

"But you assured me—"

The boy-man held up his hand. "In all candor, I lack the skill, nor could Murgen himself do better."

Melancthe's beautiful mouth drooped at the corners. "Is not your magic useful in such a case?"

The orange-haired boy-man spoke with vivacity: "It is all very well to ordain tasks by magic, but some intelligent or skillful agency must ultimately do the specified work. In such remedial work as this no entity, be it man, sandestin, halfling, demon, or other creature of controllable power, understands all the intricacies. Therefore, it cannot be done on the instant."

"Still, this was your undertaking."

"I stated that I would do my best and so I shall. Listen, and I will describe your problems. Attend me carefully; the subject is dense."

"I am listening."

"Each mind is a composite of several phases in superimposition. The first is aware, and is consciousness. The others are no less active but work for the most part in obscurity and away from the light of knowledgeable attention.

"Each phase uses its own tools. The first, or overt, phase of the mind purports to use the faculties of logic, curiosity, the differentiation of aptness from absurdity, with a corollary known as 'humour', and a certain projective kind of sympathy, known as 'justice'.

"The second and third and other phases are concerned with emotions, reflexes, and work of the body.

"Your first phase would seem to be deficient. The second phase, the agent of emotional interpretations, with great travail and inconvenience tries to fulfill this function. Here would seem to be the nature of your debility. The remedy is to strengthen the first phase, by a regimen of usage and training."

Melancthe frowned in puzzlement. "How would I train?"

"Two methods suggest themselves. I can alter your guise to that of an infant and introduce you into a noble family where you can learn by ordinary processes."

"Would I retain my memory?"

"That is at your option."

Melancthe pursed her lips. "I do not want to be an infant."

"Then you must apply yourself to learning, in the fashion of a student:

through books and study and discipline, and so you will learn to think with logic, rather than to brood in terms of emotion."

Melancthe muttered: "It would seem a horror of tedium. To study, to pore over books, to think, to intellectualize—these are the habits I derided in Shimrod."

The boy-man surveyed her with no great interest. "Make your decision."

"If I were forced to study from books, I would learn nothing and go mad in the bargain. Can you not collect a sufficiency of wisdom and experience and humour and sympathy into a node and imprint it upon the empty place in my brain?"

"No!" The boy-man responded so sharply that Melancthe wondered if he told all the truth he knew. "Make your decision!"

"I will return to Ys, and consider."

Tamurello instantly spoke a set of syllables, as if he had been waiting for nothing more. Melancthe was whirled aloft and carried high through clouds and dazzling sunlight. She glimpsed the ocean and the horizon and then felt the soft sand of the beach under her feet.

Melancthe dropped to sit in the warm sand, with arms clasped around her knees. To the south the armies of King Aillas had departed; the beach lay empty all the way to the estuary. She watched the play of the waves. Surging and churning, the surf advanced upon her in a gush of white foam and a sad sweet sound, then flowed back to the sea.

Melancthe sat an hour, then, rising to her feet, she shook the sand from her clothes and entered her quiet villa.

Chapter 7

I

KING AILLAS HAD MOVED THE HEADQUARTERS of his army to Doun Darric, a ruined village on the river Malheu, only three miles south of Sir Helwig's castle Stronson, in the very heart of South Ulfland. Doun Darric had been one of the first South Ulf villages to be despoiled by the Ska, and only tumbles of stone and rubble marked the sites of the old cottages.

The advantages of Doun Darric as army headquarters were many. The troops no longer enjoyed access to the taverns along the docks at Ys; there were no quarrels with men of the town, and the maidens of Ys were again free to visit the market without a surfeit of attention from gallant young soldiers. Even more important, the troops were close upon the high moors, where the weight of their presence was demonstrable to folk of the area.

Aillas had never dared hope that instant tranquillity, like a soft and healing balm, would settle over the mountains and moors of South Ulfland. Vendetta and clan warfare were intrinsic to the Ulfish soul. The king might issue proclamations by the dozen, but unless he cowed, bribed or otherwise persuaded the barons to preserve his laws, the land must remain wild.

The barons of the western slopes and the lower moors for the most part supported Aillas; they were intimately acquainted with the Ska. Their counterparts of the higher regions, in some cases little better than bandit chieftains, were not only the most jealous of their independence but were also the most rancorous proponents of the conduct which Aillas had vowed to obliterate. With the army at Doun Darric, the royal threats had suddenly taken on real import.

Almost immediately Aillas decided to make Doun Darric a permanent base. From everywhere across the land came masons and carpenters, to build suitable appurtenances. Meanwhile, old Doun Darric began to be resurrected: first, in temporary style, by the workmen themselves, and then to a plan more or less casually drawn up by Sir Tristano, as one evening he exercised his fancy over a bottle of wine. He ordained a market square alongside the river with shops and inns around the periphery, broad streets with sewers after the Troice system, and cottages of good quality, each with its own garden. Aillas, taking note of Sir Tristano's sketches, saw every reason why they should be realized, including augmentation of the royal prestige.

Aillas disliked Oäldes, the ramshackle and generally slovenly seat of the former Kings, and Ys was unthinkable as the capital of South Ulfland. Aillas therefore decreed Doun Darric his capital, and Sir Tristano added to his plans a small if gracious royal residence overlooking the river Malheu on one side and the square on the other. Sir Tristano now thought even farther into the future, and set aside a tract across the river for the construction of more pretentious residences by a newly prosperous upper class, which might choose to make their homes in the new town. The builders: carpenters, masons, plasterers, roofers, glaziers, painters and paint-mixers, timber-cutters and quarrymen — all rejoiced to hear the news; their own prosperity was assured for the forseeable future.

The lands in the neighborhood of Doun Darric for the most part had reverted to the wild. Aillas set aside large tracts for eventual distribution to his veterans, in accordance with his promises. Other areas Sir Maloof sold at low and long-term prices to those landless persons who would restore the land to cultivation.

Such tangible evidences of permanency tended to support the authority of the king, who no longer could be labelled a foreign adventurer, intent on wringing South Ulfland dry of what little wealth remained to it. Each day brought new platoons of both volunteers and conscripts to Doun Darric from every part of the land, and from North Ulfland as well: strong young men of great gallantry, many of noble lineage who saw in the army their only hope for glory and advancement. These newcomers were uniformly taut with pride and courage, and often displayed the concomitant qualities of obstinacy and truculence. They conducted their lives by a pair of standard rules: first, one must be constantly prepared to fight; second, in combat, there was no gracious defeat; the loser surrendered, fled or died, each outcome equally hateful.

Aillas had learned a few of the intricacies and inter-actions of the highland feuds. Plainly, many of his new troops would find themselves working in consort with their old enemies, which would seem an invitation to blood-letting. On the other hand, to reckon upon the animosities and to segregate hostile factions seemed to Aillas the worst of all solutions, since it would give the feuds official recognition. The new recruits were notified only that ancient quarrels had no place in the king's army, and must be forgotten, after which the topic received no more attention, and the soldiers were billeted without reference to their past. Typically, the erstwhile enemies, now wearing the same uniforms, after a brief period of jutting jaws, curled lips, and sidelong glances, accommodated themselves to circumstances for lack of practical alternative.

In view of Ulf self-assurance and obstinacy, the first stages of training went slowly. The Troice officers dealt patiently and philosophically with the problem. By almost imperceptible increments, the strong-minded mountain lads came to understand what was expected of them and to wear their uniforms with ease, and finally they themselves were instructing new recruits with attitudes of indulgent contempt for their awkwardness.

Meanwhile, along the upper moors and into the high glens, a tense quiet prevailed — the quiet not of restful ease, but the quiet of whispers and listening in the dark and held breath: an unnatural condition, affecting the landscape itself, as if the very mountains and crags and gorse and pine forests watched and waited for the first contravention of royal law.

Aillas sent Sir Tristano forth with a suitable escort to test the mood of the far places, and also to solicit further news of the self-proclaimed Daut knight Sir Shalles. Sir Tristano returned to report that he had received correct if somewhat cool hospitality; that the barons were disbanding their armed companies with calculated slowness; and that each house had a litany of wrongs to recite against its foes. As for Sir Shalles, he had not been idle, and appeared here and there to disseminate a wonderful variety of rumors. Sir Shalles, according to best report, was a stocky gentleman of intelligence and credibility, even though a number of his claims were either inherently ridiculous or self-contradictory; his audience could believe what it wanted to believe. He stated that Aillas and the Ska had formed a secret alliance; that ultimately the Ulf barons would find themselves fighting for the Ska. Sir Shalles reported that Aillas was subject to foaming fits, and that his sexual tastes were both freakish and rank. Sir Shalles also had it on the best authority that after King Aillas rendered the barons defenseless, he intended to impose a crushing burden of taxes upon them, and confiscate their lands when they could not pay.

"Is there more?" Aillas asked when Sir Tristano had stopped for breath.

"Much more! It is widely known that you are already sending

shiploads of Ulf maidens back to Troicinet for use in the waterfront stews."

Aillas chuckled. "What about my worship of Hoonch the dog-god? And the fact that I poisoned Oriante so as to become King of South Ulfland?"

"Neither of those, yet."

"We must strike back at this energetic Sir Shalles." Aillas thought a moment. "Announce everywhere that I am anxious to meet Sir Shalles, that I will pay him twice as much as King Casmir does to roam the back counties of Lyonesse spreading tales about King Casmir. Do not yourself go; send messengers with the notice."

"Excellent!" declared Sir Tristano. "It shall be done. Now: another matter. Have you heard the name 'Torqual'?"

Aillas reflected. "I think not. Who is he?"

"From what I can gather he is a Ska renegade, who became a bandit and took to the hills. Recently, I was told, he went to ply his trade in Lyonesse, but now he is back, in a secret keep close on the border between the Ulflands. There he has recruited a band of human brutes, and raids into South Ulfland. He has let it be known that he will attack, waylay, besiege and destroy any baron who obeys your rule; for this reason, those barons situated near the North Ulfland frontier are more than normally reluctant to fly your flag. All the while Torqual takes sanctuary in North Ulfland where you cannot go, at risk of arousing the Ska."

"A pretty problem," Muttered Aillas. "Have you a solution?"

"Nothing practical. You cannot fortify the border. You cannot usefully garrison all the castles. A sortie into North Ulfland could only amuse Torqual."

"These are my own thoughts. Still, if I cannot protect my subjects, they will not think me their king."

"It is a problem without a solution," said Sir Tristano. "Is that opinion helpful?"

"Eventually Torqual will die of old age," said Aillas. "That might be my best hope."

II

TENSIONS PERSISTED ALONG THE UPPER MOORS. With simple conviction the Ulf barons asserted the changeless reality of the old feuds; they were neither forgotten nor forgiven. Passions were dissembled; retaliations were held in abeyance, while all waited to discover who first would defy the young king, and, with even more interest, how Aillas would respond to the challenge.

The tension broke suddenly, with a majestic doom's-day inevitability to the circumstances.

The party at offense was none other than doughty Sir Hune of Three Pines House. In full and ponderous defiance of the law, he waylaid Sir Dostoy of Stoygaw Keep when Sir Dostoy ventured out on the moors for a morning's sport with his hawks. One of Sir Dostoy's sons died in the skirmish; another fled with wounds. Sir Dostoy himself was trussed and flung over the back of a horse like a sack of meal. His captors carried him up the slope of Molk Mountain to Goatskull Gap, down and across Blacken Moor, through Kaugh Forest and so across Lammon's Meadow to Three Pines House. There, Sir Hune made good his threat and nailed Sir Dostoy high on the door of the hay barn, after which Sir Hune called for his supper and ate with gusto while squires of the house used Sir Dostoy as a target for their birding arrows.

Aillas learned of the deed when the wounded second son rode reeling into Doun Darric. He was well prepared. Almost before Sir Dostoy's corpse was cold a strike-force of four hundred men, large enough to discourage intervention by Sir Hune's clan-fellows, yet not so large as to be cumbersome, was on its way to Three Pines House: up Malheu Valley with its train of wagons rumbling at best speed in the rear; along the Tin Mine Road with Molk Mountain looming into the clouds still to the east, then below Kaugh Forest and out upon Lammon's Meadow.

A half-mile to the east, on a hummock of rock, stood Three Pines House behind its fortifications.

Sir Hune received news of the royal reaction by messenger, and was taken aback somewhat by the swiftness of response. He admitted as much to Thrumbo, his Chief Archer. "Ha ha! He moves hard and he moves fast! Well then, what of that? We will hold a parley. I will declare my error, and vow to mend my ways; then we will spit a bullock and swallow a tun of good wine, and all will be well; let the Stoygaw curs yelp as they may."

Such was Sir Hune's first thought. Then, becoming uneasy, he wrote out a letter and dispatched it in haste to the houses of his clansmen:

> *Bring you and all your true men to Three Pines, where we must set this foreign kinglet into skreeking defeat! Come at once; I charge you by the bonds of blood and the tokens of the clan.*

Response to the letter was scant; only a few dozen men answered the call to war, and these lacked all zest. Sir Hune was advised a dozen times to take horse and flee over the hills into Dahaut, but by the time he had reached the same decision, the royal army had arrived at Three Pines House, and instantly placed it under investment.

Sir Hune had pulled up his gate and waited glumly for the summons to parley. He waited in vain, while with sinister efficiency the Troice contingents made their preparations. A pair of heavy mangonels was assembled; at once they began to lob great boulders up, over and down upon the roofs of the structures within the stone walls.

Sir Hune was dumbfounded and outraged; where was the call to parley he had so confidently expected? And he liked even less the sight of the gibbet which was being erected somewhat to the side. It was strong and high, and well-braced, as if prepared for much heavy work.

The barrage continued all night long. As the sun sent red rays of dawn along the misty fell, bales of straw impregnated with hot pitch and fish oil were set afire and lofted after the stones, that they might ignite broken woodwork and stores. Almost at once red flames and coils of black smoke rose above the doomed fabric of Three Pines House.

From within came hoarse calls of rage and horror; this was not the way affairs were meant to go! Here was sheer cold-blooded obliteration of Sir Hune and Three Pines in totality, and all for so trifling an offense!

Sir Hune prepared for what must now be done: a hopeless and desperate attempt to flee. The gates fell open: out galloped the warriors in an effort to break through the lines and win free across the moors. Arrows felled their horses. Some of the warriors leaped erect and fought with swords until they too were shot dead by the Troice archers; others were captured as they lay stunned in the bracken, and among these was Sir Hune. His arms were bound; a rope was tied around his neck and he was dragged stumbling to the gibbet.

Aillas stood at a distance of twenty yards. For the briefest of moments the two looked eye to eye, then Sir Hune was hoisted high.

The survivors of the battle were brought to Aillas for judgment. Two were barons in their own right, and six more were knights; these eight were considered rebels, as was Sir Hune, and they too went to the gibbet.

The remaining prisoners, some fifty men, stood haggard and woe-begone, waiting their turn. Aillas went to inspect them. He spoke: "In point of law you, like your leaders, are rebels. Probably you deserve hanging. However, I deplore the waste of strong men, who should be supporting the cause of their country rather than working to defeat it.

"I offer each of you an option. You may be hanged at this moment, or you may enlist in the king's army, to serve him with full loyalty. Choose! Those who wish to be hanged, let them step yonder to the gibbet."

There were a few uneasy mutters, a shifting of feet, and wall-eyed glances toward the gibbet, but no one moved.

"What? There are none for the gibbet? Then let those who wish to enlist in the royal army move yonder to the wagons, and place themselves under the command of the sergeant."

Sheepishly the erstwhile defenders of Three Pines House took themselves to the wagons.

The women and children of the household stood desolately by the walls of the still-smouldering castle. Aillas instructed Sir Pirmence: "Go now and console the women; advise them to find places with their kin; if need be give them assistance. Your tactfulness and perception should be invaluable. Sir Tristano, make sure that no survivors remain within the castle, whether invalids or persons whom we might wish to know better, such as Sir Shalles of Dahaut. Sir Maloof, where are you? Here is scope for your own rare talents! Speak with persons of the household and discover Sir Hune's treasure vault, together with all other precious gems, coins and objects of gold and silver. Make an inventory, then confiscate all to the interest of the royal exchequer, which should bring at least a trifle of pleasure to this melancholy day."

Sir Maloof found little enough treasure: a few salvers, cups and plates of silver; a hundred gold coins, and some trinkets of garnet, tourmaline and jasper. Sir Pirmence consoled the bereaved women with great skill, and sent them off to the places of their kin. Sir Tristano returned with grisly news. "I find no invalids nor persons in hiding. No one survives in the house, save only those in the dungeons. I counted eight prisoners and three torturers; then I could no longer bear the stench."

Aillas' heart went cold. "Torturers, then? I might have suspected as much. Tristano, you must do more. Take some men of strong stomach and go down into the dungeons. Liberate the prisoners and clap the torturers into chains. Then make use of our new soldiers." Aillas indicated Sir Hune's former henchmen. "Order them to bring into the light of day all those implements and instruments now in the dungeons, and we will make sure that no one else puts them to use."

The eight prisoners were brought up from the dungeons, limping, hopping, sidling, some moving their legs with tender delicacy, groaning and whimpering with each step: the legacy of overmuch familiarity with the rack. Two could not walk in any fashion whatever, and were carried out on pallets. All eight were in sorry state. Their garments were rags; they stank with encrustations of filth and ordure, and hair lay matted and pasted against their scalps. The six who could walk huddled together, peering from the side of their faces, half-fearful, half-apathetic.

The three torturers stood apart, surly, uncertain, but feigning a disdainful detachment from the situation. One was a ponderous big-bellied hulk, chinless and with only a hint of neck. The second was elderly, with high shoulders, a tall forehead and long chin. The third, who seemed no more than Aillas' own age, smiled with unconvincing bravado first out at the troops, then up at the bodies on the gibbet.

Aillas spoke in a sad voice to the former prisoners: "Be easy; you are free! No one will harm you now."

One of the men responded in a husky whisper: "'Now' is now, but 'then' is gone! My name is Nols; I know that only so I may hide when I am called. The rest is like a dream."

Another looked in wonder at the gibbet. He pointed a claw-like finger: "There hangs Sir Hune, heavy as lard! Is it not a marvel? Dead Sir Hune! Sweet dead Sir Hune! As dear to my eyes as the face of my mother!"

Nols also pointed. "I see Gissies and Nook and Luton! Are they still to be our jailers?"

"Indeed not," said Aillas. "They are to be hanged, which is perhaps too easy an end for them. Sergeant! Hoist high these three horrors."

"Hold!" cried the young torturer Luton in a sudden sweat. "We obeyed orders, no more! Had we not done so, a dozen others would have leapt forward to take over our posts!"

"And today they would dangle from the gibbet instead of you. . . . Sergeant, take them aloft."

"Hurrah!" quavered Nols, and his fellows joined him in a gasping chorus of cheers. "But what of Black Thrumbo? Why does he go free, and see him standing there with so kind and gentle a smile on his face."

"Who is Black Thrumbo?"

"There he stands, Chief Archer to Sir Hune. He favors the whip because its song is true. Ho, Black Thrumbo, I see you there! Why do you not greet me? You have been so familiar with me and my parts; now you are so distant!"

Aillas looked where Nols pointed. "Which is Thrumbo?"

"In the leather helmet, with a face like the moon. He is chief among the torturers."

Aillas called out: "Thrumbo, you may step over to the gibbet, if you will. I have no need for torturers in my army."

Thrumbo turned and made a desperate dash for the hillside, hoping to scramble to freedom, but, as he was somewhat corpulent and short of breath, he was quickly captured and dragged sobbing and cursing to the gibbet. An hour later Aillas returned with his troops to Doun Darric.

III

THE BARONS OF SOUTH ULFLAND were convened in a second conclave at Doun Darric. On this occasion beef turned on the spit and a tun of good wine stood ready for the broaching.

Today there were no truants; all the barons of South Ulfland were on hand. Their mood, as they conferred privately and sat at the table, was somewhat different than on the previous occasion. They seemed glum and thoughtful, troubled rather than truculent.

Before too much wine was consumed, Aillas delivered his message. Today he sat quiet while a fanfare from a pair of clarions commanded silence. Then a herald, climbing onto a bench, read from a scroll:

"All hear these words, which are those of King Aillas! I speak in his voice! 'Recently Sir Hune of Three Pines House disobeyed my explicit orders, and all present know how went the aftermath. In his dungeons he kept prisoners, contrary to the spirit if not the letter of my law.

"'I will shortly issue a code of justice, uniform with that of Troicinet and Dascinet. In each county of the land, sheriffs and magistrates will be designated. They will administer all justice: high, middle and low. The persons here today will be relieved of what can only be an onerous responsibility.

"'That responsibility is terminated. All prisoners held in durance by persons now present must be released into the custody of my representatives, who will return with each of you to your home-places. Hereafter you may no longer immure, incarcerate nor confine any of my subjects, at the risk of royal displeasure, which Sir Hune discovered to be swift and definite.

"'I further discovered that Sir Hune indulged himself in the torture of his enemies. This is vile and ignoble, no matter what the justification. I hereby declare torture, in all its categories, to be a capital offense, punishable by death and confiscation of property.

"'In all fairness I cannot punish crimes committed before my proscription, despite my inclination. You need fear no such reprisal. At this time either Sir Pirmence, Sir Maloof or Sir Tristano will interview each of you in turn. You must give information regarding prisoners in your custody, with their names and condition, and also the names of torturers in your employ. Then you will immediately depart for home, and the listed prisoners will be delivered to my representatives, who will also take your torturers into custody. Since I do not want these persons loosed into the general population, they will be brought here to Doun Darric and probably enlisted into a special corps of my army. Those among you who employed the torturers are no less culpable than they, but, as previously stated, I cannot punish you for crimes committed before my proscription.

"'Sir Pirmence, Sir Maloof and Sir Tristano are now at work among you. I urge that you cooperate and impart exact information, as these declarations will be verified.'

"Such, my lords, are the words of his Majesty, King Aillas."

IV

THE BARONS HAD DEPARTED, most to take lodging for the night with friends or kin along the way to their homes. Each had gone in company with a Troice knight and six soldiers, to ensure the exact fulfillment of King Aillas' law, which in many cases consisted of a prisoner exchange between hostile castles.

Aillas and Tristano sat long into the evening discussing the events of the day. Sir Tristano, in his conversations, had discovered no further news of Sir Shalles. He had last been seen at the remote castle of Sir Mulsant, one of the barons most intransigent of all.

"Mulsant's point of view is not without logic," said Tristano. "He lives under the Cloud-cutters, where outlaws are rife; if he disbanded his garrison, he declares that he would not survive a week, and I tend to believe him. And now Torqual has intruded on the scene. Until we can hold him in check, we cannot fairly insist that folk of the region both go defenseless and endorse our cause."

Aillas gloomily considered the statement. "Truly, our recourses are distasteful. If we strike at Torqual in North Ulfland, our chance of success is negligible and we challenge the Ska. Now, of all times, we want to let sleeping dogs lie."

"No one will argue with this point of view."

Aillas heaved a deep sigh and slumped back in his chair. "Once again dreamful hopes founder on the rocks of reality. I must adapt to the harsh facts. So long as Sir Mulsant and others like him cause us no embarrassment, I appoint them 'Wardens of the March.'"

"All this is called 'the art of practical kingship,'" said Tristano; then he and Aillas spoke of different subjects.

Chapter 8

I

SHALLES, ARRIVING IN LYONESSE TOWN, went directly to Haidion and in due course was taken to a small sitting room in the Tower of Owls where King Casmir sat studying charts and maps. Shalles performed a suitable bow and waited while King Casmir closed his portfolio, using a ponderous deliberation, which anyone with a guilty conscience could only find ominous.

At last King Casmir swung about and looked Shalles over from head to toe, as if he had never seen him before. He gestured to a chair; when Shalles had seated himself, Casmir said, "Sir Shalles, I see that you have been traveling hard; what have you to tell me?"

Encouraged by Casmir's use of the honorific, Shalles, who had been sitting on the edge of his chair, relaxed a trifle back into the seat. He considered his words carefully, since they might well make his fortune, or yield him nothing, if he failed to gain King Casmir's approval. "In general, sir, I cannot fairly give you an amplitude of good news. King Aillas has acted with decision and to good effect. He has kept his opponents off-balance and denied them a basis for insubordination. He is popular with the common folk, and also the aristocracy of the lower fells and the shore, who value order and prosperity more than an unqualified franchise, which they never had, in any case."

"Has there been measurable resistance to an alien king?"

"The most noteworthy example is that of Sir Hune of Three Pines House. He openly violated the new laws; almost before he did the deed his castle was in ruins and he swung high on a gibbet. This is language which the Ulfs understand."

Casmir gave a sour grunt. Shalles continued. "Aillas discovered full dungeons at Three Pines House. He called a conclave, where he banned private justice, and emptied every dungeon in the land. By and large, the edict won him approval, since the barons fear nothing more than their enemies' dungeons, where, if captured, they are punished for the sins of their grandfathers.

"In clearing the dungeons, Aillas confiscated all their gear. I am told that he took forty racks, seven tons of tools, and one hundred torturers. These are now a special corps in the royal army. Their cheeks are tattooed black; their uniforms are black and yellow and they wear 'maddog' helmets. They are considered pariahs and live apart from the other troops."

"Bah!" muttered Casmir. "There is a reek of over-niceness to this milk-sop king. What else?"

"I will now render an account of my own activities. They have been diligent, dangerous and miserably uncomfortable." With a somewhat forced enthusiasm in the face of King Casmir's unresponsive stare, Shalles described the range of his activities, and did not fail to mention the perils he encountered almost daily. "With a price on my head, I finally decided that I could do no more. My slanders, while always popular, were never corroborated and exerted no lasting influence. During the course of my work I discovered a strange fact, to this effect: the staid stark stupid truth carries more conviction than the most entrancing falsehoods, even though the latter sometimes receive more currency. Still, I was sufficiently irksome that Aillas tried with might and main to capture me, and I was constantly skipping away just barely clear of apprehension."

With hooded eyes and in the mildest of voices King Casmir asked: "And what do you suppose might have been your fate had you been captured?"

Shalles's sensitivities were keen. After only the most imperceptible of hesitations, he said: "That is hard to say. Aillas bruited about an offer to pay me twice your own stipend, if I became a turncoat. He intended, so I suspect, only a disparagement of my reputation, and in fact the ploy reduced my credibility to nothing."

King Casmir gave a thoughtful nod. "A rumor of this offer reached me through other sources. What of Torqual?"

Shalles paused to gather his thoughts. "I have seen Torqual at various times, though not as often as I wished. He goes his way without reference to my advice, but he seems to be serving your good interests. He is insatiable in his demands for gold, that he may the better augment his power. We were together at the reduction of Three Pines House; we stood with peasants across the meadow. Torqual tells me that, first, he has been learning the terrain, and, second, that he has recruited the nucleus of a following. He has found a bolt-hole in North Ulfland from which he can penetrate South Ulfland on raids. He has let it be known that his favored victims will be those who obey the king's command—a tactic which persuades the Ska to ignore him. Gradually he thinks to extend his power over all the high moors." Here Shalles gave a shrug.

King Casmir asked: "You would seem to doubt his success?"

"In the long run, yes. He thinks only of destruction, which is not a sound basis for a stable rule. Still, I cannot read the future. In the Ulflands anything can happen."

"So it seems," mused King Casmir. "So it seems."

Shalles said somberly: "I wish I could bring you news kinder to your ears, since my fortune depends upon pleasing you."

King Casmir rose to his feet and went to look down into the fire. At length he said: "You may go. In the morning we will talk further."

Shalles bowed and departed in a cheerless mood. Lacking compliments from King Casmir, he had not dared bring up the subject of reward.

In the morning King Casmir again conferred with Shalles, and attempted to glean more information about Torqual, but Shalles could only reiterate his statements of the day before. Finally King Casmir tendered him a sealed packet. "At the stable a good horse awaits. I have another small mission for you. Ride north into Pomperol by Icnield Way. At the village Honriot turn left and ride through Dahaut into Forest Tantrevalles. Go to Faroli and give this message into the hand of the wizard Tamurello. I expect that he will have a response for you."

II

IN DUE COURSE SHALLES RETURNED TO HAIDION. He was at once admitted into the presence of King Casmir, to whom he delivered a parcel.

King Casmir appeared in no haste to learn the contents of the parcel. He laid it on the table and, turning to Shalles, in an almost gracious manner asked: "How went the journey?"

"The journey went well, sir. I rode at speed to Faroli, which I found without undue difficulty."

"And what do you make of Faroli?"

"It is a splendid manse of silver and glass and precious black wood. Silver poles support the roof, which is like the roof of an enormous many-sided tent, but for its sheathing of green silver tiles. The gate was guarded by a pair of gray lions, double the size of the ordinary beast, with fur as glossy as fine silk. They rose up on their hind legs and called out: 'Halt, as you value your life!' I named myself the emissary of King Casmir, and they let me pass without emotion."

"And Tamurello himself? I am told that he never seems the same man twice."

"As to that, sir, I cannot say. He appeared to be tall, very thin and very pale, with black hair in a tall crest over his scalp. His eyes glowed like carbuncles and his robe was embroidered in silver signs. I gave him your message, which he read at once. Then he said: 'Await me here. Do not move by so much as a pace or the lions will tear you to bits.'

"I waited, as still as stone, while the lions sat watching. Presently Tamurello returned. He gave me that packet which I have just presented to your Majesty, and quelled his lions so that I could take my departure. I returned to Haidion at best speed, and there is no more to be told."

"Well done, Shalles." King Casmir looked toward the parcel as if he might now open it, but once again turned back to Shalles.

"And now you will wish to be rewarded for your services."

Shalles bowed. "As your Majesty so pleases."

"And what might be your desires?"

"Most of all, sir, I wish a small estate near the town Poinxter in Graywold County, where my family resides and where I was born."

King Casmir compressed his lips. "A bucolic life makes one sluggish and reluctant of foot when he goes out on the king's service. He thinks more of his hives and his calving and the set of his grapes than of the royal necessities."

"In truth, your Majesty, I have reached that time in life when I am no longer apt for midnight skulking and sinister plots. My brain has grown heavy along with my belly; it is time that I settled to a life where my great adventure of the day is a fox in the chicken-run. In short, your Majesty, pray excuse me from further service. These last months have brought me dreads in the dark and nimble escapes enough for a lifetime."

"Do you have an estate in mind?"

"I have not taken time to search the area, sir."

"And what quality estate do you consider your effort of this short period has earned?"

"If I were paid for time alone, three gold crowns would suffice. If you ask the value I put on my life, I would not sell for ten caravans laden with emeralds, not even if six shiploads of gold were added for an inducement. So I would wish to be paid with some regard for the risks I took with my costly life, for priceless plots and inspired slander, for windy nights on the moors while honest men slept snug in their beds. Your Majesty, I submit without question to your generosity. I may say that I would rejoice at a gentleman's house beside a good stream, with ten acres of woodland and three or four farms out at leasehold."

King Casmir smiled. "Shalles, if you have used as much fluency in my service as you have in your own, your requests are mild and fair, and so I must judge them." He wrote upon a parchment, performed a flourishing signature and handed the document to Shalles. "Here is the royal patent upon an unnamed property. Go to Poinxter, discover a suitable premise of the style you stipulate, and present this patent to the county reeve. Do not thank me. You may go."

Shalles bowed low and departed.

King Casmir stood brooding into the fire. The parcel from Tamurello rested on the table. King Casmir summoned his aide of all purposes Oldebor.

"Sir, your wishes?"

"You will recall Shalles."

"Distinctly, sir."

"He has returned from a brief stint in South Ulfland with exaggerated expectations and perhaps a too intimate knowledge of my affairs. Does your experience suggest a manner of dealing with Shalles?"

"Yes, sir."

"See to it. He is on his way to Poinxter in County Graywold. He carries a document signed by me which I would wish returned." King Casmir turned back to the fire and Oldebor departed the sitting room.

King Casmir at last opened the parcel to discover a stuffed blackbird mounted on a stand. A sheet of parchment, folded and tucked between the bird's legs, read:

> *To hold converse with Tamurello, pluck a feather from the belly of the bird and burn in the flame of a candle.*

Casmir examined the stuffed bird, taking critical note of drooping wings, molting feathers and a half-open beak.

The look of the bird might or might not convey an overtone of sardonic meaning. Dignity, however, prompted Casmir to ignore all but the explicit purport of bird and message. He departed the chamber, descended curving stone steps, passed through an arched portal into the Long Gallery. He walked with a ponderous tread, looking neither right nor left, and footmen at their posts along the gallery jerked quickly erect, aware that the apparently abstracted gaze of the round blue eyes in fact apprehended every detail.

King Casmir entered the Hall of Honours, a vast high-ceilinged chamber reserved for the most solemn of state occasions, to which King Casmir had vowed to restore the throne Evandig and the table Cairbra an Meadhan. The Hall of Honours was now furnished with his own ceremonial throne, a long central table and, around the walls, fifty-four massive chairs, representing the fifty-four noble houses of Lyonesse.

To Casmir's annoyance, he discovered the princess Madouc playing alone among the chairs, jumping from seat to seat, balancing on the arms, squirming through the underbraces.

For a moment Casmir stood watching. A curious child, he thought, self-willed to the point of intractability. She never cried, except sometimes in small furious gasps of vexation when someone dared to thwart her. How different yet how alike were Madouc and her mother Suldrun (such was Casmir's understanding of the case), whose dreamy docility had masked an obduracy as hard as his own.

Madouc, at last aware of Casmir's cold stare, paused in her antics. She turned to watch Casmir with a gaze of mild curiosity mingled with displeasure at this unsuitable and blundering invasion of her privacy. Like Princess Suldrun before, Madouc regarded this chamber as her personal domain.

Casmir came slowly into the room, never relaxing his cold blue stare, in order that the saucy little minx might be over-awed. Madouc's gaze dropped to the stuffed bird which Casmir was carrying. While she neither giggled nor even smiled, Casmir knew that she was amused at the picture he made.

Madouc, becoming bored with both bird and Casmir, resumed her play. She jumped from the arm of one chair to the arm of the next, then glanced around to see if Casmir were still in the room.

Casmir halted by the table. He spoke in an even voice, which, echoing against the stone walls, seemed to become grating and harsh. "Princess, what do you do here?"

Madouc supplied Casmir with the information he seemed to require. "I am playing on the chairs."

"This is not the place for your game. Go and play somewhere else."

Madouc jumped down from the chair and ran hopping and skipping from the room. Without a backward glance she was gone.

Casmir took the bird around the Great Throne of Haidion to the back wall and through the hangings into a store-room. Here he manipulated the lock of a secret door. It swung wide and Casmir was allowed access into that chamber where he kept his magical trinkets and artifacts. The most valuable of his belongings, Persilian the Magic Mirror, had been lost some five years before, and to this day Casmir was uncertain as to how the mirror had been sequestered and who was responsible. To his knowledge, no one knew of the secret chamber save himself. He would have been dumbfounded to learn the truth: that the culprits were Princess Suldrun and her lover Aillas, then Prince of Troicinet, who had taken Persilian at the behest of Persilian himself.

Casmir glanced suspiciously around the room, to assure himself that none of his other properties had disappeared. All seemed in order. A globe of swirling green and purple flame illuminated the chamber. An imp in a bottle glowered at him and tapped fingernails against the glass, hoping to engage his attention. On a table rested an object of astronomical significance, presented to one of Casmir's ancestors by Queen Dido of Carthage; and as always Casmir bent to examine the instrument, which exhibited an amazing complexity. The base was a circular ebony platter, marked around the rim with signs of the zodiac. The golden ball at the center, so Casmir had been told, represented the sun. Nine silver balls of various size rolled in circular troughs around the center, but for what purpose was a secret known only to the ancients. The third ball from the center was accompanied by a smaller ball and made its circuit in exactly one year, which only perplexed Casmir the more: if the object were a chronometer designed to measure yearly intervals, then why the other balls, some of which moved almost imperceptibly? Casmir no longer speculated in regard to the object and now gave it only a cursory survey. He placed the stuffed bird on a shelf and considered it a moment. At last he turned away. Before initiating a conversation with Tamurello, he must decide carefully what he wished to discuss.

Departing the secret chamber, Casmir passed through the Hall of Honours and stepped out into the gallery. Here, as luck would have it, he encountered Queen Sollace and Father Umphred. They had been out together in the royal carriage, inspecting sites for a cathedral.

Queen Sollace told Casmir: "The optimum site is clear; we have seen it and measured it: that area just to the north of the harbour entrance!"

Father Umphred spoke in enthusiasm: "Already a sweet sanctity surrounds your remarkable spouse! I would like to see, flanking the grand front entrance, two statues worked in imperishable bronze: on one hand the noble King Casmir and on the other the saintly Queen Sollace!"

"Have I not declared the project impractical?" demanded King Casmir. "Who will pay for such nonsense?"

Father Umphred sighed and raised his gaze to the ceiling. "The Lord will provide."

"Indeed?" asked King Casmir. "How, and in what style?"

" 'Take no other gods before me!' So spoke the Lord on Mount Sinai! Each new Christian may properly atone for his years of sin by dedicating his wealth and his labor to the construction of a great temple; thus will be eased his way into Paradise."

Casmir shrugged. "If fools so want to spend their money, why should I complain?"

Queen Sollace gave a glad cry. "Then we have your permission to proceed?"

"So long as you faithfully adhere to each and every provision of royal law."

"Ah, your Majesty, that is glorious news!" cried Father Umphred. "Still, to which provisions of the law are we susceptible? I assume that ordinary custom will here prevail?"

"I am unacquainted with these 'ordinary customs'," said King Casmir. "The laws are simple enough. First, under no circumstances, may moneys or other articles of value, be exported from Lyonesse to Rome."

Father Umphred winced and blinked. "From time to time—"

King Casmir spoke on. "All moneys collected must be declared to the Chancellor of the Royal Exchequer, who will levy the appropriate tax, which will be deducted in advance of all else. He will also fix the annual rent upon the land."

"Ah!" groaned Father Umphred. "That is a discouraging prospect! It cannot be! No secular power may levy tax upon property of the church!"

"In that case, I retract and renounce my permission! Let no cathedral be built at Lyonesse Town, now or ever!"

King Casmir went his way, with Queen Sollace and Father Umphred looking disconsolately after him.

"He is a most obstinate man!" said Queen Sollace. "I have prayed that the Lord bring the balm of religion into his heart, and today I felt that my prayers had been answered. But now he is settled; barring some miracle, he will never change."

Father Umphred said thoughtfully: "I can supply no miracles, but I know certain facts which Casmir would go to great lengths to learn."

Queen Sollace gave him a questioning look. "Which facts are these?"

"Dear Queen, I must pray for guidance! Light from above must show me the path."

Queen Sollace's face took on a petulant droop. "Tell me and allow me to advise you."

"Dear Queen, dear blessed lady! It is not so easy! I must pray."

III

TWO DAYS LATER KING CASMIR RETURNED to the secret room. He plucked a feather from the belly of the stuffed blackbird and took it away to his private parlour, at the side of his bed-room. Lighting a candle from the fire, he thrust the feather into the flame, where it burned with little puffs of acrid smoke.

King Casmir watched the wisps dissipate into the air. He called: "Tamurello? Do you hear me? It is I, Casmir of Lyonesse."

From the shadows spoke a voice: "Well then, Casmir: what now?"

"Tamurello? Is it you whom I hear?"

"What do you wish of me?"

"A sign that I truly speak with Tamurello."

"Do you remember Shalles who now lies sightless in a ditch with his throat cut?"

"I remember Shalles."

"Did he tell how he saw me?"

"Yes."

"I showed him the wizard Amach ac Eil of Caerwyddwn in the full of my black dreuhwy*."

King Casmir grunted in acquiescence. "I call your name now for a reason. My ventures stagnate. I feel frustration and anger on this account."

"Ah, Casmir, on my word you ignore such good fortune which the Cutter of Threads has allowed you! At Haidion you bask at your ease in the warmth of a dozen blazing hearths. Your table is mounded with succulence and savor! You sleep between silken sheets; your raiment is the softest cloth; gold adorns your person. There seems an adequate population of voluptuous boys; in this regard you never need fear deprivation. When someone excites your displeasure, you utter two words and he is murdered, if he is lucky. If he is unlucky, he goes to the Peinhador. All in all, I consider you a fortunate man."

Casmir ignored the gibes, which exaggerated his appetites; indeed, he was almost austere in his use of catamites. "Yes, yes; no doubt you are right. Still, these remarks fit your case as pointedly as they do my own. I suspect that you are often provoked when events fail to suit you."

From the shadows came a soft laugh. "One signal difference between the cases! You are applying to me, not I to you."

Casmir responded in even tones: "I appreciate the distinction."

"Still, you have deftly probed my sore spot. Murgen has discovered

---

*dreuhwy: from the ancient Welsh and untranslatable; approximately: a self-induced mood of morose extra-human intensity, in which any grotesque excess of conduct is possible; full identification of self with the afflatus which drives the eerie, the weird, the terrible. The adepts of the so-called 'Ninth Power' conceived of 'dreuhwy' as a condition of liberation, in which their force reached its culmination.

Tamurello mentions the idea apparently in a spirit of mockery or as an extravagant flourish in response to Casmir's rather heavy insistence upon identification.

one or two of my foibles and makes as if the world were about to end, as perhaps it will someday. Have you heard of his latest quirk?"

"No."

"A magician named Shimrod lives at Trilda, near the village Twamble."

"I am acquainted with Shimrod."

"If you can believe it, Murgen has appointed Shimrod to be my monitor and overseer, to ensure my deference to Murgen's will."

"That would seem an irksome case."

"No matter. Should Shimrod swallow himself like a revolving snake, it is all one with me. He is easily confused; I will do as I did before, and poor Shimrod will go sprawling down uncharted abysses."

King Casmir made a cautious suggestion: "Our destinies may well go hand in hand. Perhaps we can profit by an association."

Again the soft laugh from the shadows. "I can put toad-heads on your enemies! I can change the stone of their castles to suet pudding. I can enchant the surf, to bring sea-warriors with mother-of-pearl eyes charging ashore out of each breaking wave! But never may I do so! Even if, through some folly, I thought it advisable."

King Casmir said patiently: "I understand that this must be so. Still . . ."

" 'Still'?"

"Still this. Persilian the Magic Mirror once spoke out to me, though I had put no charge upon him. The utterance defies both fact and reason, and causes me a great puzzlement."

"And what was the utterance?"

"Persilian spoke like this:

> Suldrun's son shall undertake
> Before his life is gone
> To sit his right and proper place
> At Cairbra an Meadhan.
>
> If so he sits and so he thrives
> Then he shall make his own
> The Table Round, to Casmir's woe,
> And Evandig the Throne.

"So spoke Persilian, and would say no more. When Suldrun bore the girl Madouc, I went to question Persilian, but then he was gone. I have long brooded over this matter. Somewhere among those words lives wisdom, had I the wit to search it out."

After a moment the voice responded: "I care nothing for you or your prospects; and I will listen to no reproaches should your affairs go badly. Still, I am driven by my own forces in a direction which may for a time run parallel to your own. My impulse is detestation. It fixes upon Murgen, his scion Shimrod, and King Aillas of Troicinet, who at Tintzin Fyral did me savage and irreparable harm. Count me not your friend but the enemy of your enemies."

Casmir gave a grim chuckle. At Tintzin Fyral Aillas had hanged Tamurello's lover Faude Carfilhiot on a gallows grotesquely high, and gaunt as a spider's leg. "Very well; you have made yourself clear."

"Do not be too sure," said the voice, speaking sharply. "Your surmises in regard to me will surely be incorrect! At this time Murgen's calculated affronts cause me a great wrath. He uses the charlatan Shimrod as counterpoise to me, and sets him to bait me with his surveillances. Shimrod becomes self-important and pompous; he expects me to make a daily report upon my conduct. Ha! I will show him conduct to scorch his backside!"

"All very well," said Casmir. "What of Persilian's prediction? He spoke of 'son', but Suldrun bore a daughter only: is the prediction false?"

"Uncertain! These apparent contradictions often are masks for startling truth."

"If so, what might be such a 'startling truth'?"

"I suspect that she bore another child."

Casmir blinked. "That cannot be so."

"Well then: who was the father?"

"A nameless vagabond. In anger I did away with him."

"He might have had much to tell you. Who else could recite precise facts?"

"There was the serving woman, and her parents, who nurtured the baby." Casmir frowned as he thought back across the past. "The woman was a stubborn sow; she would tell me nothing."

"She might be tricked, or inveigled. The parents might also know facts not yet revealed."

Casmir grunted. "This seems to me a dry source. The parents were old; they might be dead."

"Perhaps so. Still, if you like, I can send you a man who is a ferret for smelling out secrets."

"That will suit me well."

"Let me instruct you. His name is Visbhume. He is a wizard of very limited skill and certain curious habits, owing perhaps to yellow bloom in the cracks of the brain. You must overlook his peculiarities, and give precise orders, since at times he is flighty. Visbhume lacks all qualms; if you want your grandmother strangled, Visbhume will oblige, with care and courtesy, or, if you prefer, he will strangle his own grand-mother."

Casmir gave a dubious grunt. "Can he be trusted for steadfastness?"

"Indeed! Once started he is obsessive; he never stops, as if he is pushed by an incessant rhythm inside his head. He cannot be deterred by fear, or hunger or lust; he lacks interest in ordinary sexual procedures, and I am not even curious as to his personal habits."

Casmir gave another grunt. "I care nothing for such matters, so long as he does his work."

"He is single-minded. Still, supervise him closely, as his is a strange personality."

IV

ONCE EACH WEEK KING CASMIR SAT TO DELIVER royal justice in the cold gray juridical chambers beside the old Great Hall. His chair was placed on a low dais, at the back of a massive table, with a man-at-arms, halberd at the ready, posted to either side.

At these occasions King Casmir wore always a black velvet cap encircled by a light silver crown, together with a flowing cape of black silk. This costume, so he believed, and correctly so, augmented the mood of somber and implacable justice which already hung heavy in the room.

During testimony King Casmir sat motionless, staring with cold blue eyes at the witness. He pronounced his decisions tersely, in a flat voice, without regard for rank, status or connection, and for the most part fairly, without extreme or harsh penalty, that he might enhance his reputation across the land as a wise and equable ruler.

At the end of the day's assizes, an under-chamberlain approached the table: "My lord, a certain Visbhume awaits audience; he states that he is here by your command."

"Bring him here." Casmir dismissed the court officials and ordered the guards to take up their stations outside the door.

Visbhume, entering the dour and solemn chamber, found himself alone with the king. He advanced on long bent-kneed strides, to halt close by the table, where he inspected King Casmir with placid bird-like curiosity and a total absence of awe.

King Casmir drew back from Visbhume's appraisal, which seemed over-familiar and even brash. He frowned and at once, Visbhume put on an ingratiating smile.

King Casmir pointed to a chair. "Sit." As Tamurello had indicated, Visbhume made no immediately favorable impression. He stood tall, with narrow shoulders, a gaunt chest and large hips, and hunched forward, as if in eagerness to get on with the duties at hand. His head and nose were both narrow and long; black hair seemed painted upon his scalp and made a stark contrast with his pasty skin. Arsenical shadows outlined his eyes; his mouth hung in loose-lipped folds over a sharp chin.

Visbhume seated himself. King Casmir asked: "You are Visbhume, sent here by Tamurello?"

"Sir, I am he."

King Casmir folded his hands and fixed Visbhume with his most gelid stare. "Tell me something of yourself."

"Gladly! I am a person of many talents, some unusual or even unique, though to the casual eye I seem a person of ordinary gentility. My skills transcend my appearance; I am astute and subtle; I study the arcane sciences; I have an exact memory. I am clever at dissolving mysteries."

"That is an impressive catalogue of attributes," said King Casmir. "Were you then born to nobility?"

"Sir, I have no knowledge of my birth, though certain indications lead me to suspect that I am the by-blow of a ducal amour. My earliest recollections are a farm to the far north of Dahaut, hard by the Wysrod March. As a nameless foundling I was forced into a life of stultifying toil. In due course I fled the farm and became first servant, then apprentice, to Hippolito the Magician, at Maule. I learned axioms and principles of the Grand Art; I was well on the way to great affairs!

"Alas, all things change. Ten years ago, on Glamus Eve, Hippolito flew away from Maule on a shingle and never returned. After a respectful interval I took command of the premises, and perhaps I was too bold, but that is my way; I march to music unheard by ordinary ears! Urgent trumpets, clashing—"

King Casmir made an impatient movement. "I am interested less in your inner sounds than in concrete details of your abilities."

"Very well, sir. My ambitions aroused the malice of a jealous cabal, and I was forced to flee for my life. I hitched Hippolito's iron-legged goat to a cart, and rode at a gallop away from Maule. In due course, I allied myself with Tamurello, and we have taught each other our special lores.

"At this moment I find myself at loose ends, and when Tamurello mentioned your troubles and prayed that I relieve your distress, I gave my assent. Explain, then, your difficulties, that I may subject them to my best analysis."

"The case is simple," said King Casmir. "Five years ago the then Princess Suldrun gave birth to a daughter: the present Princess Madouc. Certain circumstances in regard to the birth remain a matter for conjecture. For instance, might twins have been born? By the time these matters had come to my attention both Suldrun and the father were dead."

"And you were vouchsafed the single baby?"

"Correct. The child originally was taken by one Ehirme, a serving woman, and given into the care of her parents, from whom we recovered it. I wish to learn all the facts relevant to the case, which I neglected at the time."

"Ah hah! And quite rightly so! Who was her father?"

"This fact was never clarified. I see no other point of attack to the case than the serving woman, who at the time occupied a small farmstead south down Lirlong Way. The facts are now five years old; still their traces may persist."

"So I am confident! The full truth will surely be forthcoming."

V

VISBHUME CAME ONCE MORE TO HAIDION and there reported his findings. In his lively enthusiasm, he came forward to stand in almost intimate proximity to King Casmir, and there thrust his head forward. "Ehirme the serving woman, with her entire family, has removed to Troicinet!"

King Casmir leaned pointedly back from the waft of Visbhume's breath, and pointed to a chair. "Be seated. . . . Troicinet, you say. Where did you learn this?"

Visbhume with many a nice flourish seated himself. "I had the news from Ehirme's sister, whose spouse fishes out of Took's Hole. Further —" here Visbhume tilted his head archly sidewise " — can you guess?"

"No. Say on."

"Graithe and Wynes are the father and mother of Ehirme. They too have taken themselves part and parcel to Troicinet. The sister says that they all prosper and live as gentry, and herein I detect more than a trace of envy, which may colour the testimony."

"Indeed." Here was scope for rumination. Might King Aillas be taking an interest in his private affairs? "How long have they lived in Troicinet?"

"Several years. The woman is indefinite and I truly believe has no sense of time."

"Well, no matter. It seems that now you must cross the Lir to Troicinet."

Visbhume called out plaintively: "Ah, woe and dismay! But I will go, though I detest the uncertain motion of a boat! Nor is it easy for me to overlook the wet depths below, which were never meant for man."

"So it must be. Aillas still performs his spoliation in South Ulfland, and works opposition to my plans. Go then to Troicinet; learn the full scope of this business, since it bears upon the succession to my throne."

Visbhume leaned forward, twitching in curiosity. "How can that be? Prince Cassander is your heir!"

"Quite so," said King Casmir. "For the moment you need concern yourself only with the problems I have outlined. What are the exact details surrounding the birth of Suldun's child? Might there have been twins? If so, where is the other child? Are you clear on this?"

"Yes, of course!" Visbhume stated. "I am instantly off to Troicinet, despite my dread of every wave of the cruel black sea! Now I say, let them rear their highest! Never will they stay my passage! Casmir, I bid you farewell!"

Visbhume turned and marched on long prancing steps from the chamber. Casmir gave his head a sour shake and turned to other business.

An hour later the chamberlain announced a messenger newly arrived at Lyonesse Town. "He says he has come at haste; his message is reserved for your ears alone."

"His name?"

"He states that it would mean nothing, either to you or to me."

"Bring him here."

Into the chamber came a thin young man with a hideously scarred face. His garments were dusty and travel-worn; his station in life would not appear to be high, and he spoke with a thick peasant's accent.

"Your Majesty, I have been sent to you by Torqual, who says that you know him well."

"True. Speak on."

"He is in need of gold crowns, that he may do your bidding. He states that he sent this message by Shalles, and he would learn whether you despatched gold in the custody of Shalles, or did not do so."

King Casmir rubbed the bridge of his nose. "I gave Shalles no gold for Torqual. He asked for none. . . . Why does Torqual need gold?"

"He has not confided his business to me."

"And you are his associate?"

"I am. The new king has forbidden that men should fight, nor may they take their just revenge. But see what Sir Elphin of Floon Castle has done to me? I care nothing for Aillas and less for his law; once I do my work on Elphin of Floon, Aillas can kill me as dead as he likes."

"So what is this to Torqual?"

"We are outlaws; we roam the far fells like a wolf-pack. Recently we have found a den, where none can pursue us, and now we need gold to furnish this den and buy a store of victual, which is easier to buy than to steal."

"How much gold do you come for?"

"A hundred gold crowns."

"What? Do you plan to feed on ortolans and the honey of jasmine flowers? I will supply you forty crowns; you must eat barley porridge and drink ewe's milk."

"I can only take what you give me."

King Casmir, rising, went to the door. "Dominic!"

The man-at-arms guarding the door looked about. "Your Majesty?"

"I have a dangerous mission for a stalwart man."

"Sir, I am the man you seek."

"Prepare yourself, then; you must ride the road north with a bag of gold, and bring me news of its delivery. This gentleman, I do not know his name, will guide your way."

"It shall be done, sir."

Chapter 9

I

CASTLE CLARRIE STOOD in one of the most remote areas of South Ulfland, twenty miles from the North Ulfland border and close under the Cloud-cutters, three desolate peaks of the Teach tac Teach.

The master of Castle Clarrie and its lands was Lord Loftus, one of the barons least malleable to the rule of the new king. He based his intransigence upon the facts of recent history: namely, the raids of Ska slave-takers. These episodes had become less numerous of recent years; nevertheless parties of Ska, intent on one errand or another, still passed along the High Road, only a few miles to the east.

Further, Lord Loftus's neighbors included some, like Mott of Motterby Keep and Elphin of Floon, who were no less intractable than himself, and many were members of a hostile clan.

Castle Clarrie's traditional enemy had for centuries been the Gosse family of Fian Gosse, a castle in a glen twenty miles south of Clarrie. Unlike Lord Loftus, the young Lord Bodwy had decided to support King Aillas in all his programs, hoping to find a cessation to the bloody tangle which had killed his father, uncles and grandfather and innumerable kin long before their time.

At the Doun Darric conclave, Bodwy had approached Lord Loftus of Clarrie, and expressed the hope that trust and amity might grow between their two houses, and he pledged all his efforts to nurture a reconciliation, stating that the interests of no one were served by continued hostility.

Lord Loftus had made a rather stiff response, to the effect that he would take no new initiatives against the Gosse.

Therefore, a month later, Lord Bodwy listened with surprise to the tale of his herdsman Sturdivant: "They wore Clarrie green, with the Clarrie epaulettes; there were four, though I could recognize none by sight. Still, they were absolutely insolent and most cruel in their treatment of your good bull Black Butz, and dragged him away toward Clarrie at the run, with a chain to the ring in his nose."

Lord Bodwy at once rode to Castle Clarrie with Sturdevant, where not for a century had one of the Gosse family come in peace. Lord Loftus received him with courtesy, and Lord Bodwy looked about the great hall of Castle Clarrie with curiosity, and gave admiration to a fine hanging on the wall.

"I wish this were my only motive for coming," said Lord Bodwy. "In truth, I am anxious for my bull Black Butz. Sturdevant, tell your story."

Sturdevant said: "Sir, to make a long story short, yesterday Black Butz was taken from his pasture by four men in Clarrie green."

Lord Loftus instantly became haughty. "What? Now, in spite of all, you accuse me of stealing your cattle?"

"By no means!" declared Lord Bodwy. "I give you far more respect than that. But you must agree that the circumstances are most puzzling. Sturdevant clearly saw the Clarrie green on men he could not recognize. The tracks lead into your lands, but fail at the River Swirling."

"You are at liberty to search my premises, high and low," declared Sir Loftus in the frostiest of voices. "I will question my herdsmen at once."

"Sir Loftus, I am far less anxious to find Black Butz than to discover the motives for this peculiar act, and its perpetrators."

Despite many admirable qualities, Sir Loftus lacked easy adjustment to novel or less-than-obvious ideas. Sir Bodwy's bull had been stolen; Sir Bodwy had come at once to him. The inference was direct: Sir Bodwy thought him a cattle-thief, despite hypocritical pronouncements to the contrary.

Sir Loftus was further confounded when Black Butz was discovered in a shed at the back of his barn, slaughtered and drawn.

Transfixed with amazement, Sir Loftus at last found his tongue. He summoned his bailiff and ordered the payment of five silver florins to Sir Bodwy, though he still denied all personal responsibility for the deed.

Bodwy refused to accept the money. "You are clearly not guilty of this act; I could not bring myself to take your money. Instead I will send over a cart for the carcass and tomorrow it shall sing and sizzle on the spit." On generous impulse he added: "Perhaps you, with others of your household, might care to visit Fian Gosse and join us at the feast. This strange occurrence might thereby have an effect opposite to that which was intended."

"Sir, what do you mean by that?"

"Do you recall the self-styled Sir Shalles of Dahaut, who so clearly was an agent of Lyonesse?"

"I remember Shalles. The connection with King Casmir is not all so clear."

"It is, of course, a speculation. I also speculate that Shalles was not the only agent at work here."

Lord Loftus gave his head a shake of bafflement. "I will make a careful inquiry. Thank you for your invitation, but under the circumstances, while suspicion still hangs over my head, I fear that I must decline."

"Sir Loftus, I would wager all I own that you are absolutely free of guilt in this episode! I reiterate my invitation: let poor Black Butz, who died an ignoble death, at least perform a useful post mortem service for both our houses."

Sir Loftus' obstinacy was notable; he considered his word, once spoken, to be fixed and irrevocable, thus he might never be accused of fickleness. "Pray excuse me, Sir Bodwy, but I will be uncomfortable until this mystery is fully clarified."

Lord Bodwy returned to Fian Gosse. Five days passed; then a crofter lad rushed into the presence of Lord Bodwy with ominous news. Fourteen of Lord Loftus' finest cattle had been stolen by night, and herded south. Crofters had identified the thieves as herdsmen from Fian Gosse, on the basis of their furtive manner, and because no other folk would be prone to such a deed.

Worse news was yet to come. Slevan Wilding, Loftus' nephew, had followed the tracks into Gosse lands. At a place called Iron Tor, three men-at-arms in Fian Gosse livery loosed a flight of three arrows. Pierced three times, through heart, neck and eye, Slevan Wilding had fallen dead in his tracks. His comrades gave chase to the ambush party, but they were already fled.

Lord Loftus, learning of the ambush and examining the arrows, raised his clenched fists to the sky and sent riders over the moors and into remote glens to summon the fighting men of Clan Wilding to Castle Clarrie. King's law or none, he vowed to avenge the death of Slevan Wilding and punish those who had stolen his cattle.

Lord Bodwy instantly sent messengers riding at speed for Doun Darric, then made Fian Gosse ready to withstand both assault and siege.

The riders came into Doun Darric on dying horses, arriving at midday. By good fortune a battalion of two hundred horsemen had been ready to ride toward the North Ulfland border, on general maneuvers; Aillas ordered them instead to Fian Gosse at top speed.

All through the bright afternoon rode the troop, halting at sunset for an hour's rest, then up once more to ride by the light of the full moon: across Bruden Moor, up Werling River Road to Dead Man's Moor, and away at a slant to the northeast. At midnight, winds began gusting and clouds obscured the moon; there was danger of plunging into a bottomless bog or riding headlong into a gully, and the troop took shelter in a spinney of tamarack, to huddle over reeking fires.

At dawn the troop rode again, despite a driving wind and spatters of cold rain. With cloaks flapping, they pounded hard up Blue Murdoch Fell, and galloped under heavy gray clouds by a track across the heather. Two hours into the afternoon they arrived at Fian Gosse — only an hour after the investment of the place by Lord Loftus and his clansmen, in the number of a hundred. For the nonce they had assembled out of arrow range and were occupied at the building of ladders: particularly effective here, since the Fian Gosse walls were low and the defenders few. Lord Loftus doubted nothing but what the place must fall to the first onslaught, which he decided to conduct by the light of the moon.

The appearance of the king's troops and the king himself destroyed his plans, and instantly he knew the bitterness of total defeat. If blood flowed now, the deepest torrent would be Wilding blood. What now? he asked himself. Withdraw? Fight? Parley? He could see nothing but humiliation.

In dejection and defiance Lord Loftus stood facing the king's troops, helmet thrown back, hands resting on the pommel of his sword, point down in the turf between his feet.

A herald rode forward, dismounted with a brave flourish and faced Lord Loftus. "Sir: I speak with the voice of King Aillas. He commands you to sheath your sword, then come forward and render an explanation for your presence here. What message shall I bear to King Aillas?"

Lord Loftus made no reply. With savage force he sheathed his sword and marched across the ground. Aillas dismounted from his horse and stood waiting. All eyes, of the Wilding clansmen, of the Fian Gosse defenders, and of the royal troops, marked his every step.

At Fian Gosse the portcullis creaked up, and Lord Bodwy, with three retainers, came forth, and also approached King Aillas.

Lord Loftus came to a halt ten feet in front of Aillas. In silence, Lord Bodwy came up from the side.

Aillas spoke coldly: "Deliver your sword to Sir Glyn, who stands yonder. You are under arrest, and I charge you with conspiracy to effect an illegal assault and to commit acts of bloody violence."

Lord Loftus stonily yielded his sword.

Aillas said: "I will listen to your defense."

First Lord Loftus spoke, then Lord Bodwy, then Loftus once more, and Bodwy and finally Glannac; and now all the tale was told.

Aillas spoke in a voice more contemptuous than harsh: "Loftus, you are obstinate, over-proud and inflexible. You seem neither cruel nor vicious, merely hot-headed to a foolish degree. Can you gauge your luck that I arrived here when I did, before blood had been let? If a single life had been lost, I would have judged you guilty of murder and hanged you on the instant, and reduced your castle to broken stones."

"The blood of my nephew Slevan was shed! Who will hang for this crime?"

"Who is the murderer?"

"One of the Gosse."

"Never!" cried Bodwy. "I am not such a fool!"

"Exactly so," said Aillas. "Only someone foolishly passionate, such as yourself, would fail to perceive the pattern of this crime, which was calculated to set you at odds and to cause me grief. You have posed me a predicament and I must walk a careful path between wisdom and blind justice, nor do I want to punish foolishness for its own sake. Further, Lord Pirmence gives you a clean bill in the matter of imprisonment and torture, which weighs heavily in your favor. So then: what assurances can you give that you will never again take up arms to work your private justice, except in self-defense, or in service of the king?"

Lord Loftus blurted: "What assurance can Bodwy give that he will steal no more of my cattle?"

Bodwy gave a laugh of sheer amusement. "Did you steal my bull Black Butz?"

"No, nor would I do such a thing."

"No more would I steal from your herd."

Loftus scowled off toward the hills. "You claim that this is all a prank?"

"Worse, far worse!" declared Lord Bodwy. "Someone planned that you should invest and overrun Fian Gosse, and then suffer the consequences, to the detriment of me, you, King Aillas and all the land."

"I see the thrust of your reasoning. Only a madman could conceive a work so cunning!"

"Not a madman," said Aillas. "Unless Torqual is mad."

Lord Loftus blinked. " 'Torqual'? He is an outlaw!"

"In the service of Lyonesse. Speak now, Loftus! How will you assure me of your future faith, loyalty and obedience to the laws of the land?"

With poor grace, Lord Loftus knelt and pledged himself to the king's service, by his honour and the reputation of his house.

"That must suit the case," said Aillas. "Sir Bodwy, what do you say?"

"I have no fault to find, so long as there is an end to suspicion between Wilding and Gosse."

"Very well, so be it. Sir Glyn, return to Sir Loftus his sword."

His heart too full for words, Sir Loftus sheathed his sword.

Aillas said: "Our enemy is Torqual. He hides in North Ulfland and comes here to do dark deeds. I doubt not but what he watches at this moment from the mountain or the forest. I ask that you both learn all you can of him. At this time we cannot enter North Ulfland, lest we provoke the Ska, for which we are not yet ready. Sooner or later, however, they will take heed of us; and I doubt they will consider our convenience.

"In the meantime, instruct your herdsmen and crofters to keep a sharp watch across the moors. Man, woman or child, whoever helps to trap Torqual, his fortune is made. Make this known, if you will. Also, warn your kin and your clans-folk of Torqual and his tricks.

"Now, Lord Loftus, I cannot let you go scot-free, for the sake of my reputation. First, I place you on probation for five years. Second, I fine you twenty gold crowns, to be paid into the royal treasury. Third, you must host a festival of friendship between your clans, at which no weapons may be displayed, and only soft words spoken. Let there be music and dancing and an end to the shedding of neighborly blood."

Lord Bodwy turned to Loftus and extended his arm. "Here is my hand on it."

Lord Loftus, still somewhat stiff and utterly humiliated, felt a sudden liberation from all which had gone before. In a pulse of generosity as warm as Bodwy's own, he took the hand and clasped it. "You shall never find me lacking. I hope that we shall be good friends and neighbors."

II

No SOONER HAD AILLAS RETURNED to Doun Darric than his forebodings were realized in full degree, and his previous problems suddenly became trivial.

Aillas had long awaited a signal of Ska hostility to his rule, if only a skirmish or two, to test his mettle. Instead of a signal, the Ska dealt him a harsh and brutal blow: a challenge which allowed him only two responses. He could submit, thereby incurring ridicule and loss of face, or he could fight, which meant lunging into a conflict for which he was not yet ready.

The Ska action could not be considered a surprise. Aillas knew the Ska intimately; they considered themselves at war with the rest of the world, and took advantage of every opportunity to extend the range of their power. Since South Ulfland under King Aillas could only become stronger, his rule must be expunged promptly. As a first step, with minimum expenditure of force and Ska lives, they took the town Suarach on the south bank of the River Werling, hard by the border between the two Ulflands.

The Ska heretofore had left Suarach in peace, to serve as a neutral area where they might trade with the outer world. The town fortifications had long been broken; and Aillas, lacking both funds and troops for an adequate garrison, perforce had left Suarach undefended, hoping that the Ska would continue to regard the town as a neutral zone.

The Ska, however, moved suddenly, to make their policy in regard to South Ulfland unmistakable; they marched into Suarach with four regiments of mixed cavalry and foot soldiers, and took the town without resistance of any kind.

Immediately they impressed labor gangs from the town's population and, working with that ferocious intensity characteristic of all their conduct, they repaired the fortifications, and Suarach became a mortal insult to Aillas and the dignity of his rule, which he could not ignore without a sad diminution of prestige.

For two days Aillas kept to his Doun Darric headquarters, calculating his options. An instant counterattack to retake Suarach by frontal assault seemed the least feasible of his choices. The Ska enjoyed short lines of communication; their warriors were superior to the raw Ulfish troops in every category by which soldiery could be measured: training, discipline, leadership, weaponry, and, most telling of all, the almost religious certainty of Ska invincibility. The Troice troops, so Aillas believed, matched the Ska more evenly, but still, in sheer fighting ability, could not be held equal to the Ska*.

Aillas, sitting alone in the cottage which served as his headquarters at Doun Darric, looked out at rain sweeping down across the moor: a dreary view, but no more dismal than his present predicament. If he committed troops, ships and supplies from Troicinet, in quantity

---

*A Ska soldier feared one thing only: the disesteem of his fellows. He gained civil advancement primarily through his military exploits, and fought each battle with total ferocity, which disheartened his adversaries even before the battle was joined.

Withal, the Ska among themselves were a gentle and law-abiding people, who lived to the tenets of a unique and complicated culture, with a written history ten thousand years old, and traditions far older. Originally a small tribe which followed the retreating glaciers north, they became the true indigenes of Scandinavia, only to be at last thrust out by the Ur-Goths (later the Scandinavians and Vikings, who adopted many Ska traits and skills, including the Ska long-boat).

Ska traditions recalled battles with 'cannibal ogres' — evidently Neanderthal tribesmen — who, so they were assured, interbred with all other tribes of true men, so that only Ska were of pure human descent, and all others hybrids, soiled by the infusion of Neanderthal blood.

For further background to the fascinating Ska psychology and history, see the glossary in *LYONESSE I: Suldrun's Garden*.

sufficient to overwhelm the Ska, he not only risked disaffection at home but he also became exposed to a sudden onslaught by King Casmir of Lyonesse (who in any event would rejoice to discover Aillas trapped in a desperate war with the Ska).

At this moment, the attention of every baron, knight and lordling of South Ulfland was fixed upon him. If he failed to strike back, he lost his credibility as an effective king and became another Oriante, helpless when confronted by Ska force.

Aillas, standing by the window and looking out over the rainswept moor, finally reached a decision — which in fact was not so much a plan of action as a list of responses he must not make: no assault upon Suarach, no reinforcements from Troicinet, except for warships to harass Ska shipping, and no turning his back on the situation as if nothing had happened. So then: what remained? Only the classical weapons of the underdog: craft and cunning.

What of North Ulfland? The Ska roamed at will, using the region as a wild hinterland which eventually they would occupy. Now they exploited its resources of timber and ore, and impressed the scattered inhabitants into their labor gangs as they found convenient. Across that coastal strip known as 'The Foreshore' the Ulfs had been totally expelled. In their stead the Ska had come in numbers to build their curious many-gabled villages and to cultivate not only the fertile acreages but also those ranges which the Ulfs had relegated to grazing land. Elsewhere a few peasants clustered in squalid villages, hiding at the approach of the Ska press-gangs, even though at Xounges, King Gax still maintained his nominal rule.

Darkness settled over the sodden moor. Aillas was served a supper of bread and lentils, then sat alone by the fire for another two hours before taking to his couch, and eventually the soft sound of rain on the thatch lulled him to sleep.

In the morning by some miracle the sun shone bright from a keen blue sky, and the moors, glistening with sun-struck rain-drops, seemed not so bad a place.

Aillas took his breakfast, then despatched a message to Domreis, commanding that six warships instantly make ready and set sail for Ys, and thereafter scour the Narrow Sea for Ska shipping.

Aillas next met with his military command. He spoke for a period, defining problems and explaining how he hoped to deal with them.

The reaction of his staff surprised and gratified him; indeed, Aillas' concepts coincided generally with their own predispositions. There were even voices raised in full defiance of the Ska: "We have truckled to these black-hearted devils long enough! Now at last we will show them the stuff that Ulf warriors are made of!" "They have beat us before, true!

And why? Because they are skillfully trained, which gives each man the force of three! Now we too are trained!" "I say, march now! Full and hard into North Ulfland, then let us seek out their armies! We are not the bleating sheep they take us for!"

Aillas, half-laughing, cried out: "Ah, Sir Redyard! If only the whole army knew your determination! Our problems would be gone! But for the present we must fight with intelligence, rather than emotion. The Ska's single vulnerability is lack of numbers; they cannot afford large losses, no matter how many they take with them. But I value each of our men no less, and I do not care to trade them lives, especially our two for their one, even if it gains us victory. We must strike like bandits, take our toll, then retreat before suffering harm of our own. The war will be won gradually, but surely. On the other hand, if we attempt to battle the Ska face to face, we play their preferred game, and we shall take many losses and still not win."

"That is a tactful way of putting the facts," Sir Gahaun noted. "Also, since a good half of your soldiers began as bandits, we can take many a short-cut in their training."

"Training, always more training," grumbled Sir Redyard. "When do we fight?"

"Be patient, sir. You shall fight soon enough, I assure you."

A week later a message came to Aillas from Castle Clarrie:

> *Here is information to interest you. One of my herdsmen discovered three of my stolen cattle, high in the hills, close under Mount Noc. We rode out by stealth and managed to capture one of the thieves, by reason of an arrow in his side. Before he died he told us more of Torqual, who now commands a score of cutthroats from Ang, an ancient keep in a place called Devil-shriek Gorge, which is invulnerable to attack. He spends gold for good weapons, and for good food and drink, and it seems that this gold comes, as you averred, from King Casmir of Lyonesse, with whom Torqual maintains communication.*

III

KING CASMIR, SO IT HAPPENED, was not altogether pleased with Torqual's efforts. Once again Torqual sent a messenger demanding gold, and on this occasion King Casmir had asked for an accounting of funds already spent and results already achieved. "I am not convinced that my moneys are being spent efficiently," said King Casmir. "In sheer point of fact, my informants tell me that Torqual's style of living approaches luxury, and that he and his company of cutthroats dine on the best the land has to offer. Is my gold spent thus, on sweetmeats and raisin-cakes?"

"And why not?" demanded the messenger. "Our bolt-hole is Ang, which offers little more comfort than a pile of stones. Are we to starve while doing your work? When rain blows through the windows and the fire gutters for lack of dry fuel, Torqual can at least offer his band the solace of good food and wine!"

Casmir grudgingly paid out another twenty crowns, with instruction to Torqual that he learn to live off the country. "I suggest that he plant vacant lands to oats and barley, and that he keep cattle and sheep, and run fowl, as do the other denizens of the region, and so mitigate this remorseless erosion of my treasury."

"Sir, with the fullest respect for your wisdom, we can grow neither oats nor barley on vertical surfaces of stone, nor will cattle thrive in these areas."

While unconvinced, King Casmir said no more.

Several months went by, while events of importance occurred in the Ulflands. Secret despatches from Doun Darric and elsewhere made no mention of Torqual, and King Casmir could only speculate as to Torqual's work.

The messenger at last returned, and again required gold: on this occasion in the amount of fifty crowns.

For once King Casmir's icy composure failed him; his jaw dropped in amazement. "Have I heard you aright?"

"Sir, if you have grasped the figure 'fifty crowns', you have heard me aright. The company at Ang now numbers twenty-two strong warriors, who must be fed, clothed and armed during all seasons. Our other sources of revenue are failing us; meanwhile Torqual recuperates from a wound. He sends this message: 'If I am to maintain my force and work in your service, I must have gold!'"

King Casmir sighed and shook his head. "You shall have no more of mine — not till I see evidence that your work is worth its cost. Can you supply this information? No? . . . . Rosko! This gentleman is departing."

Toward evening of this same day Rosko, one of King Casmir's underchamberlains, using a nasal voice of deprecation, announced to King Casmir that a certain Visbhume demanded private audience.

"Bring him in," said King Casmir curtly.

Visbhume entered, thrusting past the startled Rosko and advancing with a dancing tip-toe stride of pent energy released. As before he wore a rusty black cloak and, today, a black long-billed hunter's cap, which, with his darting black eyes, long crooked nose and forward-leaning posture, gave him a look of eager curiosity. He halted close to King Casmir, doffed his hat, then, showing an arch and confidential smile, performed a bow of several flourishes.

King Casmir pointed to a seat at some distance; Visbhume's breath was far from fresh.

Visbhume seated himself with the easy attitude of a man who has done his job well. King Casmir dismissed Rosko with a wave, then asked Visbhume: "What is your news?"

"Sir, I have learned much!"

"Speak, then."

"Despite my dread of the cruel sea, I crossed the Lir in all bravery, as befits the private agent of your Majesty!"

Visbhume saw no need to mention that he had spent the better part of a month inspecting the vessels which plied the Lir, hoping to learn which offered the speediest, most secure and most comfortable passage.

Visbhume spoke on. "When service or duty is the call, then I respond with the insensate certainty of the rising sun!"

"That is good to hear," said King Casmir.

"Upon my arrival at Domreis, I took lodging at the Black Eagle Inn, which I conceived to be—"

King Casmir raised his hand. "You need not describe each incident; merely describe your findings."

"As you wish, sir. After a month or more of extremely subtle investigations, I learned the general area of Ehirme's present residence. I made my way to this locality, and there, after weeks of further inquiry, I discovered the houses of both Ehirme and her parents.

"To my surprise I found that Ehirme's sister had exaggerated not at all. These folk have been accorded the condition of gentry, and live in luxury, with servants to sweep the hearth and scour the doorstep. It is now 'Dame Ehirme' to all the world, and her spouse is 'Squire Dikken'. Her parents are 'the Right Honourable Graithe and Dame Wynes'. There is clear glass in their windows and four chimneys to their roofs, and you cannot see the ceiling to their kitchens for the sausages."

"That is an extraordinary elevation of place," said King Casmir. "Proceed, with somewhat greater compression of the weeks and months; otherwise we will be sitting here an exactly equal period of time."

"Your Majesty, I will be brief, even terse! Local inquiry yielded nothing germane to our interest, so I decided to put my questions directly to Dame Ehirme. Here I found difficulty, as she cannot speak with clarity."

"I cut her tongue in half," said King Casmir.

"Here is the explanation! Her spouse is surly, and as chary of words as a dead fish, and I took my questions to Graithe and Wynes, where I again encountered offensive taciturnity. But now I was prepared and in the guise of a wine merchant I poured them a libation which made them docile, and they babbled all they knew." Visbhume jerked his head and grinned widely at the recollection.

King Casmir waited, making no comment, until, at last, Visbhume gave over his pleasant memories.

"Ah, what a triumph!" Visbhume declared. "And now hear this news! The child originally brought out to Graithe and Wynes was a boy! When they carried the basket into the woods one day, the fairies of Thripsey Shee took the boy and left a girl. The changeling is the Princess Madouc!"

King Casmir closed his eyes and held them shut for ten seconds, but otherwise evinced no emotion, and when he spoke his voice was even as ever. "And the boy?"

"They never saw him after, near or far."

King Casmir spoke softly, as if only for the hearing of his own ears: "Persilian revealed truth, more than I could guess!"

Visbhume assumed an air of judicious wisdom, as might befit the king's trusted adviser. King Casmir appraised him for a long moment, then said in the mildest of voices: "You have spoken of this matter to whom? Tamurello?"

"To no person whatever, save yourself! That is the way of discretion!"

"You have done well."

Visbhume jumped to his feet. "Thank you, your Majesty! What is to be my reward? I hope for a pleasant estate."

"In due course. First we must pursue this matter to its ultimate."

Visbhume spoke hollowly: "You refer to the boy?"

"Of course. He would now be five years old; perhaps he still abides with the fairies."

Visbhume screwed up his face. "Not likely. They are prone to fads and foibles. Their enthusiasms never persist. The boy long since has been thrust out into the forest, and most likely devoured by wild animals."

"This I doubt. The boy must be found, identified, and brought here to Haidion. This is of paramount urgency. Do you know the location of Thripsey Shee?"

"Sir, I do not."

King Casmir smiled a grim smile. "Clearly, it is close by the old residence of Graithe and Wynes—which is to say, beyond the village Glymwode, at the edge of the forest. Find the shee and put your questions to the fairies. Subdue them with a libation of docility, if necessary."

Visbhume uttered a high-pitched sound of dismay. "Your Majesty, a word!"

King Casmir, slowly turning his head, fixed Visbhume with a stare cold and blue as a glacial lake. "You have further information to impart?"

"No, your Majesty. I must think long and well on how best to fulfill your goals."

"Waste no time. This matter is of great importance. . . . Why do you wait?"

"Your Majesty, I have needs."

"In what regard?"

"Certainly I will require a steed suitable to my condition, as well as a sum of money, for needful expenses."

"Make your application to Rosko; he will deal with your requests."

IV

THE SFER ARCT, ENTERING LYONESSE TOWN from the north, skirted the most ancient wing of Haidion, then continued across town to the Chale, the esplanade fronting the harbour. At this intersection stood the Four Mallows Inn, where Visbhume took lodging, in apparent disregard of King Casmir's order to make haste.

Visbhume dined upon a fine fresh lobster, seethed in a sauce of wine, butter and garlic, and consumed a bottle of the best wine the inn could offer. Despite the succulence of his meal, he ate without gusto, in a mood of dour foreboding. If he were to approach the fairies and annoy them with his questions, they would surely play him a round of vicious pranks—especially since they delighted in tormenting folk in whom they detected fear and loathing: both of which Visbhume felt in abundance.

After finishing his supper, Visbhume went to sit on a bench at the side of the square and while dusk fell upon the town he brooded further upon his mission. If only he had worked to better effect during his apprenticeship to Hippolito! But he had attempted only easy techniques and had never encompassed the hard disciplines required for full command of the Grand Art. When fleeing Maule in the goat-cart, he had sequestered certain of Hippolito's properties: apparatus, books, curios, and his great prize, Twitten's Almanac. He had taken these goods to a secret place in Dahaut where now they were of no use to him, and he knew none of the sleights of quick self-transfer.

Visbhume scratched his long nose. Fast travel was a lore which he must inveigle from Tamurello, when circumstances were favorable. To date, Tamurello had revealed nothing whatever; indeed his attitude was often ambiguous, and his tart comments had hurt Visbhume deeply, so that now Visbhume felt reluctant to seek help from Tamurello for fear of another hurtful rebuff.

Yet, where else could he turn? The fairies were the most capricious of creatures; to win their favor, or to gain their knowledge, one must entertain them, or delight their senses, or arouse their avarice, or perhaps only their curiosity. Or their fear.

Visbhume reflected at length, to no effect, and presently went to his couch.

In the morning, he attacked his quandary again. "I am Visbhume!" he told himself. "I am the clever, the clear-eyed, the bold! I am Visbhume the magician who pipes up the dawn and marches through life with his forehead wreathed in rainbows, riding the surge of a glorious music!"

But then, using another voice, he told himself: "Quite so and all very well, but in the present case, exactly how shall I exercise my power?"

No response vouchsafed itself, from either of the voices.

Halfway through the morning, as he sat on the bench, he was approached by a burly black-bearded Moor garbed in turban and djellaba. The Moor stood looking down at him with quizzical amusement and presently said: "So then, Visbhume! How goes it?"

Visbhume looked up sharply, then said: "Sir, you have the advantage of me. Are we truly acquainted?"

The Moor chuckled. "Ask yourself, Visbhume, who knows of your presence in Lyonesse Town?"

"They are three: King Casmir, his servant Rosko, and a certain other person whose name need not be mentioned, by reason of discretion."

"Might 'Tamurello' be the name which, in your wise restraint, you do not choose to mention?"

"Precisely so." Visbhume studied the black-bearded face. "This is an unfamiliar semblance."

Tamurello nodded. "As a matter of fact, it is close to my natural likeness, and therefore comfortable. You seem to be at loggerheads. What is your difficulty?"

Visbhume explained his problem in all frankness. "King Casmir commands that I draw information from the fairies, and I sit here among a dozen procedures, none of which serve the purpose. If truth be known, I fear fairy-tricks. They will transform me into a heron, or pull my nose out a clothyard's length, or send me riding across the sky in a whirlwind."

"The dangers are real," said Tamurello. "To avoid them you must use the skill of a lover with his coy mistress, or else seduce them with marvels."

"All very well," bleated Vishbume, "but how?"

Tamurello looked off across the harbour. After a moment he said: "Go to the market, and buy eight skeins of red yarn and eight skeins of blue yarn, and bring them here; then we shall see."

Visbhume marched swiftly away to do Tamurello's bidding. He returned to find Tamurello sitting at his ease on the bench. Visbhume started to sit also, but Tamurello made a signal. "There is room only for one. You may sit presently. Show me the yarn. . . . Aha, that will do splendidly. You must wind the red yarn into a ball, and the blue yarn into another ball. I have here a bobbin apparently carved from a maple burl; observe it, if you will." Tamurello exhibited an object about two inches in diameter. "You will notice that it is perforated by a hole, and indeed is not truly made of wood."

"What then might it be?"

"A clever little creature which has received my instructions. Now listen with all attention! Do exactly as I say; otherwise you must come to grief, and fly Madling Meadow as a heron or, more likely, a crow; the fairies at times are over-mordant in their humour."

"You need never worry; when I listen I hear and what I hear I retain forever, since my memory is like a record carved into stone!"

"A useful trait. Go to Madling Meadow, and show yourself about two hours after sunrise. At the center of the meadow you will notice a hummock. From its side grows a crooked old oak tree. This is Thripsey Shee.

"Go out on the meadow, heeding neither sounds, nor yet blows, tweaks, nor pinches: they are meaningless. The fairies idly amuse themselves, and will not truly harm you, unless you give them reason, by kicking or cursing or simply glaring about. Go with pleasant dignity, and in their curiosity they will not think even to harass you.

"When you arrive at the crooked oak tree, tie one end of the red yarn to a branch, then come back toward a pair of birch saplings, trailing the red yarn along the meadow behind you.

"Arriving at the birch saplings, toss the ball of red yarn between the trunks. Do not walk through yourself. Then thread the end of the blue yarn through the hole in the bobbin and knot it, so that it will not pull through. Toss the blue yarn after the red then utter the words which I will now teach you." Tamurello spoke aside to the bobbin: "Do not heed me now; I speak in rehearsal only. Visbhume, attention! At the proper time, utter this charge: 'Bobbin, be at your business!' Then stand back. Do not watch the bobbin; do not look between the trees. Is so much clear?"

"Absolutely, and in every respect. What then?"

"I cannot predict. If the fairies ask questions you must say: 'Who talks? Show yourself; no wise man reveals his wisdom to the air!' Then, after they show themselves you must deny knowledge of the shee, so that they may not accuse you of special purpose. When they ask what you have wrought, you must say: 'This is a nexus into Hai-Hao, but nothing can pass without my permission.'"

"Is this truly so?" asked Visbhume, charmed by the wonderful concept.

"What matters is, will the fairies believe you? The question is nuncupatory."

"Suppose in all innocence I should swindle them, and they remember and send out owls to haunt me, as they did poor Tootleman of Hoar Hill?"

"The point is well taken! However, the nexus is real but perdurable only so long as the wind allows."

Visbhume asked further questions, exploring contingencies until at last Tamurello grew restive, and rose to depart.

"One last matter!" cried Visbhume. "If they will respond to my questions, perhaps they will grant me other favors, such as a Hat of Wisdom, or Fast Shoes, or a Purse of Plenty to supply my needs."

"Ask as you like," said Tamurello, smiling in a manner which Visbhume felt might be somewhat contemptuous. "A word of caution, however: the fairies are notably unsympathetic in regard to greed." With this, Tamurello rose from the bench and strolled away, across the square and up the Sfer Arct.

Visbhume looked darkly after him. Tamurello's manner was not always gracious and kindly, as befitted a true comrade. . . . Ah well, when all was said and done, Tamurello was no doubt a worthy fellow. One must be prepared for quirks and crotchets; that was indeed the essence of friendship.

The day being still young, Visbhume also set off up the Sfer Arct. At Haidion he sought out Rosko the under-chamberlain. "I am the gentleman Visbhume. His Majesty has granted me a purse of gold and silver coins, a horse of fine quality, with proper furniture, and all else needful. By the king's command, you are instructed to fulfill these requirements."

"Wait here," said Rosko. "I must verify every detail of this request."

"That is insulting!" stormed Visbhume. "I shall report you to King Casmir!"

"Report away!" said Rosko and went off to instruct the groom.

An hour later Visbhume rode north from Lyonesse Town astride a stately white mare with a wide rump and a hanging head. In a strident and reedy voice of outrage, Visbhume had demanded of the groom a mount of braver mettle: "Must I fare forth on the king's business like some lumpkin out to deliver a sack of turnips? Is there no pride in the stables of Haidion, that they furnish sway-backed nags to gentlemen?"

The groom tapped his ears, to indicate what Visbhume half-suspected to be feigned deafness; in any event, Visbhume was forced to accept the proffered mount, nor did his purse reveal the warm shine of gold.

Coming into Old Street, he turned eastward and rode until sunset, arriving at the village Pinkersley where he took lodging at the Fox and Grapes. On the following day, he came to Little Saffield, and at the crossroad turned north. He passed the night in Tawn Timble, and the next day proceeded to Glymwode. During the afternoon he reconnoitered the neighborhood, and by dint of careful questions, learned the location of Madling Meadow, a mile along a wood-cutter's track into the Forest of Tantrevalles. Visbhume returned to Glymwode and passed the night at the Yellow Man Inn.

Early in the morning Visbhume set forth riding up the wood-cutter's lane and presently came to Madling Meadow. He alighted and tied his horse to a tree, then, standing in the forest shade, surveyed the meadow. He perceived a scene of bucolic peace, with no sound but the hum of insects. Buttercups, daisies, mallows, corn-flowers and a dozen other flowers spotted the green grass with colour. In the soft blue sky floated a few puffs of white cloud. At the center of the meadow rose a hummock on which grew a gnarled old oak. No living creature could be seen.

Visbhume readied his balls of yarn, then, stepping forward from the concealment of the forest shade, walked out into the sunlight. The silence seemed even more intense than before.

Visbhume marched confidently across the meadow, looking neither right nor left. At the hummock he halted and now something tugged at his cloak. Visbhume paid no heed. He brought out the ball of red yarn and tied an end to a low branch of the old oak.

From behind the hummock came a small mewing laugh, quickly stifled. Visbhume seemed not to hear. He turned about and, paying out the red yarn, walked back toward two young birch saplings not far from the edge of the meadow. At his back came a rustling sound, and muted whispers. Visbhume seemed to hear nothing. Again something tugged at his cloak; as before Visbhume paid no heed, and continued across the meadow leaving the red strand behind him. He stopped in front of the birch saplings and sent the ball of red yarn, now somewhat depleted, rolling between. He brought out the blue yarn, and, following Tamurello's instructions, attached the bobbin to the yarn. He rolled the blue yarn after the red, tossed the bobbin into the air and cried out: "Bobbin, be at your business!"

Mindful of Tamurello's list of heeds and cautions, Visbhume danced on nimble long legs off to the side and away from the birches. With eyes half-closed and mouth pursed in a beatific smile, Visbhume gazed benignly across the meadow, while from somewhere beyond the scope of his vision came a shrill keening sound, as of an awl drawn smartly along a taut wire.

Visbhume's narrow shoulder-blades twitched and crawled for curiosity, but even more intense was the emotion of fear; he hunched down his neck as a dog might draw its tail between its legs. "A sorry fool I would be to ignore the admonitions!" So Visbhume told himself. "And, more than all else, I am not a fool!"

Something kicked at his lean shank. Visbhume paid no heed. A pair of fingers tweaked his buttocks, provoking from Visbhume both a startled squeak and a reflexive jerk, which evoked a sputter of quiet titters.

Indignant words rose to Visbhume's lips; the fairies were taking overly broad liberties with his person. . . . Visbhume stalked ten paces to the side. Half-turning, he glanced across Madling Meadow and, marvel of marvels! Through bright mist swirling around the hummock he glimpsed a wonderful structure of jet and milk-glass. Slender columns supported domes and tall arcades and higher domes, and still more, ranked one above the other, along with a hundred terraces and balconies and, higher yet, a cluster of towers flying pennons and banderoles. In the shadowed halls hung chandeliers encrusted with diamonds and moonstones, which gave off glints of red, blue, green and purple light. . . . So much Visbhume thought to see, but as soon as he tried to trace out a form in all clarity, it swam away into the mist.

Other shapes blurred in and out of focus. The strand of red yarn which Visbhume had laid across the meadow he now apprehended as a fairy avenue of polished red porphyry, between a pair of splendid balustrades. Along this avenue fairies ran back and forth, testing the footing, pointing first to the bobbin's pattern, then to the shee. Others ran and hopped and performed foolish antics on the top of the balustrades, and all seemed to approve this marvellous novelty. At closer hand, arranged in solemn contemplation of the bobbin's work, sat clusters of fairies, quarreling, nudging and teasing, or simply frolicking among the grasses, but, most of all, they pondered the pattern created by the bobbin, which held a whole throng caught up in wonder. From the corner of his eye and almost beyond his volition, Visbhume sensed a most peculiar configuration, which even at a fleeting glimpse fascinated his mind.

A voice spoke, thin and clear: "Low human fellow, mortal fellow, intrusive fellow: why do you do what you have done?"

Visbhume looked here and there, feigning bewilderment. He spoke as if apostrophizing the sky: "How oddly the winds rustle the leaves! Almost I thought to hear a voice! Ah, voice of the wind, speak and tell me of your wild roaming! Speak, wind!"

"Fool! The wind speaks no words!"

"I heard a voice! Voice, did you speak? If so, be brave! Show yourself, as I cannot compromise myself at random."

"Look then, mortal, and see what you see."

The mists swirled away from the hummock, revealing the full splendour of the fairy castle. A host of fairies surrounded Visbhume, some sitting, others hiding in the grass. At a distance of twenty feet stood King Throbius and Queen Bossum, in full regalia. Throbius wore a crown worked from sceleone, that fragile metal forged from water-reflected gleams of moonlight. Slender cusps surrounding the crown terminated in pale blue sapphires. The robes of Throbius were blue velvet woven from the bloom of willow catkins; they trailed ten feet behind him and were carried by six round-faced skew-eyed implings, smirking sidelong with noses wrinkled. Some lagged, others tugged at the robe to bring up the laggards; sometimes they played a sly game of tug-of-war with the train, always with one eye on Throbius, the better to avoid his chastisement should their game be detected.

Queen Bossum's robes were a saffron yellow, rich as new butter, and her crown was set with topaz prisms. Her train was carried by girl-imps, whose conduct was primly correct, while they watched the antics of Throbius' implings sidelong with haughty disapproval.

Directly in front of King Throbius and Queen Bossum stood Brean the Royal Herald, who spoke again, in a voice now shrill and clear. "Mortal fellow, do you know that you trespass upon Madling Meadow? Behold their Majesties King Throbius and Queen Bossum! Explain to the royal ears and to those of the assembled notables the purpose of your investiture here on this meadow, which we include in our domain!"

Visbhume performed a bow of six flourishes. "Inform their Majesties of my pride and delight that they have deigned to notice my little concatenation, which in fact is a nexus unto Hai-Hao."

The herald spoke the message; King Throbius responded and the herald turned back to Visbhume. "The Magnificences wish to learn your name and your worldly status, that they may justly assess your conduct, and mete out the penalty for your offense, if offense it be."

"'Offense'? Surely here is no guilt whatever!" cried Visbhume in poignant contralto tones. Is this not Stangle* Meadow, where I may test my wonderful nexus?"

"Foolish mortal! You have compounded your solecism! Such words are not to be uttered in the presence of the Sempiternals; it is considered

---

*Stangle: the stuff of dead fairies, with implications of horror, calamity and putrefaction; a term to excite fear and disquiet among halflings, who prefer to think of themselves as immortal, though this is not altogether the case.

in poor taste. Secondly, this is not Stangle Meadow, but rather the halcyon Madling Meadow, and before you is Thripsey Shee."

"Ah! It seems that I have blundered, and for this my apologies. I know of Thripsey Shee and its remarkable folk; did they not even provide the royal house of Lyonesse with the Princess Madouc?"

Brean the herald looked uncertainly toward King Throbius who signaled to Visbhume. "Mortal, come forward. Why have you established your nexus on our meadow?"

"Sire, I seem to have wandered astray; the nexus was not intended for Madling Meadow, despite its many fascinations. But I wonder of the boy whom you nurtured so wisely five years ago; where is he now? I would speak with him."

"What boy is this?" Then, after Queen Bossum whispered in his ear: "He is gone; he is away through the forest. We know nothing of him."

"That is a pity; I have long felt curiosity on his account."

To the side stood a fairy with a boy's body and a girl's face, who scratched himself incessantly: head, belly, leg, buttock, nose, elbow, neck. Looking up from his scratching he took time to call out: "It was that little braggart we called Tippet! Ah, but I punished him properly, with a fine mordet*!"

King Throbius spoke to the side. "Where is good Skepe of the long arm?"

"I am here, Sire."

"Cut a fine switch and dust Falael's breeches with three and one-half smart celebrations."

Falael instantly set up a howling outcry. "Let fairness prevail! I spoke only truth!"

"Hereafter, when you speak truth, use less gusto and vainglory. Your mordet caused our humiliation! You must learn tact!"

"Ah, your Majesty, I have already been taught tact by your august example! Perhaps I already know too much, so that I cloak my awe at your Majesty's transcendent might with a possibly all too transparent film of bravado! I beg that you re-instruct Skepe from his work!"

From everywhere around the meadow came a thoughtful and approving murmur, and even King Throbius was affected. "Well spoken, Falael! Skepe, diminish by one full stroke your effort!"

Falael called out: "That is good news, your Majesty, but still it is only a start! May I continue my remarks?"

"I have heard enough."

---

*mordet: a fairy invocation, usually of bad luck; a curse.

"In that case, Sire, I will say no more, especially if you will agree to mitigate my itch."

"Impossible. The itch shall proceed, in order to cure that waspish malice which has wearied so many of us."

Visbhume called out: "Your Majesty, if you will allow me a word aside with Falael, I believe that I can persuade him to remorse."

King Throbius stroked his fine green-gold beard. "That would seem a kindly act, and surely could do no harm."

"Thank you, your Majesty." Visbhume signaled to Falael. "Step over here, if you will."

Falael dealt with an itch under his left arm-pit, then followed Visbhume to a place somewhat aside. "Mind you, I will hear no preachments and if you touch me with a Christian cross, I will transform all your teeth into barnacles."

Skepe spoke hopefully to King Throbius: "If I find them standing properly side by side, may I come up quietly behind and catch them two at a blow?"

King Throbius reflected, then signified in the negative. "Your switch is far too short."

Visbhume, overhearing the conversation, took pains to stand with Skepe in his range of vision. He spoke in low tones to Falael: "I will intercede for you with King Throbius if you satisfy my curiosity in regard to the boy Tippet, although naturally I can not promise that he will heed my advice."

Falael laughed scornfully. "You will do well to intercede for yourself. I believe that you are to be transformed into a night-crake."

"Not so! I am assured of this! Tell me of the boy Tippet."

"There is little to tell. He was obnoxious and vain; I was instrumental in expelling him from the shee."

"Where then did he go?"

"Off into the forest, but then there was more. Rhodion, Monarch of All Fairies, with great injustice dissolved my mordet and gave the girl Glyneth the power of speech with animals, while I was rendered only this offensive itch."

"Glyneth, you say. And then?"

"I paid no heed, for my own troubles were on me. If you must know more, go to the girl Glyneth."

"And who was the boy's father, and who the mother?"

"Wood-cutters, peasants, simple human folk. Bother me no more, as I know no more!" Falael made as if to turn away, but was delayed by a severe itching of the groin.

Visbhume cried out: "But where is the boy now? How is he known?"

"I care not a whit, and I hope not to see him again, for I should surely do him a mischief and suffer new vexations in consequence. Now then, intercede for me, as you promised. If you fail, I will visit a mordet upon you!"

"I can only do my best." Visbhume turned back to face King Throbius. "Your Majesty, I find that Falael is basically congenial. He has been misled by his companions, who have brought him into disgrace. As a disinterested party, before I remove the nexus and causeway from your domain, I wish to urge that your Majesty on this occasion temper justice with mercy."

"It is a large demand which you make of me," said King Throbius.

"True, but since Falael feels true remorse, further demonstration of your displeasure must be futile."

"A favor for a favor," said King Throbius. "I agree to forgive Falael and in return you must leave your fascinating nexus here on Madling Meadow."

Visbhume bowed. "Your Majesty has spoken; I am in accord."

The company of fairies gave a great yelping chortle of delight for the victory astute King Throbius had won over the peculiar mortal; there was capering, somersaults, clicking of the heels in mid-air and small joyous jigs.

Visbhume bowed low. "Your Majesty, though I have surrendered my valuable nexus, it has been in a good cause and now I crave your leave to depart."

"First things first," said King Throbius. "A single matter hangs in the air. Skepe, administer three and one-half strokes minus one stroke to Falael, as specified."

"Your Majesty!" cried Visbhume in shock. "It was precisely this beating which you agreed to spare poor Falael!"

"Not so! I agreed to forgive Falael, which I have done, fully and freely. The beating will be for other pranks which have gone undetected and which Falael no doubt richly deserves."

"Would this guilt not be cancelled by your forgiveness?"

"Perhaps so, but a weight still hangs in the air. Two and one-half strokes have been ordained; they must be effected. Since you have forfended these strokes from Falael, the logic of circumstances diverts them to your own crawling hide. Dango, Pume, Thwither: down with Visbhume's breeches; let him hold his backside at the ready. Now then, Skepe: do your duty!"

"Ai hi yi!" cried Visbhume.

"One!"

"Ai-ee ha!"

"Two!"

"Oo-oh! Oo-ha! . . . . *Zappir tzug muig lenka! Groagha teka!** But the half was stronger than the two full strokes together!"

"Yes, that is sometimes implicit in the nature of things," King Throbius agreed. "But no matter; you have had your way and Falael has been reprieved, though I am not sure of his remorse. See how he sits yonder on a post, grinning for sheer joy!"

Visbhume, after regaining his dress, bowed once again. "Your Majesty, I leave you to the enjoyment of your nexus."

"You have my leave to go. I must investigate this fascinating nexus."

Visbhume set off across the meadow, looking back over his shoulder. King Throbius slowly advanced to stand in front of the nexus, then took a slow stop forward, and another. . . . Visbhume turned and looked no more until he reached the forest shade.

Madling Meadow was as he had first seen it. The hummock supported only a gnarled old oak. Between the birches hung a tangle of blue and red yarn, which jerked and bounced and gathered itself into a sort of cocoon. . . . Visbhume untied his horse with trembling fingers, mounted and departed at speed.

V

ARRIVING IN LYONESSE TOWN, Visbhume went directly to Haidion, and on this occasion it was Sir Mungo, the High Seneschal himself, who took him to the terrace before the royal bed-chamber, where King Casmir sat cracking and eating walnuts.

At King Casmir's signal, Sir Mungo haughtily arranged a chair for the use of Visbhume, who pulled it up even closer to the table. King Casmir paused in his cracking of walnuts to turn Visbhume a mild blue gaze of mingled distaste and curiosity. "You have just arrived?"

"I have barely dismounted from my horse, your Majesty! I come in haste to report my findings."

King Casmir spoke over his shoulder to the footman: "Serve us tankards of ale; these nuts give me a thirst, and Visbhume will surely wish to wash the dust from his throat." The footman departed. "Sir Mungo, I will not need you. . . . Now then, Visbhume, what is your news?"

---

*Untranslatable: curses in the pre-Celtic dialect of the Wysrod peasantry, who were renowned for their mouth-filling epithets. Scholars will note that in this particular dialect the elision of vowels is very far advanced.

Visbhume hitched his chair even closer. "By dint of the most crafty effort I managed to draw information from a class of creature whose most joyous habit is to outwit mortal men! But I dazzled them all and they told me this: the boy whom they called Tippet had been turned out from the shee at some indefinite time in the past, whereupon he seems to have become the companion of a girl named Glyneth, and here is the core of my information."

The footman brought tankards foaming with beer along with a plate of biscuits. Without waiting for King Casmir's invitation, Visbhume seized one of the tankards and drank a deep draught.

"Most interesting," said King Casmir.

Visbhume leaned forward to rest an elbow on the table. "Now then: who is Glyneth? Can it be the Princess Glyneth of Troicinet, who occupies so anomalous a place in the court at Miraldra? Remember that Ehirme, Graithe and Wynes, all in some way associated with the boy Tippet, have removed to Troicinet, where now they prosper. Here is more of the same!"

"Your deductions would seem sound." King Casmir drank from his tankard, then brushed walnut shells to the floor, to find room to rest his own elbow. "The boy would now be five years old*. It must be that he too resides in Troicinet. But where? With Ehirme?"

"There is no such child at Ehirme's house: I can vouch for this."

"What of Graithe and Wynes?"

"I observed them for several days. They live alone."

Partly to escape Visbhume's conspiratorial nearness, King Casmir rose to his feet and went to stand by the balustrade, which allowed him a sweeping view over the roofs of Lyonesse Town and their tiles of earthen colours, the harbour and the sweep of the Lir. He looked back toward Visbhume. "There is at least an open avenue of inquiry."

Visbhume, coming to stand beside King Casmir, looked dubiously off across the Lir. "You refer to the Princess Glyneth?"

"Who else? You must return to Troicinet and discover what she knows. She is a maiden of charm and grace, with an amiable disposition and seemingly a confiding nature."

---

*Dhrun, or 'Tippet' as the fairies named him, lived at Thripsey Shee for something more than a single year, by mortal reckoning. Fairy time moves at a far faster flow, and to Dhrun's own perceptions he lived almost nine years at the shee.

King Casmir, unaware of the discrepancy, puts Dhrun's age at five rather than his actual age of close to fourteen.

"Have no fear on that score! She will answer my questions in full detail! If she attempts reticence, so much the better! I am never averse to persuading young girls and forcing them to obedience. Here is where work becomes pleasure!"

King Casmir eyed Visbhume coldly sidelong. From time to time he gratified his taste for boys of a certain manner and conformation; otherwise he eschewed the licentious excesses which enlivened King Audry's court at Avallon. "I trust that in your transports you will not forget the purpose of the inquiry."

"Have no fear! Difficulties vanish when I bring my little techniques to bear. Where would Glyneth now be found?"

"At Miraldra, so I suppose, or else at Watershade."

VI

VISBHUME TOOK LODGING ONCE AGAIN at the Four Mallows. He dined early, then went out upon the square, to sit on the same bench as before. But on this evening no burly Moor approached him, nor Tamurello in any of his other guises.

Visbhume watched the sun setting into the Lir. A breeze from the west had blown up trains of steep waves, each with a crest of white foam, and Visbhume turned away with a shudder. Were Tamurello truly a good and faithful comrade, he would have provided Visbhume means of quick transit from place to place, so that Visbhume might travel without suffering the heaving, sliding, toppling, wallowing motion of a ship, nor yet the staid gait of a sway-backed white mare.

Visbhume reflected upon the cache of magical apparatus which he had stored in Dahaut. Some of the simpler items functioned in a manner which he understood. Others, like Twitten's Almanac, might well respond to his closer investigation. The use of other objects and adjuncts remained beyond his present capabilities. Still, who could say? Among these items might be an effectuant to provide Visbhume the swift and easy transit for which he yearned so deeply.

Visbhume came to a firm decision. In the morning, instead of taking ship for Troicinet, as King Casmir might well have preferred, he rode up the Sfer Arct to the north, then off at a slant to Old Street, then east to Icnield Way, north through Pomperol into Dahaut. Arriving at the village Glimwillow, he went to a secret place and retrieved the large brass-bound chest containing the goods which he had taken away from Maule.

Visbhume lodged himself in a private chamber at the Sign of the Mandrake, and for three days worked among the contents of the chest.

When at last he returned south along Icnield Way, he carried a yellow leather wallet containing a variety of those articles he deemed most accessible to his use, and a few others of fascinating potentiality, like Twitten's Almanac. He found no obvious device or method by which he might be conveyed at speed directly to Troicinet, or elsewhere, and so rode the stately white mare as before. At Slute Skeme he sold the white mare and with many misgivings took passage aboard a lumbering cargo vessel bound for Domreis.

Three days of cautious inquiry at last yielded information that, in the absence of Prince Dhrun — now making a ceremonial visit to Dascinet — the Princess Glyneth had taken herself off to Watershade.

In the morning Visbhume set off along the coast road. A storm of roaring winds and driving rain persuaded him to break his journey at the town Hag's Head, under Cape Haze, where he took lodging at the Three Lampreys. To pass the time he composed himself to a study of Twitten's Almanac, and became so enthralled by the vistas of opportunity suddenly displayed before his imagination that he extended his visit another day, and yet another, and another, even though the weather had once again become fine.

Meanwhile, the Three Lampreys was comfortable and convenient; Visbhume ate well, drank well, and sat long hours in the sunshine, pondering Twitten's wonderful calculations and the no less remarkable conversion of theory into fact. Visbhume called for ink, quill and parchment, and attempted calculations of his own, to the wondering curiosity of others at the inn, who at last decided him to be an astrologer calculating the moods, surges and retrogressions of the several planets: a conjecture which pleased Visbhume and which he took no pains to disabuse.

Visbhume enjoyed other activities as well. He dozed in the sunlight, took short strolls along the shore, and tried to induce the serving maids to accompany him on these strolls. He was especially interested in the flaxen-haired butter-and-milk girl, whose body, despite her youth, had started to show a number of appealing aspects.

Visbhume's interest in her attributes became so forthright that the inn-keeper came out to chide him: "You, sir, I must ask you to mend your ways! These little maids do not know how to cope with your lewdness. I have told them to throw a good drench of cold water on you if you fondle them again."

Visbhume said haughtily: "Fellow, you are presuming far out of your place!"

"That is as may be. In any case, let us have no more of your leers and probing fingers and invitations down the shore."

"This is sheer insolence!" stormed Visbhume. "Be warned! I am almost prompted to take my custom elsewhere!"

"Do as you like; there will be no grief at Three Lampreys! Truth to tell, with your constant tapping and prancing of the feet, you are alarming my regulars; they think you a natural and as I reflect on it, so do I. By the statutes of law I cannot turn you out unless you commit a nuisance, and you have veered yourself very close. Beware!"

Visbhume declared in all dignity: "Innkeeper, you are surly and dull. The girls enjoy my little play; if not, they would never come so often, lilting and tittling, flirting and showing their things; just so."

"Aha! You will find how they like it when they cool your play with good cold water. Meanwhile, you may also pay your score as of this moment, in case you become suddenly indignant and prance off by night."

"That is a churlish remark to make to a gentleman!"

"No doubt. I am careful never to do so."

"You have offended me," said Visbhume. "I will pay the score and depart your premises at once. As for your gratuity, expect not even a groat."

Visbhume departed and took up residence at the Sea Coral Inn on the other side of town, where he stayed another three days, continuing his studies of the Almanac. At last his calculations prompted him to be off about his affairs. He purchased a small cart drawn by a dainty little pony, which carried him along the road at a spanking pace, with a twinkling clack-clack-clack of varnished hooves. Past the Three Lampreys rode Visbhume, sitting proudly high on the seat, then along the road to Rundle River Valley, up the River Road to Green Man's Gap, over and down upon the Ceald.

VII

A STRANGE SWEET MOOD had come over Glyneth of late. When in the company of her friends, or even with Dhrun, she often would have preferred solitude. And sometimes, when she had slipped away and was truly alone, then: perversity of perversities! an indefinable uneasiness afflicted her, as if somewhere wonderful events were in progress, and there she longed to be, though, poor forlorn girl, she had not been invited and no one even noticed her absence.

Glyneth became wistful and restless. At times fascinating images came to tease her, glimpses less substantial than daydreams, figments and fancies, of madcap revelries by moonlight; of fêtes where she was adored by gallant strangers; of drifting over land and sea in a magic ship of the air, in the company of the one she loved most of all and who loved her no less.

With Dhrun gone from Domreis and their schooling at recess, Glyneth dithered and wavered for a day or so, but without the presence of Dhrun or Aillas, Miraldra held no charm, and she took herself to Watershade, where she resolved that she would read all the books in Ospero's library. She made a brave start, and read *Lagronius: his Chronicles*, and *Memories of Nausicaa* and even started to pick her way through *The Iliad*, but the dreamy moods came on her often, and the books were put aside.

When the lake lay calm and blue in the sunlight, she liked to row out into total solitude and lie back to watch the tall white clouds. There was no sweeter occupation; she seemed to become one with this world she loved so dearly, which was hers to enjoy and possess during her term. And sometimes the feelings became too intense and she rose up quickly, to sit with arms clasped around her knees, blinking back tears for the passing of halcyon moments.

So Glyneth indulged herself with romantic excesses, and at times wondered if someone had cast a glamour upon her. Dame Flora became vaguely worried because her darling Glyneth had not gone out to climb trees or jump fences.

As the days passed, Glyneth began to feel lonely. Occasionally she rode into the village to visit her friend the Lady Alicia at Black Oak Manor; as often she walked into the Wild Woods to pick strawberries.

The day before Dhrun was due to arrive, Glyneth arose early and after due consideration, decided to gather strawberries. She kissed Dame Flora goodbye and taking her basket, set off into the Wild Woods.

By noon Glyneth had not returned to Watershade, nor yet by sunset, and servants went out to search. They found nothing.

Early the next morning a messenger was despatched to Domreis; he met Dhrun along the way and both rode in haste to Castle Miraldra.

Chapter 10

I

For Aillas, the Ska occupation of Suarach posed him more than a military dilemma; the action, so coldly deliberate, also inflicted a notable personal humiliation upon him. In the purview of the Ulfs, such a provocation compelled retort, since a person who suffered shame by the purposeful act of another carried the stink of the occasion upon him until his enemy had been punished or until he had died in the attempt. Hence, as Aillas went about his affairs, he felt conspicuous and tainted, and knew that every eye watched him.

Aillas ignored the covert attention as best he could and pressed the training of his brigades with even greater diligence. Of late he had noticed a gratifying new spirit among the troops: a briskness and precision where before the Ulfish slouch and reluctance to move to unfamiliar cadences had been more apparent. The changes would seem to reflect a grudging confidence in the army's fighting efficiency. Aillas still wondered as to their stamina and cohesiveness in the face of ponderous and ominously careful onslaughts of the Ska, which in the past had destroyed not only North Ulfish armies, but also Godelian and Daut forces of superior number.

It was a cruel problem, with no comfortable solutions. If Aillas risked a confrontation and events went badly, his troops' morale would be shattered and he would lose his credibility as a commander. The Ska, by occupying Suarach, apparently hoped to provoke him into a reckless set battle, where their heavy cavalry could demolish the Ulfish army as a hammer smashes a nut. Aillas had no intention of risking such an engagement, certainly not at this time. Still, if he waited too long before taking any action whatever, the Ulfs, who were temperamentally prompted to quick and savage response to provocation, might well become cynical and stale.

Sir Pirmence, returning from the high fells with a levy of conscripts, reinforced Aillas' own fears. "You will never train them finer than they are now," said Pirmence. "They need to test themselves and make sure that your heathen ideas are practical."

"Very well," said Aillas. "We shall put them to the test. But on ground of my own choosing."

Pirmence hesitated and seemed to conduct an internal dialogue. At last he took a swaggering step forward and said: "I can also impart to you this report, which is well-founded: Castle Sank is a fortress across the border to the north."

"As a matter of fact, I know it well," said Aillas.

"The lord is the Duke Luhalcx. At this moment he has taken his family and much of his retinue to Skaghane, so that Sank is only lightly defended."

"That is interesting news," said Aillas. Two hours later he issued marching orders to six companies of Ulfish light cavalry and archers, two companies of Troice heavy cavalry, two companies of Troice infantry and a platoon of thirty-five Troice knights. They would depart Doun Darric at tomorrow's sunset, that they might evade Ska surveillance.

Aillas was well aware that Ska spies monitored his movements. In order to neutralize their activity he had organized a squad of secret counterespionage police. Even before the issuance of marching orders Aillas sent his secret police out to strategic places around the camp, where they would be sure to intercept couriers attempting to carry information from Doun Darric.

The sun dropped into the west and twilight settled upon the camp. Aillas sat at his work-table studying maps. Outside he heard a scuffle of steps and muttered voices; the door opened and Sir Flews, his aide, looked into the room. "Sir, the police have made a capture."

Sir Flews spoke with awe and suppressed excitement. Aillas straightened up from the table. "Bring them in."

Six men entered the room, two with arms tied behind their backs. Aillas looked in slack-jawed wonder to see, first, a slim black-eyed young man with black hair cut in the Ska style, and, second, Sir Pirmence.

The captain of the police was Hilgretz, younger brother to Sir Ganwy of Koll Keep, and now he made his report. "We took up our posts, and almost immediately after dark noticed a flashing light from the camp. We deployed with care and captured the Ska at the crest of the hill, and when we followed the light to its source we came upon Sir Pirmence."

"This is a sad situation," said Aillas.

Sir Pirmence gave his full agreement. "It is cheerless indeed."

"You betrayed me at Domreis, and I brought you here that you might redeem yourself; instead you have betrayed me again."

Sir Pirmence looked at Aillas askance, like an old silver-haired fox. "You knew of my work in Domreis? How is this possible when it was so discreet?"

"Nothing is discreet when Yane starts looking into it. Both you and Maloof are traitors. Rather than kill you I thought to make use of your talents."

"Ah Aillas, it was a gracious thought but over-subtle; I failed to grasp your intention. So poor Maloof has also transgressed."

"He did and now he pays his debt. You also worked well and might have earned back your life, as I hope will Maloof."

"Maloof dances to a different tune than I. More just to say, he hears no tune whatever and could not lift a leg if Terpsichore herself came to lead the measure."

"At least he has desisted from his treachery, or so I suppose. Why have you not done likewise?"

Sir Pirmence sighed and shook his head. "Who knows? I hate you, and yet truly I love you. I sneer at your callow simplicity, but I glory in your enterprise. I crave your success, but I strive for your despair. What is wrong with me? Where is my flaw? Perhaps I wish that I were you, and since this cannot be I must punish you for the fault. Or if you prefer the crude facts, they are these: I was born to duplicity."

"And what of Castle Sank? Was your information no more than bait to lure me and many good men to their deaths?"

"No, on my honour! Do you smile? Smile then. I am far too proud to lie. I gave you only the purest truth."

Aillas looked to the Ska. "And you, sir: do you have anything to say?"

"Nothing."

"You are a young man, with a long life ahead of you. If I spare this life, will you give me your parole never to work again to my detriment, or that of South Ulfland?"

"I could not in good faith make this guaranty."

Aillas took Hilgretz aside. "I must put this matter into your hands. We can not excite the camp by dangling Sir Pirmence and the Ska from a gibbet just before we march; there would be too many questions and too much conjecture."

"Leave it to me, sir. I will take them into the woods, where all will go quietly."

Aillas turned back to his maps. "Let that be the way of it."

II

AFTERGLOW STILL COLOURED THE WEST; in the east a soft yellow moon rose above the Teach tac Teach. Aillas climbed upon the bed of a wagon and addressed his troops: "Now we go forth to fight. We are not waiting for the Ska to attack us; we are marching to attack the Ska. They are to know a new experience, and perhaps we can avenge a few of those crimes which they have worked upon this land.

"Now you know the reason for your long and hard training: that you may match the Ska in military skills. We are their equal except in one respect. They are veterans. They make few mistakes. I tell you now once more: we must carry out our battle-plans, no more and no less! Never be tempted by feints or by a seeming sudden advantage. Perhaps it is real, whereupon we will exploit the situation, but cautiously. More likely, it is false and you will lose your lives.

"We have a true advantage. The Ska are few in number. They cannot afford large losses, and this is our strategy: to maximize their losses and to minimize our own. That means: strike and break away! Attack! Retreat! Attack again! With the strictest attention to orders! Let us have no heroics, no proud gallantries: only competence and toughness.

"There is no more to be said. Good luck to us all."

Four of the Ulfish companies and the two companies of Troice heavy cavalry, under the command of Sir Redyard departed into the northeast, where they would guard the road between Suarach and Castle Sank. The other companies set off to the north toward Castle Sank itself, across a landscape of which Aillas already had bitter experience.*

Sank served as an administrative node for the district and as a way-point for labor-gangs and slaves on the way to the great western fortress Poëlitetz. The household at Sank, during Aillas' stint as a domestic slave, consisted of Duke Luhalcx, his spouse Chraio, their son Alvicx, their daughter Tatzel, with numerous retainers. Aillas, dejected and lonely, had become to some extent infatuated with Tatzel, who, by the very nature of things, barely noticed his existence, if at all.

Tatzel at the time had been fifteen years old: a slim girl of verve and flair who carried herself in a jaunty carefree manner unique to herself: a style purposeful, extravagant and exuberant, if somewhat too abrupt and personal to qualify as pure grace. Aillas saw her as a creature luminous with imagination and intelligence, and he found every detail

---

*See *LYONESSE I: SULDRUN'S GARDEN*, where the circumstances of Aillas' sojourn at Castle Sank are chronicled in detail.

of her conduct entrancing. She walked with steps somewhat longer than necessary, with a kind of reckless swagger and an expression of pensive concentration and purpose, as if she were bound on a mission of the utmost importance. In typical Ska style her black hair was cut ear-length but retained enough curl to flow loosely. While slender and energetic, her contours were adequately rounded and feminine, and often, as Aillas watched her saunter past, he ached to reach out and seize her. Had he performed so rash an act and had she reported it to her father, he might well have been gelded, and he carefully kept his inclinations in check. Tatzel would now be in Skaghane with her family: a fact which caused Aillas more than a twinge of disappointment, since to meet Tatzel again under changed circumstances had been for a long period the stuff of his day-dreams.

As the moon rose into the sky the columns departed Doun Darric. Aillas planned to march by night, with moonlight to show the way and scouts to warn of bogs and quagmires. During daylight hours, the troops would take concealment in a copse or a fold of the moors. If not intercepted or distracted by unforeseen circumstances, Aillas estimated that four nights of marching should bring the expedition close to Castle Sank. The land had been ravaged; they would meet no one along the way excepting a few crofters and small herdsmen, who cared nothing for the passage of troops by night, and Aillas had reason to hope that his band might arrive at Castle Sank unheralded.

Toward morning of the third day scouts led the troops out upon the main road leading down from the old tin mines: a road sometimes used by the Ska on forays into South Ulfland: a road which Aillas had once walked with a rope around his neck.

The troops took shelter and rested during the day, and at sunset continued their march. Still they had encountered no Ska parties, either small or large.

Shortly before dawn an odd droning rasping sound was heard in the distance, which Aillas recognized and identified: the voice of the sawmill, where heavy steel blades ten feet in length were driven up and down in reciprocating motion by the power of a waterwheel, to cut planks from pine and cedar logs carted down from the high Teach tac Teach by timber-cutters.

Castle Sank was close at hand. Aillas would have preferred to rest his troops after the night's march, but now there was no effective cover. By proceeding they would arrive at Sank during that languid hour before sunrise, when blood ran slow and responses were sluggish.

Not so in the South Ulfish troops; with pulses pounding they came at speed down the road, hooves slurring in the dust, harness jingling and metal clanking, dark shapes hunching across the pre-dawn sky.

Ahead loomed Castle Sank with a single great tower rising from the central citadel. "Straight on!" Aillas cried out. "Drive inside before they drop the outer gate!"

Fifty horsemen charged in a sudden pounding lunge, with the foot soldiers running behind. In their arrogance the Ska had neglected to swing shut the timber and iron doors in the outer walls; the Ulfish troops burst into the courtyard unchallenged.

Before them the portal into the citadel and the inner castle also stood wide, but the sentries, recovering from their initial immobility, reacted and the portcullis slammed down in the face of the charging knights.

From their barracks came a dozen Ska warriors, only half-dressed and half-armed; they were cut down and the battle, such as it was, came to an end.

On the walls of the citadel archers appeared, but the Ulfish archers, mounting the outer wall, killed several, and wounded several more, and the others took to cover. From the citadel a man jumped out on the roof, ran crouching to the stables, where he seized upon a horse and pounded away across the fells. Aillas ordered pursuit. "Chase him a mile or two, then let him get away. Tristano! Where is Tristano?"

"Here, sir." Tristano was the second in command.

"Take a strong force to the sawmill. Kill the Ska and whomever resists you. Burn the warehouses and break the wheel, but leave the mill intact; someday we will find it useful. Work swiftly and bring back the labor-gangs. Flews! Send out scouts in all directions, that we may not be surprised in our turn."

The outbuildings, shops and sheds surrounding Castle Sank gave birth to soaring flames. The castle horses were led from the stables, which were also burned. The man-hunting dogs were destroyed, and the kennels put to the torch. From the dormitory at the back of the kitchen garden came the household servants, and the dormitory was fired.

The household slaves were brought before Aillas. He looked from face to face. There: the tall bald man with the vulpine yellow-skinned face and drooping eyelids: that was Imboden, the major domo. And there: the slender handsome man with the mercurial flow of expression and the prematurely silver hair: he was Cyprian, the slave superintendent. Aillas knew them both for sycophants who used the men under them for their own advantage.

Aillas motioned them to step forward. "Imboden, Cyprian! It is a pleasure to see you! Do you remember me?"

Imboden spoke no word, aware that words were useless no matter what the identity of the man who addressed him; he looked up toward the sky as if he were bored. Cyprian was more sanguine. He studied Aillas and cried out in glad surprise: "I remember you well! Though now your name escapes me. Are you bent on suicide, to have returned like this?"

"That I am here is the stuff of desperate longing and hope fulfilled!" declared Aillas. "Do you remember Cargus, who was cook? And Yane, who worked in the laundry? How they would rejoice to be here today, rather than in Troicinet, where both command the rank of 'earl'.'"

Cyprian, smiling easily, said: "I can imagine your satisfaction! It is shared, to greater or less degree, by all of us! Hurrah! We are now free men!"

"For you and Imboden freedom will be short and bitter."

"Come, sir!" cried Cyprian in anguish, his great gray eyes moist. "Were we not all comrades in the old days?"

"I remember very little comradeship," said Aillas. "I remember the constant fear of betrayal. How many men you have sent to their doom no one will ever know. A single one would be enough. Flews, throw up a gibbet and hang these two high, in full view of the citadel."

Imboden went wordlessly to his death, and managed by his conduct to convey a sense of bored contempt for everyone associated with the circumstances. Cyprian, however, burst into tears, and cried out his complaints: "This is sheer infamy! That I, who have done so many good things, should know such cruelty! Have you no mercy? When I think of my many kindnesses —"

From those who had been his staff came jeers, ironic laughs, and calls: "Hang him high!" "He is even more sly than Imboden, who at least made no pretenses." "For this reptile hanging is too good!"

"Up with him," said Aillas.

Down from the sawmill came Sir Tristano with his troops, followed by a bewildered cluster of sawmill slaves. Among these Aillas discovered another old acquaintance: Taussig, who had been his first foreman. Taussig, who was crippled, cantankerous and knew a single goal in life: the fulfillment of his work quotas, recognized Aillas immediately and without pleasure. "I see you have taken your vengeance upon Imboden and Cyprian; am I to be next?"

Aillas gave a sour laugh. "If I hanged everyone who has served me ill, I would leave behind an avenue of corpses wherever I went. I will do you no favors, nor will I do you a harm."

"The harm you already have done me! Seventeen years I have toiled for the Ska; I needed but three years more, and then I might enjoy my reward: five acres of good land, a cottage and a spouse. You have taken this from me."

Aillas said: "From your point of view the world is a sorry place, and you may well be right."

Aillas turned his attention back to the household servants. He learned what he already knew: that the Duke Luhalcx with the Lady Chraio and the Lady Tatzel were absent on a visit to Skaghane. Rumor had it that the Duke Luhalcx was to be sent afar on a special mission of great importance, while the Ladies Chraio and Tatzel were expected home at any time. Sir Alvicx was at the moment lord of the castle, and commanded a garrison of about forty warriors, including several knights of notable achievement.

Aillas knew well the fortifications of the Castle Sank citadel: the walls were high and the stone was sound. Traveling light, he had brought no seige engines, nor was there time for a protracted investment of the fortress; he hunted larger game.

Aillas spoke to the erstwhile slaves, of castle and sawmill. "You are once again your own men, as free as the air, and the way lies open to the south. Go to Doun Darric on the Malheu River; there present yourselves to Sir Maloof, who will find you employment. Should you feel inclined to kill Ska, you may join the army of the king. Take food from the commissary yonder and load it on the horses; arm yourselves as best you can and take to Sir Maloof these horses captured from the Duke's stables. You, Narles, whom I remember as a decent fellow, I place in command. For utmost security, travel by night and sleep by day in the coverts. You should find no trouble; the region is free of Ska."

"There are Ska up at the tin mines," spoke one.

"In that case, do not go near the tin mines, unless you elect to fall on the Ska from ambush and strike a sound blow for your new king."

Narles said in a subdued voice: "I fear that is beyond our powers at the moment; we require every iota of our courage simply to run away."

"You must do as you see fit," said Aillas. "In any case, leave at once, and may good luck go with you."

Diffidently, the former slaves took their departure.

A day passed, and another, during which Aillas did as much damage as possible to Castle Sank and its precincts. Three times his scouts rode back announcing the approach of Ska riders, all from the direction of Poëlitetz. The first two parties were small groups of a dozen riders each; they rode blindly into ambush, and suddenly found themselves surrounded by archers with drawn bows. In both cases they ignored the command: "Surrender or die!" Spurring their mounts and bending low in the saddle they tried to break free from the trap, and were instantly killed, thus relieving Aillas of the awkward problem of dealing with prisoners.

The third party was a different matter, and consisted of about eighty heavy cavalry coming down from Poëlitetz, evidently for reassignment elsewhere.

Again Aillas set up his ambush of archers and mounted knights in a copse beside the road. Presently the Ska contingent riding four abreast, came into view: seasoned troops, confident but far from reckless. They wore their conical black-enameled steel helmets and shirts of chain mail, as well as greaves. They carried short lances, swords, chain-balls — the so-called "morning-stars" — with bow and arrows in quivers at their saddlebows. As they came placidly along the road, thirty-five Troice knights charged from the copse and galloping downhill with lances leveled, struck into the rear third of the column. To cries of horror and shock the lances drove through chain mail and lifted the riders from their horses, to drop them into the dust beside the road.

Riding up the hill and reforming, they charged once more. From the copse poured arrows, each aimed with careful intent. The commander bawled orders to depart this place of death, and the column started off at full gallop. On the hillside four ropes were cut, allowing a great oak tree to topple across the road, and the Ska troops for a period lost their organization.

Finally, battling desperately, hand to hand, the Ska managed to collect in a small group. Three times Aillas called for surrender, before pounding them again with his knights; three times the Ska absorbed the blows and reformed as best they could, and with stern faces hurled themselves upon their enemies.

There was to be no surrender; all would die on the sun-dappled road.

III

IN A SOMBER MOOD Aillas led his troops back to Castle Sank. A victory such as this, which had been, in fact, sheer slaughter of valiant men, brought no exultation. The deed was necessary, no doubt as to this, since it was how the war must be won. Still, Aillas could feel no pride in the event, and was gratified to discover his troops were of similar mind.

All taken with all, he had reason for satisfaction. His casualties had been light; his units had conducted themselves with flawless precision; for the Ska the loss of so many veteran troops was a major disaster.

"If ambush I must, then ambush I will," Aillas muttered to himself. "A fig for chivalry, at least until the war is won."

From Castle Sank Aillas sent back wagons to salvage weapons; Ska steel, forged with infinite patience, equalled the best in all the world, including the fabulous steels of far Cipangu, and the lesser blades of Damascus.

The time had come to move west, to deal with those troops coming up from Suarach which might have evaded the attentions of Sir Redyard.

At dawn the investing force made ready to depart. The events of the next few days were unpredictable and all carried rations of hardtack, cheese and dried fruit in their saddlebags.

Minutes before departure one of the scouts rode pell-mell into camp, bringing news of a Ska company approaching from the northwest, along that road which led to the Ska Foreshore and Skaghane. This company consisted of several persons of quality and their escort, including one who might well be Lady Chraio, spouse of Duke Luhalcx, along with another lady of middle years, and a youth. The escort consisted of a dozen lightly-armed horsemen; clearly no news of the events at Sank had yet been made known across North Ulfland.

Aillas listened with keen interest. He asked: "What of the Lady Tatzel? Was she not among the group?"

"As to that, sir, I cannot say surely, since I am not acquainted with the lady, and I necessarily spied upon the column from a distance. If she is in her middle years, she might be one of the two ladies I have mentioned."

"She is young, and almost like a boy in the shape of her body."

"A youth rides with the group. I took him for a lad; he could be the Lady Tatzel riding in a boy's garments. This is not unusual among the Ska."

Aillas called Sir Balor, one of his Ulfish captains, and gave instructions. "Select your ground so that you can surround the group, and kill only when you must. Under no circumstances harm the ladies or the youth. Send off your captives to Doun Darric with an appropriate guard, then rejoin us at your best speed."

Sir Balor rode off with fifty men to the northwest. At the same time the balance of the army set out toward Suarach, leaving only a detachment at Sank to hold the siege and destroy any further small groups coming down from the mountains.

Aillas had been restless ever since he had learned of the approaching company. He made an impulsive decision, and placing Sir Tristano in command of the army, rode off after Sir Balor, already half a mile to the north.

The day was warm and bright; the moors were at their finest, fragrant with the sweetness of heather, the tang of furze and the smoky reek of the dank soil itself. The clear air seemed to enhance the detail of far objects, and as Aillas rode over a rise, he commanded a view of panoramic scope: to right and left the rise and fall of the gray-green moors, marked by outcrops of rock and occasional copses of larch, alder or cypress. Ahead, the landscape fell away to the horizon, with far dark marks to indicate forests. About a mile to the west Aillas saw the company of Ska bound carelessly for Castle Sank.

Sir Balor and his company, riding in a swale, were not yet visible; the Ska idled along placidly, oblivious to their imminent peril.

The two cavalcades converged. The Ska, breasting a little rise, paused at the ridge: perhaps to rest their mounts, perhaps to admire the view, or possibly because some subliminal signal had aroused their uneasiness: a wisp of dust, a far jingle of metal, a muted drumming of hooves. For a moment they surveyed the landscape. Aillas was still too far to discern detail, but the thought that one among that far clot of forms might be the Lady Tatzel caused him a thrill of excitement mingled with a darker sardonic pleasure.

The Ska rode forward, and now to Aillas' dismay, the troops of Sir Balor, rather than keeping to cover and waiting to encircle the Ska, rode pell-mell up over a swale only a few hundred yards to the south of the Ska. Aillas cursed under his breath; Sir Balor should have sent a single man to reconnoiter, and now all chance of surprise was lost.

The Ska paused only a moment to take stock of the situation, then veered to the northeast on a course which, so they hoped, would bring them closer to Castle Sank: perhaps more close than their assailants might wish to approach. Sir Balor altered his course to intercept them, and again Aillas cursed Sir Balor and his hot-headed tactics. If he were to allow them to approach Castle Sank, they would have been met by those troops left to hold the siege. Then, if Lord Alvicz had attempted a desperate sortie to rescue his mother and sister, Castle Sank itself might have been taken.

But Sir Balor, like a hound on a hot scent, could think only of closing with his quarry, and took his troops pounding across the moors in hot pursuit. The Ska bore away to the north, toward a small forest and, beyond, a rocky knoll surmounted by the ruins of an ancient fort. Sir Balor and his forces came on apace, the faster horses gaining ground perceptibly on the Ska, with the slower strung out behind. Farther still to the rear came Aillas, and presently he could discern the individual Ska riders. He took note of the so-called 'youth'; it was clearly Tatzel, and she wore a suit of dark green cloth, low boots and a loose black cap.

The Ska were obviously making for the old fortress, where they could most readily withstand the superior numbers of the attackers. They rode into the forest and a few moments later emerged; Sir Balor and his men followed.

The Ska began to climb the knoll; Aillas sought through the group: where was Tatzel? Where the youth in dark green with the black cap?

She was nowhere to be seen.

Aillas laughed. He pulled up his horse, and watched as Sir Balor and his troop rode pell-mell through the forest and out, now with only a hundred yards between the two parties.

Aillas kept his eyes on the forest. As soon as the Ulfish troops had passed, a lone rider emerged and rode away at full speed toward Castle Sank, from which she no doubt intended to bring succor to those at bay in the old fortress.

Her course would take her somewhat to the north of Aillas. He examined the terrain, then swung around his horse and rode to where he might hope to intercept her most easily.

Tatzel drew near, crouched low over the horse's surging neck, with locks of black hair blowing back on the wind. She turned her head and her face became shocked to discover Aillas riding hard down upon her, and she could not restrain a cry of consternation. Snatching at the reins, she turned her horse to the north, away from Castle Sank, in a direction Aillas was not at all anxious to explore. Rashly or wisely, Aillas hesitated not an instant; never before had he flushed quarry so precious into the open, and for better or worse he could not abandon it now, no matter where it took him; and so began a wild chase across the North Ulfish moors.

Tatzel rode a young black mare, sleek, long of leg but with no great depth of chest and perhaps less stamina. Aillas' roan was larger and heavier, and bred for durability; Aillas doubted not that sooner or later he could overtake Tatzel, especially in hard going, and as he pursued, he sought to drive her toward the mountains, ever higher: away from both Castle Sank and the lower moors where she might discover help in the form of a Ska settlement or another party of travellers.

Tatzel seemed intent only upon using the speed of her mare to its best advantage, but the moors afforded uncertain and sometimes dangerous footing, and neither horse could gain on the other. Aillas carried no bow, and so could not put an arrow into the mare's withers to bring it to a halt.

A mile went by, and another; and the horses flagged. With the advantage in endurance, Aillas began to gain, yard by yard, and soon Tatzel must be taken. In a desperation she had never in her lifetime known before, she swung sharply up into a rocky gulch which, between a pair of spurs, led up to the higher moors, hoping, perhaps, to dodge into a convenient covert and lose Aillas as he blundered past.

To no avail. No such covert offered itself, and in any case Aillas came only twenty yards behind, and was not likely to be so deceived. The gulch became choked with sedge and alder thicket; Tatzel turned up the side of the canyon, and, dismounting, pulled her horse up over ledges of rotten black rock and through small furze bushes, and at last clambered up to the stony top-surface of the spur. Aillas followed, but halted when Tatzel began to roll stones down upon him, and so was obliged to climb to the top by a different route, which allowed Tatzel a few yards vantage.

Aillas reached the face of the spur. Gullies dropped away to either side. Behind him it seemed that he could see forever under the windy Atlantic sky: across heather-gray moors, dark declivities, the black smears of far forests. Tatzel staggered up toward the high ridge, pulling her distressed mare behind her. Aillas followed and once more began to close the distance between.

Tatzel mounting her horse, rode at best speed, up to the plateau, with the final thrust of the great Teach tac Teach now looming close at hand, and, most notably, Noc, the first of the Cloud-cutters.

Aillas followed, but found to his great discouragement that his horse had somehow wrenched its leg and had gone lame. Aillas cursed, pulled the bridle from the horse's head, threw off the saddle and let it go free. This was serious misfortune, and suddenly his folly in setting off in pursuit of Tatzel, leaving no word nor message, was brought home to him.

Still, all was not lost, by any means. He shouldered his wallet and set out after Tatzel afoot. So winded was her mare and so difficult the footing among the loose stones that once more he found himself rapidly gaining upon her. Another two minutes should bring her to bay.

Tatzel recognized as much. She cast a despairing glance around the landscape, but no help offered itself; Aillas, observing her face as she looked back at him, could not help but feel a qualm of pity.

He hardened his heart. "Tatzel, dear little Tatzel with your haughty head so high! You have known much of despair and fear and sorrow in others; why should you not feel some of your own?"

Tatzel came to a decision. If she rode onward Aillas would have her at once. On her left hand opened a valley with steep stony walls. Tatzel paused an instant, took a deep breath;, then, jumping from her horse, pulled it over the edge of the slope. Sliding, squatting on its haunches, eyes glaring white, nickering in terror, the mare floundered down the slope. Her footing gave way; she fell and began to roll with a grotesque thrashing of legs and torso and contorted neck. The slope increased in pitch; far down the horse struck full into a boulder and lay still.

Tatzel, sliding and clawing, holding for dear life to shrubs and bushes, encountered a patch of loose scree. It slid treacherously from under her feet, to create a landslide which carried her to the bottom, and there she lay dazed. After a minute she tried to move but her left leg could not support her and she sank back in pain, staring at the broken limb.

Aillas watched the disastrous descent, then, with haste no longer of overriding concern, chose a more careful route to the bottom.

He found Tatzel slumped against a rock, face white with pain. He looked to her horse, which had broken its back and lay wheezing and blowing bloody foam. Aillas stabbed it quickly with his sword and the horse became still.

Aillas returned to Tatzel and dropped to his knee beside her. "Are you hurt?"

"My leg is broken."

Aillas carried her to a bed of river sand, and as gently as possible tried to straighten the leg. It seemed cleanly broken, without splintering of the bone, so he thought, and needed principally the support of splints.

Aillas rose to his feet and surveyed the valley. In olden times the river meadows had supported a series of farmsteads, which had disappeared leaving only the crumble of stone fences and a few decaying ruins. He saw no living creature and neither saw nor smelled smoke. Still, beside the river ran the vestige of a trail; the valley could not be altogether unknown to traffic, which might prove to his disadvantage.

Aillas went to the river's edge and cut two dozen willow withes. Returning to Tatzel he peeled off bark and gave it to her. "Chew it; it will help relieve the pain."

From the dead horse he brought Tatzel's cloak, the saddle blanket, and her small wallet of black leather clasped with gold, together with straps and buckles from the bridle and saddle.

Aillas gave her more willow bark to chew, then with his knife slit the leg of her trousers up past her slender knee. He folded aside the cloth to bare the leg.

"I am no bone-setter," said Aillas. "I can only do for you what I have seen done for others. I will try not to cause you pain."

Tatzel had nothing to say, since, in the first place, she found the circumstances confusing. Aillas' demeanor seemed neither ferocious nor even ominous; if he were intent upon a sexual attack would he pause to tie her leg in a splint, which could but interfere with his activity?

Aillas cut a strip from her cloak, and wrapped it around her leg that it might serve as a cushion, then arranged the withes, cut to proper length. Finally, he pulled the leg straight. Tatzel gasped, but made no other outcry, and Aillas strapped the splints into place. Tatzel sighed and closed her eyes. Aillas made a cushion of his cloak and put it under her head. He brushed the damp curls from her forehead and studied the clear, wan features with mixed feelings, recalling other times at Castle Sank. Then he had longed to touch her, to make her aware of his presence. Now that he might fondle her as he chose, his inclination was restrained by a whole new set of strictures.

Tatzel opened her eyes, and studied his face. "I have seen you before. . . . I cannot remember where."

Aillas thought: Already she had forgotten her fear; perhaps he was too transparent. Indeed, she seemed to be demonstrating that ineffable Ska certainty of place, which, had it been less innocent, might be considered arrogant. In such case, the game became more interesting.

Tatzel said: "Your voice is not Ulfish. Who are you, then?"

"I am a gentleman of Troicinet."

Tatzel grimaced, either from pain or from unpleasant recollection. "One time at Sank we had a servant from Troicinet. He escaped."

"I escaped from Sank."

Tatzel looked at him with dispassionate curiosity. "At the time everyone spoke harshly of you, because you poisoned us. Your name is 'Halis' or 'Ailish': something of the sort."

"Ordinarily I call myself 'Aillas'."

Tatzel seemed to make no connection between Aillas the houseservant and Aillas, King of Dascinet, Troicinet and South Ulfland, even had she known the latter's name.

Tatzel spoke without accent. "You are foolish to haunt these parts. When you are captured, you may well be gelded."

"I hope, in that case, I shall not be captured."

"Were you in company with the bandits who attacked us?"

"They were not bandits; they were soldiers in the service of the King of South Ulfland."

"It is all the same." Tatzel closed her eyes and lay quiet. After a moment of thought, Aillas rose to his feet and considered the surroundings. Shelter for the night was important, but even more so, security and concealment. The trail along the river-bank gave evidence of at least some small traffic, and would seem to connect the High Windy Way with settlements and Ska depots along the lower moors.

Some small distance up the valley Aillas noticed a dilapidated hut which might even now afford refuge to herders and wanderers of the hills. The sun was falling behind the mountains; soon the valley would be in shadow. He looked down. "Tatzel."

She opened her eyes.

"There is a hut yonder, where we can shelter for the night. I will help you to stand. Put your arms around my neck. . . . Up you come."

Aillas found that his heart was beating much faster than was normal. The warm pressure of Tatzel's body against his own, her arms clasping him, her clean fragrance commingled of pine-needles and lemon verbena and crushed geranium: they were intensely stimulating. Aillas did not want to release her. "Put your arm around me and I will support you. . . . Take a step."

Chapter 11

FOR AN INSTANT, after Aillas had raised Tatzel to her feet, they stood immobile, her arms around his neck, face only inches from his own, and across Aillas' mind flashed recollections of dreary days at Castle Sank. He heaved a deep sigh and turned away.

Step by step, the two moved along the trail, Tatzel hopping and Aillas supporting her weight. At last they reached the hut which was all that survived of an old farmstead. The site was pleasant, on a rise beside a small stream coursing down from a wooded ravine at the back. Rude stone walls supported cedar poles for rafters and tiles of mica schist for the roof. A door of old gray wood sagged in the doorway; within, on one side was a table and a bench; on the other a hearth and a makeshift chimney to carry away the smoke.

Aillas lowered Tatzel to the bench and eased her leg. He looked into her face. "Do you feel pain?"

Tatzel replied only with a single short nod and a quick glance of wonder for so foolish a question.

"Rest as well as you can; I will be back in a moment."

Aillas gathered fresh willow shoots with thick bark from the river-bank. He noticed crayfish in the shallow pools and a noble trout lazing in the shadows. He took the willow back to Tatzel and peeled away the bark. "Chew this. I will bring you water."

At the side of the hut the stream had been deepened and dammed to form a small pool, in which Aillas discovered a wooden bucket, submerged that it should not dry out and crack. Aillas gratefully brought up the bucket and carried water into the hut. He gathered grass, sedge and shrubbery, and piled it on the floor to make a bed. By the river's edge he found drifts of dry wood, which he carried into the hut. Then, striking a spark, he blew up a fire.

Tatzel, sitting at the table, seemed absorbed in her own thoughts and watched him without interest.

Dusk had come to the valley. Aillas once more left the hut. On this occasion he was gone almost half an hour. He returned with several pieces of fresh red meat wrapped in reeds and also a branch loaded with elderberries, which he placed beside Tatzel. Kneeling at the hearth he lay the meat on a flat stone and cut off thin strips which he threaded upon twigs and set to toast over the fire.

When the meat was cooked to his satisfaction he brought it to the table. Tatzel had been eating elderberries; now she ate the meat, slowly and without great appetite. She drank from the pail, then, pouring water on a kerchief from her wallet, she cleaned and rinsed her fingers.

Aillas chose his words carefully: "It might be difficult for you to relieve yourself comfortably. Whenever you wish I will help you as best I can."

"I need none of your help," said Tatzel shortly.

"As you like. When you are ready to sleep I will make up your bed."

Tatzel gave her head a fretful toss, to indicate that she would much prefer to sleep elsewhere, such as her own bed at Castle Sank, then sat staring stonily into the flames. Presently she turned to inspect Aillas, as if now, for the first time, she were ready to recognize his presence in the hut. "You stated that soldiers and not bandits attacked my party?"

"So I did, and such is the case."

"What will they do with my mother?"

"They are under orders to spare life whenever possible. I expect that your mother will be captured and sent into South Ulfland as a slave."

"A slave? My mother?" Tatzel wrestled with the idea, then put it aside, as something too grotesque to be considered. She looked sidelong at Aillas, thinking: What an odd person! At times as grim and careful as an old man, and the next moment he appears little more than a boy. Amazing what turns up among one's slaves! The episode is most puzzling! Why did he pursue me so remorselessly? Does he hope to collect ransom? She asked: "What of you? Are you a soldier? Or a bandit?"

Aillas reflected a moment, then said: "I am more nearly a soldier than a bandit. But I am neither."

"What are you then?"

"As I told you before, I am a gentleman of Troicinet."

"I know nothing of Troicinet. Why did you wander so far from safety? Even in South Ulfland you were secure."

"I came partly to punish the Ska for their looting and slave-taking, and also, if the truth be known. . ." Aillas stopped short. Looking into the flames, he decided to say no more.

Tatzel prompted him. " 'And if the truth be known'?"

Aillas shrugged. "At Castle Sank I was forced into servitude. Often

I watched you as you went here and there, and I came to admire you. I promised myself that someday I would return and we would meet on somewhat different terms. That is one of the reasons I am here."

Tatzel mused a moment. "You are most pertinacious. Very few slaves have escaped Castle Sank."

"I was recaptured and sent to Poëlitetz," said Aillas. "I escaped from there as well."

"All this is confused and complex," said Tatzel crossly. "It is beyond both my comprehension and my interest. All I know is that you have caused me pain and inconvenience. Your slavish yearnings seem disgusting and truly insolent, and you show a gracelessness in bruiting them about."

Aillas laughed again. "Quite right! My hopes and day-dreams now seem nothing less than callow when I put them into words. Still, I have only answered your question, and with candor. In the process I have clarified my own thinking. Or, better to say, I have been forced to admit certain things to myself."

Tatzel sighed. "Again you speak in riddles. I care nothing for their solving."

"It is simple enough. When the day-dreams and romances of two persons run alike, they become friends, or, as it may be, lovers. When this is not the case, they find no pleasure in each other's company. It is an easy concept, though but few take the trouble to understand it."

Tatzel looked into the fire. "Personally, I care not a fig for your mournings and vagaries. Explain them to persons whom you think they may fascinate."

"For the present I will keep them to myself," said Aillas.

After a few moments Tatzel stated: "I am surprised that your band dared venture so far from South Ulfland."

"The explanation again is simple. Since we came to attack Castle Sank, it was necessary to come at least so far."

Tatzel at last showed startlement. "And you were repelled?"

"To the contrary. We left the citadel intact only because we had brought no siege engines. We destroyed everything in sight, then rode off to do battle elsewhere."

Tatzel stared at him in wonder. "That is a cruel deed!"

"It is no more than long-delayed justice, and it is only a start."

Tatzel looked glumly into the flames. "And what do you propose to do with me?"

"I have impressed you into servitude after the Ska style. You are now my slave. Henceforth, conduct yourself accordingly."

"That is not possible!" cried Tatzel furiously. "I am Ska and of noble birth!"

"You must adjust yourself to the idea. It is a pity that you have broken your leg and so cannot obey my commands."

Tatzel, leaning on the table with chin on her two fists, scowled into the fire. Aillas rose to his feet and spread her cloak across the bed of grass. "Chew some of the willow bark, that you may sleep without pain."

"I want no more bark."

Aillas bent over her. "Put your arms around my neck and I will carry you to the bed."

After a moment's hesitation Tatzel obeyed, and Aillas transferred her to the bed of grass. He unlaced the thongs of her boots and drew them from her feet. "Are you comfortable?"

Tatzel looked up at him blank-faced as if she had not heard the question. Aillas turned away, and went outside to listen to the night.

The air was still. He heard the murmur of water in the river but otherwise silence. He returned into the hut. Tilting up the table, he placed it across the doorway, and wedged it in place with the bench. He banked the fire and after removing his own boots, lay down beside Tatzel and covered them over with his cloak. He looked toward the pale blotch of Tatzel's face. "Have you ever slept with a man before?"

"No."

Aillas gave a noncommittal grunt. "Thanks to the broken leg your virginity is secure. It would be too much distraction to hear you yelping in pain because your leg was hurting. . . . I suppose that I am a man of too many niceties."

Tatzel made a scornful sound but otherwise had nothing to say. She twisted about so that her back was toward Aillas, and presently he heard her regular breathing.

In the morning the sun rose into a cloudless day. Aillas brought hard-tack and cheese from his wallet for their breakfast. Immediately after he took Tatzel to a secluded little glen fifty yards up the ravine behind the hut. Tatzel protested and grumbled but Aillas was firm. "These hills are not unknown to true bandits who are little more than wild animals. I lack bow and arrow and if there were more than two I could not protect you. If more than two Ska found us, I could not protect myself. So you must hide during the day until we leave this place."

"When will that be?" demanded Tatzel, somewhat peevishly.

"As soon as possible. Do not stir from here until I come for you. Unless several days go by; then you will know that I am dead."

Aillas returned to the valley. From a crook of driftwood and a pole cut from a birch sapling he contrived a crutch. He cut a strong willow branch, scraped and shaved it and produced a bow of no great quality, since willow lacked the strong resilience of ash or yew. Hickory and oak were too brittle; alder was too weak; horse-chestnut served tolerably well, but none grew to hand. He cut willow shoots for arrows and fletched them with ribbons of trailing cloth. Finally he contrived a fishing-spear by splitting one end of a birch pole into four prongs, sharpening each, wedging the prongs apart with a pebble, and lashing a foot from the end to prevent the pole from splitting along its whole length.

The time was now an hour into the afternoon. Aillas took his fishing spear to the river, and after an hour of the most patient and crafty effort, managed to spear a fine brown trout of three or four pounds. As he cleaned the fish by the water's edge he heard the sounds of approaching horses and instantly took to cover.

Up the road came two mounted men, followed by a wagon drawn by a pair of shaggy farm-horses. A tow-headed peasant boy of fourteen drove the wagon. The riders were of a different, more sinister sort. They wore makeshift vests of chain and leather helmets with neck- and ear-flaps. Heavy long-swords slanted back from their belts; bows and arrows hung at their saddlebows, along with short-handled battle-axes. The larger of the two was somewhat older than Aillas, dark, burly, with small mean eyes, a coarse beard and a fleshy beak of a nose. The other, older by perhaps fifteen years, rode crouched in the saddle, as lean, sinewy and tough as the leather on which he sat. His face was pale and disturbing; strangely wide cheekbones with round gray eyes and a small thin-lipped mouth gave him an almost ophidian semblance.

Aillas instantly knew the two for outlaws, and he congratulated himself on his foresight in hiding Tatzel up the gully, inasmuch as the riders had taken note of the dead horse, and were somewhat puzzled as to its significance.

Arriving at the hut the horsemen halted and muttered together, then bent to examine tracks in the sand. Warily dismounting, they tied their horses to the wagon and started to approach the hut, then stopped short in surprise.

Aillas went cold and stiff with shock. Tatzel had also heard the approach of the horsemen. She came hobbling around the side of the hut and, facing the two, spoke in a voice of confident authority, though Aillas could not hear her words. She gestured toward the wagon; Aillas assumed that she had given instructions that she wished to be transported to the nearest Ska castle or administrative depot.

The two men looked at each other, grinning in some mutuality of understanding, and even the boy, gaping open-mouthed from the wagon, blinked in perplexity.

Aillas seethed with contradictory emotions: fury at the enormity of

Tatzel's folly, then a gust of great sadness for what she must endure, then another surge of anger, of a different sort: no matter how he raged and cursed, he could not now withdraw from her troubles and hope to keep his self-respect. In her arrogance and vanity, Tatzel had endangered not only herself, but Aillas as well.

The two men approached Tatzel and halted close in front of her. They looked her up and down, and exchanged appreciative comments. Tatzel, drawing back, issued a set of desperate new commands.

The thin bent man put questions to Tatzel. She answered in icy tones and again gestured toward the wagon.

"Yes, yes," the men seemed to say. "All in good time. But first things first! Great good fortune has brought the three of us together and we must celebrate our luck in proper style. A pity only that there are not two of you!"

Tatzel stumbled back another pace and looked desperately around the landscape. Aillas thought sardonically: 'Now she wonders why I do not rush forward to teach the ruffians a lesson.'

The burly bearded man leaned forward and seized Tatzel around the waist. He drew her close, and tried to kiss her. Tatzel twisted her head this way and that, but presently he found her mouth. The lean man tapped him on the shoulder and the two exchanged words, and the younger man sullenly drew back, either by reason of fear or by difference in status.

The older man spoke gently but with effect, and the younger man gave a shrugging acquiescence. Together they prepared for a game, to determine who first would amuse himself with Tatzel. The younger man pushed a stick into the ground, and drew a line in the dirt at a distance of ten feet. Taking coins from their pouches, they stood behind the line and in turn tossed coins toward the stick. The boy, jumping down from the wagon, came to watch with what seemed a more than casual interest.

While their attention was distracted, Aillas ran behind the wagon. In front of the hut there was argument as to a possible breach of the rules, and the boy was called on as an arbiter. He rendered a decision, and the game was played once again to the amended rules, though not without grumbling and the exchange of heated words between the two. Tatzel at the same time made furious expostulations, until she was commanded to silence, whereupon she stood back and watched with mouth drawn into a grimace.

During these events Aillas moved quietly to the horses and availed himself of a bow and a handful of arrows.

The game ended; the victor was the burly black-bearded man who laughed proudly and congratulated Tatzel on her luck. Once again he

seized her and, with a leer and a wink toward his comrade, took her
into the hut.

The older man gave a dreary shrug, and growled an order to the boy,
who ran off to the wagon and brought back a wallowing leather sack
of wine. The two went to squat in the sunlight at the side of the hut.

Aillas quietly approached, arrow nocked to the string. He sidled to
the doorway and, softly as a shadow, stepped inside. Tatzel lay sprawled
naked on the grass bed. The bandit had dropped his breeches and kneeling at the ready groped to insert his monumental genital member. Tatzel
saw the still silhouette in the doorway and gasped; the bandit looked
over his shoulder. He uttered an inarticulate curse and clambered to
his feet, groping for his sword. He opened his mouth, to call out his
rage; Aillas loosed the arrow. It hissed across the room, entered the open
mouth, to pin the head to a post in the back wall, where the man died
in dancing spasms of arms and legs.

Aillas returned outside as quietly as he had entered. Stepping around
the corner, he found the older man leaning back with the wine-sack
tilted high, while the boy watched in fascinated envy. The boy's eyes,
looking past the wine-sack, focused upon Aillas; he gave a strangled
falsetto call. The bandit, rolling his pale gray eyes to the side, saw Aillas.
He dropped the bag and scrambled to his feet, snatching at his sword.
His face somber and grave, Aillas loosed his arrow. The bandit's knees
buckled; he clawed briefly at the shaft protruding from his chest, then
sagged to the ground.

Aillas went to look for the boy, and discovered him fleeing in great
bounds and leaps down the road the way he had come, and a moment
later he was gone from sight.

Aillas looked into the hut. Tatzel with eyes pensively downcast, was
dressing herself, back turned to the corpse. Aillas, also thoughtful, went
to the wagon, which was covered by a tarpaulin of good waxed linen
canvas. Below were a variety of provisions, in large quantity, sufficient
to feed a dozen men for a month or more.

Aillas chose goods from the wagon: a sack of meal, two flitches of
bacon, salt, two round cheeses, a sack of wine, a ham, a goodly bundle
of onions, a crock of preserved goose, a rack of salt fish, a bag of raisins
and dried apricots. He packed the supplies in the tarpaulin and loaded
it upon the best of the draught horses, which now would carry the pack.

Tatzel came to sit in the doorway of the hut, where she demurely
combed the short curling locks of her hair. Aillas remembered the crutch
he had contrived for her use. After the briefest of hesitations, he went
to get it, along with the trout he had speared. The crutch he gave to
Tatzel. "This may help you to walk."

Aillas entered the hut, took up the two cloaks, shook them out, and gave a final glance to the corpse. The next person to enter the hut would discover a sight to startle him.

Returning into the wholesome outer air, Aillas said: "Come! Before long this place will be swarming with Ska, depending on how far the boy must run with his news."

Tatzel pointed up the trail. "Someone is coming now; best that you flee while you can save yourself."

Turning to look, Aillas discovered an old man approaching with four goats. He wore garments of bast, straw sandals and a low wide-brimmed hat of woven straw. Each of his goats carried a small pack. As he drew abreast of the hut, he turned an incurious glance from Aillas to Tatzel and would have passed without a word, had not Aillas called out: "Hold a moment, if you will."

The old man halted, politely but without enthusiasm.

Aillas said: "I am strange to these parts; perhaps you can direct me."

"I will do my best, sir."

Aillas pointed down the valley. "Where does the road lead?"

"It is ten miles down to Glostra, which is a village and a Ska outpost, where they keep a goodly barracks."

"And up the road?"

"There are several turnings. If one keeps to the main trail he comes to the High Moor, and there he will find the Windy Way to Poëlitetz."

Aillas nodded; this was more or less what he had expected. He signalled to the old man. "Come with me, and tie your goats to the wagon, if you like."

The old man dubiously followed Aillas to the hut. Here Aillas showed him the two corpses. "They came up the road with the wagon. They attacked me and I killed them. Who are they?"

"In the hut with the beard: he is a half-breed Ska. The other is known as Fedrik the Snake. Both were bandits in the service of Torqual, or so it is said."

"Torqual. . . . I have heard the name."

"He is chief of the bandits, and his lair is Castle Ang, where he cannot be attacked."

"Much depends upon who is attacking, and how," said Aillas. "Where is the fort, so that we may avoid it?"

"Fifteen miles along the trail you will discover three pines by the road, with a ram's skull nailed to each. Here the road forks. The way to the right leads to Ang. I have seen it once only, and the entry was guarded by two knights in full armour impaled on stakes. I will go there never again."

"I see that the second of your goats carries a good iron pannikin," said Aillas. "Will you trade this pannikin for a horse, a wagon and a supply of victual as to keep you fat for a year?"

"The trade would seem to be fair, from my point of view," said the old man cautiously. "These articles are naturally yours to bestow."

"I have claimed them and no one disputes me. However, should we make the trade, I suggest that you take the goods as quickly as possible to some secret place, if for no other reason than to forestall envy."

"That is wise counsel," agreed the old man. "I hereby effect the trade."

"Further, you have never seen us and we have never seen you."

"Precisely so. At this moment I hear only the echo of ghost-voices carried on the wind."

II

THE SUN SANK BEHIND AILLAS AND TATZEL as they rode up the valley, with the line to the pack horse tied to the back of her saddle. Aillas carried both bows and both quivers.

The valley narrowed and rose at a gradient which caused the river to gurgle and tumble and leap when it came upon a boulder in its bed. Soft pines and cedars appeared in copses and single sentinels; draws and gullies entered the valley from either side, each with its trickle of a stream.

Late in the afternoon the wind began to rise and clouds raced overhead; rain might be approaching from the sea: a dismal prospect.

Sunset gilded the high mountain ridges; the valleys began to fill with dusk. Aillas turned up one of the tributary valleys, and after about a hundred yards of leading his horse along the banks of a rivulet, came upon a grassy glade protected from the wind and where their fire could not be seen by night-wanderers along the road.

Tatzel was not pleased with the campsite and looked back and forth with disapproval. "Why do we stay at this rude place?"

"So that we may not be troubled during the night by strangers," explained Aillas.

"We are plunging ever more deeply into wilderness. Where are you taking us, or do you know?"

"I hope to find a way serene and peaceful over the high moors, thence down into South Ulfland and so back to Doun Darric. Eventually I will take you to Domreis in Troicinet."

"I do not care to visit these places," said Tatzel coldly. "Do not my wishes carry weight?"

Aillas laughed. "You will discover that, as a slave, your wishes are entirely ignored."

Tatzel scowled and seemed not to hear. Aillas collected wood, arranged rocks to form a fire-place, and while doing so discovered a fine sheet of hard green serpentine almost a foot square and no more than half an inch thick. He struck up a fire, laid out the trout, and turned to Tatzel who sat on a log nearby, watching the preparations with an air of boredom.

Aillas said: "Tonight you shall cook, while I put up a shelter against the weather."

Tatzel shook her head. "I know nothing of such things."

"I will explain what you must do. Cut fat from the ham, try it out slowly in the pannikin, so that the fat does not smoke. Meanwhile cut the trout into pieces. When the fat is ready, fry the fish, with great care that the fish does not scorch. When the fish is nicely browned, put the pan aside. Then mix some meal with water, and make thin cakes. Press them down on the griddle, which will now be hot." Aillas indicated the sheet of serpentine. "Turn the cakes when they are done on one side, and cook on the other side."

"This is knowledge I do not care to learn."

Aillas reflected. "I can cut a switch and beat you well, until you cry for mercy, even though I am tired. Or I can do these tasks myself and serve you politely to your pleasure. Or I can let you go hungry and cold, which is the course of least exertion to myself. Which would you suggest?"

Tatzel cocked her head judiciously to the side, but made no recommendation.

Aillas said: "Truly, I do not care to beat you. I wish to serve you even less. So it seems that you must cook or go without your supper. And remember, in the morning, it will be the same all over again."

Tatzel said scornfully: "I will eat apricots and drink wine."

"You will do nothing of the sort. Further, you may arrange your own bed. Or sit in the rain all night, for all I care."

Tatzel looked glumly into the fire with arms clasped around her knees. Meanwhile Aillas contrived a tent from the tarpaulin, then, gathering armfuls of rank grass, arranged a bed.

Tatzel, taking note that the bed was intended for a single person, uttered a sibilant curse, and furiously set about preparing the supper. Aillas thereupon gathered more grass and extended the bed.

The two ate in silence. For Aillas, food had never tasted better than this fried trout and griddle-cakes, with slices of onion and gulps of wine. Overhead the wind sighed through the trees and the flames swirled back and forth. Aillas at last went to water the horses, and then tethered them where they could graze to advantage.

Tatzel watched him sidelong, but when he returned to the fire, she was once more brooding into the flames.

Aillas drank a final gulp from the wine-sack. Tatzel watched him covertly. Aillas smiled into the fire. "Where did you hide my knife?" This was the knife with which Tatzel had cut the trout into pieces.

Tatzel pondered a moment, then reached inside her tunic and drew the knife from the waist-band of her trousers. Aillas reached out quickly and took the knife.

Tatzel rubbed her wrist. "You hurt me."

"Not so much as you might have hurt me while I slept."

Tatzel responded with a bored shrug. After a moment Aillas rose to his feet. He carried such of the provisions as might be damaged by rain to the shelter of the tent. Now he took up the bows and tested first one, then the other, gauging smoothness, power and strength of construction. Both were good bows, but one was better and this, with the arrows, he tucked under the grass where he would sleep, convenient to his hand, but not available to the reach of Tatzel's fingers. The other bow he put on the fire and burned.

Tatzel watched with her mouth drooping. "I am truly perplexed."

"Indeed? What is it this time?"

"Why do you stubbornly hold me captive? My own preference is to be free, and I only impede you on your journey. Apparently you do not even intend to use me as a woman."

Aillas thought back across the events of the day. He muttered: "I could not bring myself to touch you."

"Most peculiar! Suddenly you respect my rank!"

"Wrong."

"Because of the bandit, then." Tatzel blinked, and Aillas thought he saw tears glistening in her eyes. "What could I gain by fighting? I am in the power of Otherlings: escaped slaves and bandits; now I am apathetic. Do as you like with me."

Aillas made a scornful sound. "Save your dramatics. I told you last night and again tonight: I would never force myself upon you."

Tatzel looked at him sidelong. "Then what are your plans? I am mystified by your conduct."

"It is quite simple. I was enslaved and compelled to serve you at Castle Sank, to my abiding fury. I swore that some day there would be an accounting. Now you are the slave and you must serve me according to my whims. What could be simpler? There is even a kind of beauty in the symmetry of events. Try to enjoy this artful beauty as much as I do!"

Tatzel merely compressed her lips. "I am not a slave! I am the Lady Tatzel of Castle Sank!"

"Those bandits, were they impressed with your rank?"

"They were Otherlings, but partly of Ska blood."

"What is the relevance of that? They were both depraved. I killed them with pleasure."

"With arrows and ambushes," sneered Tatzel. "You dare not confront the Ska otherwise."

Aillas made a wry face. "In a certain sense, that is true. So far as I am concerned, war is neither a game nor an occasion for gallantry, but rather an unpleasant event to be settled with the least possible hurt for one's self. . . . Do you know of a Ska named Torqual?"

At first Tatzel seemed disinclined to answer. Then she said: "I know of Torqual. He is a third cousin to me. But I have seen him only once. He is no longer considered Ska, and now he is gone to another land."

"He has returned, and his den is up yonder, under Noc. Tonight we have drunk his wine and consumed his onions. The trout was my own."

Tatzel looked off down the gully where a nocturnal beast had caused a rustling among the leaves. She looked back to Aillas. "Torqual is said to keep close reckonings. I suspect that you will pay a dear price for your feast."

"I much prefer to enjoy Torqual's bounty free of charge," said Aillas. "Still, no one knows how the future will go. It is a dark and awful country, this North Ulfland."

"I have never found it so," said Tatzel in a reasonable voice.

"You have never been a slave until now. . . . Come. It is time we were asleep. The wagon-boy will talk everywhere of the noble Ska lady, and the valley will swarm with Ska soldiers. I want to make an early start."

"Sleep, then," said Tatzel indifferently. "I will sit up for yet a little while."

"Then I must tie you with rope lest you wander off during the night. In these places odd creatures move about in the dark; would you want to be dragged down into a cave?"

With poor grace Tatzel limped over to the bed. "We still must use the rope for the sake of security. I sleep soundly, and I might never awake if during the night a rock fell upon my head." He passed the bight of a rope around Tatzel's waist, made it fast in a bight-bowline which she could not untie, and secured the ends to his own waist, thus constraining her close beside him.

Tatzel lay down and Aillas covered her with her cloak. The moon, three-quarters full, shone through a rift in the leaves and played full upon her face, softening her features and causing her to seem entrancingly pretty. For a moment Aillas looked down at her, wondering as to the quality of the half-sleepy half-scornful smile which momentarily twitched at her mouth. . . . He turned away, before images could form in his mind and, lying down beside her, covered himself with his own cloak. . . . Had he overlooked anything? Weapons? All secure. Rope? The knots were out of her reach. He relaxed and presently fell asleep.

III

AILLAS AROSE AN HOUR BEFORE DAWN. There had been no rain and he discovered a live coal among the ashes. He covered it with dry grass and blew up a fire. Yawning and shivering, Tatzel crept from her bed and huddled before the blaze, warming her hands. Aillas brought out bacon and the sack of meal, which Tatzel pretended not to notice. Aillas spoke a few terse words; after scowling and darting a glance at his back, Tatzel set herself to frying bacon and baking griddle-cakes. Aillas saddled the horses and made them ready for the trail.

In the dewy pre-dawn stillness Aillas and Tatzel ate their breakfast, and neither chose to speak.

Aillas loaded the pack-horse, helped Tatzel into the saddle and they departed the ravine. Coming to the trail Aillas stopped to look and listen, but discovered no evidence of traffic, and once again the two set off up the valley, and all the while Aillas kept a close watch down the valley behind them.

They rode through perilous territory. Aillas pushed the horses to their best speed, that they might pass by the fork to Castle Ang as early in the day as possible.

As the miles passed by, the landscape became ever more grand. At the sides of the valley cliffs reared high, sometimes lofting above tumbles of boulders, sometimes rising from stands of massive pines and firs.

The sun appeared above the eastern ridge and shone upon three pines standing tall beside the trail, with a ram's skull nailed to the trunk of each. At this place the road forked, one way leading off to the right. With alacrity and a lightening of the spirit Aillas rode past the ominous fork and put it out of sight behind them.

The horses began to labor, both for the pace Aillas had set and for the gradient of the trail. Up, up, and up, traversing and twisting, back and forth under hanging ledges and bulging boulders, across an occasional mountain meadow: so went the trail, thence once again up on a new slant.

An hour after passing the fork to Ang, Aillas led the way to a secluded nook at the back of a forest of pines. He dismounted, and helped Tatzel to the ground. Here they would rest during the middle of the day, and so lessen the chances of meeting other riders, who, in these regions, could only be sources of danger. Tatzel seemed to feel that prudence of this sort was both furtive and ludicrous. "You are as timid as a rabbit," she told Aillas. "Do you live your life in fear, always peeking and peering, and jerking about wide-eyed at a whisper?"

"You have found me out," said Aillas. "I cringe to a thousand fears. It must be the ultimate abasement when a man is considered a coward by his own slaves."

Tatzel uttered a jeering laugh and stretched herself out on a sunny patch of sand.

Aillas leaned back against a tree and looked around the skyline. Despite all, Tatzel's comments had irked him. Could she truly think him timid, merely for exercising ordinary caution? More than likely so. In her own experience, men travelled the countryside without dreading unpleasant events. "Before long the Ska will be peeking and peering too," Aillas told her. "They are no longer chivvying a few poor peasants from pillar to post; now they have the Troice to contend with and this is a far different matter."

"If all Troice are as prudent as you, we are in little difficulty."

"So it may be," said Aillas. Again he searched the skyline, but discovered only rock and air. Ragged clouds racing along the wind, passed from time to time in front of the sun, with their swift shadows following up the valley.

Tatzel, lying with her head on her arms watched him. "What are you looking for?"

"Someone keeping watch from the ridge. . . . Rest while you can. From now on we ride by night."

Tatzel closed her eyes and presently seemed to sleep.

At noon they ate ham and cheese and cold griddle-cakes. The sun passed across the zenith. Clouds came in greater numbers, and soon the sun was lost behind an overcast. Tatzel, huddling in her cloak, grumbled at the chilly gusts of wind, and recommended that Aillas erect the tent.

Aillas shook his head. "This is coward's weather! Scouts and sentinels are blinded by the mist, and bandits rob only when the weather is fine. Come! We ride!"

He bundled away the ham and cheese and once more they set off up the trail.

The afternoon passed slowly and without comfort. An hour before sunset the winds decreased to puffs and gusts, while the overcast cracked and broke. A dozen beams spurted down at the wild landscape, bringing clots of color to the otherwise drab scenery.

Aillas halted to rest the horses. As he looked back the way they had come, the full scope of the valley opened before him, and now, only a mile ahead, the edge of the plateau cut across the sky.

Aillas led the way up the trail, though once again he felt exposed to the observation of any who might be guarding the valley.

The trail arrived at the final steep slope; Aillas dismounted to spare his horse. Back and forth he trudged: step after slow step, until he too became winded and paused to catch his breath. The horses, bobbing their heads and snorting softly, gradually recovered from their exertions. Deep shade surrounded the group, with beams from the low sun breaking through rifts to illuminate banks and reefs of cloud to the east.

Aillas once more started up the trail: back, forth, back, forth, and with a last surge, came up and out upon the plateau. To the south stood the Cloud-cutters; to the east rose the final ridge of the Teach tac Teach, now burning in the sunset light; to the north the plateau became lost in fog and low clouds.

A hundred feet away a tall man in a black cape brooded over the landscape. He stood as if in deep thought, hands resting on the pommel of his sword, with the tip of the scabbard resting on the ground before him. His horse stood tied to a nearby shrub. He glanced aside at Aillas and Tatzel, then seemed to ignore them, which suited Aillas well enough.

Aillas set off along the trail, passing the man by as if he were not there.

The man turned slowly to face them, so that the sunset light modeled his features in dark gold and black. He spoke a single word: "Hold!"

Aillas politely reined up his horse, and the man came slowly forward. Black hair hung close beside a low forehead with saturnine eyebrows and luminous hazel eyes below. Harsh cheek-bones, a mouth wide and shapely, if somewhat heavy, above a short heavy chin, along with a flickering muscle of the left cheek, gave an impression of passionate strength dominated, if only barely, by a sardonic intelligence. He spoke again, in a voice at once harsh and melodious: "Where do you go?"

"We travel along the Windy Way and down into South Ulfland," said Aillas. "Who, sir, are you?"

"My name is Torqual." His eyes became fixed upon Tatzel. He murmured: "And who is this lady?"

"She is in my service, at the moment."

"Lady, are you not Ska?"

"I am Ska."

Torqual moved somewhat closer. He was a strong man, thought Aillas: broad of shoulder, deep of chest, narrow in the flanks. Here was a man, he thought, whom Tatzel would think neither furtive nor timid, nor even prudent.

Torqual spoke in lilting melodious tones: "Young man, I claim your life. You trespass upon a territory which I consider my own. Dismount and kneel before me, that I may strike off your head with fullest ease. You shall die in this tragic golden light of sunset." He drew sword from his scabbard with a whine of steel on steel.

Aillas said courteously: "Sir, I prefer not to die, and certainly not upon my knees. I will ask your permission to cross this land which you claim, with my goods and my company put to no peril."

"The permission is denied, though indeed you speak with a good and easy voice. Still, it is all one."

Aillas dismounted and drew his own sword, which was slim and light, and which suited the style of sword-play he had learned in Troicinet. His knife? Where was his knife, upon which he relied? He had cut cheese for their noonday meal, and had packed the knife away with the cheese.

Aillas said: "Sir, before we continue with this matter, may I offer you a bite of cheese?"

"I care for no cheese, though it is an amusing concept."

"In that case, allow me a moment while I cut a morsel or two for myself, as I hunger."

"I have no time to spare while you eat cheese; prepare instead for death." With this, Torqual advanced a step and slashed out with his sword. Aillas jumped aside and the stroke went for naught. Torqual swung again but the stroke slid off Aillas' blade.

Aillas feinted a lunge, but Torqual's heavy blade darted up and Aillas would have been spitted had he attempted more, and he understood that Torqual was a swordsman of skill as well as strength.

Torqual again attacked, driving Aillas back, and Aillas fended off a series of blows any of which might have cut him in two, apparently each time by a hair's-breadth. On the last stroke Aillas counterthrust savagely, touching Torqual's shoulder, and Torqual was forced to jerk back with an effort in order to recover. Aillas now took note that Torqual carried a knife at his belt.

Torqual's mouth drooped in concentration; he had not expected quite so much exercise. Again he struck, and Aillas lunged hard, throwing up his left arm in an awkward manner which exposed his left side. Torqual attempted a tricky backhanded blow, which Aillas effortlessly slid aside, and lunging again threw up his left arm in the the same awkward fashion.

Torqual lunged; Aillas countered and thrust home, drawing blood from the side of Torqual's chest, missing his heart only by inches. Torqual's mouth drooped and his eyes widened; otherwise he ignored the wound. Aillas noticed now that his hand had gone to his knife.

Torqual again made play and again Aillas fended away his blows, and Torqual seemed to allow an opening for a lunge. Aillas stepped foward, thrust his left arm high, exposing his left side; instantly Torqual struck out with the knife, except that Aillas stabbed out his sword and plunged the blade through the inner side of Torqual's elbow, so that the point emerged beyond and the knife dropped from the suddenly nerveless hand.

Aillas pounced upon the knife and caught it up almost before it struck the ground. He grinned at Torqual, and now began to press the fight: thrusting, lunging, the tip of his sword moving beyond Torqual's ability to fend it off. "Kneel, Torqual," said Aillas, "so that I may kill you with less effort." Aillas swung the tip of his sword in a circle, dodged, feinted, thrust, and Torqual was forced back, step by step.

Torqual drew a deep breath, and venting a great yell, charged with sword swinging like a scythe. Aillas retreated and momentarily Torqual's chest was exposed. Aillas threw the knife with all his force; it sank to the hilt into Torqual's chest. He staggered backward, dumbfounded. Aillas lunged and thrust his sword through Torqual's neck. Torqual cried out in woe and tottered backward over the edge of the plateau. He fell and rolled: down, down, and down, and at last, coming to rest, was merely a black anonymous bundle.

Aillas looked around. Where was Tatzel? She was already two hundred yards away, riding at best speed to the north, though somewhat slowed by the pack animal which Aillas had tied to her horse, as well as Aillas' horse which he had tied to the pack horse. Tatzel therefore rode at an awkward canter which still would have been sufficient to leave Aillas behind, had it not been for Torqual's horse.

Tatzel looked back over her shoulder; Aillas saw the desperate flash of her face, and might have been angry except for the exultation of his victory over Torqual.

He untied Torqual's horse, mounted and gave chase. And again he became angry that Tatzel had chosen to flee north, ever farther into the wilderness which extended all the way to the Godelian border.

At the thought a new concept entered Aillas' mind, which he considered a moment, then rejected. It was too flamboyant, too brash, and probably impractical. . . . The thought recurred. Was it truly impractical? Probably, and reckless as well. On the other hand, when all was said and done, it might be the boldest and bravest stroke of all.

Tatzel rode on with grim determination, hoping that Aillas' horse would fall and break a leg. She had a long lead; miles went by before Aillas caught her. Without comment he took up the reins of her horse, and slowed it to a walk.

Tatzel sat glowering, but had nothing to say. By the light of the afterglow Aillas made camp in a little spinney of mountain larch, and on this evening for their supper they dined upon Torqual's preserved goose.

Chapter 12

I

WINDS BLEW ACROSS THE HIGH MOORS, moaning and sighing through the larch trees. Covered by the tarpaulin, with Tatzel taut and sullen beside him, Aillas watched clouds flying across the moon.

There was much to consider. Even now in South Ulfland his absence may not yet have been noticed, each of his staff believing him to be elsewhere. Still, when all was weighed in the balance — here Aillas smiled a rueful smile to the moon — he would have done the same deeds, and endured the same hardships all over again, if only to gain those fresh perceptions which had banished some of the clutter from his mind. Further and beyond all else, a wonderful new scheme had burst into his mind. Tatzel would discover a new bewilderment, and the thought prompted Aillas to chuckle aloud.

Tatzel, also lying awake and staring up at the moon, found Aillas' amusement totally at discord with her own mood. She asked resentfully: "Why are you laughing?" Then, as Aillas made no immediate reply, she said: "When men are bereft of their senses, they laugh up at the moon."

Aillas chuckled once more. "Your ingratitude has curdled my brain. I laugh so that I may not cry."

Tatzel made a scornful sound. "Your vanity is inflated because Torqual stumbled and fell."

"Poor Torqual! I neglected to warn him that fighting with strangers might be dangerous, and he suffered a fearful injury! Kindly Torqual, modest and good! His demise* brings sorrow to us all!"

---

*Torqual survived both his wounds and his fall. He managed to crawl to the trail, where he was rescued by a pair of his henchmen. They took him to Castle Ang where in due course he recovered his strength.

Tatzel said no more, and so the night passed.

In the morning, as they ate their breakfast crouched over a small reeking red fire, Aillas looked across the moors and discovered, not half a mile distant, a caravan of Ska horsemen leading a dozen wagons piled high with bales and, behind, a column of two or three dozen men linked neck to neck with ropes.

Aillas instantly extinguished the fire lest a wisp of smoke draw attention from the riders. He told Tatzel: "Yonder is the Windy Way; it leads to Poëlitetz. I have come this way before."

Tatzel watched wistfully as the caravan passed by, and Aillas could not suppress a pang of pity and even a trace of guilt. Was it just to visit vengeance for all the wrongs done to him upon the head of one young girl?

He gave an angry answer to himself: Why not? She was Ska; she shared and endorsed the Ska philosophy; she had shown never an iota of pity or concern for the slaves at Castle Sank: why should she be exempt from retribution?

Because the Ska style of life was not of her contriving, came the answer. She had assimilated Ska precepts with her mother's milk; they had been given to her as axioms of existence; she was Ska willy-nilly, through no choice of her own!

But the same could be said of any Ska, man or woman, old or young, and she showed no sign whatever of altering her point of view. She simply refused to accept Aillas' assertion that she was now herself a slave. In short, she was as guilty as any other Ska, and tender emotions in this case were irrelevant.

Still, there was no denying that Aillas had singled out Tatzel for special attention, although he had envisioned none of their present hardships. He had wanted only to—what? To force her to recognize him as a person of worth. To make real the daydreams he had fabricated at Castle Sank. To indulge himself in the pleasure of her companionship. To enter intimately into her life and thoughts, to gain her good opinion, to excite her amorous yearnings. . . . Again Aillas felt sardonic amusement. These goals, formed with such innocent fervor, now all seemed absurd. At any time he could put Tatzel to those erotic uses which she apparently at least half-expected, and which, so Aillas' instinct told him, she might not have found entirely unwelcome. Often, when he felt her warm presence beside him, the urge to abandon all restraint was almost overpowering. But whenever lust started to cook inside his brain, a whole cluster of ideas intervened to quench the fire. First, what he had seen upon entering the hut had sickened him and the image hung in his mind. Second, Tatzel had possessed herself of his knife, and he could only believe that she had meant to kill him, a thought which dampened his ardor. Third, Tatzel, a Ska, thought him a hybrid of the ancient beetle-browed cannibals and true man, and a creature lower in the evolutionary scale than herself: in short, an Otherling. Fourth, since he could not woo Tatzel in the ordinary fashion, pride dissuaded him from taking her by force, for the sheer relief of his glands, with no thought for all the other considerations. If Tatzel were amorously inclined, let her make the first move: naturally, a far-fetched possibility. Although — perhaps he only imagined this — sometimes he felt as if Tatzel were taunting him, daring him to take her, and possibly she burned with some of the same urges which beset him.

An irksome problem. Perhaps some day, or some evening, when conditions were right, he would learn the truth of how she felt, and perhaps the daydreams would be realized in full and breathtaking totality. Meanwhile, the caravan had passed.

"Come!" he said gruffly. "It is time we were riding."

Aillas had long since recovered his knife from the cheese. He made up the pack, which he loaded upon the horse he had previously ridden, while he mounted Torqual's strong black stallion, and the previous packhorse carried nothing. Aillas helped Tatzel into the saddle and they were once more underway, but now they rode into the north.

As Aillas had expected, Tatzel was sorely bewildered by the choice of direction, and finally blurted out a question: "Why do we ride to the north? South Ulfland is behind us!"

"True: a long hard journey, with Ska and other bandits as thick as flies along the way."

"Still: why ride north?"

"Ahead is the road from the Foreshore to Poëlitetz. Beyond is wilderness, all the way to Godelia. The land is empty; there are neither bandits nor Ska to plunder us. At Dun Cruighre we will find a Troice ship and return to South Ulfland in comfort."

Tatzel looked at him as if she doubted his sanity, then gave her apathetic shrug.

An hour later they came upon the road leading from the Foreshore to the great mountain redoubt Poëlitetz. Discovering no traffic to right or to left, Aillas put the horses to their best speed, and crossed the road unchallenged.

All day they rode across trackless moor. Far to the east stood the guardian ridge which here separated Dahaut from North Ulfland. To west and north the moor melted into haze. On this high tableland only furze and sedge and coarse grasses prospered, with an occasional cluster of windbeaten yews or a spinney of ragged larches. Sometimes a hawk flew overhead, on the lookout for quail or young rabbits, and crows flapped across the desolate distance.

As the afternoon passed, a float of heavy black clouds appeared in the west: first a line of scud which quickly advanced to loom across the sky; a storm was surely in the offing, with a dreary night ahead. Aillas accelerated the pace of his company and gave keen attention to the landscape, in the hope of discovering some semblance of shelter.

The outriders of the storm passed across the sun, creating a scene of melancholy magnificence. Beams of golden light played across the moor, and shone full upon a low cottage with walls of white-washed stone and a roof slabbed over with thick turf from which grew tufts of grass and clover. Smoke issued from the chimney, and in the yard adjacent to the byre Aillas noted a dozen sheep and as many fowl.

With hopes high he approached the cottage, and dismounted near the door. At the same time he signaled to Tatzel: "Down from your horse! I am not in the mood for another crazy chase across the moors."

"Help me then; my leg pulses with pain."

Aillas lifted Tatzel to the ground, then, together, the two approached the cottage.

Before they could knock, the door swung wide to reveal a short sturdy man of middle years, round and red of face with orange-red hair cut to overhang his ears like the eaves of a house.

"Our good wishes to you, sir," said Aillas. "Our business here is ordinary: we seek food and shelter during this stormy night for which we will pay in suitable degree."

"I can provide shelter," said the crofter. "As for payment, 'suitable' for me might be 'unsuitable' for you. Sometimes these misunderstandings put folk at the outs."

Aillas searched the contents of his wallet. "Here is a silver half-florin. If this will suffice, we have eliminated the problem."

"Well spoken!" declared the crofter. "The times of the world would flow in halcyon joy, if everyone were so open-hearted and forthright as you! Give me the coin."

Aillas tendered the half-florin piece. "Whom do I address?"

"You may know me as Cwyd. And you, sir, and your mistress?"

"I am Aillas, and this is Tatzel."

"She seems somewhat morose and out of sorts. Do you beat her often?"

"I must admit that I do not."

"There is the answer! Beat her well; beat her often! It will bring the roses to her cheeks! There is nothing better to induce good cheer in a woman than a fine constitutional beating, since they are exceptionally jolly during the intervals in an effort to postpone the next of the series."

A woman came to join them. "Cwyd speaks the truth! When he raises his fist to me I laugh and I smile, with all the good humour in the world, for my head is full of merry thoughts. Cwyd's beating has well served its purpose! Nevertheless Cwyd himself becomes gloomy, through bafflement. How did the roaches find their way into his pudding? Where except in Cwyd's small-clothes are household nettles known to grow? Sometimes as Cwyd dozes in the sunlight, a sheep wanders by and urinates in his face. Ghosts have even been known to skulk up behind Cwyd in the dark and beat him mercilessly with mallets and cudgels."

Cwyd nodded. "Admittedly, when Threlka is beaten for her faults, there is often a peculiar aftermath! Nonetheless, the basic concept is sound. Your mistress has the look of costive asthenia, as if she were an arsenic-eater."

"I think not," said Aillas.

"In that case, a thrashing or two might well release the bile into her blood, and soon she would be skipping and singing and larking about with the rest of us. Threlka, what is your opinion?" Aside, he told Aillas: "Threlka is a witch of the seventh degree, and is wise beyond most others."

"In the first place, the girl has a broken leg," said Threlka. "Tonight I will mend the break, and then she will know less dole. But singing and larking? I think not. She is fey."

"Sound opinions," said Cwyd. "Now then, Aillas, let us deal with your horses, while the storm still gathers strength. Tonight it will be a mighty display, and conceivably a single silver coin is poor recompense for the misery I am sparing you."

"This sort of afterthought often spoils a promising friendship," said Aillas.

"No matter how reasonable its basis?" asked Cwyd anxiously.

"Trust, once established, must never become the plaything of avarice! This was my father's wise dictum."

"The proposition seems generally sound," admitted Cwyd. "Still, it must be remembered that 'friendship' is temporal, while 'reason' transcends both human caprice and time itself."

"And 'avarice'?"

Cwyd pondered. "I would define 'avarice' as a consequence of the human estate: a condition arising from turbulence and inequality. In none of the paradises, where conditions are no doubt optimum, does 'avarice' exert force. Here, we are men struggling toward perfection and 'avarice' is a station along the way."

"That is an interesting point," said Aillas. "Am I correct in my belief that I have felt the first drops of rain?"

The horses were stabled and fed generous wisps of hay. Aillas and Cwyd returned to the main room of the cottage.

For supper Threlka set out a savory soup of onions, greens, barley and mutton, with milk, bread and butter, while Aillas contributed what remained of the potted goose, as well as a goodly portion of cheese. Meanwhile the wind howled and roared and rain battered in a steady hard tattoo on the turf roof. A dozen times Aillas gave thanks to the providence which had afforded them shelter.

The same ideas had occurred to Cwyd. He said: "Hear how the storm yells, like a giant in pain!" And again, with russet eyes fixed knowingly upon Aillas: "Pity the poor traveller who must brave such ferocities! And all the while we sit snug before our fire!" And again: "In conditions like this the word 'avarice' loiters sickly by the wayside while the concept 'gratitude' marches forward in triumph, like Palaemon's conquering army!"

Aillas responded: "When storms rage, then is when folk become aware of their common humanity, and like you and Threlka, they willingly extend hospitality to those unfortunate enough to be at disadvantage, just as you, in your hour of inconvenience, will hope for the same! In these cases, the thought of payment is cause for embarrassment, and the host cries out: 'What do you take me for? A jackal?' It is heart-warming to meet such folk out here on the high moors!"

"Exactly so!" cried Cwyd. "Out here on the high moors where conditions are hard, 'sharing' is the watchword, and each gives of what he has without stint! I open my larder wide and light my best and most cheerful blaze; you are of the same disposition with your superfluity of silver coins; thus we honour each other!"

"Precisely to the point!" declared Aillas. "I will reckon up my little store of coins and whatever I find to be superfluous you shall have! We are in accord; let us say no more on the subject."

When supper was done, Threlka sat Tatzel in a chair with her leg propped upon a stool. She cut away the dark green breeches, which were now soiled and stained. "This is not a good color for healing. We will find you ordinary clothes, by which you will profit. You may remove your tunic as well. . . . Come, girl," she said as Tatzel hesitated. "Cwyd cares nothing for your breasts; he has seen them by the hundreds on cows and sheep, and they are all the same. Sometimes I think that modesty is merely a ploy so that we can pretend a difference to the animals. Alas! We are very much alike. But here! If you are uncomfortable, wear this blouse."

Threlka cut away the splint and threw it into the fire. "Burn, wood, burn! Pain, in smoke fly up the chimney; disturb Tatzel no longer!" From a black jar she poured a syrup upon Tatzel's leg, then sprinkled on crushed dry leaves. She wound the shin with a loose bandage and tied it with a coarse red string. "And so it goes! In the morning you shall know no more weakness."

"Thank you," said Tatzel with a wan smile. "The splint was most tiresome. How may I pay you for your healing?"

"I want nothing but the pleasure of your smile," said Threlka. "Oh, if you wish, give me three hairs of your head for remembrance; that shall suffice."

"It is not enough," said Aillas. "Here is a silver penny, worth a whole head of hair, and also useless in magic, should it fall into improper hands."

"Yes, that is wisdom," Cwyd agreed. "And now it is time to sleep."

All night long the storm wailed and roared across the moors, and only began to slacken with the coming of day. The sun rose in a cataclysmic welter of black, white, red, pink and gray; then seemed to assert itself and from a peculiarly black sky sent long low shafts of rose-coloured light across the moors.

Cwyd blew up the fire and Threlka prepared porridge, which the group consumed with milk, berries and rashers of fried bacon provided by Aillas.

Threlka removed the bandage from Tatzel's leg, and threw the bandage into the fire with an incantation. "Rise now, Tatzel, and walk! Once more you are whole!"

Cautiously Tatzel tested the leg and discovered neither pain nor stiffness, much to her pleasure.

Aillas and Cwyd went to saddle the horses, and Aillas asked: "If I were to question you about the lands I intend to travel, would you be happy if in gratitude I made you a present of several copper pennies?"

Cwyd mused. "Our conversations have raised a number of interesting points. I could describe every turn of a long road, reciting each of the perils to be found along the way and its remedy, thus saving your life a dozen times, and you would gratefully reward me with a bag of gold. However, if I casually mentioned that the man you wished to see at the end of this road were dead, you might thank me but give me nothing, though all went to the same effect. Is there not an inherent disequilibrium at work here?"

"Yes indeed," said Aillas. "The paradox resides once again in the distortions worked upon the fabric of our life by greed. I suggest that we free ourselves of this ignoble vice, and seek to help each other with full and wholehearted zeal."

Cwyd grumbled: "In short, you refuse to pay me what my information is worth?"

"If you saved my life even once, how should I pay you? The concept is meaningless. For this reason such services are generally held to be free."

"Still, if I saved your life a dozen times, as well as your father and mother and the virtue of your sister, and you gave me a single copper groat, at least I could put my belly up to the board and drink a mug of beer to your health."

"Very well," said Aillas. "Tell me all you know. It may be worth a copper groat."

Cwyd threw his hands in the air. "At least in dealing with you I exercise my tongue. . . . Where do you fare?"

"North to Dun Cruighre in Godelia."

"You have come the proper route. A day's ride to the north the moors end at a great declivity: the Cam Brakes. This is a series of ledges or terraces arranged like steps, which, according to myth, the giant Cam laid out to ease his way from Lake Quyvern up to the moors. On the first, or topmost, brake, you will find many ancient tombs; give them all due respect. This place was sacred to the ancient Rhedaspians, who inhabited the land three thousand years ago. Ghosts are common, and it is said that sometimes old friendships are renewed and old antagonisms find vent. If you by chance see such ghosts, make no sound and give no interference, and above all, never agree to act as arbiter at one of their ghostly tribunals. Act as if you see nothing nor hear nothing and they will ignore you. There is my first information."

"And a good information it is!"

"On the second brake lives a ghoul who has the power to change his guise. It will meet you in sweet friendship, and offer wine and food and kindly shelter. Accept nothing — not so much as a sup of cold water — and cross down over this brake, no matter what the cost, while the sun is in the sky; at sunset the ghoul assumes its true shape and your life is in the balance. If you take its gift you are lost. That is the second information."

"It is even better than the first!"

"The third brake, which is in the middle, is fair and wholesome, and here you may rest, if you choose. . . . Still, I advise against entering any enclosure, hut or hole, and whatever benefits the land provides, give thanks to the god Spirifiume, who rules this place and also a goodly duchy on the planet Mars. That is the third information."

"Interesting, as always."

"The fourth and fifth brakes are generally safe to the traveller, though all the brakes are haunted in some degree. Pass these by without delay. When you come to Lake Quyvern, you will discover Kernuun's Antler, which is the inn of Dildahl the Druid. He is, so it seems, a kindly man, and offers a hospitality of moderate cost. This is hardly true and you must eat none of his fish! He will serve it in many guises: as roe, and croquettes, and pickles, and pudding, and in soup. Eat only the items whose cost is specified. This is the fourth information."

"These are all valuable instructions."

"The east shore of Lake Quyvern is unsafe owing to mires and bogs and morasses. The western shore is a place beyond my understanding. Arch-druids are rife, as well as a complementary sect of Arch-druidesses, with whom they hold social intercourse and discuss topics relating to their creed. At grand banquets it is said that they eat the flesh of children, in accordance with ancient ritual. The islands of Lake Quyvern are sacred to the druids, and if you set foot on them your life is forfeit. This is the fifth information."

"Once more: most interesting! I am impressed by your knowledge!"

"Lake Quyvern empties into the River Solander, which flows north to the Skyre, and Godelia spreads before you like a bad smell. That is the sixth information." And Cwyd made a gesture to signify that his tale was told, and stood smiling modestly, as if waiting for Aillas' further applause.

Aillas said: "Ah, Cwyd, my dear fellow, your informations are most helpful. Are there more?"

Cwyd asked dolefully: "Have I not told enough?"

"You have done so, but you would not be withholding three or four other informations, just in case I prove an ingrate for the first six?"

"No. I have fully and frankly disclosed all I know to your advantage."

"Then here is a gold crown in exchange, and know that I have enjoyed this evening with you. Further, I will tell you this: I am favorably known to the magician Shimrod, and to the King of South Ulfland and Troicinet as well. Should events ever bring you near these persons, you need but mention my name and your needs will be met."

"Sir, I am sorry to see you go: so much so that I offer you another day and night at three-quarter rate!"

"Most generous!" said Aillas. "But we cannot delay."

"In that case, I wish you good luck on your venture."

II

AILLAS AND TATZEL RODE AWAY from the cottage of Cwyd and Threlka, Tatzel now wearing a peasant's blouse and baggy breeches, cut of oatmeal-coloured homespun. She had bathed; the fresh garments and the curing of her leg put her almost in a cheerful frame of mind, sullied only by the presence of the odious Aillas, who still pretended to regard himself as her master. . . . His manner was puzzling. At Sank, by his own admission, he had come to admire her, but now, out on these lonely moors, where he could do as he pleased, he acted as if under frigid constraint — perhaps the deference a house-servant owed a Ska lady of high birth?

Tatzel covertly studied Aillas. For an Otherling he was personable enough, and she had already noticed that he seemed quite clean. Last night, as she had listened to his conversation with Cwyd, she had been mildly surprised to hear talk so flexible and easy coming from the mouth of a one-time house-servant. She recalled his duel with Torqual; he had attacked this universally feared Ska warrior with almost casual confidence, and in the end it was Torqual who had quailed.

Tatzel decided that Aillas did not think of himself as a house-servant. Why, then, had he kept so remote, even when, for sheer caprice and experiment, she had sought to arouse him? To just a trifling degree, of course, with events very much under her control, but still he had ignored her.

Might the deficiency lie in herself? Did she smell bad? Tatzel shook her head in puzzlement. The world was a strange place. She looked around the landscape. After the storm the day was still and fresh, with a few lost clouds wandering the sky. Ahead the moors seemed to dissolve into air, partly by reason of water-haze and partly due to the Cam Brakes, where the land fell away in descending ledges.

At sunset Aillas elected to make camp, with the Brakes only a mile ahead. In the morning he waited until the sun was half an hour high before setting off to the north. Almost immediately they came to the verge of the brakes, with far regions spread before them and Lake Quyvern extending away from the foot of the fifth brake.

The faintest of trails led along the side of a stream which tumbled down into the first brake. After a few hundred yards the stream entered a steep-sided gulch and the trail, which evidently had been traced by wandering cattle, disappeared.

Dismounting, Aillas and Tatzel picked their way afoot down the slope and in due course arrived at the first brake: a pleasant meadow a mile or so wide spattered with red poppies and blue larkspur. Solitary oaks of great size stood at intervals, each with a hoary individuality of its own. At the back of the meadow an irregular line of tombs defied weather and time. Each displayed a plaque carved in the sinuous Rhedaspian characters now incomprehensible to living men. Aillas wondered if the ghosts mentioned by Cwyd might be persuaded to read the inscriptions and thus contribute to the knowledge of contemporary scholars. It was an interesting idea, thought Aillas, which he must discuss at some later occasion with Shimrod.

Giving the tombs a wide berth, and observing no ghosts, Aillas and

Tatzel rode to the edge of the brake, over and down toward the second brake. Again they traversed carefuly back and forth, slipping and sliding on occasion, and at length came out upon the second brake.

Aillas instructed Tatzel: "Now we must be wary! According to Cwyd, an evil creature lives here, and he may appear in any guise. We must accept neither gifts nor favors! Do you understand? Take nothing whatever, from anyone or anything, or the ghoul will take your life! Now! Let us cross this brake with all possible speed."

The second brake, like the first, was a long ribbon of meadow a mile or so wide. At intervals grew solitary oaks and on the left a forest of elm and horse-chestnut obscured their view to the west.

Halfway across they met a young man trudging up the brakes. He was stalwart and handsome, with a fresh complexion, a crisp golden beard, and a head of short golden curls. He carried a staff, a rucksack and a small lute; a dagger hung at his belt. His brown smock and trousers were plain and serviceable; his green cap boasted a jaunty red feather. As he drew near Aillas and Tatzel he halted and raised his hand in greeting. "Bonaventure, and where do you ride?"

"Toward Godelia; that is our immediate destination," said Aillas. "What of you?"

"I am a vagabond poet; I wander where the wind blows me."

"It would seem a pleasant and careless life," said Aillas. "Do you never yearn to find a true home for yourself?"

"It is a bittersweet dilemma. I often find places which urge me to tarry, and so I do, until I remember other places where I have found joys and marvels, and I am compelled again to my journey."

"And no single place satisfies you?"

"Never. The place I seek is always beyond the far mountain."

"I can offer you no sensible advice," said Aillas. "Except this: do not delay your wandering here! Climb to the top of the brakes before this day is done; you will live a longer life."

The vagabond gave a carol of easy laughter. "Fear comes only to those already frightened. Today the most alarming sights have been several hummingbirds and a tangle of fine wild grapes which now I am tired of carrying." He proffered fresh purple grapes in a pair of clusters to both Aillas and Tatzel.

Tatzel reached out in pleasure; Aillas, leaning, struck aside her arm and reined back the horses. "Thank you; we do not care to eat. On these brakes you are well-advised to take nothing and to give nothing. Good-day to you."

Aillas and Tatzel rode away, with Tatzel resentful. Aillas said shortly: "Did I not warn you to accept nothing while on this brake?"

"He did not seem a ghoul."

"Would that not be his intent? Where is he now?" They looked back the way they had come but the young vagabond had vanished from view.

"It is very strange," muttered Tatzel.

"As the ghoul himself asserted: the world is a place of marvels."

Almost as Aillas spoke, a little girl in a white frock jumped up from under a tree where she had been tying garlands of wild-flowers. Her hair was long and golden; her eyes were blue; she was as pretty as one of her own flowers.

The girl came forward and spoke: "Sir and lady, where do you ride, and why in such haste?"

"To Lake Quyvern and beyond," said Aillas. "We ride in haste the sooner to join those we love. What of you? Do you always wander these wild places so freely?"

"This a region of peace. True, on moonlit nights the ghosts come out and march to their ghostly music, and it is a sight to behold, since they wear armour of gold, black iron and silver, and helmets with tall crests. It is a fine sight to see!"

"So I should think," said Aillas. "Where do you live? I see neither house nor hut."

"Yonder, by the three oak trees: there is my home. Will you not come to visit? I was sent out to gather nuts but I have delayed among the flowers. Here: this garland is for you, since your face is so handsome and your voice so soft."

Aillas jerked back his horse. "Away with you and your flowers! They make me sneeze! Hurry now, before Tatzel pulls your nose! You will find no nuts under the poplar trees."

The girl moved back and cried out: "You are a coarse cruel man, and you have made me cry!"

"No great matter." Aillas and Tatzel rode away, leaving the little girl forlorn and wistful, but after a moment, when they turned to look back, she was gone.

The sun rose up the sky, and without further interruption they came to the edge of the brake. Aillas halted to pick out the best way down the slope; the pack-horse, meanwhile, took advantage of the occasion to lower its head and snatch a mouthful of grass from the meadow. Instantly, from behind a nearby tree came running an old man with a shock of white hair and a long white beard. "Hola!" he cried. "How dare you steal my good pasturage for your use, and almost under my very nose? You have compounded larceny and trespass with insolence!"

"Not so!" Aillas declared. "Your charges have no merit."

"What! How can you contradict me? Each of us saw the dereliction in process!"

"I could testify to no dereliction," said Aillas. "First, you have not marked off your property with a fence, as the law requires. Second, you have erected neither sign nor way-post challenging what in any case is our right by the common law: which is to say, harmless passage across untilled meadows and pastures. Third, where are the cattle for which you are conserving this pasturage? Unless you can prove a damage, you have suffered no loss."

"Legalisms! Sophistries! You have the sleight of words, by which poor peasants like me are mulcted and left helpless! Still, I would not have you think me a curmudgeon, and I hereby make you a gift of that fodder sequestered from my private reserve by your horse."

"I reject your gift!" declared Aillas. "Can you show articles from King Gax? If not, you can prove no title to the grass."

"I need prove nothing! Here on the second brake, the giving of a gift is certified by acceptance. Your horse, acting as your agent, accepted the gift, and you therefore become an extensionary donee."

At this moment the pack-horse raised high its tail and voided the contents of its gut. Aillas pointed to the pile of dung. "As you see, the horse tested your gift and rejected it. There is no more to be said."

"Fie! That is not the same grass!"

"It is near enough, and we cannot wait while you prove otherwise. Good-day, sir!" Aillas and Tatzel led their horses over the brink and descended toward the third brake. From behind came a rageful howling and a tirade of curses, then a melodious voice calling: "Aillas! Tatzel! Come back, come back!"

"Make no acknowledgment," Aillas warned Tatzel. "Do not even look back!"

"Why not?"

Aillas pulled his head down and bent forward. "You might see something you would rather not see. I have this hint from my instinct."

Tatzel struggled with her curiosity but at last followed Aillas' advice, and soon the calls were heard no more.

The descent was steep and the going slow; two hours into the afternoon they came down upon the third brake: another pleasant parkland of trees, meadows, grassy banks, ponds and small meandering streams.

Aillas looked around the serene landscape. "This is the brake in which the god Spirifiume takes a special interest, and it seems as if he has dealt lovingly with the land."

Tatzel looked about with no great interest.

Half an hour later, while riding through a grove of oak trees, they surprised a young boar rooting for acorns. Aillas instantly nocked an arrow to his bow, and said: "Spirifiume, if yonder beast is of special value to you, cause the boar to jump aside or, if you prefer, divert my arrow." He let the arrow fly, and it struck deep into the heart of the boar.

Aillas dismounted and, while Tatzel looked fastidiously in another direction, he did what needed to be done and presently came away with the choicest parts strung on a twig for convenience of transport.

Mindful of Cwyd's third information, Aillas called out: "Spirifiume, we thank you for your bounty!" . . . . Aillas blinked. Something had happened. What? A twinkling of a hundred colours across the sunlight? A whisper of a hundred soft chords? He looked at Tatzel. "Did you notice anything?"

"A crow flew past."

"No colours? No sound?"

"None."

Once more they set off, and entered a forest. Noticing a clump of morels growing soft and graceful in the shade, Aillas pulled up his horse and dismounted. He signalled to Tatzel. "Come. You no longer have the excuse of a tender leg. Help me gather mushrooms."

Tatzel wordlessly joined him, and for a space they picked mushrooms: morels, delicate shaggy-manes, golden chanterelles, pepper-tops, savory young field mushrooms.

Again Aillas acknowledged Spirifiume's bounty, and the two rode onward.

With the sun still two hours high they arrived at the edge of the brake, with a steep and difficult descent below. Lake Quyvern now dominated the landscape to the north. A dozen forested islets rose from the surface and on two of these the ruins of two ancient castles faced each other across a mile of water. The air between them seemed to quiver with the memory of a thousand adventures: griefs and delights, romantic yearnings and dreadful deeds, treacheries by night and gallantries by day.

Aillas found within himself no inclination to scramble down yet another slope on this day. Cwyd had recommended the third brake for an overnight camp, and the advice seemed good. Aillas turned away from the edge and rode to a little meadow where a stream trickled from the forest; here he decided to camp.

Dismounting, he dug a shallow trench in which he built a fire of dry oak. To the side he arranged the meat on a spit, where it might roast and drip into the pannikin, with Tatzel turning the spit as needful. The drippings in the pannikin would later be used to fry the mushrooms, which Tatzel also had been ordered to clean and cut. Glumly accepting reality, she set to work.

Aillas staked out the horses, set up the tent and gathered grass for a bed, then, returning to the fire, sat with his back to a laurel tree with the wine sack ready to hand.

Tatzel knelt beside the fire, her black locks tied back with a ribbon. Thinking back to his time at Castle Sank, Aillas tried to remember his first sight of Tatzel: then a slender creature of thoughtless assurance walking with long swaggering strides by reason of natural verve.

Aillas sighed. Upon a heartsick young man, Tatzel, with her fascinating face and jaunty vitality, had made a deep impression.

And now? He watched her as she worked. Her assurance had been replaced by sullen unhappiness, and the bitter facts of her present existence had taken the luster from her verve.

Tatzel felt the pressure of his attention and turned a quick glance over her shoulder. "Why do you look at me so?"

"An idle whim."

Tatzel looked back to the fire. "Sometimes I suspect you of madness."

" 'Madness'?" Aillas considered the word. "How so?"

"There would seem no other reason for your hatred of me."

Aillas laughed. "I feel no such hatred." He drank from the wine-sack. "Tonight I am kindly disposed; in fact, I see that I owe you a debt of gratitude."

"That debt is easily paid. You may give me a horse and let me go my way."

"In this wild country? I would be doing you no favor. My gratitude, moreover, is indirect. You have earned it despite yourself."

Tatzel muttered: "Again the madness comes on you."

Aillas raised the wine-sack and drank. He offered the sack to Tatzel, who disdainfully shook her head. Aillas drank again from a sack now sadly flabby. "My remarks are probably somewhat opaque. I will explain. At Castle Sank I became enamored of a certain Tatzel, who in some respects resembled you, but who was essentially an imaginary creature. This phantom which lived in my mind possessed qualities which I thought must be innate to a creature of such grace and intelligence.

"Ah well, I escaped from Sank and went my way, encumbered still with this phantom, which now only served to distort my perceptions. At last I returned to South Ulfland.

"Almost by chance my most far-fetched daydreams were realized, and I was able to capture you: the real Tatzel. So then — what of the phantom?" Aillas paused to drink, tilting the wine-sack high. "This impossibly delightful creature is gone, and now is even hard to remember. Tatzel exists, of course, and she has freed me from the tyranny of my imagination, and here is the source of my gratitude."

Tatzel, after a single brief side-glance, turned back to the fire. She rearranged the spit, where the roasting pork exhaled a splendid odor. She prepared batter for griddlecakes, then started the mushrooms to fry in the drippings from the roasting pork, while Aillas went to gather a salad of watercress from the stream.

In due course the pork was done to a turn; the two dined on the best the land could afford. "Spirifiume!" called Aillas. "Be assured that we take great pleasure in your bounty, and we thank you for your hospitality! I drink to your continued health!"

Spirifiume gave back neither flux of colour nor whisper of sound, but when Aillas went to lift the wine-sack, which had arrived at a state of discouraging flatness, he found that it bulged to its fullest capacity. Aillas tasted the wine; it was soft and sweet and tart and fresh, at one and the same time. He cried out: "Spirifiume! You are a god after my own heart! Should you ever tire of North Ulfland, please establish yourself in Troicinet!"

The sun still illuminated the panorama. Tatzel came to sit under the tree and idly picking little blue daisies, strung them into a chain. Suddenly she spoke. "I have been thinking of what you told me. . . . I feel a whole torrent of emotions! Because you brooded over your daydreams, I all unwittingly must suffer! Discomforts, dangers, indignities — I have known them all! Even though at Sank I spoke never a word to you —"

"Ah, but you did! After a trifle of sword-play with your brother! And do you not recall stopping in the gallery to talk with me?"

Tatzel looked blank. "Was that you? . . . I barely noticed. Still, no matter how closely I resembled your illusion, the realities remain."

"And what are they?"

"I am Ska; you are Otherling. Even in dreams, your ideas are unthinkable."

"Apparently so." Aillas looked back across his memories. "Had I known you better at Castle Sank, I might never have troubled to capture you. The joke is on both of us. But again, no matter. You are you and I am I. The phantom is gone."

Tatzel took up the wine-sack and drank. Then, raising to her knees, and sitting back on her heels, she swung around to face squarely upon Aillas, displaying for almost the first time the animation of the old Tatzel. She spoke with fervour: "You are so wonderfully wrong-headed I can almost find it within myself to laugh at you! After chasing me over the moors, breaking my leg and causing me a dozen humiliations, you expect me to come creeping to you with adoration in my eyes, happy to be your slave, soliciting your caress, hoping with all my heart that I may compare favorably with your erotic daydream. You profess to find the Ska lacking in pathos, but your conduct toward me is absolutely self-serving! And now you sulk because I do not come sobbing to you and begging for your indulgence. Is it not a farce?"

Aillas heaved a deep sigh. "Everything you say is true. In all justice, I must admit as much. I have been driven by romantic passion to act out a dream. I will say this, with only glancing reference to the fact that the Ska made me their slave and that I am entitled to retaliation: you are a prisoner of war. Had the Ska not taken our town Suarach, we would not have attacked Castle Sank. If you had submitted at once to capture, you would not have broken your leg, nor been exposed to humiliation, nor isolated here on the moors with me."

"Bah! In my place, would you have done other than try to escape?"

"No. In my place, would you have done other than try to capture me?"

Tatzel looked at him for a full five seconds. "No. . . . Still, prisoner of war or slave or whatever, I am Ska and you are Otherling, and that is the way of it."

III

In the morning, while packing the wine-sack, Aillas found it bulging full as if it had never been broached, and he gave a most fervent thanks to the genial god Spirifiume for what would seem an incalculable treasure. After ordering the campsite with meticulous care, out of respect for their host, Aillas and Tatzel set off down the slope. There was an easier quality to their relationship, as if the air had been cleared, though cameraderie was still lacking.

The slope was steep, the brambles and thickets troublesome, but in due course they came down upon the fourth brake: the narrowest and most heavily forested of all the brakes, and in some areas less than half a mile in width. Tall trees: maple, chestnut, ash, oak, held high green umbrellas of foliage to shroud the brake in sun-flecked shadow.

Cwyd had ignored the fourth brake in his informations; Aillas, therefore, had no reason to dread some imminent danger. Still, an odd and troubling odor hung in the air, of a sort Aillas found both mystifying and, at a primordial level, frightening, the more so since he could not identify it.

Tatzel looked about with a puzzled expression, glanced at Aillas; then, observing his own perplexity, she said nothing.

The horses, taking note of the odor, jerked their heads and sidled stiff-legged, adding to Aillas' uneasiness. He pulled up and searched the forest aisles in all directions, but found only shaded ground, carpeted with dead leaves and dappled with morning sunlight.

Aillas bestirred himself; nothing could be gained by delay. He shook the reins and once more the party set off across the brake.

They rode through an uncanny quiet. Aillas watched warily to right and left, and twisted in the saddle to look back the way they had come. He saw nothing. Tatzel, absorbed in her own thoughts, rode with her gaze directed between the ears of her horse, at a point in the middle distance, and ignored Aillas' tension.

For ten minutes they rode through the silence; sunlight, filtering through foliage, working odd tricks on the vision. Suddenly a remarkable illusion appeared to Aillas so that he sucked in his breath, blinked and stared with bulging eyes. . . . Illusion? No illusion whatever! Two great creatures fifteen feet tall watched placidly from a distance of barely thirty yards. They stood on squat yellow legs, of human conformation. The torsos and arms might have been those of monstrous gray-yellow bears. Stiff yellow bristles surrounded the round heads, producing an effect much like enormous yellow satin pincushions, with no discernible facial features. Here, clearly, was the source of the stench.

The creatures stood motionless, their bristling great heads turned— toward Aillas and Tatzel? Hairs prickled at the back of Aillas' neck; these were not ogres or giants, or anything else of this world, nor would they seem to be demons. They were things beyond both knowledge and hearsay, and they would haunt his memory for a very long time. Tatzel, riding ahead, observed not the silent creatures, nor did she hear Aillas' startled gasp.

The creatures passed from sight; Aillas kicked his heels into the flanks of his horse and took his troop loping through the forest; the horses needed no urging.

A few moments later they arrived at the edge of the brake and there discovered a trail which led them by an easy route down to the fifth brake, across and down the final slope to the shores of Lake Quyvern. Here the trail met the shoreside road and once more they had returned to the society of men.

Along the eastern shore grew a thick pine forest; to the west were coves and rocky headlands. Two hundred yards ahead appeared a huddle of timber structures, including a hospice, or an inn.

As Aillas and Tatzel rode along the road they came upon a boatwright's workshop at the water's edge and, nearby, a dock to which were moored half a dozen small boats.

Out on the lake, a skiff approached the dock, sculled by a tall thin man with a long pallid face and lank black hair hanging to his shoulders. He brought the skiff close to the dock, made fast the painter, lifted out a basket of fish and stepped ashore. Here he paused to survey Aillas, Tatzel and their four horses with a slow and measured gaze.

The fisherman brought his catch to the road where he set down the basket and addressed Aillas in a deep voice: "Travellers, whence have you come and where do you go?"

Aillas replied: "We have come a goodly distance, over the moors from South Ulfland. Our destination will be decreed by Tshansin, Goddess of Beginnings and Endings, who walks on wheels."

The fisherman showed a smile of mildly amused contempt. "That is pagan superstition. I am not by nature a proselyter, but, truly, a unified wisdom rules the Tricosm, seeping from the roots of the Foundation Oak Kahaurok, to form the stars in the sky."

"That is the belief of the druids," said Aillas. "It would seem that your own thinking is based on Druid doctrine."

"There is a single Truth."

"Perhaps someday I will look more deeply into the matter," said Aillas. "At the moment I am interested in yonder inn, if such it be."

"The house you see is Kernuun's Antler, and I am Dildahl, keeper of the house, which I maintain for the Arch-druids on their peregrinations out to the sacred places. Still, if wayfarers are prepared to pay my charges, I will extend them very comfortable facilities."

"What might be the order of these charges? Are they dear or modest? It is well to know such things in advance."

"All in all, my charges are fair. They vary from item to item, as might be expected. Lodging for the two of you in a private chamber equipped with pallets of clean straw and ewers of fresh water, I value at two copper pennies. A supper of lentils and bread, with a breakfast of porridge will cost another penny. Other dishes command higher prices. I serve excellent quail, four to the spit, for two copper pennies. A generous cut off a haunch of venison, with barley, currants, apples and nuts, is valued similarly. Fish is sold according to the season and the supply."

"I have heard that certain of your charges are exorbitant," said Aillas. "Still, these quotations are not unreasonable."

"In this regard you must make your own assessment. In the past I have been victimized by swindlers and impoverished guttricks, so I have learned to protect myself from indigence." Dildahl lifted his basket of fish. "Will I expect you then at the Antler?"

"I must consider the contents of my wallet," said Aillas. "I am not by any means a wealthy Arch-druid, to whom a handful of coppers is like an equal number of acorns."

Dildahl appraised the horses. "Still, you ride sound and valuable steeds."

"Ah, but these horses are all of value that I own."

Dildahl shrugged and departed.

IV

By the time Aillas completed his transactions along the lakeshore the time was late afternoon. All wind had left the sky; the lake lay flat as a mirror, with each of the islands reflected in duplicate below.

After considering sky, lake and landscape, Aillas told Tatzel: "It seems that we must entrust ourselves to the mercies of the voracious Dildahl. Restraint may be necessary, since I carry no large store of coins on my person. What of you?"

"I have nothing."

"With ordinary caution, we should fare well enough, even though there is something about Dildahl which arouses my distrust."

The two presented themselves to the common room of Kernuun's Antler, where Dildahl, now attired in a white apron and a white cap which to some extent confined his long black locks, seemed gratified to see them. "For a time I thought that you had decided to proceed on your way."

"We transacted a trifle of business, and then remembered the comforts of the Antler. Hence, you see us now."

"So be it! I can offer a suite of rooms customarily occupied by the most august of the druids, complete with baths of warm water and soap of olive oil, should you feel inclined to a measure of luxury—"

"Still at a cost of two copper pennies? If so—"

"There is a substantial difference in the rate," said Dildahl.

Aillas felt in his wallet and rattled the few coins which he found there. "We must moderate our desires to our means. I would not wish to lodge and dine like a priest and then find myself embarassed when it came time to pay the tally."

Dildahl said: "In this regard, I usually insist that unreferenced guests post a declaration of surety with me, just precisely to avoid any awkward dilemmas. Please sign this paper." So saying, Dildahl tendered a sheet of good parchment inscribed in a fine hand with the notification:

Be It Hereby Known That I, Who am the undersigned, now propose to take food and lodging for myself and my entourage at that inn known as Kernuun's Antler, of which the Honourable Dildahl is the landlord. I agree to pay the proper and designated charges for chamberage, and also for such food and drink as may be consumed by me and my entourage. As surety for the payment of these charges, I offer those horses now in my possession, together with their saddles, bridles, and other furniture. If I do not pay the charges stipulated on the account rendered by Dildahl said horses and adjuncts become the property of Dildahl in fee whole and simple.

Aillas frowned. "This declaration has a somewhat menacing tone."

"It could alarm only a person who planned to avoid payment of his debt. Are you this sort of person? If so, I have no interest in placing before you the goods of my kitchen and the comforts of my rooms."

"That is fairly said," remarked Aillas. "However, I could not sleep well unless I added a small proviso. Give me your pen."

"What do you intend to write?" demanded Dildahl in suspicion.

"You shall see." Aillas inscribed an addendum:

This document shall not be held to encompass the clothes worn by Aillas and his companion, nor their weapons, personal effects, ornaments, wine-sacks, keepsakes or other possessions.

Aillas of Troicinet

Dildahl scrutinized the addendum, shrugged, and placed the parchment under the counter. "Come; I will show you to your chamber."

Dildahl took them to a pair of large pleasant rooms with windows overlooking the lake, and a separate bathroom. Aillas asked: "For these rooms the charge is two pennies?"

"Of course not!" declared Dildahl in astonishment. "I understood that you wished to test the luxury of the Antler!"

"Only at a price of two pennies."

Dildahl scowled. "The cheap chamber is dank, and furthermore is not ready."

"Dildahl, if you wish to hold me to payment of my account, then I must hold you to the charges quoted by you."

"Bah!" muttered Dildahl, drooping his loose lower lip to show a purple maw. "For my own convenience, you may occupy these rooms for three pennies."

"Please render that quotation in writing, here and now, to avoid later misunderstanding." Then, as he watched Dildahl writing: "No, no! Not three pennies apiece! Three pennies in total!"

"You are a troublesome guest," muttered Dildahl. "There is little profit in serving such as you."

"A man can spend only what he can afford! If he over-reaches, he loses his horses!"

Dildahl only grunted. "When will you dine?"

"As soon as we freshen ourselves in this convenient bath."

"For such a price, I include no hot water."

"Ah well! Since we have incurred your displeasure, cold water must be our lot!"

Dildahl turned away. "It is only your petty frugality which I find reprehensible."

"I hope you will instruct us in the ways of open-handed bounty when we take our supper."

"We shall see," said Dildahl.

At supper the two sat alone in the common room except for a pair of brown-cloaked druids bending low over their food in a corner of the room. They finished their meal and came to the counter to pay the score. Aillas strolled across the room and stood by as each laid down a copper penny and departed.

Dildahl was somewhat annoyed by Aillas' proximity to the transaction. "Well then? What will you eat?"

"What is on your board tonight?"

"The lentil soup is burned, and is off."

"The druids appeared to be eating fine brown trout. You may fry us a pair of these, with a salad of cress and garden stuff. What were the druids eating in their side dish?"

"That was my specialty: crayfish tails with eggs and mustard."

"You may also serve us such a side dish, with some good bread and butter, and perhaps a fruit conserve."

Dildahl bowed. "At your order. Will you drink wine?"

"You may bring us a flask of whatever wine you deem a good value for the price, but at all times, please keep our parsimony in mind. We are as niggardly as druids."

Aillas and Tatzel were served a dinner with which they could find no fault and Dildahl seemed almost civil. Tatzel eyed him with foreboding. "He seems to be making a large number of marks on his board."

"He can mark until doomsday for all of me. If he becomes insolent, you need only announce that you are Lady Tatzel of Castle Sank, and instantly he will moderate his manner. I know his kind."

"I thought that I was now Tatzel the slave-girl."

Aillas chuckled. "True! Your protests might not carry weight, after all."

The two retired and went to their couches; the night passed without incident.

In the morning they ate a breakfast of porridge, bacon and eggs. Aillas then, counting on his fingers, arrived at what he considered a fair reckoning for the hospitality provided by Dildahl: a sum of ten copper pennies, or a silver half-florin.

Aillas went to the counter to pay the score; here Dildahl, rubbing his hands briskly together, presented him a statement of charges, the grand total of which was three silver florins and fourpence.

Aillas laughed and tossed back the statement. "I do not even intend to argue with you. Here is a silver half-florin, with an extra two pennies because the mustard was good. I now offer you this sum in payment; will you accept it?"

"Certainly not!" declared Dildahl, his face flushing red and his lax lower lip drooping.

"Then I will take the money back, and we will bid you good-day."

"Do you think to alarm me?" roared Dildahl. "I have your pledge at this moment next to my very hand! You have refused to pay my charges; therefore I claim ownership of your horses."

Aillas and Tatzel turned away from the counter. "Claim all you like," said Aillas. "I own no horses. Yesterday, before our arrival, I traded them for a boat. Dildahl, farewell!"

V

THE BOAT WAS A CLINKER-PLANK SKIFF fifteen feet long with copper-riveted seams, a sprit-sail, lee-boards and a rudder swung off the transom in the new manner.

Aillas rowed the skiff out into the lake, raised the sail to a morning breeze from the west and the boat scudded northward down the lake with the wake gurgling behind.

Tatzel made herself comfortable in the bow, and Aillas thought that she seemed to be enjoying the freshness of the morning. Presently she looked over her shoulder: "Now where are you bound?"

"As before, to Dun Cruighre in Godelia."

"Is that close to Xounges?"

"Xounges is immediately across the Skyre."

Tatzel said no more. Aillas wondered as to her interest but forebore to ask.

For two days they sailed the lake, passing the twelve Druid islets, and discovering on one a giant crow built of wickerwork, which provoked Tatzel's wonder. Aillas told her: "In the fall, on the eve of the day they call 'Suaurghille', they will set the crow afire and conduct a great orgy below. Inside the crow will burn two dozen of their enemies. If we set foot on the island we would burn with the others. Sometimes it will be a horse, or a man, or a bear, or a bull."

At its northern end the lake became shallow and choked with reeds, but at length spilled out to become the head-waters of the River Solander. Three days later Aillas looked ahead to see the bluffs which flanked the Solander Estuary. On the right was the Kingdom of Dahaut; on the left, North Ulfland still.

The estuary opened into the Skyre, and the skiff rode over larger waves than it might have liked, and far larger than Tatzel found comfortable, while the scent of salt water hung in the air. With the wind blowing brisk from the west, the skiff plunged ahead at four or five knots, throwing back cold spray, to add to Tatzel's discomfort.

Ahead, on the left, at the end of a stony peninsula, rose the fortified town Xounges; on the right now was Godelia, the land of the Celts, and at last Dun Cruighre came into view.

Aillas looked along the docks and to his delight discovered not only a large Troice cargo cog, but also one of his new warships.

Aillas sailed the skiff up to the side the warship. The sailors on deck looked curiously down. One called: "Ahoy there, fellow! Stand clear! What do you think you are up to?"

Aillas called up: "Drop me a ladder and call the captain."

A ladder was lowered; Aillas made fast the skiff, steadied the ladder while Tatzel climbed to the deck, then he too followed. By this time the capain had appeared. Aillas took him aside. "Sir, do you recognize me?"

The captain looked hard, and his eyes widened. "Your Majesty! What do you here in this condition?"

"It is a long story which I will tell you presently. For now, know me merely as 'Aillas', no more. I am, so to speak, incognito."

"Just as you say, sir."

"The lady is Ska and under my protection. See if you can find her a place of privacy; let her bathe and give her clean clothes; she has been sick for three days now and would as soon die as live."

"At once, sir! And you will be wanting something of the same, I take it?"

"If it is not too inconvenient for you, I would welcome a bath and a change of clothes."

"My convenience, sir, is not to be considered. Our facilities are not luxurious, but they are yours to command."

"Thank you, but first: what is the news from South Ulfland?"

"I can only give a third-hand report, but it is said that a Ska army from Suarach was caught in the open country by one of our armies. There was a great battle of a sort which will long be remembered. The Ska were sorely beset, and then another of our armies marching down from the east struck them from the rear and they were destroyed. I am told that Suarach is once more an Ulf city."

"And all this occurred during my absence," said Aillas. "It appears that I am not as indispensable as I would like to think."

"As to that, sir, I cannot say. We have been sailing the Narrow Sea, interdicting the Ska, and we have caused them great trouble. We are here now only to take on supplies. In fact, we were close upon casting off when you came aboard."

"What of King Gax across the way in Xounges? Is he still alive?"

"It is said that he is finally dying and a Ska puppet will be the next king; that is the news which has come to us."

"Hold off your departure, if you will, and also show me where I can clean myself."

Half an hour later, Aillas encountered Tatzel in the captain's cabin. She had discarded her old garments, bathed and now wore a gown of dark maroon linen which one of the seamen had been sent ashore to buy in the market. She came slowly close to Aillas and put her hands on his shoulders. "Aillas, take me, if you please, to Xounges and put me ashore on the dock! My father is now there on a special mission. I want nothing so much as to join him." Tatzel searched Aillas' face. "You are not truly an unkind man! I implore you, let me go free! I can offer you nothing but my body which you seem not to want, but you may have me now, and gladly, if you will deliver me to Xounges! Or if you want none of me, my father will reward you!"

"Indeed!" said Aillas. "How?"

"First, he will remit your slavery forever; you need never fear recapture! He will give you gold, enough that you may take up a piece of land in Troicinet, and never know want."

Aillas, looking into the mournful face, could not resist a laugh. "Tatzel, you are most persuasive. We shall go to Xounges."

Chapter 13

I

WHILE AILLAS with his unsatisfactory slave Tatzel traversed the wilds of North Ulfland, events elsewhere about the Elder Isles were not therefore held in abeyance.

At Lyonesse Town, Queen Sollace and her spiritual adviser Father Umphred inspected drawings for the prospective cathedral which they hoped might rear a magnificent façade above the end of the Chale and bring an ecstasy of religious awe upon all who saw it.

Queen Sollace, should the cathedral be built, had been assured of sanctification and eternal bliss by Father Umphred, whose own rewards would be somewhat more modest: the Archbishopric of the Lyonesse Diocese.

In view of King Casmir's obdurate resistance, Queen Sollace had become less confident in her hopes. Father Umphred, time and time again, reassured her: "Dear lady, dear lady! Never allow the shades of despair to mar the regal beauty of your cheeks! Discouragement? Expel the word: down, down, down! Into the odious quagmire of guilt, heresy and vice where wallow the benighted folk of this world!"

Sollace sighed. "Your words are good to hear, but virtue alone, even when joined with a thousand prayers and tears of holy passion, will not melt the soul of Casmir."

"Not so, dear lady! I have words to whisper in the ear of King Casmir which might mean two or even four cathedrals! But they must be whispered at the proper moment!"

Father Umphred's encouragement was nothing new; he had hinted in this manner on other occasions, and Queen Sollace had learned to control her curiosity with a sniff and a toss of the head.

As for King Casmir, he wanted no dilution of his authority. His subjects espoused a great variety of beliefs: Zoroastrianism, a whiff or

238

two of Christianity, Pantheism, Druidical doctrine, a few fragments of classic Roman theology, somewhat more of the Gothic system, all on a substratum of ancient animism and Pelasgian Mysteries. Such a melange of religions suited King Casmir well; he wanted nothing to do with an orthodoxy deriving from Rome, and Sollace's talk of a cathedral had become a vexation.

At Falu Ffail in Avallon, King Audry sat with his feet in a basin of warm soapy water, in preparation for the royal pedicure, meanwhile listening to despatches from sources near and far, as read by Malrador, the under-chamberlain entrusted with this thankless task.

King Audry was especially distressed by the news from Sir Lavrilan dal Ponzo, who, at King Audry's orders and using tactics suggested by two of Audry's intimates, Sir Arthemus and Sir Gligory, had conducted a grand sortie into Wysrod, where he had been repulsed by the Celts.

Sir Lavrilan earnestly requested reinforcements, and cited the need for light cavalry and archers; the pikemen and young knights recommended by Arthemus and Gligory had fared poorly against the boisterous Celts.

King Audry sat back into the cushions of his chair, and threw his hands high in disgust. "What went wrong this time? I am baffled by these ineptitudes! No, Malrador, I will hear no more! Already you have soured my day with your croaking; sometimes I suspect that you enjoy making me miserable!"

"Your Majesty!" cried Malrador. "How can you think that of me? I do my duty, no more! And, respectfully, I urge that you hear this last despatch; it came in only an hour ago from the marches. It seems that notable events are afoot in the Ulflands, regarding which your Majesty must be apprised."

King Audry surveyed Malrador through half-closed eyelids, his head thrown back into the cushions. "Often I toy with the notion of requiring you not only to read the despatches, but also to answer them, thus sparing me the vexation."

At this humourous sally, Sir Arthemus and Sir Gligory, sitting nearby, gave appreciative chuckles.

Malrador bowed. "Sire, I would never dare to so presume. This then is the news from Sir Samfire of the marches." Malrador went on to read the despatch, which told of Troice and Ulfish successes against the Ska. Sir Samfire went on to make recommendations, using language which aroused King Audry to forget the situation and stamp his feet. Two maidens and the barber came running to remove the basin and prop Audry's feet on a cushioned stool, so that the pedicure might proceed. The barber said politely: "Sire, I suggest that you hold your feet motionless while I am cutting your toenails."

Audry muttered: "Yes, yes. . . . I am astonished by Samfire's language! Does he think to dictate my strategies?"

Arthemus and Gligory clicked their tongues and made sounds of perturbation. Malrador incautiously said: "Your Majesty, I believe that Samfire merely attempts to put the significance of the events into clear perspective, for your maximum information."

"Ta-ta-ta, Malrador! Now you take his part against me! These are distant events, beyond the marches, and all the while we are mocked by these infuriating Celts! They lack all awe of great Dahaut! Bah! They must be punished. I will drown them in their own blood, since that seems to be their choice. Arthemus? Gligory? Why are we so bedevilled? Answer me that! By boors and lumpkins smelling of cow! What is the explanation?"

Arthemus and Gligory made indignant gestures and pulled at their mustaches. King Audry turned bitterly back to Malrador. "Well then, you have had your way; now are you done? Always you bring me worries when I am least in the mood to deal with them!"

"Sire, it is my task to read the despatches. If I concealed unfavorable news from you, then indeed you would have cause to reprimand me."

King Audry heaved a sigh. "That is true enough. Malrador, you are a faithful fellow! Go, and write these words on parchment: 'Sir Lavrilan dal Ponzo: we extend our best regards! It is time that you wiped the butter from your chin and, perhaps by example, inculcated your troops with a mood of full pugnacity! Only last month you assured me that we would break the heads of a thousand Celtic fools; what fol-de-rol will you tell me next?' Then affix my seal, subscribe my signature and send off this despatch by fast courier."

"Very good, sire. It shall be done, and your reprimand shall be effected."

"It is more than a mere reprimand, Malrador! It is an order! I want to see Celtic heads grinning from the ends of our pikes; I want the might of Dahaut to send these buffoons flying and hopping like frightened rabbits!"

Malrador said gravely: "Sir Arthemus and Sir Gligory command crack brigades; why restrain their fire? They are both spoiling for a good fight!"

Arthemus and Gligory clapped their hands as if in enthusiasm. "Well said, Malrador! Go now and stir up Sir Lavrilan while we discuss affairs with his Highness!"

As soon as Malrador had departed, Arthemus and Gligory soothingly explained away the latest debacle in Wysrod, and turned the conversation to more pleasant subjects, and the three immersed themselves in plans for the entertainment of King Adolphe of Aquitaine, and so went affairs in Dahaut.

In other parts of the Elder Isles, Torqual, by sheer force of will resurrected himself from the edge of death. In her villa on the beach near Ys, Melancthe thought unfathomable thoughts. At Swer Smod and Trilda respectively, Murgen and Shimrod kept to their manses, and occupied themselves with their researches. Tamurello, however, was absent from Faroli, and according to the magician Raught Raven, had taken himself to the peak of a high mountain in Ethiopia, for a period of meditation.

And the Green Pearl? A pair of young goblins, coming upon Manting's naked white skeleton, played games with the bones: kicking the skull back and forth, wearing the pelvis as a helmet, and throwing the vertebrae at a party of dryads, who quickly climbed into the trees and taunted the goblins in sweet high voices.

Forest mold covered the pearl ever deeper. So passed the summer and autumn and winter. With the coming of spring, seeds began to germinate in that area close upon the buried pearl. Young plants sent up shoots, which grew with unusual vigor, sending out a profusion of lush leaves followed by wonderful flowers, each different from the rest and like no other flower ever seen before.

II

XOUNGES HAD BEEN A FORTIFIED PLACE since before the beginning of history. The town occupied a flat-topped knob of stone bounded on three sides by cliffs rising a sheer two hundred feet from the water. On the fourth side a narrow saddle of granite something over a hundred yards long connected the town with the mainland.

The Ulfland of four centuries ago had been a powerful kingdom, comprising both North and South Ulfland (though not Ys or the Vale of Evander), Godelia and what were now the Marches of Dahaut, out past Poëlitetz. At this time King Fidwig, in the full exercise of his megalomaniac might, decreed the total security of Xounges. Ten thousand men toiled twenty years, to achieve a system of fortifications based on walls of granite forty feet wide at the base and a hundred and twenty feet high, closing the causeway at its narrowest width, again where the causeway entered the town, then hooking out into the Skyre to protect the harbor from attack by sea.

Almost as an afterthought, King Fidwig ordained a palace, and Jehaundel was built to a scale as prodigious as the walls of Xounges.

Much reduced from its old magnificence, Xounges remained as secure against attack as ever. The aristocracy had maintained tall stone town-houses; and formed the nucleus of the small army which defended the city from the Ska.

Jehaundel, now the palace of King Gax, showed a massive façade to the market square, but, like the palaces of the lesser nobility, made no pretense of ancient glory. The wings were closed off, as were the upper floors save for the suite used by King Gax: a dreary set of chambers carpeted with woven rushes and furnished with massive pieces scarred by the hard usage of centuries. Fuel was an item of expense; the bedroom where King Gax lay dying was warmed only minimally by a mean little smolder of turves.

In his prime Gax had been a man of noteworthy stature and strong physique. For thirty years, while the Ska advanced their black battalions, first into the Foreshore, then across North Ulfland, his rule had gone badly. He had fought hard and suffered wounds, but the Ska were relentless. They destroyed his forces and crushed three proud Daut armies fighting under a treaty of mutual assistance. At last the Ska drove Gax to bay, behind the walls of Xounges. Stalemate came into being. The Ska were powerless to strike at him; and he could exert even less pressure against the Ska.

From time to time Ska emissaries brought Gax lukewarm offers of amnesty, if he would open the gates of Xounges and abdicate in favor of the Ska designate. Gax rejected all such overtures, in the wistful hope that King Audry might once again honour the ancient pact and send a great army to drive the Ska into the sea.

In this policy he was generally supported by his subjects, who saw no advantage for themselves under Ska rule. Sir Kreim, next of the royal succession, also endorsed Gax's intransigence, if for reasons quite at variance with Gax's own. Sir Kreim was a burly heavy-faced man of middle maturity, with black hair, lowering black brows and a short curling black beard in stark contrast to the pallor of his complexion. His appetites were large; his tastes were coarse; his ambitions were unbridled. When he himself assumed the throne, he hoped to use the office for his best personal advantage, either through alliance with the Ska, or abdication at a price which would afford him a luxurious estate in Dahaut.

Time passed and King Gax was unconscionably slow about his dying. If rumor were to be believed, Sir Kreim contained his impatience only by dint of great effort and perhaps had even considered methods to hasten the natural processes.

The chamberlain Rohan, upon learning that Sir Kreim had shown great favor to a pair of the guards outside King Gax's bedchamber, ordered new dead-bolts affixed to the doors and reassigned the guards to permanent night duty on the outer parapets, where rain and storm were merely signals for augmented vigilance. Rohan also devised a system which guaranteed that King Gax's food was the most wholesome in all Xounges; each of the kitchen cooks was required to eat of Gax's food before it was served.

Sir Kreim, taking note of the precautions, congratulated Rohan for his fidelity and grimly set himself to wait for King Gax to die at his own pace.

Meanwhile, the stalemate persisted. King Audry not only failed to succor his ally King Gax; the Ska insolently drove into Dahaut and occupied the fort Poëlitetz. In outrage King Audry issued a series of ever more emphatic protests, then warnings, then threats. The Ska paid no heed, and King Audry finally turned his attention elsewhere. In due course he would assemble an invincible army, with a hundred carriages of war, a thousand knights in full regalia, and ten thousand valiant men-at-arms. In a magnificent glitter of sharp steel and silver crests, with banderoles streaming overhead, the great army would fall upon the Ska and send them reeling and skreeking into the sea; and Audry sent King Gax a document asserting his firm decision in this regard.

King Gax seldom stirred from his bed. He could sense the ebbing of his vitality, and sometimes thought to feel the passing of hours and minutes as if they were grains of sand in an hour-glass. His face, once ruddy, was drawn and gray, but his eyes still burned with the smoky yellow gleam of intelligence. He lay motionless, propped up on a pillow, arms arranged on the coverlet, and spent long hours watching the flicker of fire on the hearth.

Occasionally, under Rohan's watchful eye, he conferred with his staff and received visitors, including a deputation of high-ranking Ska: the Dukes Luhalcx and Ankhalcx, and an entourage of lesser lords. While they spoke bluntly and to the point, they conducted themselves with all propriety, and King Gax could find no fault with their general behavior.

During the Ska's first audience with King Gax, necessarily in his bedroom, Sir Kreim and two others were also in attendance. Duke Luhalcx stated the deputation's business: "Your Highness, we regret to find you unwell, but all men die, and it appears that your time is close upon you."

King Gax managed a weary smile. "While life remains, I live."

Duke Luhalcx bowed curtly in acknowledgment. "I intended the comment only as a step-board for the burden of my message, which I now state. The Ska nation rules North Ulfland, and intends to restore the ancient glory. We will expand our power: first to the south, then to the east. The city Xounges is a nuisance to us: a stone in our path. We must guard its approaches lest the Dauts attempt a reinforcement, which would place an enemy force full on our flank and threaten our control of Poëlitetz. We want both the city Xounges and the titular rule of North Ulfland, that we may rescind the treaty with Dahaut. With our flank secure, we are free to subjugate South Ulfland, where the new king is becoming obstreperous."

"I am not interested in expediting your conquests. To the contrary."

"Still, you die, and events will pass you by. There is no royal prince in the statutory line of succession — "

Here Sir Kreim indignantly thrust himself forward. "Absurd and incorrect! I am in the direct line of succession, and I shall be the next king of North Ulfland!"

Duke Luhalcx smiled. "We understand your ambitions very well, since you have communicated them to us on several occasions already. We intend to buy neither Xounges nor the title from you." He turned back to King Gax, who had watched the interchange with a wintry smile. "Your Highness, we request that you immediately anoint our designate as the king of North Ulfland."

Sir Kreim cried out: "Your Majesty, the insolence of this proposal is exceeded only by its cold-blooded arrogance! We obviously reject it with indignation!"

Duke Luhalcx paid him no heed. "We will thereupon grant you and all present inhabitants of this place amnesty for acts committed to our detriment and we will confiscate neither wealth nor property. Will you agree to this proposal?"

"Certainly not!" declared Sir Kreim.

Gax spoke in irritation: "Sir Kreim, please allow me to formulate my own responses." He turned back to Duke Luhalcx. "We have survived the displeasure of the Ska for many years. Why should we not continue to do so?"

"You can assure this policy only while you live. Upon your death, Sir Kreim, should he become king, will attempt to extort treasure from us. Our easiest recourse is to pay, then recover this treasure by a levy upon all the folk of Xounges. I assure you that not one groat of Sir Kreim's fee will come from our own coffers."

"There would be no negotiations!" snapped Sir Kreim. "On this I am firm! But if there were, you would be forced to stipulate financial as well as physical amnesty for our entire population!"

King Gax spoke sharply: "Sir Kreim, I have heard enough of your interpolations! You may leave the room at once!"

Sir Kreim bowed and departed.

King Gax asked: "Suppose the next king for a fact continued my policies: what then?"

"I do not care to reveal all the details of our plans. Suffice it to say, we would feel that we must take Xounges by force."

"If this is so simple, why have you not done so before?"

Duke Luhalcx considered a moment, then said: "I will tell you this: we do not regard Xounges as impregnable. If we decide upon siege, then you will know a total blockade and full deprivation. Rain will be your only drink, and grass your only meat. If we were to take Xounges by force, and if a single precious Ska life were lost, every man, woman and child in Xounges would know the shackles of slavery."

King Gax made a flickering gesture of frail white fingers. "Go. I will consider my opportunities."

Duke Luhalcx bowed and the deputation departed.

A week later the Ska returned. Sir Kreim was again present, on condition that he maintain full silence, unless his opinions were solicitied.

Duke Luhalcx presented his compliments to King Gax, and asked: "Your Highness, in connection with our proposal, have you reached a decision?"

Gax gave a hacking cough. "You are right in that my life is leaving me. I must choose my successor and soon, or I shall die with the deed undone."

"Whereupon Sir Kreim becomes king?"

"True. Unless I anoint him, or someone else, such as good Rohan here, before I die."

"The Ska preference, even over the excellent Rohan, is the Duke Ankhalcx. His nomination would ensure for Xounges the advantages of which I spoke."

"I will keep your recommendation in mind."

"When will you undertake the ceremony of coronation?"

"Soon. I have sent a courier to King Audry, asking his advice. A response should arrive before the week is out. Until then I will have nothing further to say."

"But you have not ruled out our candidate Duke Ankhalcx?"

"I have come to no firm decision. If King Audry instantly mobilizes a great army and marches west, naturally I will not throw open the gates to you."

"In any case, you will still wish to nominate and anoint your successor?"

Gax reflected a moment. "Yes."

"And when will this ceremony occur?"

Gax closed his eyes. "Seven days from today."

"You will give me no prior indication of your intentions?"

Gax spoke with his eyes closed. "Much depends upon the news from Avallon. In truth, I expect very little, and I will die a bitter death."

The Ska departed, tight-lipped and muttering among themselves.

III

THE TROICE WARSHIP TIED UP TO A DOCK in the Xounges harbor. Aillas disembarked with Tatzel, the captain and two others from the ship's crew.

The group passed under a raised portcullis, through a tunnel thirty feet long and out upon a narrow cobbled street which wound up to the market square. The façade of Jehaundel loomed opposite: a set of ponderous stone blocks, devoid of grace or delicacy. The group crossed the square, entered Jehaundel by the front portal, which was opened for them by a doorkeeper.

In an echoing stone foyer a footman came forward. "Sir, what is your business here?"

"I am a gentleman of South Ulfland and I request an audience with King Gax."

"Sir, King Gax is ill, and sees few persons, especially if their business is casual or inconsequential."

"My business is neither one nor the other."

The footman brought the High Chancellor from his office, who asked: "You are surely not another courier from Avallon?"

"No." Aillas took the official aside. "I am here on a matter of urgency. You must take me directly to King Gax."

"Ah, but that I am not allowed to do. What is your name and how is your business so urgent?"

"Mention my presence only to King Gax and in private. Tell him that I am intimate with Sir Tristano of Troicinet, whom perhaps you yourself will remember."

"I do indeed! What name, then, shall I announce?"

"King Gax will want my name spoken to himself alone."

"Come this way, if you please."

The High Chancellor led them into the main gallery and indicated benches along the wall. "Please be seated. When the king is able to see you, Rohan the chamberlain will so inform you."

"Remember! Not a word to anyone but King Gax!"

Half an hour passed. Rohan the chamberlain appeared: a stocky short-legged person of mature years, with a few wisps of gray hair and an expression of chronic suspicion. He inspected the group with automatic distrust. He spoke to Aillas, who had risen to meet him. "The king has taken favorable notice of your message. He now confers with the Ska, but will speak with you shortly."

The conference in King Gax's bedchamber was short indeed. Sir Kreim, already on hand, stared sullenly into the fire. As soon as Dukes Luhalcx and Ankhalcx entered, King Gax indicated a blond young gentleman dressed in the flamboyant style of the court at Avallon.

"There is the Daut courier. Sir, read out King Audry's message once again, if you please."

The courier snapped open a scroll and read: " 'To the attention of Gax, King of North Ulfland: Royal cousin, I send you my dearest regards! In the matter of the Ska brigands, I counsel that you fall on them tooth and nail and defend your great city for yet another brief period, until I can mitigate one or two carking local problems. Then together we will destroy this black-hearted human plague once and for all! Be of good cheer, and know of my hopes for your continued good health. I am the undersigned, Audry, King of Dahaut.' "

King Gax said: "That is my message from Audry. It is as I expected; he intends to do nothing."

Luhalcx, with a grim smile, nodded. "So then: what of my proposal?"

Unable to repress his fury, Sir Kreim called out: "I beg you, sir, make no commitments until we have conferred!"

Gax ignored him. To Luhalcx he said: "Put your proposal in the form of a written protocol, with your guarantees delineated in bold black ink. In three days will be the coronation."

"Of whom?"

"Bring me your solemn handwritten document."

Luhalcx and Ankhalcx bowed and left the chamber. They descended the stairs and turned down the great gallery. To the side sat a group of five persons. A young woman in their midst cried out in a poignant voice: "Father! Do not pass me by!"

Tatzel jumped to her feet and would have run across the gallery had not Aillas caught her around the waist and pulled her back down upon the bench. "Girl, sit quiet and make no bother!"

Luhalcx stared incredulously from Tatzel to Aillas and back once more to Tatzel: "What are you doing here?"

Aillas spoke: "Address your remarks to me! The girl is my slave."

Luhalcx's jaw dropped in new bewilderment. "What idiocy is this? My man, you are mistaken! This is the Lady Tatzel, a Ska noblewoman; how can she be your slave?"

"By the usual process, which you of all people must know in every detail. In short, I captured her and subdued her to my will."

Duke Luhalcx slowly came forward, eyes glowing. "You cannot do such a deed to a noble Ska lady, and then dismiss it so casually in front of her very father!"

"It is no hardship whatever," said Aillas. "You have never strained at the deed. Now the shoe is on the other foot, and suddenly you find the idea incredible. Do you not sense a taint of unreality?"

Duke Luhalcx showed a wolfish grin and put his hand to his sword. "I will kill you dead; then the unreality, and reality itself, will disappear."

"Father!" cried Tatzel. "Do not fight him! He is a very demon with the sword! He cut Torqual to pieces!"

"In any event, I will not fight you," said Aillas. "I am in this palace under the protection of King Gax. His soldiers will come to my call and put you in a dungeon."

Duke Luhalcx looked uncertainly from Aillas to a pair of armed pikemen who stood immobile nearby, watching the encounter with the cool gaze of lizards.

Rohan the chamberlain came into the hall, and approached Aillas. "His Highness will see you now."

"He must see me as well," declared Duke Luhalcx with sudden vehemence. "This is an intolerable case, which he must adjudicate!"

Rohan tried to argue that turmoil might excite King Gax, but his protests went unheeded. However, at the door to the bedchamber, he excluded all but Aillas, Tatzel and the Duke Luhalcx, who strode forward and addressed King Gax from close by his bed.

"Your Highness, I bring my complaint to your attention. When I walked along your gallery I discovered this fellow and with him my daughter, whom he holds by force and claims as his slave! I bade him to relinquish her to me; as a Ska noblewoman she cannot be subjected to such indignities!"

King Gax asked huskily: "Did the enslavement occur here at Jehaundel, while she was under the protection of my roof?"

"No; the deed was done elsewhere."

King Gax looked at Aillas. "Sir, what have you to say?"

"Your Highness, I plead natural law. Duke Luhalcx has enslaved many free folk both of South and North Ulfland, including, so it happens, myself. He does not remember me, but for a goodly period of my life he forced me to serve him as his servant at Castle Sank, where I became acquainted with Tatzel. I escaped from Sank; I became a free man, and then, when opportunity offered, I captured Tatzel and made her my slave."

King Gax looked at Duke Luhalcx. "Do you have Ulfish slaves in your custody?"

"I do." Luhalcx spoke with lame dignity, for already he saw how his case was going.

"Then how, in logic, can you protest this instance? Even though it must cause you pain."

Duke Luhalcx bowed his head. "Your adjudication is fair and just; I stand reprimanded for my protests." He turned to Aillas. "How much in gold will you take, that I may recover my daughter?"

Aillas said slowly: "I know of no gauge which measures the value of a human life. Luhalcx, take your daughter; she is useless to me. Tatzel, I give you into the care of your father. Now, if you please, you may depart, and allow me to consult with good King Gax."

Duke Luhalcx gave a short nod. He took Tatzel's hand and the two departed the chamber. Remaining were Rohan and the two guards by the door.

Aillas turned to King Gax. "Sire, our business must be transacted in total secrecy."

Gax croaked: "Rohan, leave us together. Guards, stand outside the door."

With poor grace Rohan departed the chamber, and the guards moved into the hall. Aillas turned back to King Gax. "Sire, my name is Aillas."

Half an hour later Rohan became uneasy and looked through the doorway. "Sir, are you well?"

"Quite well, Rohan. I need nothing; you may go."

Rohan departed. Aillas asked: "Do you trust Rohan?"

King Gax uttered a wry chuckle. "It is generally felt that Kreim is to be the next king; profit and place go with him, and I am deemed, accurately enough, as good as dead."

"Not quite," said Aillas.

"Rohan devotes himself to my welfare by night and by day. I count him among my few true friends."

"In that case, let us include him in our discussions."

"As you wish. Rohan!"

Rohan appeared with a promptitude which suggested an ear to the door. "Sir?"

"We wish you to contribute your wisdom to our discussions."

"Very well, sir."

Aillas said: "The ceremony of coronation will take place three days from now. Apparently your best hope is to surrender the city to the Ska along with the crown. Therefore Sir Kreim must act either tonight or tomorrow night, or his dreams will be forever shattered."

Gax stared forlornly into the fire. "Were he king, could he not hold Xounges as I have done?"

"Perhaps, had he the will to do so. Still, Xounges is not so impregnable as you may think. Do sentries patrol the cliffs by night?"

"For what reason? What could they see but foam and black water?"

"If I were attacking Xounges, I would choose a dark calm night. A rope ladder would be lowered from somewhere along the cliffs, and warriors waiting below in small boats would climb this ladder, then lower more ladders and more warriors would climb the cliffs. In short order hundreds of men would have arrived to enter your city."

King Gax nodded weakly. "No doubt you are right."

"As another case, how is your harbour guarded?"

"At sunset two heavy chains close off the entrance; no ship, large or small, can enter. Then the portcullis is lowered."

"Chains will not hold back swimmers. On a dark night a thousand men could ease into the harbour, towing their weapons on floats, then hide aboard ships already at the docks until morning. As soon as the portcullis was raised, a pair of posts could be positioned to make any attempt to lower it impossible. Leaving the ships immediately and charging into the city, the army would have control of Xounges within the hour."

King Gax gave a dismal groan. "The years have made me heavy. Needless to say, changes will be made."

"A good idea," said Aillas. "But for now, more urgent affairs press on us, and we must plan for all contingencies. By that I mean Sir Kreim."

The afternoon passed. At sunset King Gax took his evening meal of gruel with a few morsels of mince-meat, chopped apple and a goblet of white wine. An hour later the guards at the door were changed, and new guards came on duty. Rohan indignantly reported that the two new guards were cousins to Sir Kreim's spouse, of rank far too high to be standing guard duty by night. Bribes had clearly been paid and influence exerted: so declared Rohan, furious, if for no other reason than the contravention to his personal authority.

Darkness came to Xounges. King Gax composed himself for sleep and Rohan retired to his own chambers.

Jehaundel became quiet. In Gax's bedchamber the fire burned low on the hearth. A pair of wall-sconces on the back wall cast soft yellow light, leaving the high groined ceiling in shadow.

A faint thud of footsteps sounded from the hall. The door eased open with a quavering creak. A heavy shape stood silhouetted against the light of torches in the hall.

The figure came quietly into the room. From his bed Gax croaked: "Who is there? Ho, guards! Rohan!"

The dark shape spoke softly. "Gax, good King Gax, you have lived long enough and now your time has come."

Gax called out huskily: "Rohan! Where are you? Bring the guards!"

Rohan appeared from his chamber. "Sir Kreim, what does this mean? You are disturbing King Gax!"

"Rohan, if you wish to serve me both here and later in Dahaut, hold your peace. Gax has outlived his time and now must die. He will smother under a pillow and it will be as if he died in his sleep. Interfere at your peril!"

Sir Kreim went to the bed and picked up a pillow.

"Hold!" said a voice. Sir Kreim looked up to discover a man watching him from across the room with sword drawn. "Sir Kreim, it is you who are about to die."

"Who are you?" rasped Sir Kreim. "Guards! Carve me the liver of this importunate fool!"

From Rohan's chamber three Troice seamen came to stand by the door; when the guards entered they were seized and stabbed. Sir Kreim rushed to attack Aillas; steel clashed and Sir Kreim reeled back from a wound in his chest. Before he could renew the attack, one of the seamen leapt on his back, bore him to the floor and stabbed him through the heart.

Again silence held the room. Gax spoke: "Rohan, call porters; have them carry these hulks out and throw them over the cliff. See to it; I am going back to sleep."

IV

ON THE DAY BEFORE THE CORONATION, Aillas went out upon Xounges' fabled walls. They were, he decided, as proof against assault as tradition had asserted, if guarded by alert defenders.

He stood on the battlements, looking out across the Skyre, one foot in an embrasure and leaning against the lichen-stained merlon. Farther along the battlements he noticed Duke Luhalcx, with his brother Duke Ankhalcx, both in flowing black cloaks, and Tatzel, wearing a gray wool knee-length frock, a black cape, gray stockings which left her knees bare and black ankle boots. A red felt cap with the shortest of bills controlled her hair against the efforts of the wind. After a single glance, Aillas paid no more heed to the three, and he was moderately surprised when Duke Luhalcx came purposefully toward him, leaving Ankhalcx and Tatzel together fifty yards along the parapet.

Aillas brought himself erect, and as Luhalcx stopped before him, gave a formal half-bow. "Good day, sir."

Luhalcx bowed curtly. "Sir, I have given much thought to the circumstances which have brought us into contact. There are certain ideas which I feel compelled to place before you."

"Speak."

"I have tried to put myself into your position, and I believe that I can understand how you might be prompted to pursue and capture the Lady Tatzel; I too consider her a person of great charm. She has described to me in detail your journey across the wilderness, and your general courtesy and concern for her comfort, which clearly was not due to any regard you might have felt for her status."

"That is quite true."

"You showed more forebearance than I myself might have used in a similar case, or so I fear. I am puzzled by your motives."

"They are personal, and reflect no discredit upon the Lady Tatzel. Essentially, I cannot bring myself to use a woman by force."

Luhalcx gave a wintry smile. "Your motives would seem to do you credit, even if, in so saying, I seem implicitly to be denigrating the policies of the Ska. . . . Well, no matter. My own feelings translate into gratitude that Tatzel escaped harm, and so, for want of anything better, I give you my thanks, for at least this particular phase of the affair."

Aillas shrugged. "Sir, I recognize your courtesy, but I can not accept your thanks, since my acts were not intended for your benefit; if anything, to the contrary. Let us simply leave matters as they are."

Duke Luhalcx showed a rueful half-smile. "You are a prickly fellow; this is for certain."

"You are my enemy. Have you received recent news from home?"

"Nothing fresh. What has happened?"

"According to the captain of the ship, Ulf troops, with the aid of a Troice contingent, have retaken Suarach and destroyed the Ska garrison."

Luhalcx's face became still. "If true, that is grim news."

"From my point of view, you had no business in Suarach to begin with." Aillas paused a moment, then said: "I will advise you, and if you are wise you will follow my instructions to the letter. Return to Castle Sank. Pack all your precious relics, your portraits and mementos from antique times, and your books; remove these to Skaghane, because soon, soon, soon, Castle Sank must burn to the ground."

"You make me a harsh forecast," said Luhalcx. "It is futile; we will never forsake our dream. First, we will take the Elder Isles, then we shall exact our great revenge upon the Goths who drove us from Norway."

"The Ska have a long memory."

"We dream as a people; we remember as a people! I myself have seen visions in the fire, and they came, not as illusions, but as recollections. We climbed the glaciers to find a lost valley; we fought red-headed warriors mounted on mammoths; we destroyed the cannibal half-men who had lived in the land for a million years. I remember this as if I had been there myself."

Aillas pointed. "Sir, look where those waves come sweeping in from the Atlantic! They seem irresistible! After a thousand miles of steady onward motion they strike the cliff and in an instant they are broken into foam."

Duke Luhalcx said shortly: "I have heard your remarks and I will give them due attention. One final matter which preys on my mind: the safety of my spouse, the Lady Chraio."

"I have no knowledge of her. If she were captured, I am sure that she has been treated no less courteously than you would deal with a captive Ulfish woman."

Duke Luhalcx grimaced, bowed and, turning away, rejoined Duke Ankhalcx and Tatzel. For a few minutes they stood looking across the battlements, then turned and went off in the direction they had come.

During the late afternoon, a dense purple-gray overcast rose from the west to obscure the sun, and early twilight settled over Xounges. The night was totally dark and brought torrents of rain at irregular intervals, which dwindled as dawn tinted the sky with a wet glow the colour of eggplant.

Two hours into the morning, the rain had become a misty drizzle, and the sky showed signs of clearing for the coronation later in the day. Aillas came running up from the harbour: through the tunnel, along cobbled passages, across the market square, now deserted, and entered Jehaundel by the massive front portal.

In the foyer Aillas gave his wet cloak into the care of a footman, then set off down the main gallery. From the great hall came Tatzel, where she had been observing preparations for the coronation. She saw Aillas, hesitated, then came forward, looking neither right nor left. Aillas felt a pang of déjà vu; once again he stood in the gallery at Castle Sank, with Tatzel marching toward him, unheeding of all save her private thoughts.

Tatzel approached, her eyes fixed on a point far down the gallery; clearly Aillas was not in her good graces. For a moment Aillas thought that she might pass him by without speaking, but at the last instant she came to a grudging halt, and swept him up and down with a quick cool glance. "Why do you look at me so oddly?"

"A peculiar mood came over me. I fancied myself back at Castle Sank. I still feel the chill."

Tatzel's drooping mouth twitched. "I am surprised that you are still here. Is not the ship's captain anxious to put to sea?"

"He has decided to delay sailing for still a day or so, which allows me time to finish my business."

Tatzel looked blank. "I thought that you came here to bring me to my father."

"That, for a fact, was one of my purposes. Then, King Gax has graciously allowed my attendance at today's ceremony, which will certainly be a historic occasion, and I would not care to miss it."

Tatzel gave an indifferent shrug. "It does not seem all that important to me, but perhaps you are right. Now I must go and make my own preparations, though no one will be paying attention to me."

"Perhaps I will watch you," said Aillas. "The expressions of your face have always intrigued me."

V

RAIN CONTINUED INTO THE AFTERNOON, sweeping down upon Xounges from a sky of black gloom: rattling on the tiles, hissing into the slate-green waters of the Skyre.

Within the great hall of Jehaundel, a dank half-light entered through high narrow windows. Four great fires cast a more cheerful glow, which which was augmented by a series of wall-sconces.

A dozen gonfalons, representing the glory of Old Ulfland, hung on the stone walls, their colours faded, the deeds they celebrated now forgotten; still, the sight of the ancient standards brought moisture to many eyes among those Ulfs who had come to witness the coronation of the new king—a transition which all felt must extinguish the last remaining sparks of ancient honour.

In addition to the lords of the great old houses, there were present a company of lesser nobility, as well as a party of eight Ska, standing austerely to the side, the ambassadors of Godelia and Dahaut, and a group from the Troice warship.

A pair of middle-aged heralds blew fanfares; Sir Pertane, the High Chancellor, called out: "I announce the imminent arrival of His Majesty, King Gax!"

Six footman carried in a platform supporting a throne in which sat King Gax. By a ramp the footmen mounted to a low dais, lowered the platform and departed. King Gax, wearing a robe of red plush trimmed with black fur, and wearing the crown of North Ulfland over a red cap, raised a fragile hand to the company. "I bid you all welcome. Be seated, those who so desire; those who prefer the support of their feet to that of their haunches: let them stand."

A shifting and a murmur stirred the company.

King Gax spoke again. "Death has come to knock at my door. I am loath to let him enter my house; he is said to be a pertinacious guest. Hark! I hear his knock even now! Can others hear this sound, or does it tap-tap-tap for my ears only? No matter, no matter; but still I must do a last deed before I receive my caller.

"Notice all! I wear the ancient crown! Once it spoke loud of glory and place! This was the crown of Ulfland, when ours loomed large among the states of the Elder Isles! Then there was no 'North' and no 'South' to our land; it united all the west of Hybras, from Godelia to Cape Farewell! Today I wear a symbol of helplessness and defeat. My realm extends only as far as the sound of my voice. The Ska have conquered our land, and made a wilderness where folk once tilled the soil of their farmsteads."

King Gax gazed around the room. He pointed a white finger. "There stand the Ska. Duke Luhalcx advises me to abdicate in favor of Duke Ankhalcx. Duke Luhalcx knows our ancient laws and his candidate is at hand. Duke Luhalcx argues that by naming a Ska ruler I do no more than legitimize actuality.

"Luhalcx argues with a good voice, but others have argued with voices even better. They assert that if the crown passed not to the Ska but to the present King of South Ulfland, then once again the land would be joined under a rule which is committed to expulsion of the Ska and restoration of the old order. These arguments are compelling, as in South Ulfland there is already a new sense of pride and adequacy. South Ulfish forces have already dealt hard blows to the Ska, and are only just starting to bring their power to bear.

"Such arguments cannot be ignored. The same head that wears the crown of South Ulfland shall wear this crown which now graces my unworthy old head."

Duke Luhalcx cried out in a passion: "The ceremony is void unless the South Ulfish king is on hand to receive the crown from your head, and by your hand! You have cited the law yourself!"

"Indeed I have done so. We will go through the form. Sir Pertane, utter your summons!"

The High Chancellor called out to the company: "Where is he whom Gax, King of North Ulfland, has commanded to appear before him? I refer in specific, to Aillas, King of Dascinet and Troicinet, Scola and

South Ulfland. Let him announce himself if indeed he is present."

Aillas stepped forward and approached the dais. "I am here."

"Aillas, will you accept from me this crown of our mutual ancestors, and wear it with all possible honour?"

"I will do so."

"Aillas, will you defend this land against its enemies and meanwhile nurture the weak and succor the impoverished? Will you guard the lamb from the wolf, restore the waif to its parent, and give the same justice to high and low alike?"

"I will do all these, so far as I am able."

"Aillas, will you conduct yourself in full kingly fashion, eschewing both gluttony and venery, and restraining the cruel display of your wrath, and ever let mercy temper your justice?"

"I will do all these, insofar as I am capable."

"Aillas, come forward." Gax kissed Aillas' forehead and Aillas saw that tears were streaming down the haggard cheeks. "Aillas, my son, and I wish that you were my son indeed, you have made me a happy man! In joy I tender you this crown and place it on your head. You are now Aillas, King of Ulfland, and let none in all the world dispute my decree! Druids, where are you? Come forth and sanctify this deed to Cronus the Father, to Lug the Bright, and to Apollo the Wise."

From the shadows came a gaunt man in a hooded brown robe. Around Aillas' neck he hung a necklace of red holly berries, then crushing a berry in his fingers, he rubbed it on Aillas' cheeks and forehead, meanwhile chanting in a tongue incomprehensible to Aillas. Then, with no further ritual, he returned to the shadows.

Sir Pertane called out in a sonorous voice: "Let all know that, by the laws of this land, here stands the new King of Ulfland, and let none be at confusion in this regard! Heralds, go forth about the city and announce this great glad news!"

The footmen, at a signal from Gax, came forward and lifting the platform carried him from the room.

Aillas went to sit in a chair on the dais. "Gentlemen and ladies: for the moment I can tell you this. In South Ulfland we have already made life somewhat better for gentility and commoner alike. Our navy controls the Narrow Sea; where the Ska once sailed out like pirates, now they dare not leave port. On land we will continue our successful tactics; we shall inflict casualties upon the Ska while taking as few as possible ourselves. This is a kind of warfare which they cannot support, and sooner or later they must draw back to the Foreshore. Luhalcx, you have heard me; I make no secret of our strategy. You have never blenched at the sight of Ulfish blood; prepare yourself for the colour of your own Ska blood! Would you send a grand army south to take my town Doun Darric? Do so! You will find the town empty, with all the troops pillaging your Foreshore, so that not a single Ska house is left standing. Then we will turn south and meet you, and harass your army as hounds bait a bear, and very few of you will win back to Skaghane."

"That is a grim prediction."

"It is only the start. Troice warships now sail the Narrow Sea as easily as they do the Lir. Presently the raids on Skaghane will begin: smoke will rise from this town and that, and again and again, to your despair. Take my advice and end your rapacity!"

"I will convey your message to my peers."

"Truly I hope that they will be swayed by my words. As for your stay here in Xounges, be at comfort. You came as guests; you may leave as guests, at your own best convenience. And when you describe these events to your fellows, I hope that you will stress my prediction: to the effect that, unless they renounce their ancient obsession, as I have renounced my revenge against you, they will know great grief."

"King Aillas, we are accustomed to grief."

Looking beyond Duke Luhalcx, Aillas took note of Tatzel standing somewhat apart. He looked into her pale face, and for a moment was urged to cross the room to speak to her. Certain of the Ska moved so as to cross his line of vision and block her from his view; he turned away, and went, rather, to Gax's bedchamber, where he thought that he might sit in company with the old man.

Arriving at the royal suite he knocked at the door, which was opened by Rohan. Aillas spoke quietly: "I came to sit with King Gax, if he is not too tired after the ceremony."

"Sire, you are not in time. King Gax will never tire again; he is dead."

VI

AILLAS SPENT THREE BUSY DAYS in Xounges. He participated in ceremonies of gloomy pomp, to the braying of druid horns at the funeral of King Gax; he reorganized the system of guards and sentries, and tried to appoint Rohan as his viceroy, without success. "Appoint Sir Pertane to this post," said Rohan. "He has been more than faithful to King Gax and is a great one for place and status. He is also indecisive and even a trifle dull; instruct him, therefore, that I will direct policy and that he must follow my instructions, which will trouble him not at all."

"In short order I hope to base three or four companies of good troops here at Xounges. Since we can attack anywhere along the Skyre, the Ska will know great anguish and trouble in defending themselves. In this region they are obviously much over-extended; they must either commit two or three battalions to guard the Skyre and the river Solander, and perhaps even Lake Quyvern, or they must retreat from this entire area, and then the road to Poëlitetz comes under our attack. If they send their battalions here, they weaken themselves elsewhere. No matter how valiant they are, they cannot defend so large a territory from an enemy who will not fight them in the manner they prefer."

"I am convinced that you are right," said Rohan. "For the first time in many years I see a glimmer of hope for us. Be assured that in your absence, Xounges will be guarded. Further, I suggest that you send a military commission here, to train our men so that they may take their place in your army. Our years of passivity are at an end."

In the early morning Aillas sailed from Xounges. Rounding Tawzy Head, the warship sailed south down the Narrow Sea, encountering only another Troice ship along the way, the Ska now making their passages by night.

Aillas left the ship at Oäldes and, taking horse, rode at speed to Doun Darric, where he received a great welcome from Sir Tristano, Sir Redyard, and others of his staff, who, after three weeks, had become much concerned by his absence.

"I assured them of your safety," said Sir Tristano. "I have an instinct in this regard; it told me you were off on some remarkable adventure. Was my instinct correct?"

"Absolutely!" Aillas reported the events which had taken him so far afield, to the fascination of his audience.

"We can in no way match your tale," said Sir Tristano. "Nothing of note has occurred since the taking of Suarach. We now range into North Ulfland at will, alert for cheap victories, but these are hard to come by, since the Ska no longer venture abroad in small parties." He brought out a packet. "These are the despatches from Domreis, which, in your absence, I have taken the liberty to read. There is one which I find somewhat mysterious. It is signed 'S-T', which would seem to indicate Sion-Tansifer, but the words are not his."

"That is how Yane keeps his invisibility. If the despatch is intercepted and something in it is discreditable or off-colour, then Sion-Tansifer gets the blame." He read the despatch:

The cog Parsis, sailing from Lyonesse Town, has arrived at Domreis. The passengers include a certain Visbhume, who would appear to be a sorcerer of no great force, and also a spy in the service of King Casmir. Once before he came over on the Parsis, and put many sly questions regarding Dhrun and Glyneth, to Ehirme and other members of her family, regarding which they have only recently informed me. Visbhume now has taken himself to

the village *Wysk*, near *Watershade*, where he roams the forest, purportedly
in search of rare herbs. He is being kept under surveillance, but something
bulks below the surface and the bodes are not good. *Casmir* of course is at
his striving, but who stands behind *Casmir*? *J* am tempted to suggest that
you come home, preferably in company with *Shimrod*.

S-T

Aillas re-read the despatch, frowning at every word. He looked to
Sir Tristano: "Have you seen Shimrod?"

"Not recently. Were you expecting to find him here?"

"No. . . . It appears that I must return to Domreis at all speed. When
terriers bark, one may ignore them. When the old hound bays, then
one leaps for his weapons."

VII

THE WARSHIP *PANNUC* arrived at Domreis harbour on the morning of
a sunny summer day and tied up at a dock hard under the walls of
Miraldra. Without waiting for the gangway, Aillas jumped ashore and
ran up into the castle. He found the seneschal Sir Este dozing in the
chamber off the great hall which he used for his office.

Sir Este jumped to his feet. "Your Highness, we had no word of your
coming!"

"No matter. Where is the Prince Dhrun?"

"He has been gone three days, sir: out to Watershade for the summer."

"And the Princess Glyneth?"

"At Watershade as well."

"And Sir Yane?"

"He is somewhere about the castle, sir, or perhaps in the town.
Or he might be at his estate. In truth, I have not seen him since yesterday."

"Search him out, if you please, and send him to my chambers."

Aillas bathed in hastily provided ewers of warm water and changed
into fresh garments. When he came out into his parlour, he found Yane
waiting for him. "At last!" said Yane. "The far-ranging king returns,
preceded by startling rumor."

Aillas laughed and threw his arms around Yane's shoulders. "I have
much to tell you! Would you be surprised to learn that I am now King
of all Ulfland, in full formality? And no doubt to a bitter griping of
Casmir's royal bowels. No? You are not surprised?"

"The news came two days ago by pigeon."

"I have other surprises still! You remember Duke Luhalcx of Castle Sank?"

"I remember him well."

"You will be pleased to learn that I twisted his nose in a most satisfying style! He now rues the day that he offended Cargus, Yane and Aillas!"

"Now there is fine news indeed! Tell me more!"

"I captured the Lady Tatzel and took her across the moors as my slave. Had I bedded her as she expected, she would have hated me as an insolent brute. I gave her back to her father untouched and now she hates me even more."

"Such is the nature of the female race."

"True. I expected effusive thanks and tears of joy and invitations from Tatzel, but I had none of these: only a surly ingratitude. More urgently, what of your bodes and premonitions which brought me home at such haste? Evidently they have come to nothing!"

"Not so! Nothing has changed, and I feel imminence as heavy as before."

"All on account of the sorcerer Visbhume?"

"Exactly so. He excites my deepest suspicions. He is Casmir's agent: so much is incontrovertible, even though the facts lead to more mysteries."

"And what are the facts?"

"Three times he has visited Haidion, where he was favoured with immediate audiences. He came to Troicinet aboard the *Parsis* and made careful inquiries in regard to Dhrun and Glyneth, and took the news back to Casmir. Recently he came again aboard the *Parsis* and at this moment sojourns in a village not ten miles from Watershade. Now do you understand my suspicion?"

"Not only do I understnd it; I share it. He is still at Wysk?"

"He lodges at the Cat and Plough: needless to say, under surveillance. Sometimes he studies a book with leather covers; sometimes he rides in an absurd little pony cart; sometimes he walks out into the forest, searching for rare herbs. The village girls give him a wide berth; he is always after them to cut his hair or rub his back or sit on his lap and play a game he calls 'Pouncing Ferrets'. When they will not go into the woods to hunt herbs with him, he becomes peevish."

Aillas heaved a fretful sigh. "Tomorrow I must consult my ministers, or they will think harshly of me. Then I will ride out to Watershade. . . . With magic at hand I would be happy to see Shimrod. But I can not send for him every time one or the other of us feels a bode. He would quickly lose patience with me. Ah well, we shall see. Now I am ravenously hungry. The food aboard the *Pannuc* is at best only adequate. Perhaps the kitchen can find us something savory for our dinner:

a fowl, or some ham and eggs, with some turnips in butter and some leeks."

As they ate, Yane told of King Casmir's secret warship. With many precautions the hull had been launched from the ways in Blaloc, and according to all reports it was a fine hull indeed, built of staunch oak and sound bronze nails, with low freeboard and lateen rig for crisp sailing, and ports for rowing with forty oars when the winds went calm.

To evade notice, the hull had been towed by night from the shipyard to a fitting-out dock further up the Murmeil Estuary, where the rigging would have been installed. Instead, Troice ships had closed in; the tow-lines were cut and the hull drifted down the estuary and out into the open sea. At dawn, Troice ships picked up the line and towed the hull to the south of Dascinet and into one of the deep narrow inlets, where the hull, suitably rigged, would eventually join the Troice navy. Yane reported that Casmir, raging over the loss, had pulled half the hair from his beard.

"Let Casmir build ships by the dozen!" cried Aillas. "We will continue to take them until not a hair remains to his face!"

As Aillas and Yane took their cheese and fruit, Dhrun burst into the chamber, travel-worn and wild-eyed. Aillas jumped to his feet. "Dhrun! What is amiss?"

"Glyneth is gone! She has disappeared from Watershade! I could not prevent it; it happened the day before I arrived!"

"How did she disappear? Did someone take her?"

"She went wandering into the Wild Woods as she often has done; she never came back! No one is sure but a certain odd fellow named Visbhume is thought to be responsible. He is also gone."

Aillas sagged into a chair. The world, only minutes before so bright and fair, had suddenly gone gray. A dull weight pressed upon his heart. "Naturally you made a search?"

"I went out at once with Noser and Bunce. They traced her well enough to a glade in the forest and there the trail died. I called out searchers, and a hundred men sought her high and low, and they are still searching. I rode here to get help, and I have not stopped along the way except to change horses! I am greatly relieved to find you, for I am at my wit's end!"

Aillas threw his arm around his son's shoulders. "Good Dhrun, I could have done no more or no better! There is magic at work, and we cannot cope with it."

"Then we must send for Shimrod!"

"That we will do! Come!"

Aillas led the way to the study at the side of his parlour. On a taboret a stuffed owl sat on a perch. From the owl's beak dangled a blue cord by a string with a gold bead at the tip. "Ah!" cried Aillas. "Shimrod has preceded us!"

He gently pulled at the blue cord and the stuffed owl spoke: "I have gone to Watershade. Join me there."

Chapter 14

I

THE SEASON CAME AROUND to the high solstice, a time of great significance for astronomers. The night skies were ruled by the gentle constellations of summer: Ophiuchus, Lyra, Cepheus, Deneb the Swan. Arcturus and Spica, noble stars of spring, sank in the west; from the east rose Altair to stare down upon sullen Antares, where Scorpio sprawled across the south.

Under the cool stars and everywhere across the Elder Isles folk conducted their endeavors: sometimes in joy, as at King Gax's coronation of Aillas; sometimes in fury, as in the case of King Casmir and his stolen ship. Elsewhere husbands chided wives and wives discerned flaws in their husbands; at village inns and wayside taverns boasting, gluttony and wine-swilling were rife, to the thud of mugs, the clinking of coins and gusts of laughter. At Kernuun's Antler, on the shore of Lake Quyvern, avarice was embodied in the person of the innkeeper Dildahl, and here, perhaps, is an appropriate occasion to recount further incidents in regard to Dildahl which otherwise might be lost in the spate of larger events.

Two days before the solstice, a group of druids came to Kernuun's Antler for their midday meal. Despite double portions of Dildahl's good boiled beef and braised lamb shanks, their conversation was pitched in tones of vehement indignation. At last Dildahl could no longer contain his curiosity. Putting a question, he learned that a band of sacrilegious outlaws had stormed the sacred islet Alziel, put torches to the great wicker crow and liberated the sacrificial victims, so that the usual rite was no longer feasible. The circumstance, so the druids asserted, was somehow connected with the accession of a new king at Xounges, who had sent out gangs of cutthroats to harass and ambush the Ska.

263

"Outrageous!" declared Dildahl. "But if they were in pursuit of Ska, why did they destroy the crow and so spoil the rite?"

"We can only believe that the new king's personal fetish is the crow. Next year we will construct a goat, and no doubt all will be well."

Later in the afternoon a pair of middle-aged travellers arrived at the inn. Dildahl, watching from a window, adjudged them persons of no great distinction, although their garments and the silver medals on their hats indicated a decent level of prosperity, and each rode a horse of obvious spirit and quality.

The two dismounted, tied their horses to a rail and entered the inn. They found Dildahl, the tall, saturnine innkeeper, behind the counter in the common room and requested food and lodging for the night, giving their names as Harbig and Dussel.

Dildahl agreed to supply their needs in whatever style they desired, then, citing the unalterable rule of the house, he tendered to each a document for signature. Harbig and Dussel, reading, discovered a firm stipulation that should the visitor fail to pay his score, he must surrender and forfeit his horse, saddle and bridle, in full and even discharge of his debt.

Harbig, the elder of the travellers, frowned at the uncompromising terms used in the contract. "Is not this language somewhat harsh? After all, we are honest men."

Dussel asked: "Or are your prices so high that one must pay the worth of a horse for a night's accomodation?"

"See for yourself!" declared Dildahl. "There on the board I advertise my menu for the day. Tonight I serve boiled beef with horseradish and cabbage, or, should one prefer, a good platter of lamb shanks braised with peas and garlic, or a savory soup of lentils. The prices are marked plain and clear."

Harbig studied the board. "Your tariffs would seem wholesome but not severe," he stated. "If the portions are of satisfactory size, and the garlic is not scamped in the cooking, you shall find no complaint in this quarter. Dussel, am I correct in this?"

"In every respect, save one," said Dussel, a person moonfaced and a trifle portly. "We must verify the charges and subcharges for our lodging."

"Quite so; a wise precaution! Landlord, how do you quote our room-rent, stated in toto, inclusive of all extras, imposts, fees for water, heating, cleaning and ventilation, and with free access to the latrine?"

Dildahl quoted rates for his various styles of accomodation, and the two travellers settled upon a chamber with rates and amenities to their satisfaction.

"Now then," said Dildahl. "All is in order, except your signatures on the documents. Here, and here, if you please."

Harbig still held back. "All seems in order, but why must we subject our poor horses to the shameful burden of liens? Somehow I find the condition a source of anxiety."

Dussel nodded in thoughtful agreement. "It seems to ensure a nervous visit for the traveller."

"Aha!" cried Dildahl. "You can not imagine the sly tricks and feats of criminal cunning which the ordinary innkeeper must endure! Never will I forget this apparently innocent young couple who rode down from the Brakes and commanded from me my best. I kindly obliged and served to their order, so that the whole kitchen was in an uproar with the preparation of special dishes and the serving of fine wines. In the morning, when I presented my modest little account, they claimed penury. 'We have no money!' they told me, merry as larks. I said: 'Then I fear I must take your horses!' They laughed again. 'We have no horses! We traded them all for a boat!' That day I learned a bitter and costly lesson. Now I keep custody of my surety, in my own barn!"

"A sorry tale!" said Dussel. "Well then, Harbig: what of this paper? Shall we sign?"

"What harm can come of it?" asked Harbig. "These prices seem fair and we are neither paupers nor fly-by-nights."

"So be it," said Dussel. "However I must, in all conscience, add a notation. Landlord, I write: 'My horse is extremely valuable and must have excellent care.'"

"A good idea!" said Harbig. "I will write the same. . . . There! And tonight I shall put prudence behind me! Though it cost a round penny or more, I vow that I will partake of Dildahl's special boiled beef with horseradish sauce and good bread and butter!"

"I am heartily of your persuasion!" declared Dussel.

At suppertime, Harbig and Dussel came handily to the common room, and took their places at the table. When Dildahl came to see to their pleasure, Harbig and Dussel both commanded a goodly portion of boiled beef. Dildahl dolefully reported that the meat had burned in the pot and all had been thrown out to the dogs. "Still, we have fine fish to offer: indeed, fish is our specialty!"

Harbig said: "I think that, in lieu of good beef, I will make do with lamb shanks, and let there be no stinting with the garlic!"

"For me the same!" declared Dussel. "And shall we not also crack a bottle of good but inexpensive red wine?"

"Exactly in order!" declared Harbig. "Dussel, you are a man of exquisite discrimination."

"Alas!" sighed Dildahl. "At noon six druids arrived and each ate lamb shanks with both cheeks, so that tonight the kitchen boy ate the remaining scraps for his supper. But no matter; I can offer a succulent pie of crayfish tails, or a brace of fine brown trout, at their prime, sizzling in butter and vinegar."

Harbig scanned the board. "They are not written on the menu. How are the prices? Fair, or so I expect, with the whole lake at your doorstep?"

"When it comes to fish, we are at our best! What of two dozen pilchard, with lemons and sorrel?"

"Toothsome, no doubt, but price, man! What of the price?"

"Oh ha ha, I am not certain; it varies with the catch."

Harbig dubiously eyed the menu. "Lentil soup might be tasty."

"Soup is off," said Dildahl. "What of a plate of splendid salmon roe, with capers and butter, with a salad of cress and parsley?"

"And the price?"

Dildahl gave his hand a deprecating wave. "It might be more or it might be less."

"I rather fancy the salmon roe," said Dussel. "Tonight that shall be my meal."

"I shall dine on trout," said Harbig. "Let there be an adequacy of side-dishes."

Dildahl bowed and rubbed his hands. "So it shall be."

The two were served their fish, which they consumed with gusto, along with two bottles of wine. Soon thereafter they sought their beds.

In the morning, Dildahl provided a breakfast of porridge with curds. Harbig and Dussel ate briskly, and then called out for their scores.

With a grim smile Dildahl brought each man his tally.

Harbig cried out aghast. "Am I reading correctly? Or are the figures upside-down? My score comes to nineteen silver florins fourpence!"

Dussel was likewise dumbfounded. "For a platter of roe I am accustomed to paying no more than a few groats or maybe a good red penny; I seem to see here a demand for twenty-one silver florins! Harbig, are we awake? Or still asleep and roaming some never-never land?"

"You are awake and my prices are real," said Dildahl shortly. "At Kernuun's Antler, fish is very dear, since it is prepared by secret recipes."

"So be it," said Harbig. "If pay we must, then pay we will."

The two travellers glumly opened their wallets and paid over silver coins, to the sum required. Harbig said: "Now, if you please, bring us our horses, as we are in a hurry to be off and on our way."

"Immediately!" Dildahl called an order to the kitchen boy, who ran out to the barn. A moment later he returned faster than he had gone.

"Sir, the barn is broken open! The door hangs loose and the horses are gone!"

"What!" cried Harbig. "Do I hear aright? My great champion Nebo which I value at a hundred pieces of gold? Or even two hundred?"

In shock Dussel cried: "And my prize steed from Morocco, which cost me one hundred golden crowns, but which I would not sell for three hundred?"

Harbig said sternly: "Dildahl, your joke has gone far enough! Produce our horses upon this instant, or else pay us over their value, and precious horses indeed they were! For Nebo I demand two hundred crowns of gold!"

Dussel declared his loss to be even greater: "For Ponzante I need two hundred and fifty gold crowns even to approach a settlement."

Dildahl finally found his tongue. "These cited prices are absolutely outrageous! For a single gold crown I can buy the finest of steeds!"

"Ah ha ha! Our horses are like your fish. Pay on this instant four hundred and fifty gold crowns!"

"You cannot enforce this insane demand!" declared Dildahl. "Be off with you, or the stablemen will beat you well, and cast you into the lake!"

"Trouble yourself only to look along the road," said Harbig. "You will notice an encampment of twenty soldiers, from the army of Aillas, King of Ulfland. Reimburse us our stolen horses, or prepare to kick from the royal gibbet."

Dildahl ran to the door and with pendulous lower lip sagging, took note of the encampment. Slowly he turned back to Harbig. "Why have these soldiers come to Lake Quyvern?"

"First, to attack Ska and drive them from the region. Second, to burn the wicker crow and to liberate druid captives. Third, to investigate rumours of villainy at Kernuun's Antler, and to hang the landlord if the charges seem well-grounded."

Dussel said sternly, "Once more: pay us for our horses or we will call for the king's protection!"

"But I own no such sum!" Dildahl grimaced. "I will return your florins; that must suffice."

"Bah! Not enough! We now take title to the inn, as you take title to your guests' horses, 'in full and even exchange'. Dussel, at last you fulfill your dreams! You are the landlord-in-residence at a fine country inn! As a first step, impound all the coins in yonder drawer and the gold in Dildahl's strong-box."

"No, no, no!" cried Dildahl. "Not my precious gold!"

Dussel ignored the outcry. "Dildahl, show me the strong-box. Then you must go, and promptly. We will allow you the clothes on your back."

Dildahl still could not accept his fate. "This is an unthinkable turn of events!"

Harbig raised his eyebrows dubiously. "Surely you did not believe that you could continue robbing your guests forever?"

"It is a mistake! Somewhere there must be recourse!"

Harbig said: "Be grateful that you deal with us, not the sergeant of yonder platoon, who already has selected a tree and measured a rope."

Dildahl growled: "I detect strange coincidences. How do you know so much about yonder troop?"

"I am their captain. Dussel, if you must know, has been chief cook at Jehaundel, but with King Gax gone, his services are no longer required, and he has always hoped to keep a country inn. Dussel, am I correct in this?"

"In every respect! Now, Dildahl, show me the strong-box, then be on your way."

Dildahl set up a great moaning. "Have mercy! My spouse is afflicted in the lower limbs and cannot walk; the veins circle her legs like purple snakes! Must we crawl on our hands and knees in the dust?"

Harbig spoke to Dussel: "Dildahl seems to manage well enough at the stove, and deals especially kindly with fish. Why not keep him at work as pot-boy and under-cook, while his spouse makes herself useful milking the cows, making cheese and butter, digging turnips, carrots and leeks, and working the soil, all from a kneeling position, to spare her sore legs? Entirely by the mercy of King Aillas, of course."

"Dildahl, what do you say?" demanded Dussel. "Will you serve me faithfully, without complaint or shiftlessness, at my direction?"

Dildahl rolled his eyes high, and clenched his fists. "If I must, I must."

"Very good. First, point out the location of your, or, better to say, my strong-box."

"It is under the flagstone of my private parlour."

"Now my parlour. You must move at once, out to one of the cottages. Then scour this floor until each plank glows the colour of new straw! I wish to see neither soil nor stain on the floor of the Lakeshore Inn, which is certain to become a rustic resort for the gentility of Xounges!"

II

TWITTEN'S CORNERS, in the Forest of Tantrevalles, was the site each year of three fairs, to which came traders and buyers from all across the Elder Isles, human and halfling alike, each hoping to discover some wonderful charm or trinket or elixir to bring advantage to his life or gold to his wallet.

The first and the last of these so-called 'Goblin Fairs' marked, respectively, the spring and autumn equinoxes. The second, or middle, fair started on that evening known to the druids as 'Pignal aan Haag', to the fairies of Forest Tantrevalles as 'Summersthawn', to the Ska archivists as 'Soltra Nurre', in the language of primaeval Norway: a time marking the start of the lunar year, defined as the night of the first new moon after the summer solstice. For reasons unknown this night had come to be a time of unusual influences and oblique pressures from entities aroused to sentience. Wanderers of high places often thought to hear the echo of windy voices and the drumming of far galloping hooves.

At the inn known as 'The Laughing Sun and the Crying Moon', hard by Twitten's Corners, the night was known as 'Freamas', and meant a spate of incessant toil for Hockshank the innkeeper. Even before Freamas the inn was crowded with folk of many sorts who had come to mingle in unconventional cameraderie, to sell, to buy, to trade, or only to watch and listen, or perhaps to seek out some long-lost friend, or some defaulted enemy, or to recover an item of which they had been deprived; the yearnings were as disparate as the folk themselves.

Among these folk was Melancthe, who had arrived early to take up the apartment reserved for her use.

For Melancthe the fair was surcease from introspection, an occasion where her presence aroused little attention and less curiosity. Hockshank the landlord was casual in regard to his clientele, so long as they paid in good silver and gold, caused no nuisance, and exuded no vile, foul nor arresting odors, and his common room knew a wide variety of halflings and hybrids, oddities and nonesuches, as well as persons, like Melancthe, apparently ordinary in their qualities.

Arriving early on the day before Freamas, Melancthe went to watch construction of the booths around the periphery of the meadow. Many merchants already displayed their wares, hoping to engage the visitor of limited means before he spent all his coin elsewhere.

Melancthe went slowly from booth to booth, listening without comment to the excited calls of the hucksters, showing a faint smile when she saw something which pleased her. Along the eastern edge of the meadow she came upon a sign painted in green, yellow and white:

HERE ARE THE PREMISES OF
THE NOTABLE AND SINGULAR
ZUCK
DEALER IN OBJECTS UNIQUE UNDER THE FIRMAMENT!
MY PRICES ARE FAIR; MY GOODS ARE OFTEN REMARKABLE!
NO GUARANTIES! NO RETURNS! NO REFUNDS!

Zuck himself stood behind the counter of his booth: a person short, plump, round-faced, near-bald, with an innocent inquiring expression. A button of a nose and round plum-coloured eyes pointed at the corners hinted of halfling blood in his heritage, as did a sallow green cast to his complexion.

Zuck regularly sold at the fair, and specialized in *materia magica*: the substances from which potions and elixirs were generally compounded. Today his wares included a novelty. Between a tray of small bronze bottles and cubes of clear gum a single flower stood displayed in a black vase.

Melancthe's attention was instantly attracted. The flower was notable both for its odd conformation and its colours, so vivid and intense as to be almost palpable: brilliant black, purple, frosty blue and carmine red.

Melancthe could not remove her gaze from the flower. She asked: "Zuck, good Zuck: what flower is that?"

"Lovely lady, that I cannot say. A fellow of the forest brought me this single bloom that I might gauge the mood of the market."

"Who might be this wonderful gardener?"

Zuck laid his finger beside his nose and showed Melancthe a knowing grin. "The person is a falloy and of a distant nature; he insists upon anonymity, so that he will not be subjected to lengthy theoretical discussions, or stealthy attempts to learn his secret."

"The flowers, then, must grow somewhere in the forest nearby."

"Quite so. The flowers are sparse and each is more magnificent than the next."

"Then you have seen others?"

Zuck blinked. "As a matter of fact: no. The falloy is a great one for hyperbole, and avaricious to boot. However, I have insisted upon moderate prices for the sake of my reputation."

"I must buy the flower; what, in fact, is your price?"

Zuck looked blandly up toward the sky. "The day is almost done, and I like to end with an easy sale, to serve as an omen for tomorrow.

For you, lovely lady, I will quote an almost trifling sum: five crowns of gold."

Melancthe looked at Zuck in innocent surprise. "So much gold for a single flower?"

"Ah bah, does the price seem high? In that case, take it for three crowns, as I am in a hurry to shutter my booth."

"Zuck, dear Zuck: I seldom carry coins of gold!"

Zuck's voice became somewhat flat. "What coins then do you carry?"

"Look! A pretty silver florin! For you, good Zuck, for your very own, and I will take the flower." Melancthe reached across the counter and lifted the flower from the vase.

Zuck looked dubiously at the coin. "If this is for me, what remains for the falloy?"

Melancthe held the flower to her nose and kissed the petals. "We will pay him when next he brings us flowers. I want them all, every one!"

"It is a poor way to do business," grumbled Zuck. "But I suppose that you must prevail."

"Thank you, dear Zuck! The flower is superb, and its perfume likewise! It exhales a draught from the very shores of paradise!"

"Ah well," said Zuck. "Tastes differ, and I sense only a rather disreputable chife."

"It is rich," said Melancthe. "It opens doors into rooms where I have never looked before."

Zuck mused: "A bloom of such evocation is definitely undervalued at a single silver bit."

"Then here is another, to guarantee my interests! Remember, all the flowers must be sold to me, and me alone!"

Zuck bowed. "So it shall be, though you must be prepared to pay the fair price!"

"You shall not find me wanting. When does the gardener come again?"

"As to that, I cannot be sure, since he is a falloy."

III

WHEN DUSK FELL OVER THE MEADOW Melancthe returned to the inn, and presently appeared in the common room. She went to a table in the shadows. For her supper she was served a tureen bubbling with a stew of hare, mushrooms, ramp, parsley and wine, with a crust of new bread, a conserve of wild currants, and a flask of currant wine. A mote of dust drifted down from above to settle into the wine, where it formed a bubble.

Melancthe, observing the event, instantly became still.

From the bubble issued a small voice, so faint and soft that she bent forward to hear it.

The message was brief; Melancthe sat back, her mouth drooping in annoyance. With a touch of the forefinger she broke the bubble. "Once again," she muttered to herself. "Once again I must use my purple fire to warm this icy sea-green monument to decorum. But I need not mix one with the other — unless the caprice comes on me." She contemplated her flower and inhaled its perfume, while far away at Trilda, Shimrod, studying an ancient portfolio in his workroom, was visited with a shudder of uneasiness.

Shimrod set the portfolio aside and slowly stood erect. He closed his eyes, and into his mind drifted the image of Melancthe, as if she floated in dark water, nude and relaxed, hair drifting loose beside her face.

Shimrod frowned off across the room. At a basic and elementary level, the image was stimulating; on another level, it aroused only skepticism.

Shimrod pondered a moment or two in the silence of his work-room, then reached out and tapped a small silver bell.

"Speak!" said a voice.

"Melancthe has come floating along a dark stream and into my mind," said Shimrod. "She wore a minumum of garments, which is to say, none at all. She broke into my studies and started my blood to moving; then she departed, smiling in a manner of cool insolence. She would not have troubled herself without a purpose."

"In that case, discover her purpose. Then we will know better how to respond."

"Tonight is Freamas," said Shimrod. "She will be at Twitten's Corners."

"Go then to Twitten's Corners."

"Very well; I will do so."

Shimrod brought other books and portfolios to his work-table and by the light of a single fat candle, turned the heavy parchment pages until he came upon the text he sought. He read in all concentration, storing the acrid syllables in his mind, while a moth circled the candle flame and finally died in a puff of dust.

Shimrod packed a wallet with articles of convenience and necessity. His preparations were complete. He went out to the road before Trilda, spoke a few words, closed his eyes and stepped three paces backward. When he opened his eyes he stood beside the tall iron post which marked Twitten's Corners, at the very heart of Forest Tantrevalles. Twilight had given way to night; soft white stars shone down through gaps in the foliage. Fifty yards to the east cheerful yellow light poured from the windows of the Laughing Sun and the Crying Moon into the road, and Shimrod bent his steps in this direction.

The iron-bound door had been propped open to admit the airs of the night. At one side Hockshank stood behind his counter, carving a haunch of venison; elsewhere were tables, benches and chairs, tonight occupied to capacity. In a far shadowed corner Shimrod noted the quiet shape of Melancthe, where she apparently sat absorbed in the reflections on the surface of her wine, seemingly oblivious to Shimrod's presence.

Shimrod approached the counter.

Hockshank glanced at him from the side of his golden eyes; halfling blood ran in Hockshank's veins. His hair was like fur the colour of decaying straw; he stood with a slight forward stoop; his feet were covered with gray-yellow fur and instead of toenails he had small black claws. Hockshank said: "I seem to recognize you from past custom, but I have no head for names, and in any case, should you be seeking accommodation, there is none to be had."

"I am Shimrod, from Trilda. In the past, by dint of careful thought, or again, by housing certain of your guests in the stable, we have discovered a chamber for my use and your own profit, and both of us have been the happier men for the effort."

Hockshank never paused in his work. "Shimrod, I recall you of old, but tonight the stable is already full. If you put down a purse of gold, I still could not find you a room."

"A small purse, or a large purse?"

"Tonight either will buy you a bench in the common room, but nothing better. Custom presses in on all sides; already I have made some difficult compromises." Hockshank pointed his knife. "Notice at the table yonder the three sturdy matrons of imposing mien?"

Shimrod turned to look. "Their dignity is impressive."

"Just so. They are Sacred Virgins at the Temple of Dis, in Dahaut. I have assigned them to a dormitory of six beds along with the three gentlemen yonder with the grape-leaves in their hair. I hope that they may reconcile their philosophical differences without disturbing others in the inn."

"What of the lady sitting alone in the corner?"

Hockshank glanced across the room. "She is Melancthe the demiwitch and occupies the apartments behind the Door of the Two Green Lizards."

"Perhaps you might induce her to share her apartments with me."

Hockshank paused in his carving. "If only all were so deftly done, I would be there myself, and you could share the top of the oven with Dame Hockshank."

Shimrod turned away and went to a table at the side of the room, where he dined on venison, with currants and barley.

Melancthe at last chose to notice his presence. Crossing the room, she slipped into the chair opposite him. In a light voice she asked: "I have always considered you a very paragon of gallantry! Am I so wrong in my judgment?"

"In most respects: yes. How is my gallantry at fault?"

"Since it was I who called you here, surely you might have joined me at my table."

Shimrod nodded. "What you say is valid, in the abstract. Still, in the past I have found you unpredictable, and sometimes pungent in your recriminations; it is one of your little quirks. I hesitated to make a public demonstration of our acquaintance and perhaps cause you embarrassment. I therefore waited upon your signal."

"Good modest self-effacing Shimrod! I was right after all! Your chivalry is irreproachable!"

"Thank you," said Shimrod. "Furthermore, I wanted to dine before you told me something to destroy my appetite."

"Now are you replete?"

"I have dined well, though the venison was somewhat tough, and meanwhile you decided what you wished to tell me."

Melancthe smiled down at the flower she held in her fingers. "Perhaps I have nothing whatever to tell you."

"Why then was I summoned by so explicit a signal? Unless at this moment thieves are ransacking Trilda."

Melancthe's smile, as she twirled the flower in her fingers, became vague. "It might be that I merely wanted to be seen in company with the famous Shimrod, to enhance my reputation."

"Bah! Not a person here knows me, except Hockshank."

Melancthe looked around the room. "For a fact, no one seems to be noticing. The reason is simple: your modesty. Tamurello's dramatic guises are for the most part self-defeating. You are more clever; you conceal yourself in a form which allows you great advantage."

Shimrod looked blankly across the table. "Indeed? How so?"

Melancthe inspected Shimrod through half-closed eyes with her head tilted sidewise. "You simulate the universal man with total conviction! Your hair is hacked short across your face peasant-style, and is even the colour of well-used stable-straw. The features of your face are bony and gaunt, but you relieve their coarseness by a simpleton's drollery which reassures everyone. You wear what appears to be a peasant's smock, and as you dine, elbows high, you display the appetite of one who has toiled long hours among the turnips. All these aspects make for a great advantage, as well you realize! No adversary would ever associate what purports to be a gaunt, blinking loon for the dangerous and debonair Shimrod! It is a cunning disguise."

"Thank you!" said Shimrod. "Your compliments are hard to come by; I accept them all with pleasure. . . . Boy! Bring more wine!"

Melancthe smiled down at her flower. "Has Hockshank found you a chamber for the night?"

"He has offered me a bench here in the common room. Something better may still come to light."

"Who knows?" murmured Melancthe.

The boy brought wine in a gray faience decanter decorated with blue and green birds, and a pair of squat faience goblets. Shimrod poured both goblets full. "Now then: you have called me here; you have characterized me as a boor and a loon; you have distracted me from my work. Was there any other purpose in your signal?"

Melancthe shrugged. Tonight she wore a dark brown robe, in which she seemed childishly slight. "I might have called you because I was lonely."

Shimrod raised high his eyebrows. "Among all these quaint folk? They are your familiars and the songsters who join you out on the rocks!"

"Truly, Shimrod, I wanted to see you that I might ask your opinion of my flower." She displayed the blossom; the petals, black, purple, ice-blue and carmine-red, seemed as fresh now as if the flower had just been plucked. "Smell! The odor is unique."

Shimrod sniffed and looked askance at the flower. "Certainly it is vivid, and its petals are nicely shaped. I have never seen another like it."

"And the perfume?"

"I find it a trifle too heady. I am reminded of . . ." Shimrod paused and rubbed his chin.

"Of what?"

"A strange picture came into my mind: a scene of flowers at war and a great carnage. Flowers with green arms and legs lay dead or mortally wounded; others tall in pride and cruelty cut down at those who were doomed, and so smelled the battlefield."

"That is a complex and subtle way to describe a scent."

"Perhaps so. Where did you come by the flower?"

"At the booth of the trader Zuck, who will tell me nothing as to its source."

Shimrod drank from the goblet. "We have discussed my disguise and your flower; what other topics interest you?"

Melancthe gave her head a rueful shake. "When first we met you lacked all suspicion. Now you dart cynical glances over your wine-cup."

"I am older," said Shimrod. "Is that not the ordinary course of life? When I first knew myself as Shimrod, I felt an exuberance I cannot describe! Murgen despaired of me, and would not so much as hear my voice. I cared nothing; I frolicked like a young goat, and travelled the land with a new adventure at every turning."

"Aha, tonight your secrets are emerging. Do they include a spouse from this time of rashness, along with a bevy of sons and daughters?"

Shimrod laughed. "There is definitely no spouse. As for children, who knows the truth, if all were sorted out? I enjoyed a vagabond's life; I was as careless as a bird, and only too susceptible to the charms of winsome maidens, be they fairy, falloy or human. If I fathered children, how many or how they fare today is unknown to me. Sometimes I wonder but in those days I never gave thought to such things. All is past; tonight here sits Shimrod, sedate and crafty, in his peasant disguise. Meanwhile, how goes your life?"

Melancthe sighed. "Tamurello is back from Mount Khambaste and the air is immediately rife with intrigue and rumor, which might or might not interest you."

"I am willing to listen."

Melancthe studied the flower as if seeing it for the first time. "I pay little heed. Occasionally I hear a name I recognize; then I turn my head to listen. For instance, are you acquainted with the magician Visbhume?"

"Not by such a name. What of this Visbhume; why is he notable?"

"For nothing in particular. Apparently he was at one time apprentice to a certain Hippolito, now dead."

"I have heard of Hippolito. He lived in the north of Dahaut."

"Visbhume approached Tamurello with some mad scheme, and Tamurello sent him packing." And Melancthe added primly: "Visbhume lacks all principle."

"How so?"

"Oh—this way and that. Lacking Tamurello's support he declared himself ready to serve King Casmir of Lyonesse. They think to attack King Aillas of Troicinet."

Shimrod tried to feign disinterest. "And so: what are his intentions?"

"There was talk of using the Princess Glyneth in their plans. . . . You appear to be stunned by this little rumor."

"Truly? I admit to affection for the Princess Glyneth. I would do my best to ward her from harm."

Melancthe leaned back in her chair and thoughtfully sipped wine from her goblet. Presently she spoke, in a soft even voice, though a subtle ear might have detected nuances of mockery and annoyance. "Amazing how chaste little virgins like Glyneth can excite such wild extravagances of gallantry, while other persons of equal worth, perhaps blemished by a goiter or a pock-mark or two, can lie suffering in the ditch, eliciting little if any notice."

Shimrod uttered a melancholy laugh. "The fact is real! The explanation derives from day-dreams and ideal concepts far more powerful than justice, truth and mercy all combined. But not in the case of Glyneth. She spills over with kindness; and she would never ignore those lying in the ditch. She is always merry; she is clean and fresh as the sunlight; she brings pleasure to the world by her sheer existence."

Melancthe seemed taken aback by the fervor of Shimrod's remarks. "In Shimrod she has a dedicated champion. I was unaware of your devotion."

"I know her well, and I love her as I would my own daughter."

Melancthe rose to her feet, mouth drooping. "I had forgotten; the subject bores me."

Shimrod also rose to his feet. "Melancthe, are you retiring for the night?"

"Yes; the common room grows noisy. You may join me if you like."

"Lacking all better alternative, I accept." Shimrod took Melancthe's arm and the two retired to the apartment behind the Door of the Two Green Lizards.

Shimrod put light to the candles in the candelabra on the table. Melancthe, standing in the center of the room, fixed the flower into her hair, watching Shimrod all the while. She let fall her brown robe and stood nude in the candlelight. "Shimrod: am I not beautiful?"

"Beyond all doubt; beyond all question! But put aside the flower; it detracts from you."

Melancthe pouted. "But I like it! Shimrod, come kiss me."

"Put aside the flower! I find it repellent."

"As you like." Melancthe tossed the flower to the table. "Now will you kiss me?"

"I will do better than that," said Shimrod, and so passed the first hours of the night.

At midnight, as the two lay pressed close together, Shimrod said: "I have an uneasy feeling that you were about to tell me something more of the wizard Visbhume."

"Yes, that is so."

"Then why will you not tell me?"

"Because I feared that you would become agitated and perform some instant and unnecessary act."

"What sort of act might that be?"

"There is nothing you can do now; Visbhume has already gone to

Watershade and departed, for one of his private bolt-holes: a place known as Tanjecterly."

A cold chill came over Shimrod. "And he took Glyneth with him?"

"That is the rumor. But you can do nothing to prevent it. The deed is done."

"Why did Visbhume do this?"

"He worked at Casmir's behest. Also, if Tamurello is to be believed, such projects are dear to Visbhume's heart."

"He must know that he has just put a short term to his life," said Shimrod.

Melancthe held him close. "I like you best when you are like this."

Shimrod thrust her away. "You should have told me at once, if you meant to tell me at all."

"Ah Shimrod! You must remember my mixed feelings for you. I am at ease and even happy with you, but soon I find that I want to hurt you and cause you every conceivable pain."

"You are lucky that I lack similar yearnings, even though you provoke them." Shimrod dressed himself.

"It is exactly as I feared," said Melancthe. "The impractical Shimrod hurries off to Tanjecterly and there rescues his dainty Glyneth."

"Where is Tanjecterly? How does one get there?"

"The route is detailed in the rarest of all books: one which Visbhume stole from Hippolito."

"And the name of the book?"

"Twitten's Almanac, or some such thing. . . . Shimrod! Are you truly going?"

The only response was the sound of the door closing behind Shimrod. Melancthe shrugged and presently fell asleep.

In the morning Melancthe went in great anticipation to the booth of Zuck the trader, where she was disappointed anew.

"I have spoken to the falloy," said Zuck. "There will be no more flowers at this fair; the plants yielded only the single blossom. There will be more in the fall, as the buds are already forming, and the falloy says that you must bring gold, as silver is not enough for wares so heady."

Melancthe spoke a soft sound under her breath. "Zuck, I will come in the autumn, and you must reserve the blooms for me alone! Is it agreed?"

"So long as you pay in gold."

"There will be no difficulty here."

IV

RETURNING TO TRILDA, Shimrod went at once to the workroom. In the Pantological Index he discovered a reference to 'Tanjecterly':

> *The source of information in regard to Tanjecterly is derived from the exceedingly rare and somewhat suspect "Twitten's Almanac'. Tanjecterly is described as one of a set, or cycle, of ten superimposed worlds, which includes our own. Interconnections are difficult to find and evanescent in nature.*
>
> *According to Twitten, Tanjecterly, similar in certain ordinary respects to our world, is notably different in others. The inhabitants are said to be various and include even tribes of human-seeming folk, and others in which the similarity is at best cursory. The environment of Tanjecterly is described as noxious, and indeed lethal to those persons who would travel here without making adaptations. Again, Tanjecterly may be no more than one of Twitten's idle fables; his caprices and pranks are well-documented elsewhere. On the other hand, the 'Almanac' is said to be a work of great complexity and inner coherence, which would seem to lend the volume credence.*

Shimrod tapped the silver bell. A voice said: "Shimrod, you work late."

"I was summoned to a rendezvous by Melancthe the Witch. I met her at the Laughing Sun and Crying Moon Inn, and I thought surely that she had called to give me news, and so it was, though she took her own time in the telling.

"She mentioned a low sorcerer by the name of Visbhume, formerly apprenticed to Hippolito. Visbhume conferred with Tamurello, who sent him to King Casmir of Lyonesse. Thereafter, according to Melancthe, Visbhume went to Watershade and for reasons not entirely clear, kidnapped Glyneth and took her to the place Tanjecterly.

"The Index lists Tanjecterly as a possibly imaginary place, mentioned by Twitten in his 'Almanac'."

"So then: what are your plans?"

"I can only do as Melancthe, and perhaps Tamurello expect. I will go to Watershade; there I hope either to find this is all a mare's-nest, or is a situation where I can interfere with Visbhume's plans. Failing this, I must go wherever Visbhume has taken Glyneth, which may mean Tanjecterly itself."

The cool voice said: "This seems a complicated intrigue. Several motivations are suggested. Like you, I suspect that Tamurello has instructed Melancthe. She had very good success urging you to leap like a fool into interworld chaos before; she and Tamurello no doubt have theorized that, if the scheme worked so well before, why should it not work again? Clearly they want you to plunge with full bravado into Tanjecterly, whence you will never return: for them a fine feat! They destroy you and cripple me. Under no circumstances are you to venture into Tanjecterly. It is a palpable trap!

"Second: if Visbhume is working at the behest of Casmir, then the object might also be to confuse, distract and harm King Aillas. I have recently sensed, and this confirms, that Tamurello at last has discovered the insolence to ignore my edicts, and I must punish him."

"All very well," said Shimrod. "But what of Glyneth?"

"I know nothing about Tanjecterly; it seems that I must make inquiries. In the morning I will tell you my findings; then you must counsel King Aillas. But neither he, nor you, nor the prince Dhrun, may venture the way into Tanjecterly."

"Then how shall Glyneth be rescued?"

"We will send our agent. Now I must go to study."

V

AT SUNSET AILLAS AND DHRUN, on horses sweaty and spent, crossed the moat by the old timber drawbridge and so arrived at Watershade.

Shimrod came out to meet them. Aillas and Dhrun searched his face, hoping to read some trace of cheer. Shimrod gave his head a shake. "I know a few sparse facts, and their indications are worse than ever. I cannot even speculate on what is happening to Glyneth. Come; let us go inside, and I will tell you what I know. At this moment, hysterical haste will avail us nothing; tonight at least we will sit quietly and rest and form plans as best we can."

Aillas said: "You do not infect me with optimism."

"There is none to be had. Come; Weare has laid out our supper and I will tell you of Tanjecterly."

Dhrun asked: "Where is Tanjecterly?"

"You shall hear."

Aillas and Dhrun ate cold beef and bread while Shimrod spoke. "I will start at the starting," said Shimrod. "Some hundreds of years ago Twitten the Wizard either himself compiled, or obtained from another source, a volume which became known as Twitten's Almanac. This same Twitten, for purposes unknown, placed the iron post at a crossroads in the Forest of Tantrevalles, despite legends which state otherwise.

"The almanac, so I learn, describes a cycle of worlds one of which is Tanjecterly.

"Hippolito the Magician owned the almanac, and apparently instructed his apprentice Visbhume in its use; when Hippolito disappeared, presumably to his death, Visbhume made off with the almanac."

Aillas said: "I know something of this Visbhume. By all reports he is a strange and unpleasant person, and works in the service of Casmir. He came before to Troicinet, and put assiduous inquiries regarding Dhrun to Dame Ehirme and her family, who seem to have given him hints as to the circumstances of Dhrun's birth, of which Casmir still knows nothing."

"Here may be the basis of Visbhume's acts," said Shimrod. "He has taken Glyneth that he may learn all there is to be known in this regard."

Dhrun groaned. "Let him give us back Glyneth! I will tell him all he wants to know and more!"

Aillas spoke between clenched teeth: "Show me the gate into Tanjecterly; if he has laid a rude finger on her, I will break all his bones!"

"Just so," said Shimrod with a sad smile. "Murgen feels that Tamurello is responsible, and Tamurello hopes that all who love Glyneth most will recklessly hurl themselves into Tanjecterly, and there be lost forever. Murgen has forbidden any such acts."

"Then what can we do?" demanded Dhrun.

"Nothing, until we receive word from Murgen."

VI

IN THE MORNING DHRUN LED THE WAY to the woodcutter's hut deep in the Wild Woods to which his dogs had followed Glyneth's trail. As before, the hut stood alone in a little glade, and appeared to be deserted.

Aillas approached and started to step through the doorway. He was stayed by a sharp cry: "Hold, Aillas! Stand back! As you value your life, do not enter the hut!"

Murgen came forward. Today he seemed a tall erect woodsman with close-cropped white hair. He spoke to Dhrun: "When you traced Glyneth to this place, did you enter the hut?"

"No, sir. The dogs stopped at the doorway, and acted in a peculiar manner. I looked through the doorway and saw that the hut was empty; the place gave me an eerie feeling and I came away."

"That was well-considered. See this golden shine around the doorway? It is barely visible in the light. It marks the way into Tanjecterly, and the way is still open. If you wish to bring great rejoicing to the heart of King Casmir, step through the doorway."

Aillas asked: "May I call out through the doorway?"

"Call away! Your voice can do no harm."

Aillas stepped close to the doorway and called through the opening: "Glyneth! It is Aillas! Can you hear me?"

Silence was profound; Aillas reluctantly turned away and watched as Murgen scratched an outline in the turf before the hut, in the shape of a square twenty feet on the side. With the most meticulous care he scratched a number of other marks inside the perimeter and then stood back. From his wallet he brought a small box carved from a single block of red cinnabar and tossed the contents toward the delineated square.

Dense white vapor filled the interior of the square, to dissipate with a sudden soft explosion, leaving behind a structure of gray stone. The single means of ingress was a tall black iron door, adorned with a panel displaying the Tree of Life.

Murgen went to the door, swung it wide, beckoned to the company. "Come!"

Aillas, passing through the portal, felt a puzzling sense of familiarity, as if he had come this way before. Shimrod knew their location precisely: the entry to the great hall at Swer Smod.

"Come," said Murgen. "There is reason for haste. The ten places slide and move past each other. Visbhume's passage seems firm but who knows when it will break. Since we cannot pass through, we need an agent of suitable sort. I have done the needful study; now the synthesis. Come; to my workroom."

Murgen took the company to a chamber furnished with shelves, cabinets, and tables burdened with unfamiliar machinery. Windows to the east overlooked the foothills of the Teach tac Teach and, beyond, the dark expanse of Forest Tantrevalles.

Murgen pointed to a bench. "Sit, if you will. . . . Notice this cabinet. It has cost me large toil and a dozen obligations in unseemly places. Still, what must be, is. The cabinet glows with a green-yellow light; it is in fact the stuff of Tanjecterly. The creature within is a young syaspic feroce from the Dyad Mountains of Tanjecterly. Now he is a mere schematic; when activated he will also manifest the stuff of Tanjecterly and will form the armature of our construction. It has other virtues as well: it is strong, alert, agile and cunning. It is immune to fear and is loyal to the death. Its flaws are the other side of the same coin: it is savage and becomes a monster of destructive fury when provoked, or sometimes even in the absence of provocation. It is also prone to unpredictable frivolities which propel its kind on expeditions of ten thousand miles that they may dine on a particular fruit. This is the basis of our agent."

Aillas eyed the creature dubiously. It stood a few inches over six feet tall and displayed a rudely man-like form, with a heavy head resting on massive shoulders, long arms with taloned hands and prongs growing from the knuckles. A black pelt covered its scalp, a strip down its back and about the pelvic region. Its features were heavy and crude, with a low forehead, a short nose and ropy mouth; tawny-gold eyes looked through slits between ridges of cartilage.

Murgen spoke again: "This is not the beast itself, which would be of no use to us, but its constructive principles, which define its nature. Last night I sought across a hundred worlds and a million years of time. I still am not content but in so short a time I can discover none better." He closed the cabinet on the syaspic feroce, and opened another to reveal the simulacrum of a strong young man wearing leather trousers buckled at the belt. "This creature appears to our eyes as a man because our brains make such an interpretation; it is unnecessary to think differently. He lives among the far moons of Achernar, and he is accustomed to the most extreme outrages of terror and the hourly proximity of death. He survives because he is ruthless and intelligent; his name is Kul the Killer. To our eyes and our brains he seems a handsome clean-limbed young man of fine physique, and we will make use of this matrix when we join him to the feroce, as we do now."

Murgen joined the cabinets, then, at a table, took what appeared to be a sheet of paper cut into patterns and laid it on another similar set of patterns. He worked for a moment with patterns, cabinets and machinery. "Now!" said Murgen. "The synthesis is done. We shall call the product 'Kul'. Let us observe him."

Murgen opened the cabinet door, to reveal a new being with attributes of both its constituent beings. The head rode on a short heavy neck; the face was less brutally modeled; the arms, hands, legs and feet were more distinctly human. Kul wore his short leather trousers, while the pelt of black hair now covered only the scalp, the neck and part of the back.

Murgen said: "Kul is not yet alive, and needs still another component: direction, full intelligence, and sympathetic juncture with our own humanity. Any of you three can supply these qualities; each of you, in his own way, loves Glyneth. Shimrod, I deem you the least suitable. Dhrun, you would gladly give your life for Glyneth; but the quality I seek I find in Aillas."

"Whatever you need, I will give it."

Murgen looked at Aillas. "It will mean discomfort and weakness, for you must invest the strength of your spirit and a goodly quantity of your red human blood in this creature. Kul will have no knowledge of you, but his human virtues, if such words apply, will be yours."

Murgen nodded. "Shimrod, Dhrun: wait in the hall."

Dhrun and Shimrod departed the workroom. An hour passed.

Murgen appeared. "I have sent Aillas to Watershade. He gave more of himself than I expected and he is weak. Let him rest; in a week or so he will be himself."

"And what of the creature Kul?"

"I have instructed him, and already he has fared through the hole into Tanjecterly. Come; let us learn what news he sends back."

The three returned through the foyer to the glade in the Wild Woods. Murgen dissolved the gray stone structure; the three approached the woodcutter's hut.

A black glass bottle flew through the doorway and landed at their feet. Murgen extracted a message:

> *I find neither Glyneth nor Visbhume close at hand. I have questioned one who watched all that happened. Glyneth took flight from Visbhume, who went in pursuit. The trail is plain. I will follow.*

Chapter 15

I

ON A BRIGHT SUMMER'S MORNING Glyneth rose with the sun. She washed her face, and combed out her hair, which had grown to hang in loose dark golden curls somewhat past her ears. It was beautiful hair, so she had been told: full of glints and gleams, but perhaps a trifle longer than truly convenient, since now the wind could blow it into a tousle, so that it needed attention to keep it neat. To cut, or not to cut? Glyneth pondered carefully. Gallants of the court had assured her how nicely her hair set off the contours of her face. Still, the one person whose opinion truly mattered to her never seemed to notice whether her hair was long or short.

"Ah ha," said Glyneth to herself. "We will soon put a stop to that kind of nonsense, since now I think I know what to do."

On this bright morning she made a breakfast of porridge, with a boiled egg and a glass of fresh milk, and the whole day lay ahead of her. On the morrow, Dhrun would be arriving for the summer; today was her last day of solitude.

Glyneth considered riding her horse into the village, but only yesterday, when she rode to visit her friend Lady Alicia at Black Oak Manor, a peculiar man in a pony cart had signaled her to a halt and had put the most surprising questions.

Glyneth had politely acknowledged her identity. Yes, she knew Prince Dhrun very well; no one knew him better. Was it true then that Dhrun had lived for a period in a fairy shee? At this point Glyneth had excused herself from further conversation. "I cannot assert this of my own personal knowledge, sir. Why not put your questions to King Aillas at the court if you are truly interested? There you would learn which facts are real and which are idle speculation."

"That is good advice! Today is a fine day for riding to horse! How far do you go?"

"I ride to visit my friends," said Glyneth. "Good day to you, sir!"

On this morning Glyneth decided that she did care to risk another encounter with the odd gentleman—it was almost as if he had been waiting for her to ride past—and so she decided to wander in the woods.

She took up her berry basket, kissed Dame Flora, and promised to be home in time to eat the berries she planned to pick for her lunch. So saying, she set off into the Wild Woods.

Today the forest was at its best. The foliage glowed a thousand shades of green in the sunlight, and a breeze from the lake made a pleasant murmur as it passed.

Glyneth knew a place where wild strawberries grew in abundance, and never seemed to fail, but as she walked along the trail her attention was attracted by the most beautiful butterfly she had ever seen. It floated before her, on wings of orange, black and red fully six inches across, and of a most unusual shape. Glyneth increased her pace hoping that it would settle, that she might examine it at her leisure, but it flew even faster, and eventually, entering a glade, it flew into a woodcutter's hut.

Most odd, thought Glyneth. What a foolish butterfly! She looked through the door, and seemed to notice an odd greenish-yellow glow, but paid it no heed. She stepped into the hut, and looked all around, but the butterfly was gone. On an old table across the room lay a scrap of parchment. Glyneth read:

You may be surprised but all is well, and all will be well. Your good friend Sir Visbhume will help you and is about to bring you a great happiness. Once again! Feel no fear! Put all trust in noble Sir Visbhume, and do his bidding.

Most strange, thought Glyneth. Why should she be surprised? And put her trust in Visbhume and do his bidding? Not likely! Still, undeniably, something strange was in the air! First the butterfly, then the peculiar light which now pervaded the room. Magic hung in the air! Glyneth had known a surfeit of magic and wanted no more of it. She turned to the door; never mind the butterfly, and the berries; she wanted only to be safe home at Watershade as quickly as possible.

She stepped from the hut, but where was the forest? She looked out on a strange landscape; where could she be?

Two suns hung at the zenith of a heather-gray sky, lazily circling each other: one green, the other lemon-yellow. Short blue grass grew along a hillside sloping down to a slow gentle river, which flowed from right to left and out on a wide flat plain. Where the river met the horizon an object like a black moon hung in the sky, and the very look of the object caused Glyneth a spasm of unreasonable fear, even horror. Feeling ever more frightened, Glyneth turned away to look elsewhere.

Across the river, low hills and dales rolled in a majestic rhythmic succession, finally blending together. A range of mountains, black and yellow-brown, slanted down from the far left, to disappear over the horizon. Closer at hand, along the banks of the river, grew trees with nearly spherical crowns, dark red or blue or blue-green. At the riverside a short man hunched over to dig in the mud with a spade. He wore a dark brown smock, and a wide-brimmed brown hat concealed his features. A hundred yards along the shore a boat swung at a rude dock.

Scanning the countryside, Glyneth could not help but marvel at the brightness and clarity of the colours. They were not the colours of Earth! Where had she wandered? . . . From behind her came the sound of a small polite cough. Glyneth whirled around. On a bench beside the hut sat the strange man who had spoken to her on the previous day. She stared at him in mingled wonder and consternation.

Visbhume rose to his feet and bowed. He wore neither cloak nor cape, only a voluminous shirt of black silk with loose overlong sleeves almost to his finger tips; the collar was tied with a flowing cravat of patterned black and red silk. His trousers were also voluminous black silk, hanging to the ground and barely showing long narrow black slippers.

"Have we not met before?" asked Visbhume in the most refined of accents.

"We spoke on the road yesterday," said Glyneth. Then, her voice trembling in hope, she asked, "Can you please tell me the way back to the forest? I am wanted home for my lunch."

"Aha ha hah!" said Visbhume. "It must be somewhere about."

"So I should think but I see it nowhere. . . . Why are you here?"

"At the moment, I stand admiring the splendid scenery of Tanjecterly. You are Glyneth, I believe. If I may say so, your person in no small measure enhances the beauty of these already charming vistas."

Glyneth frowned and pursed her lips but could think of nothing to say which did not seem ungracious.

Visbhume went on, as before using a voice of refinement and gentility. "You may know me as Sir Visbhume. I am a knight of excellent degree, versed in all the phases of chivalry, and in all the courtly arts now the rage of Aquitania. You will derive enormous benefit from my protection and instruction."

"That is kind of you, sir," said Glyneth. "I hope that you will indeed instruct me how to return to the forest. I must be home to Watershade within the hour; otherwise Dame Flora will worry greatly."

"That is a vain hope," said Visbhume grandly. "Dame Flora must find a means to assuage her concern. The gate functions in only one direction, and we must discover the corresponding crevice of return."

Glyneth searched dubiously all around. "How is that crevice found? If you tell me, I will search it out."

"There is no hurry," said Visbhume with a trace of asperity in his voice. "I regard this as a delightful occasion, with none to trouble us or say us nay, as is so often the case! We shall relax at ease and each take pleasure in the other's capabilities. I am accomplished in a dozen ways; you will clap your hands in happiness for your luck."

Glyneth, darting one quick side-glance at Visbhume, remained thoughtfully silent. . . . Visbhume was possibly unworldly. Cautiously she suggested: "You do not seem alarmed by this strange place! Would you not prefer to be at home with your family?"

"Ah, but I have no family! I am a wandering minstrel; I know music of palpable energies, music to cause your blood to pump and your feet to tap!" Visbhume pulled a small fiddle from his wallet and using an inordinately long bow, played a fine jig and danced as well: kicking and jerking, raising high his elbows, producing all the while his strident, if sprightly, music.

At last, with eyes glowing, he came to a halt. "Why are you not dancing?"

"In truth, Sir Visbhume, I worry about finding my way home. Please, can you help me?"

"We shall see, we shall see," said Visbhume airily. "Come sit beside me and tell me an item or two of information."

"Sir, let me conduct you to Watershade, where we may talk at leisure."

Visbhume held up his hand. "No, no! I know all there is to be known of clever young ladies who say 'yes' when they mean 'no' and 'no' when they mean 'Visbhume, please and by all means!' I wish to talk here, where candor will make you my absolute favorite, and will not that be a pleasant treat? Come now, sit; I enjoy the sense of your delectable presence!"

"Sir Visbhume, I prefer to stand. Tell me what you wish to know."

"I am curious as to Prince Dhrun and his early youth. It would seem that he is quite old in years for so young a father."

"Sir, the folk concerned might not wish me to gossip at wholesale with strangers."

"But I am not a stranger! I am Visbhume, and much attracted by your fresh young beauty! Here on Tanjecterly there are none to cavil and none to glare and none to cry out 'impudicity!' We can indulge ourselves in the most daring of intimacies. . . . But ah, I have perhaps hinted at too much! Think only of my search for truth! I need but a few facts to ease my curiosity. Tell me, my dear! Tell me, do!"

Glyneth tried to seem casual. "Better that we return to Watershade, you and I! There you may put questions to Dhrun himself, and he will surely give you a gracious response. You will gain my good opinion, and I will know no guilt."

Visbhume chuckled. "Guilt, my dear? Never! Come closer to me; I would caress your glossy hair, with perhaps a kiss for your reward."

Glyneth drew back a step. Visbhume's evident intent was bad news indeed, since, if he misused her, he would not dare liberate her for fear that she would carry tales. In such a case her only protection lay in denying him the information he sought.

Visbhume watched her sidelong, smiling like a fox, as if he were able to read the flow of her thoughts. He said: "Glyneth, I am a person who dances to a merry tune! Still, sometimes I must, by necessity and rightness, tread to a more portentous strain. I dislike excesses where events go wildly awry and affectionate trust is forever shattered. Do you apprehend my meaning?"

"You want me to obey you, and you promise me harm if I will not."

Visbhume chuckled. "That is blunt and direct; the music to these words is not pretty. Still—"

"Sir Visbhume, I care not a twig for your music. I must also tell you that unless you in all courtesy allow me to leave this place, you will answer to King Aillas, and this is as sure as the sun rises and sets."

"King Aillas? Oh la! The suns of Tanjecterly neither rise nor set; they curvet in graceful rounds about the sky. Now then! The fabric of our love is not yet rent! Tell me what I wish to know—after all, it is no great thing—or I must compel you to a sweet obedience. I will show you, so that you will know my power. Watch!"

Visbhume went to a nearby hedge and plucked a flower of twenty pink and white petals. "See this bloom? Is it not dainty and innocent? See how I do." Visbhume pushed his long thin white fingers from the black sleeves and, petal by petal, pulled the flower apart, with each petal smiling up at Glyneth, who watched with dread growing large in her mind.

Visbhume tossed away the dead flower. "By this means I have taken a richness into my soul. But it is only a taste, when I would dine full. Watch!"

Visbhume rummaged through his wallet and found a little silver whistle. Going once more to the hedge, he blew on the pipe. Glyneth stared to where a sheath sewed to the side of the wallet showed the haft of a little stiletto. She moved a step toward the wallet, but Visbhume had turned so that her movements were under his gaze.

A bird with a blue-crested head flew to the hedge to hear Visbhume's piping. With nimble white fingers Visbhume played flourishes, trills and wild little arpeggios, and the bird cocked its head askance to hear such mad and wonderful notes.

Glyneth, through fairy magic, had been gifted with the language of all things, and she cried out to the bird: "Fly! He means you harm!"

The bird chirped uneasily, but Visbhume had seized it, and carried it back to the bench. "Now, my dear, watch! And remember, everything I do has its reason."

While Glyneth watched aghast, Visbhume performed atrocious deeds upon the bird, and finally let the tattered thing drop to the ground. He wiped his fingers fastidiously upon a tuft of grass, and smiled at Glyneth. "Such are the ways in which my blood is stirred, and a sweet savor is added to our knowledge of one another. So come closer, sweet Glyneth, I am ready to caress your warm person."

Glyneth took a deep breath and twisted her face into the caricature of a smile. Slowly she came toward Visbhume, who crowed in delight. "Ah, sweet, sweet, sweet! You come like a dear maiden should!" He reached out his arms; Glyneth shoved him smartly on the narrow chest and sent him stumbling backward, mouth pursed in a purple O of astonishment. Glyneth seized the wallet, and drew the stiletto. As Visbhume staggered back toward her she struck out. Her arm was deflected; the stiletto plunged through Visbhume's left cheek, across his mouth and out his right cheek. The stiletto, of magic properties, could not be withdrawn save by the hand which had thrust it. Visbhume gave a crazy chortling cry of pain and whirled in a circle; Glyneth seized his wallet and ran at full speed down the slope to the river. A hundred yards downstream she spied the dock. Visbhume came bounding after her, the stiletto yet protruding from his cheek.

Glyneth ran to the dock and jumped into the boat. The fisherman who dug in the mud along the shore cried out in anger: "Halt! Do not molest my boat! Away with you and your tricks!"

The language was strange, but her sleight of tongues allowed Glyneth complete understanding; nevertheless, she cast off the line and pushed out into the river just as Visbhume came running out on the dock. He stood waving his arms and trying to call, but the stiletto impeded his tongue, and his words were barely comprehensible: ". . . my wallet! . . . Glyneth! Come back; you do not know what you do! . . . the holes to our world, we will never return!"

Glyneth looked for oars, but found none. The boat was caught in the current and swept off downstream, with Visbhume bounding along the bank, uttering strangled orders and pleas, until he was halted by the influx of a second river, so that he was obliged to stop and watch Glyneth, in her boat, float beyond his reach of vision, along with his wallet.

Presently Visbhume came upon a ferry operated by a pair of lumpish men, who demanded coin before they would convey him across the river. Visbhume, lacking coin, was compelled to surrender the silver buckle from his shoe for the passage.

At the ferry terminus Visbhume discovered a blacksmith shop. Upon payment of the remaining buckle, the smith sawed the handle from the shaft; then, while Visbhume shrieked in pain, he seized the tip with a pincers and pulled the blade out through Visbhume's right cheek.

From a pocket in his voluminous sleeve, Visbhume brought a round white box. He removed the top and shook out a tablet of waxy yellow balm. With sighs and exclamations of gratification he rubbed the balm on his wounds, easing his pain and healing the cuts. He returned balm into box and box into the pocket in his sleeve; the pieces of stiletto he dropped into a pocket in the side of his trousers, and once more set off in pursuit of Glyneth.

At length Visbhume reached the shore of the main river. The surface of the water lay blank; the boat had drifted far out of sight.

II

THE BOAT FLOATED ALONG THE RIVER, with the banks sliding by at either side. Glyneth sat rigidly fearful that somehow the boat might rock and pitch her into the dark deep water, and Glyneth thought that she would not like to explore the depths of this river. She looked sadly over her shoulder; with every instant she floated farther from the hut and passage back the way she had come. She told herself: "My friends will help me!" No matter what the circumstances, she must cling to this conviction — because she knew it was true.

Another dismal idea: what if she became hungry and thirsty? Dare she eat and drink the substances of Tanjecterly? More than likely they would poison her. In her mind's-eye she saw herself eating a morsel of fruit, and instantly choking, then turning black and swelling into a disgusting parody of herself.

"I must stop thinking such things!" she told herself resolutely. "Aillas will help me as soon as he finds that I am lost, and Shimrod as well, and of course my dear Dhrun. . . . The sooner the better, for this is a dreadful place!"

Spherical trees with foliage of red and blue and blue-black lined the banks. On several occasions Glyneth saw beasts at the river's edge: a white bull with the head of an insect and spikes along his back; a spindly stilt-man fifteen feet tall with a narrow neck and a sharp face adapted to looking into foliage for nuts and fruit.

Glyneth explored the contents of the wallet. She found a book bound
in leather entitled *Twitten's Almanac*, evidently newly copied from an
older work. She found a small bottle of wine and a little box containing
a hunch of bread and a slab of cheese. These were Visbhume's rations,
and Glyneth surmised that both bottle and case were magically refilled
after use. She noticed other articles whose utility was not so clear,
including a half-dozen small glass bulbs swarming inside with insects.

Glyneth, in the absence of Visbhume, began to feel less desperate.
Sooner or later her friends would find her, and bring her home; of this
she felt sure. . . . Why should Visbhume so insistently inquire upon
the circumstances of Dhrun's birth? He could only be acting in the
interests of King Casmir, and hence disclosure of the knowledge most
probably would not be to the advantage of Dhrun.

The boat drifted into marshy shallows. Glyneth reached into the
water and secured a floating branch, which she used to pole herself to
the shore. She climbed the bank and searched upriver, but discovered
no sign of Visbhume. She turned to look downriver and discovered a
line of stony crags descending from a high ridge, at last to thrust into
the water. Glyneth eyed these crags with distrust, speculating that they
might be the haunt of ferocious beasts. The boat and the squat person
in the wide brown hat, digging in the mud, indicated the existence of
a human population — but where? And what sort of human beings?

Glyneth stood on the shore, dubiously considering the landscape: a
woeful figure in a pretty blue frock. Conceivably all the best magic of
Shimrod might not be able to find her, and she would spend all the
days of her life under the green and yellow suns of Tanjecterly — unless
Visbhume came upon her and hypnotized her with his silver pipe.

She blinked away her tears. As her first urgency she must find a refuge
secure from Visbhume.

The crags which came down to the river intrigued her. If she climbed
to the near ridge she could overlook a great sweep of country and
perhaps discover a human settlement. The idea was not without its
dreary possibilities! Strangers were not everywhere accorded kind hospitality, not even among the lands of Earth.

So Glyneth hesitated and wondered how best to survive. The boat
offered a measure of security and she was reluctant to leave it behind.

Her indecision was suddenly vacated. From the water rose a sinewy
member, as wide as her own waist, ending with a wedge-shaped head,
a single green eye and a great fanged mouth. The eye fixed upon her;
the mouth gaped wide, showing a dark red interior; the head lunged
forward, but Glyneth had already jumped back.

The head and neck slowly subsided into the river. Shuddering,

Glyneth backed away from the boat, which no longer seemed a source of security. . . . Well, then: up to the ridge.

She broke away twigs from her branch, so that it might be used as a club, or a staff, or a makeshift lance. Throwing the strap to Visbhume's wallet over her shoulder, she set out as bravely as possible downstream along the riverbank toward the crags.

Without incident she arrived at the base of the crags and climbed the first rise of ground. Here she paused to catch her breath and, looking back the way she had come, with dismay thought to see a far bounding black form: almost certainly Visbhume.

The rocks were close at hand, where she could possibly find a hiding place. She climbed up a slope among hummocks of curiously convoluted stones. . . . As she passed among them, they abruptly uncoiled and jerked erect.

Glyneth gasped in terror; she was surrounded by tall thin creatures gray as stone, with tall pointed heads. Eyes like disks of black glass and long leathery nasal flaps produced an effect of droll dejection, by no means reassuring, especially when one of the group dropped a cord over Glyneth's neck and led her away at a scuttling trot along a trail through the rocks.

Ten minutes later the group came out upon a flat area with crags rising steep at the back. The goblin-eels thrust Glyneth into a pen also occupied by a rotund six-legged creature with a dull pink body surmounted by an object like an enormous orange polyp, fringed by a hundred eyes growing on stalks.

The eyes veered around to peer at Glyneth, who was now in a state beyond terror, with her emotions anaesthetized. . . . Unreal. She closed her eyes and opened them again. Nothing had changed.

The walls of the pen were woven of branches, in a rude and untidy style. Glyneth stealthily tested the tightness of the weave and decided that without too much effort she could open a hole large enough to permit her passage. She watched the goblin-eels for a moment, wondering what might be the best time to attempt an escape. At the moment the group stood assembled around a pit in the stone, with an opening about four feet in diameter, from which exuded wisps of vapor, or steam.

Several of the goblin-eels stirred the substance in the pit with long-handled paddles. Occasionally one or another touched the stuff on the paddles and tasted it with the nice judgment of connoisseurs. Conversing in whispers, they arrived at a consensus. Several entered the pen and deftly chopped two legs from the pink beast. Ignoring its squeals of pain as it hobbled to the side of the pen the goblin-eels dropped the legs into the pit. Others tossed a bale of vegetation into the steaming vent. A black shrimplike creature, which roared and bellowed and strove mightily against its bonds, was also dragged to the opening and thrown in. Its cries reached a crescendo of roaring, then subsided into plaintive gurgling, dwindled and went silent.

Eyes doleful and droll were now turned toward Glyneth, and tears at last coursed down her cheeks. "How dreadful and dreary that I must die in this vile pit, when I do not want to do so, not in the least!"

A shrill wild sound came from the trail: the fluting and warbling of Visbhume's silver whistle. The goblin-eels became still, then turned and gave signals of perturbation.

Visbhume appeared, marching smartly to the meter of his music, with an occasional caper of sheer extravagance, when he struck some phrase he considered particularly felicitous.

The goblin-eels began shaking and jerking, as if impelled despite all inclination, and began to hop up and down, in place, while Visbhume played fiery jigs and fare-thee-wells.

At last he halted, and cried out in a reedy voice a language Glyneth knew to be that of the goblin-eels: "Who is master here, lord of the irresistible tap-tap-a-tapping?"

All whispered: "It is you, it is you! The Progressive Eels are your minions! Put down your fearful weapon; must we hop and jump to exhaustion?"

"I will show you my mercy, but first, one last little quickstep, for your health's sake, and so that you remember me the better!"

"Spare us!" cried those who had termed themselves the Progressive Eels. "Come; taste the good slime of our pit!" And: "Put away your magic; eat slime!"

Glyneth had been thrusting at the weave of the pen; she created a hole and squeezed through. "Now! Away, be away! Run, run, run!"

Visbhume pointed: "I will desist, and I will take away with me that creature who even now thinks to escape the pen. Seize her, and bring her to me."

The Progressive Eels leapt to surround Glyneth, and one seized her hair. A heavy stone, larger than a pair of clenched fists, hissed down to strike the Progressive Eel's face and crush it to instant pulp.

Stones rattled down the mountainside; Glyneth jerked around in a state close to hysteria; she was not soothed by the silhouette of what appeared to be a monstrous half-human beast, black against the lavender sky. The creature stood a moment, appraising the scene below, then lunged down the rocks with what seemed a total contempt for gravity: bounding, running, sliding, and at last leaping into the midst of the Progressive Eels. It snatched a sword from the scabbard at its leather belt, and with furious zeal set about hacking and chopping. Glyneth shrank back, appalled by the frightful sounds which rose from the combat. Heads with eyes wide in blank surprise rolled along the ground; torsos half-severed fell down, to crawl about with foolish kicks, usually to tumble into the pit.

Hissing and sighing, the Progressive Eels ran off into the rocks, despite Visbhume's raging commands. At last he blew a great blast on his pipe which brought the eels to a sudden halt.

Visbhume screamed: "Stand fast! Attack this footling beast, with full force, from all directions! It will cringe before your onslaught!"

The Progressive Eels considered the scene of carnage with large blank eyes. Visbhume exhorted them again: "Strike great blows! Hurl stones and hurtful objects, or even nauseous refuse! Take up spears; stab the thing through and through!"

Certain of the eels heeded the instructions and picked up rocks to throw, but Visbhume's wrath was not yet appeased. He cried: "Attack! Capture! Marshall the battle-worms! To action, all!"

The man-beast wiped its sword on a corpse and showed Glyneth a grimace of drawn lips and white teeth somewhat difficult to interpret. Shrinking back, she stumbled and started to slide into the pit, but the creature seized her arm and pulled her to safety. Glyneth stared wildly around the landscape, seeking an easy route away from this dreadful place; from the corner of her eye she glimpsed the downward trajectory of a great stone. She lurched aside, and the stone crashed to the surface where she had stood. Another stone slanted down to strike the man-beast's shoulder; he spun around roaring in rage, but chose not to attack. He slung Glyneth over his shoulder and bounded away up the mountain-side.

Visbhume set up an instant scream of indignation. "You are taking my wallet, my personal property! Drop it at once! Theft is a crime! The wallet is mine alone, with my valuable things!"

Glyneth only clutched the wallet more closely, and was whisked up the slope at a speed which made her dizzy.

The creature at last halted and swung Glyneth to the ground. Glyneth prepared to be devoured or used in some unthinkable fashion, but the creature went to look back the way they had come. It turned around, almost casual in its conduct, showing no signal of menace, and Glyneth drew a deep breath. She ordered her clothes which had become disarranged, then stood hugging Visbhume's wallet in her arms, wondering woefully how the creature meant to deal with her.

The man-beast made sounds, straining as if it found its larynx a new and unfamiliar tool. Glyneth listened intently; if it meant to harm her, why should it labor to make her understand? Suddenly Glyneth saw that it intended reassurance; fear left her and despite all efforts at self-control, she began to cry.

The creature continued to make sounds, and began to approach intelligibility. Glyneth, trying to listen, forgot her tears. She prompted him: "Speak slowly! . . . . Say it once again."

Using a voice thick and slurred, he began to form understandable words. "I will help you. . . . Do not be afraid."

Glyneth asked tremulously: "Did someone send you to help me?"

"A man with white hair sent me. His name is Murgen. I am Kul! Murgen instructed me in what I must do."

With dawning hope Glyneth asked: "And what is that?"

"I must take you to where you came into this place, as fast as I can. There is little time, since I had to come so far to find you. We are already here too long."

Glyneth asked with new foreboding: "And what if we are too late?"

"I will tell you then." Kul went to look down the slope. "We must go! The rock-worms are coming with long-point spears, to draw my blood. A man in black gives them orders!"

"That is Visbhume. He is a magician, and I took his wallet, which has made him angry."

"I will kill him presently. Can you walk, or shall I carry you?"

"I can walk very nicely, thank you," said Glyneth. "It is not dignified to ride over your shoulder with my bottom in the air."

"Let us see how fast you can run with dignity."

They climbed the slope until Glyneth began to pant, whereupon Kul threw her over his shoulder once again and bounded up the rocks. Looking backwards, Glyneth could see only space and far downward perspectives; Kul seemed to ignore gravity and equilibrium, and Glyneth finally closed her eyes.

Arriving at the ridge, he set her down. "Now, if we go yonder, behind that forest, we will come down upon the little house. I believe that an hour or two still remain to us, before the gate closes. If all is proper, you will soon be home."

Glyneth looked at Kul sidelong. "And what of you?"

Kul seemed puzzled. "I have not been told."

"Do you have a home here, or friends?"

"No."

"That seems strange!"

"Come," said Kul. "Time is short."

The two ran along the ridge, with Kul ever more urgent for speed, and when Glyneth could run no further, he again lifted her and carried her, bounding at a slant down the slope. Finally, at a place behind the forest, he set her down. "Come now; let us see how the land lays."

They went under the balls of dark blue and plum-red foliage and looked across the sward. The hut stood at a distance of a hundred yards. Along the riverbank came Visbhume riding a great black eight-legged beast, flat as a plank across its dorsal surface, with a complicated tangle of horn, flexible eye-stalks, feeding tubes for a head and a wide flat back twenty feet long, where Visbhume rode in fine style on the cushioned top bench of a white howdah. Behind came a band of twenty Progressive Eels carrying spears, along with a dozen other creatures wearing armour of a black metallic substance and tall conical helmets which connected directly to their epaulettes. These goblin-knights carried maces and lances and marched on heavy short legs.

Kul said: "Listen carefully, because time is short. I will go to the far end of the forest and show myself. If they march to attack me, you run to the hut. At the door you will notice a rim of golden light. Stop and listen. If you hear nothing, the way is safe; you may pass through. If you hear harsh sounds, or any sounds whatever, do not venture yourself; the hole is closing and you will be chopped into a thousand motes. Is this all clear?"

"Yes, but what of you?"

"Have no fears for me. Quickly now; be ready!"

Glyneth cried out: "Kul! Should I wait for you?"

Kul made an urgent gesture. "No!" He lunged off through the forest.

A few moments later Glyneth heard Visbhume's shrill outcry: "There stands the beast! To the attack! Pierce both with long-points and lances; break him with your maces! Strike with all force and accurate direction! Cut the horrid creature into minute parcels; let his red blood spurt and run! But attention all! Do not strike or pierce the maiden!"

The black goblin-knights ran heavily forward, with the Progressive Eels skipping to the side, while Visbhume rode well to the rear.

Glyneth waited as long as she dared, then, choosing her time, darted out of the forest.

Visbhume saw her instantly, and swinging about his long steed, sent it cantering across the sward to intercept her. Behind ran the Progressive Eels, hissing and whispering.

Glyneth stopped short; she could never reach the hut in time; she retreated to the forest. Visbhume called out: "Halt! Would you return to Watershade? Stand then, and hear me!"

Glyneth paused uncertainly. Visbhume brought his steed lumbering about in a grand curve, and halted directly between Glyneth and the hut. "Glyneth, make response! What will you say to me?"

Glyneth called out: "I want to go back to Watershade!"

"Just so! Then you must tell me what I want to know!"

Glyneth screwed up her face in sick indecision. Both Dhrun and Aillas would wish her to tell all she knew, if thereby she could save herself. But would Visbhume stand by his terms?

She knew very well that he would not do so.

Certain of the Progressives were crouching and slinking toward her, thinking to make a sudden leap so as to catch her. She backed toward the forest. On sudden inspiration, she halted. Reaching into Visbhume's wallet, she brought out one of the glass eggs full of insects; this she hurled into the midst of the Progressive Eels.

For a moment they stood immobile, staring with disk-eyes glazed over with consternation; then, letting fall their long-point spears they lurched hissing and singing across the sward, dropping from time to time to roll and flail arms and legs in the air. Some plunged into the river and were seen no more; others wallowed in the mud along the shore, and crawled at best speed downstream.

Visbhume cried out: "Glyneth, the minutes fly! I will be safe, since my way is mysterious, but you will be lost forever!"

Glyneth called out in her most cajoling voice: "Visbhume, let me go back to Watershade; do! And I will thank you, even though you brought me here; and King Aillas himself will answer your questions."

"Ha ha! Do I seem such a fool? King Aillas will have me quickly hanged! Do you quibble with me while the precious minutes flow by? I see the portal; it is still open, but already the golden rim is starting to fade! Tell me now!"

"Let me go first!"

Visbhume screamed in rage. "I make the conditions, not you! Tell me now, or I go through the portal and leave you to the vile Progressives!"

Kul suddenly burst from the forest, and bounded toward Visbhume, who cried out in alarm and put his steed into a posture of defense, with a pair of coiled tentacles snapping out toward Kul.

Kul picked up one of the long-point spears and came forward, circling and feinting with spear poised to throw, but always Visbhume protected himself behind the high-reared neck, and now from the forest came the goblin-knights.

Visbhume began to make a wailing outcry. "The time is short! Leave me be, that I may return to Earth! How dare you molest me so! Knights, kill me this beast, and quickly! The rim is fading; must I bide on Tanjecterly?"

Kul shouted: "Glyneth! Through the gate!"

Glyneth sidled around Kul and the eight-legged carpet-beast, and made a new dash for the hut. She stopped short. The knights had come to attack Kul with maces on high. They chopped, but he slid away and plunged into their midst. Glyneth could see only a welter of movement, and then the knights submerged Kul under sheer weight of numbers.

Glyneth, crying out in anguish, seized up a lance; running forward, she stabbed one of the knights; a heavy mailed leg kicked her in the stomach and sent her toppling backwards. Then, as she watched, knights seemed to explode up and out, as Kul thrust up from among them. With a mace in each hand, he smashed heads and sent knights reeling. Taking note of Glyneth, he shouted: "Go to the hut! Escape while you can!"

Glyneth cried out desperately: "I can not leave you to fight alone!"

Kul groaned in frustration. "Must I be killed for nothing? Save yourself; at least do this for me!"

To Glyneth's horror a black knight reared high; it swung up its mace and with full power brought it down upon Kul, who slid to the side to avoid the blow, but fell once again to the sward. Sobbing in despair Glyneth turned and ran for the hut, to find Visbhume in front of her, running on long prancing pointed-toe strides, his anxiety now only to extricate himself from Tanjecterly.

Visbhume arrived at the hut with Glyneth close behind. Visbhume gave a croak of despair and stopped short. "Ah, what sorrow, and grief piled on sorrow! The gold is gone! The gate is closed!"

Glyneth likewise came to a shocked standstill. The gold rim around the door-opening had faded completely, leaving only weathered wood.

Slowly Visbhume turned upon Glyneth, his eyes yellow. Glyneth shrank back. Visbhume spoke in a voice glottal with passion: "Now I must pronounce justice! By your deed I am locked here on Tanjecterly, to bide a long and uncertain time! The blame is yours and so shall be the punishment! Prepare yourself for events both bitter and sweet, and of long duration!" With face contorted he lurched forward, Glyneth dodged aside, but Visbhume held his arms wide with thin fingers outspread. Glyneth threw a despairing glance over her shoulder, but discovered only a field of corpses. In that case, she would throw herself in the river. . . . Above Visbhume loomed a shadow. Kul, with blood streaming from a dozen wounds, seized Visbhume by the neck, lifted him high and threw him to the ground, where Visbhume lay whimpering and writhing. Kul stepped forward with his sword, but Glyneth cried out: "No! We need to learn from him!"

Kul slumped to sit upon the steps of the hut. Glyneth went to him. "You are wounded; you drip blood! I have no way to care for you!"

Kul gave his head a dreary shake. "Do not concern yourself."

Glyneth spoke to Visbhume. "What medicines and balms are in this wallet?"

"None!"

Glyneth looked at him closely. "How did you cure the wounds where I stabbed you?"

Visbhume said thinly: "I carry only stuffs for my personal use! Give me now my wallet, as I will need it."

"Visbhume: how did you heal your cheek?"

"No matter!" said Visbhume angrily. "That is my private affair."

With an effort Glyneth took up Kul's sword. "Visbhume, tell me now, or I will cut off your hand and watch to see you deal with your hurt!" She raised the sword in the air. Visbhume, looking up startled into the pale clenched face, reached into a pocket sewn to the inner side of his sleeve. He brought out first his silver pipe, then his fiddle and bow, in magically diminished form, then the two pieces of the broken stiletto, then a round white box, which he gave disdainfully to Glyneth. "Rub this wax to the wound. Do not waste it; it is most valuable."

Glyneth warily put down the sword, and rubbed the wax upon Kul's cuts, slashes, bruises and stab-wounds, despite Visbhume's protests against her lavish employment of his personal commodities. With wonder Glyneth saw the cuts seal and the flesh become whole, to the magic of the balm. Kul sighed; Glyneth, working as gently as she could, spoke in alarm: "Why do you sigh? Do I hurt you?"

"No. . . . Odd ideas enter my mind. . . . Scenes of places I have never known."

Visbhume rose to his feet and arranged the set of his garments. He spoke with frigid dignity: "I will now take my wallet and mount my carpet wole and be away from this unhappy site! You have done me incalculable harms, hurting my body and restraining my rightful exit from Tanjecterly! Still, in the circumstances, I will control my bitterness and make the best of affairs. Glyneth, my wallet, on this instant! Then, on my running carpet wole I will take my leave of you."

Kul said shortly: "Sit down on the ground; if you run I am too tired to chase you. Glyneth, go to the carcasses yonder and find some straps and cords from their harness."

Visbhume cried out in a brassy voice: "What now? Have you not dealt me trouble enough?"

Kul grinned. "Not nearly enough."

Glyneth brought straps, from which Kul fashioned a collar for Visbhume's neck with a leash twenty feet long. Meanwhile Glyneth gingerly explored Visbhume's garments for secret pockets and removed all his magical adjuncts, which she tucked into the wallet. Visbhume at last stifled his protests and sat crouched in surly silence. The eight-legged wole on which he had arrived had strayed no great distance and placidly cropped the sward with its feeding tubes. Kul climbed to its long flat back and threw down a pair of anchors to prevent it from coursing away.

Glyneth addressed Visbhume: "Now: will you answer questions and tell us all we should know?"

"Ask away," snapped Visbhume. "I must now serve you or risk damage to my poor body, where I already feel the pain of purple bruises. A person of my status is much demeaned."

"If we are hungry, what shall we eat?"

Visbhume considered a moment, then licked his lips. "Since I too hunger, I will tell you how to find bounty. In the wallet you will find a box. Take therefrom a scrap of cloth, and spread it smooth. Let fall upon it a drop of wine, a crumb of bread and a sliver of cheese."

Glyneth followed instructions and the trifle of cloth instantly expanded to became a fine damask cover laden with all manner of viands, and the three ate to their satiation, whereupon the cloth once more became small.

Glyneth said: "Visbhume, you have been forming quiet plots. If they help you, then we have only ourselves to blame, and we will therefore be vigilant, and show you little mercy if you anger us."

"Bah!" muttered Visbhume. "I could form a dozen plots a minute, or wear them like yonder tree wears its leaves, but to what avail?"

"If I knew, you would never learn from me."

"Ah, Glyneth, your words are hurtful! At one time tender feelings existed between us; have you forgotten so soon?"

Glyneth grimaced but made no comment. "How can we send a message to Murgen?"

Visbhume seemed genuinely puzzled. "To what purpose? He knows you are here?"

"So that he can open a new gate, and rescue us."

"Murgen, no matter what his power, cannot break a new gate when the pendulum is swinging."

"Explain, if you will."

"I spoke in parable. There is no pendulum. At a certain pulse, time is static both here and on Earth, and the gate can be opened at one node or another. See the black moon which moves around the northern sky? It strikes a radius with a central pole and somewhere along the radius a node can be opened, if pulses are in synchrony. It is a matter of exacting calculation, since time moves at different rates here and on Earth. Sometimes here time goes fast and on Earth slow, and sometimes the opposite. Only when time runs at the same rate, as determined by the pulses, can the gates be opened. Otherwise, gates could be opened anywhere at any time."

"How can the gate be opened again, and when, and where?"

Visbhume rose to his feet and, as if in boredom or perhaps abstraction of thought, started to remove the collar from his neck. Kul gave the leash a tug which sent Visbhume jumping in a ridiculous caper to keep his balance. "Do that no more," said Kul. "Be happy the strap is only around your neck and not through holes in your ears. Answer the question, and do not try to confuse us with verbiage."

Visbhume growled: "You would take all my valuable knowledge and give me nothing, and still tie me by the neck, as if I were a cur dog or a Progressive."

"But for your doing, we would not be here; have you forgotten?"

Visbhume blew out his thin cheeks. "No good cause is served in dredging up ancient history. That which is done is done, whether we rejoice or grieve! That is my slogan! At that twist in the prism known as 'Now' we are to concern ourselves only with immediate cases."

"Just so. As of 'now' answer the question."

Visbhume said loftily: "Let us work practically! I must take the lead, since the knowledge is mine, and you must trust me to consider our mutual interests. Otherwise I must in intricate detail school you in all the—" Visbhume stopped short as Kul began to draw taut the leash. Kul said: "Answer!"

Visbhume said plaintively: "I was preparing my careful response! Your conduct lacks all gentility." He cleared his throat. "The matter is complex, and, so I fear, beyond your understanding. Time moves by one phase on Earth and by another here. Each phase consists of nine quavers, or pulses, or, even better, constrictions in and out from the central node of what we call 'synchronicity'. Is this clear? No? As I supposed. There is no point in going farther. You must trust my best judgment."

Glyneth said: "You still have not answered me. How do we return to Earth?"

"I am so doing! Between Earth and Tanjecterly, the synchrony lasts six to nine days, and, as we have seen has just ended. Then it sweeps away, along the radius of the black moon with the center node. At the next pulse, the gate will open into another place, but none so easy as Tanjecterly. Hidmarth and Skurre are demon-worlds; Underwood is empty save for a moaning sound; Pthopus is a single torpid soul. These were discovered and explored by Twitten the Arch-mage, and he compiled an almanac, which is of great value."

Glyneth brought a long narrow book with black metal covers from the wallet. The spine was like a sheath housing a black nine-sided metal rod with a golden knob at the end. Glyneth, withdrawing the rod, saw that each of the nine sides was engraved in crabbed golden characters.

Visbhume casually held out his hand. "Let me instruct myself; I have forgotten my calculations."

Glyneth drew the book away. "What is the purpose of the rod?"

"That is a subsidiary instrument. Replace it in the sheath and hand me the book."

Glyneth replaced the rod and opened the book. The first page, indited in queer crawling marks with straggling tails and looping risers was illegible, but someone, perhaps Visbhume, had attached a sheet which would seem to be a translation of the original text. Glyneth read aloud:

> "*These nine places, along with Gaean Earth, form the ten worlds of Chronos, and he has skewered them all on his axis. By cunning effort I have constrained the axis, and held it fixed: such is the magnitude of my achievement.*
>
> "*Of the nine worlds I warn against Paador, Nith and Woon; Hidmarth and Skurre are purulent places infested with demons. Cheng may well be home to the sandestins, but this is uncertain, while Pthopus is truly insipid. Only Tanjecterly will tolerate human men.*
>
> "*In each section the almanac details the cycle of quavers and indicates the standard by which ingress and exit may be obtained. With the almanac is the key, and only this key will strike through the weft and allow passage. Lose not the key! The almanac is thereby useless!*
>
> "*The calculations must be worked with precision. At the periphery of the quaver the key opens a gate where it is struck. The central node is immutable. On Earth it stands where I have fixed it. On Tanjecterly, it resides at the center of the Parley Place, at the town Asphrodiske, where dwell many sad souls.*
>
> "*Such is the domain of Chronos. Some say he is dead, but if one would discover the wraith, he need only tweak the axis, and he shall learn his own truth.*
>
> "*So say I, Twitten of Gaean Earth.*"

Glyneth looked up from the almanac. "Where is Asphrodiske?"

Visbhume made a petulant gesture. "Somewhere off across the plains — a journey of far distance."

"And there we can return to Earth?"

"At the low pulse."

"When will that be?"

"Let me see the almanac."

Glyneth extracted the key, and gave the almanac to Kul. "Let him look but keep your fingers at his throat."

Visbhume cried out in a tragic voice: "Replace the key! Will you not heed Twitten's warning?"

"I will not lose it. Read what you wish to read."

Visbhume studied the indexes and those calculations which he had already made. "The time will be measured by the black moon, on its way to opposition with now."

"How long is that?

"A week? Three weeks? A month? There is no measure but the black moon. On Earth there will be a time much different, short or long: I do not know."

"And if we use the key at Asphrodiske, where will we come out on Earth?"

Visbhume chuckled. "At Twitten's Corners; where else?"

"Do we have time to reach Asphrodiske?"

"It is exactly as far as is Watershade from Twitten's Corners."

Glyneth mused: "The distance is far but not too far." She held out her hand. "Give me the almanac."

"And I took you for a pretty flirtatious little softling!" growled Visbhume. "You are as hard as steel!" With poor grace Visbhume obeyed the order.

"Yonder is Visbhume's carpet wole or whatever it is called; it stands placid and ready. Should we not ride to Asphrodiske in comfort and style?"

Kul jerked the leash. "On your feet! Go command your beast to our use."

Visbhume ungraciously obeyed the order. The anchors were drawn aboard; with Glyneth and Kul riding in the pergola and Visbhume sitting disconsolately with legs dangling over the stern quarters, the wole set off across the plains of Tanjecterly.

Chapter 16

I

THE WOODCUTTER'S HUT STOOD DESOLATE in the forest, with all its magic gone. A shaft of sunlight slanted through the doorway and laid a skewed rectangle along the width of the floor, leaving the old table and bench in gloom. The silence was disturbed only by the sigh of wind among leaves.

Everything which had happened at the hut, or which might have happened, was part of the sad and arid past, and gone forever.

At Watershade Aillas, Dhrun and Shimrod passed a forlorn seven days. Shimrod, for once somber, could report only that Murgen had not abandoned his interest in the matter.

The dear familiar chambers, with the merry presence of Glyneth only a memory, were too melancholy to be borne. Shimrod took himself to Trilda while Aillas and Dhrun returned to Domreis.

Castle Miraldra was dreary and dull. Aillas occupied himself with routine business of the kingdom, while Dhrun made a desultory effort to resume his studies. Despatches from South Ulfland caught Aillas' attention. The Ska had carefully assembled and fitted out a powerful army in the Foreshore, with the clear purpose of striking into South Ulfland, to destroy the Ulf armies and occupy Suarach, Oäldes and perhaps even Ys itself.

Aillas and Dhrun took ship for South Ulfland with new troops from Dascinet and Scola. They landed at Oäldes and rode at once to Doun Darric.

In conference Aillas learned that, of late, no major engagements had occurred, which suited him well. His strategy dictated the infliction of maximum enemy losses, while incurring a minimum of his own: a kind of war for which he had shaped his army and which put the Ska at disadvantage. Effectively the Ska had lost control of North Ulfland's southern half, save where Castle Sank still served as a strongpoint.

Aillas drafted a letter to Sarquin, Elector-king of the Ska:

> **To the attention of the noble Sarquin, Elector-King:** *I am the legal and ordained King of Ulfland. I find that your armies still tread upon my soil and hold my people in thrall.*
>
> *I ask that you withdraw your armies to the Foreshore, that you liberate all Ulfish thralls still in servitude, and that you renounce your aggressive attempts against my land. If you act at once, I will demand no reparations.*
>
> *If you fail to heed my request, your people will be killed and Ska blood will flow deep. My armies now exceed yours in number. They are trained to strike and strike again, but to take no blows in return. My ships control the Narrow Sea; we can burn your coastal towns at will. Shortly you will see black smoke rising along the shores of Skaghane, and your folk will know the same woe you have visited upon my people.*
>
> *I call upon you to end your futile dream of conquest; you can not harm us; we can destroy you, and bring you great grief.*
>
> *These are the words of*
> **Aillas, King of Troicinet, Dascinet, Scola**
> **and Ulfland.**

Aillas sealed the letter and sent the parcel to be delivered by a captive Ska knight. A week went by and the only response was a sudden movement of Ska troops. East from the Foreshore came the great black army, moving with ominous deliberation.

Aillas had no slightest intention of attacking so massive a force. Immediately however he sent skirmishers out to lure the Ska light cavalry within range of his archers. Small parties circled to attack the baggage trains and to harass generally the lines of communication.

The Ska army split into two units of about equal strength, the first proceeding to the town Kerquar on the west and the second moving east to Blackthorn Heath, at the center of North Ulfland.

Ulf patrols became ever bolder, riding to within shouting distance of the Ska to call insults, in the hope of enticing a group away from the main body, where they could be ambushed and cut to pieces. At night Ska sentries went in fear of their lives and were as often murdered as not, and finally the Ska themselves began sending out night patrols, and setting up their own ambushes, which to some extent diminished Ulf pressures, though the Ska still lost more than they gained.

Small signs indicated an erosion of Ska morale. Previously they had attacked, with flair and impunity, and had regarded themselves as invincible. Now that they had become quarry and victim, the mantle of invincibility quickly proved to be a thing of no substance and they long and well had mulled over the recollection of their recent defeat, which could not be explained away.

Aillas wondered if they could be provoked into new errors of strategy which the Ulfish forces could exploit. He and his commanders, poring over maps, drew up a variety of battle-plans, each with notes to deal with contingencies.

So began an intricate and carefully timed set of operations: attacks, withdrawals, and ever more daring feints against the towns of the Foreshore, until these feints became actual raids, combined with assaults from the sea. At last, as Aillas hoped, the army based at Kerquar shifted to the north-west, with the effect of isolating the army on Blackthorn Heath from reinforcement in the case of sudden massive attack. Now, any plans for a Ska invasion of South Ulfland seemed to have been postponed.

Aillas instantly sent a force of light cavalry to harass and engage the attention of this army, without actually coming to grips with the highly disciplined core of heavy cavalry. At the same time he sent a special siege army, equipped with two dozen massive arbalests, catapults and other siege engines against Castle Sank, the fortress guarding the southeast. He envisioned a quick and brutally powerful assault, and so it was, despite the rebuilding and reinforcement of the garrison.

In six hours the outer walls had fallen and the citadel was under attack, with archers stationed upon high wooden towers keeping the parapets under fire. The machines sent great stones high to break open the roofs, then sent in fireballs to ignite the wrecked timbers. The defenders fought with desperate courage, and twice sallies of armoured knights were broken.

On the second night during the final stages of the operation, with flames roaring high, Aillas thought to glimpse Tatzel on the parapets. She wore an archer's helmet and carried a bow, with which she discharged arrow after arrow at the attacking forces. Words rose in Aillas' throat, but he held them back, and watched in fascination. She looked down and saw him; nocking an arrow to the string of her bow, she drew far back with all her power, but before she could release, an arrow arched across space and plunged into her chest. She looked down in dismay and let the arrow fly against the merlon beside which she stood, and it glanced away. She seemed to sink to her knees, and fell backward out of sight.

Aillas was still not certain of her identity, in the flickering red light, but later she was not found among the survivors and Aillas lacked all inclination to sort through the charred corpses in search of gallant young Tatzel.

The Ska army on Blackthorn Heath, learning of the assault on Castle Sank, broke camp and made a desperate effort to arrive at Sank in time to lift the siege. In their haste they departed from their usually tight formation of march, and raced north in a column, and here was the mistake for which Aillas had not only prepared but had prompted the Ska to commit. At a place called Tolerby Scrub, the Ska met an ambush of Ulf main forces, with sixty Troice knights leading the charge into the very heart of the Ska army, then wheeling and withdrawing, while from the other side came a similar charge of the Ulf barons.

The battle was far from easy, and only when troops coming down from the victory at Sank collapsed the Ska flank was the battle won.

There were few Ska survivors, and many casualties among both Ulf and Troice. Aillas, observing so much carnage, turned away in revulsion. Still, he was now master of all North Ulfland, save only the areas near the Foreshore, the Foreshore itself and the approaches to the great fort Poëlitetz.

Two weeks later, Aillas, riding with fifty knights, approached the remaining Ska army near the town Twock. He sent a herald out under a flag of truce, with a message:

Aillas, King of Troicinet, Dascinet, Scola and Ulfland, requests a parley with the chief commander of the Ska army.

A pair of heralds set a table out upon the fell, spread it with a white cloth, set down chairs and on poles hung a gonfalon with the black and silver Ska emblem, and a gonfalon, quartered, displaying the arms of Troicinet, Dascinet, Ulfland and Scola.

With two knights by his side and a pair of heralds, Aillas went out to wait ten yards back of the table. Ten minutes passed, then, from the Ska army came a similar group.

Aillas advanced to the table, as did his counterpart: a tall spare man, keen-featured, with black eyes and black-gray hair.

Aillas bowed. "I am Aillas, King of Troicinet, Dascinet and Ulfland."

The Ska said: "I am Sarquin, King-elect of Skaghane and all the Ska."

"I am happy to meet a person of ultimate authority," said Aillas. "My work is thereby eased. I am here to arrange peace. We have reconquered our territory; the war is effectively won. Our hatred of you remains but it is not worth the spilling of any more blood. You might still fight but now you are outnumbered, by warriors at least equal to your own. If you choose to fight on, there will be only boys, women and old men left on Skaghane. At this moment, I could land a force of three thousand men upon Skaghane and no one could halt me.

"I wish to wound or kill no more brave men, either yours or mine. These are the terms of my peace.

"You shall withdraw all your forces from Ulfland, including Poëlitetz. You shall not carry with you wealth or treasures accumulated in Ulfland, nor may you herd horses, cattle, sheep nor swine. Knights may ride their mounts; all other horses must be surrendered.

"You shall maintain sovereignty over the Foreshore, for the use and welfare of your people.

"You shall release all slaves, serfs, thralls and captives now in your custody, on Skaghane, along the Foreshore, and elsewhere, and deliver them with all kind and clement treatment to the town Suarach.

"You will agree not to conspire nor ally yourself with, nor give counsel, comfort nor assistance to, the enemies of my rule: specifically, King Casmir of Lyonesse, nor to anyone else.

"Otherwise I make no demands upon you, for reparations or indemnities, or punitive damages for the lives of my people whom you have ravaged in your acquisitive lust.

"These terms are generous. If you accept them, you may return to Skaghane with honour, since your warriors have fought bravely, and surely these are conditions which will allow you comfort, prosperity, and in due course fellowship among the nations of the Elder Isles. If you reject them, you not only gain nothing but you bring disaster to your subjects and to your country.

"We cannot be friends, but at least we need not be enemies. Those are my proposals. Do you accept or reject them?"

Sarquin, Elector-King of the Ska, spoke three words. "I accept them."

Aillas rose to his feet. "In the name of all the men who otherwise would die, I thank you for your wise decision."

Sarquin rose, bowed, turned and rejoined his army. Half an hour later the army broke camp and marched west into the Foreshore.

II

THE WAR WAS WON. Ska troops departed Poëlitetz, and were instantly replaced by a garrison of Ulf warriors. Audry, King of Dahaut, in due course protested this act to Aillas, claiming that Poëlitetz was situated on the soil of Dahaut.

Aillas replied that while King Audry cited several points of technical interest, and used the resources of abstract logic in an adroit manner, he had actually made no connection with reality. Aillas pointed out that historically Poëlitetz guarded Ulfland from Dahaut, but served no useful purpose whatever when controlled by the Dauts. The line of the

Great Scarp more realistically defined the boundary than did the Teach tac Teach watershed.

King Audry in a rage threw Aillas' letter to the floor and never bothered to reply.

Aillas and Dhrun returned to Troicinet, leaving Sir Tristano and Sir Maloof to oversee the details of the Ska withdrawal, which in any event went with scrupulous exactitude.

A few days after the return of Dhrun and Aillas to Domreis, Shimrod appeared at Castle Miraldra. After supper Aillas, Dhrun and Shimrod went to sit by a blazing fire in a small side parlour. After an awkward moment Aillas forced himself to ask: "I suppose that you have nothing new to tell us."

"There have been certain strange circumstances, but they change essentially nothing."

"What strange circumstances are these?"

"Order in more wine," said Shimrod. "They make long and dry telling."

Aillas summoned the footman. "Two more — no, three more flasks of wine, since we must keep Shimrod in good voice."

Shimrod said: "Good voice or not, much is still unknown to us."

Aillas, noting an indefinable hesitancy in Shimrod's manner, seized upon the word: "'Still'?"

"Still, yet, then and now. But I will tell you what I have come to learn. You will see that it is little enough. First, I will say that Tanjecterly is only one of ten worlds, including our good Gaean Earth, which old Father Chronos swings on a noose. Some are the realms of demons, others are not even so useful as this. Visbhume opened a hole into Tanjecterly with his key, but it seems that sometimes holes open of themselves to let men fall through willy-nilly, to their vast surprise, and so to disappear forever. But this is all to the side. A certain indomitable sorcerer by the name of Ticely Twitten made a study of these worlds and his almanac measures what he calls 'pulses' and 'quavers'. Time does not go in Tanjecterly, for instance, in consonance with time here. A minute here may be an hour there, or the opposite may be true."

"Interesting," said Aillas. "So then?"

"My tale begins with Twitten. Hippolito of Maule acquired his almanac, and it was purloined by Visbhume. For reasons unknown, Casmir sent Visbhume to ask questions of Glyneth, and he took her to Tanjecterly, for various reasons: one of these being Tamurello's hope that I or Murgen would foolishly trap ourselves forever. Instead, as you know, we sent Kul, that he might rescue Glyneth. In the absence of facts, it is hard to judge his success . . ."

III

THE CARPET-WOLE COURSED OFF in a direction which Glyneth decided to call east, opposite to the point in the sky where she had first noted the black moon. This odd celestial object had already shifted perceptibly, veering toward the north while remaining the same distance above the horizon.

For ten miles the wole ran along the riverbank, with open plains to the south. In the distance a band of long-legged beings took interested note of their passage and even began to make a rather menacing approach, but the wole increased its pace and the creatures lost interest in pursuit.

The river swung away to the north and the wole set off across a seemingly limitless steppe, with short blue grass below and spherical trees scattered at far intervals.

Kul rode forward on the first shoulders of the beast, standing flat-footed with legs somewhat apart. Glyneth, perched high on the cushioned bench of the pergola, sat where she could see in all directions. Had she chosen to do so, she might have stepped down to the rug which covered the wole's back and walked aft to where Visbhume sat hunched over the wole's hindquarters, his eyes liquid with resentment for the indignity of the leash around his neck.

For a period Glyneth ignored Visbhume, save for an occasional glance to ensure that he might not be about his crafty tricks. Finally she descended to the rug and went aft. She asked Visbhume: "Is there no night here?"

"None."

"Then how do we keep time, and know when to sleep?"

"Sleep when you are tired," snapped Visbhume. "That is the rule. As for keeping time, the black moon must serve as the clock."

"And how far is Asphrodiske?"

"That is hard to say. Several hundred leagues, perhaps. Twitten has not drawn maps for our ease and delectation." An idea came into Visbhume's mind; he blinked and licked his lips. "Still, his surveys are exact. Bring the almanac and I will make the calculations."

Glyneth ignored the request. She looked to the side, gauging the passing landscape. "At this pace we are surely travelling four or five leagues each hour. Will the wole tire?"

"It wants to rest and eat grass for the same time that it runs."

"Then in fifty hours it will take us a hundred leagues. That is my reckoning."

"The reckoning is fair and equable, but accounts neither for dangers nor delays."

Glyneth looked up at the circling suns. "I am so tired now that I could sleep standing on my feet."

"I too am tired," said Visbhume. "Let us stop so that we may refresh ourselves. Tired as I am, I will keep the first watch, so that you and the beast may sleep."

"'Beast'? Kul?"

"Just so."

Glyneth went forward to Kul. "Are you tired?"

Kul considered the state of his being. "Yes, I am tired."

"Should we stop to sleep?"

Kul surveyed the landscape. "I see no urgent threat."

"Visbhume has kindly offered to take the first watch, so that you and I might sleep in comfort."

"Ah! Visbhume shows a rare magnanimity!"

"He also knows some dreadful tricks."

"Just so. Our sleep might be sound and deep—and long. Still, in the harness box I have discovered a fine length of rope, and Visbhume perhaps will oblige us after all."

Arriving at a spot where two trees grew fifty feet apart, Kul brought the wole to a halt and dropped its anchor.

With eager interest Visbhume inquired: "What now? Do we rest? Shall I keep the first watch? If so, remove this leash, so that I may look right and left with all possible facility."

"In good time," said Kul. From the harness box at the back of the pergola he brought a coil of strong rope. He tied one end to one of the trees, then signaled to Visbhume. "Stand exactly here, halfway between the trees."

With a wincing scowl Visbhume obeyed. Kul removed the leash, knotted the rope around Visbhume's neck, then, going to the other tree, drew the rope tight so that Visbhume was fixed between the two trees, unable to move in either direction far enough to free himself, even though his arms and legs were free.

Glyneth watched with approval. "Now you must search him well! There are pockets in his sleeves and his trousers and perhaps even his shoes."

Visbhume cried out in fury: "Am I to be allowed no privacy of person? This sort of search is contrary to every known rule of gentility."

Kul carefully searched Visbhume's garments, and it became clear that Glyneth, through diffidence, had failed to search Visbhume with sufficient care. Kul discovered a short tube of unknown employment, a brown box containing what seemed to be a miniature cottage, and in the seams of Visbhume's pantaloons, two lengths of stiff if resilient steel wire. The inside of Visbhume's belt yielded a dagger. The boots, the cravat and the gathering of the pantaloons at Visbhume's bony ankles seemed innocent of contraband.

Glyneth examined the miniature cottage. "This would seem a magic cottage. How is it made large?"

"That is a most valuable property," said Visbhume. "I do not allow its general use."

Kul said: "Visbhume, so far your skin is largely whole. You have eaten well and you have ridden on the wole. If these conditions agree with you, answer each question directly and with truth; otherwise you shall come upon a great sadness."

Visbhume blurted angrily: "Put the miniature on the ground and cry out: 'House, grow big!' When you wish it to reduce, cry out: 'House, grow small!'"

Glyneth put the miniature house on the ground and cried out: "House, grow big!" Immediately she was yielded a cottage of comfortable aspect, with smoke already rising from the chimney.

Kul said: "Visbhume, you shall keep first watch, as you so kindly offered. If any tricks are left to you, which I do not doubt, try none of them, since I will be alert."

Entering the house, Glyneth found a comfortable couch and throwing herself down, fell instantly asleep.

She awakened after an unknown period to find Visbhume sleeping on the ground beside the cottage while Kul sat dozing in the doorway. Glyneth went across the room and stroked the black fur covering his scalp. Kul looked up. "You are awake."

"I will keep watch. Now you sleep."

Kul rose from the chair and looked around the room. For a moment Glyneth thought that he might stretch out on the floor, but he lay down on the couch and was at once asleep.

Visbhume presently awoke. Glyneth pretended not to notice. Visbhume studied the situation through eyelids barely slitted open, through which his eyes glinted like the yellow eyes of a fox.

Visbhume studied Glyneth a moment or two. He whispered: "Glyneth!"

Glyneth looked toward him.

Visbhume asked: "Is the creature asleep?"

Glyneth nodded.

Visbhume spoke in the most cajoling of voices: "You know truly that your interests lie with me, the powerful and mighty Visbhume! So then: will you join with me in sacred and absolute cabal? We will defeat the monster beast, with his slavering threats and objectionable attitudes!"

"Indeed? And then?"

"You know the love I bear for you! Can you feel the quiver of a like feeling for me?"

"What then?"

"Then: away to Asphrodiske, and back to Earth at the coming of the quaver."

"And that will be when?"

"A short time, shorter than you might think!"

"Visbhume! You alarm me! Have we enough time?"

"If all goes well and I am in command."

"But how do we know how long or short is our time?"

"By the black moon! When the radius swings to the diameter exactly opposite the gate by which we entered, that is the time! Now, will you join me in deep and unassailable cabal?"

"Kul is terrible and strong."

"So am I! Does he think all my power is gone? I hope so! Then you are with me?"

"Of course not."

"What! You prefer the beast to me, Visbhume who lives and dances to the thrilling musics?"

"Visbhume, sleep while you have the chance. Your foolishness is keeping Kul awake."

Visbhume spoke in a low and almost sibilant tone: "For the last time you have flouted me, and how you shall regret it!"

Glyneth made no response.

Kul awoke; the three made breakfast upon milk, bread, butter, cheese, onions and ham from the pantry, then Glyneth called: "House, grow small!"

The cottage shrank quickly to miniature size, and Glyneth carefully returned it to its box. They climbed aboard the wole and once again set off across the plain.

Today Visbhume wished to share the comforts of the pergola with Glyneth. "From this vantage I command a wide view! In a flash I can apprehend danger at a great distance!"

"You are the rearguard," said Kul. "You must spy out dangers overtaking us from behind; that is your duty, and your best vantage is over the hindquarters, exactly as yesterday. Quick now! The black moon rolls around the sky, and we must arrive at Asphrodiske in good time."

Across the plain of blue grass ran the wole, the splayed legs coursing forward and back so that the tassels of the rug jerked to the motion. Kul knelt at the base of the pergola, leaning forward so that his massive shoulders almost filled the space between the wole's ocular horns.

Glyneth reclined at her ease across the pergola's cushioned bench, one slim leg idly dangling, while Visbhume hunched at the far end of the rug, glumly looking back the way they had come.

To the north appeared a deep forest of dark blue and purple trees. Drawing near they saw a tall manse of dark timber, built to a style elegant and stately, with many narrow glass windows, turrets and cupolas, as well as a dozen elaborate follies and crotchets included apparently for the sheer relief of boredom. To Glyneth's taste, the style verged upon the eccentric, though out here, overlooking this changeless plain, anyone's taste would seem as sound as any one else's, and Glyneth straightened in her seat, so as not to present a careless or untidy image to possible observation through the tall narrow windows.

As they passed by, a portal opened and out rode a knight in full armour of glossy black and brown metal. From his helm rose a high crest, beautifully wrought, of rods, disks and barbed prongs. The knight rode a creature somewhat like a black splay-legged tiger with a row of sharp horns down its forehead, and carried a tall lance from which fluttered a purple banner, engaged with an emblem of dark red, silver and blue.

The knight halted at a distance of a hundred feet, and Kul politely brought the wole to a halt. The knight called out: "Who are you, that crosses the breadth of my domain, with neither let nor leave?"

Glyneth called out: "We are strangers to this place, Sir Knight, and no one informed us of your rule. This being the case, will you kindly grant us leave to pass on our way?"

"That is well and softly spoken," declared the knight. "I would be tempted to clemency, did I not fear that others, less courteous than yourself, might be emboldened to take liberties."

Glyneth declared: "Sir, our lips are sealed as if with bars of iron! Never will your forbearance be bruited abroad, and our reports will extol only the splendor of your carriage and the gallantry of your conduct. With our best regards to you and your dear ones, we will now hastily withdraw from your presence."

"Not so fast! Have I not spoken? You are in detention. Dismount and proceed to Lorn House!"

Kul rose to his feet and shouted: "Fool! Return to your manse while life remains to you!"

The knight lowered his lance. Kul jumped down from the wole, to Glyneth's distress. She cried out: "Kul, get back up here! We will run away, and he may chase us if he wishes!"

"His steed is too fast," said Visbhume. "Give me the tube you took from me and I will blow a fire-mite at him. No! Better! In my wallet is a trifle of mirror; give that to me."

Glyneth found the mirror and gave it to Visbhume. The knight aimed his lance at Kul; the triple-horned black tiger sprang forward. Visbhume made a sweeping motion with his hand; the mirror expanded to reflect the knight and his steed. Visbhume snapped away the mirror; the knight and his reflected image clashed together; both lances shivered and both knights were pitched to the ground where they drew swords and hacked at each other, while the tiger-mounts rolled and tumbled in a snarling screaming ball.

Kul jumped aboard the wole; it lumbered away to the east, with the combat still raging behind.

Glyneth went to Visbhume. "That was good work and it will earn you consideration when the final accounting is made. Give me back the mirror."

"Better, far better that it remains with me," said Visbhume smoothly. "In emergencies I will therefore be swift to act."

Glyneth asked pointedly: "Do you recall Kul's admonition? He was anxious to fight the knight; you denied him his exercise and now he may be short-tempered."

"Aaagh, the monstrous brute!" growled Visbhume under his breath, and with unwilling fingers relinquished the mirror.

Time passed; leagues were thrust astern. Glyneth tried to puzzle through the computations in Twitten's almanac, but met no success. Visbhume refused to teach her, declaring that first she must learn two arcane languages and an exotic sytem of mathematics, each with its particular mode of graphic representation. Glyneth also found a chart, which Visbhume gracelessly interpreted for her. "Here is the Lakkady Hills, the River Mys and the hut; this is the great Tang-Tang Steppe, inhabited only by a few rogue knights and bands of nomad beasts. This is where we now travel."

"And this town here, by the river: is it Asphrodiske?"

Visbhume squinted at the chart. "That seems to be the town Pude, by the River Haroo. Asphrodiske is here, beyond these woods and the Steppe of Sore Beggars."

Glyneth looked dubiously at the black moon, which had moved a considerable distance around the horizon. "It is yet a long way. Have we time?"

"Much depends upon the flow of circumstances," said Visbhume. "If an experienced captain of far travels, such as myself, were in charge of the voyage, events might well go with facility."

"We will give your advice every consideration," said Glyneth. "You may also keep a sharp look-out for robber knights and nomad beasts."

The travellers proceeded across Tang-Tang Steppe, but encountered no molestation either by robber knights or by nomad beasts, though occasionally in the distance they saw heavy long-necked beasts grazing upon the fruit of the trees, and a few sparse packs of two-legged wolves hopping and loping across the middle distance. From time to time the creatures paused to stand high, the better to appraise the wole, with Glyneth lolling on the bench of the pergola, Kul below and Visbhume crouched at the rear.

Visbhume became drowsy and lay back on the rug to doze in the warmth of the suns' light. Glyneth, at a sudden sound, looked around to find that one of the wolves had trotted furtively up behind the wole, then jumped to the rug, where now, sitting on Visbhume's face, it sucked blood from his chest through the rasping orifices in the palms of its forepaws.

Kul jumped aft, seized the wolf, wrung its neck and threw it astern. Visbhume, with a lambent glare first at Kul, then back toward the corpse of the wolf, now being torn apart by four of its fellows, at last regained his composure. "Had I not been deprived of my things, this outrage could not have occurred!"

Glyneth gave him a scornful glance. "You should not have brought me here in the first place."

"You must not blame me; I was so commissioned, by a highly placed person!"

"Who? Casmir? That is no excuse. Why does he want to know about Dhrun?"

"A portent, or something of the sort, has caused him alarm," said Visbhume sourly, candid only through the discomfiture of the wolf's attack, for which it was convenient to blame Casmir. Glyneth pressed for further details, but Visbhume would say no more until she first responded to his questions with equal frankness, a suggestion which prompted from Glyneth only a laugh of contemptuous amusement, and Visbhume said darkly: "I will never forget such insults!"

The journey proceeded as before. The wolves ran behind for a period, hopping and bounding on long legs, but at last uttered howls of rebuke after the wole and turned away to the south.

Leagues were vanquished by the wole's running feet, while the black moon drifted around the sky. The group halted to rest a second and then a third time. On each occasion Glyneth raised the magic cottage and caused a fine banquet to appear on the table, at which all dined to repletion. Visbhume, however, was not allowed to drink overmuch wine lest he become large and annoy the others with his boasting. He then went into a fit of tearful complaints for the plight in which he found himself.

Glyneth refused to listen to him. "Again I will point out that these troubles are of your own making!"

Visbhume started to refute her statement, but Glyneth stopped him short. "Neither Kul nor I care to waste our time with foolishness. Instead—" she brought the wallet to the table "—tell me, and I remind you of Kul's views in regard to evasiveness, how I may blow fire-mites from this tube."

"You cannot do so," said Visbhume, smiling and tapping his hands on the table in time to some internal tune.

"And how would you do so?"

"First I would need the fire-mites. Are there any in the wallet?"

Glyneth looked blank. "I do not know." She brought out a flask. "What is in this little flagon?"

"That is Hippolito's mental sensitizer. One drop stimulates the mind and helps one achieve an enviable reputation for hilarity and wit. Two drops enhances the aesthetic propensities to an exquisite degree, so that the person so stimulated can translate the patterns of spiderwebs into song-cycles and epic sagas."

"Three drops?"

"It has never been attempted by human man. Kul might wish to experience a sublime and aesthetic experience; for such as Kul, I recommend four or even five drops."

"Kul is not an aesthete," said Glyneth. "These are your healing salves and balms, and this is your hair tonic. . . . What is in this green bottle?"

Visbhume said delicately: "That, my dear Glyneth, is a tincture of erotic sublimations. It melts chaste maidens previously proof to both season and reason, and induces a wonderful emotion. When ingested by a gentleman, even of stately years, it lends a surge to the flagging zest and invigorates that person who, for whatever reason, finds himself growing, let us say, absentminded."

"I doubt if we will need this disgusting tonic," said Glyneth coldly. She drew further objects from the wallet. "Here are your insect-bulbs; here is the tube and here the mirror. Cloth, bread, cheese, wine. Fiddle and bow; also pipes. Wires. What is their purpose?"

"They are useful when one wishes to cross a chasm, or to batter open stone walls. The peremptory spells are difficult to use."

"And the fire-mites?"

Visbhume made a negligent gesture. "The question is nuncupatory."

Glyneth screeched: "Kul! Do not kill him!"

Kul slowly subsided to his chair. Visbhume huddled mournfully in the corner. In sudden inspiration, Glyneth pointed to a line of what seemed decorative buttons running along the length of Visbhume's sleeves. "The buttons! Visbhume, are these the fire-mites? ... Kul, be patient. Pull off the buttons."

"Better yet, Visbhume shall eat several of them."

Visbhume looked up in startlement. "Never!"

"Then give them here!"

"I dare not!" cried Visbhume. "As soon as they are detached they must be blown through the tube."

Kul cut from Visbhume's loose sleeves long strips of black cloth to which the fire-mites were affixed, and thenceforth, as Visbhume walked or moved his arms, his bony white elbows protruded from the rents.

Glyneth rolled the strips of cloth around the tube and so made a bundle. "Now then! Explain, if you will, how these are to be used."

"Pull the button from the fabric and put it in the tube so that the head looks away, then blow at the person you wish to discommode."

"What other trickeries are you concealing from us?"

"None! No more! You have scoured me bare! I am helpless!"

Glyneth repacked the wallet. "I hope that you are telling the truth, for your own sake, since, truly, your misery only makes me ill."

As before, the three slept in sequence. Visbhume protested loudly about sleeping outside for fear of the running wolves. He was at last allowed to sleep in the pantry with the door secured against his escape.

In due course the wole once more set off across the steppe: a rolling savannah dotted with spherical trees, of somewhat different colour than before, with occasional trees of mustard-ocher or black and maroon, rather than the carmine-red of the trees along the Mys River.

Ahead stood a gigantic tree six hundred feet tall. The first boughs left the trunk in a cluster of six, spaced symmetrically around the trunk, each terminating in a great ball of dark yellow-brown foliage, with other layers of branches similarly spaced, all the way to the top. In the distance could be seen several other such giant trees, some even taller.

As the wole passed by the first, the passengers noted to their fascination that in the bark of the trunk, two hundred feet above the ground, arboreal two-legged creatures had cut out apartments interconnected by rickety balconies. The tree-dwellers showed great excitement as the wole passed by, and came out to crowd the balconies, pointing, signalling and performing gesticulations of defiance. Visbhume's obscene gestures only stirred them to a new pitch of indignation.

Inexorably the black moon veered around the sky. Glyneth tried to estimate how long and how far they had travelled but only succeeded in confusing herself. Visbhume pretended a like uncertainty and was ordered to the ground to run behind the wole until his comprehensions sharpened, and almost at once he was able to render a precise report.

"Observe the pink star yonder! When the black moon passes under the star the way is open to Twitten's Corners. That is my estimate. The reckoning is not certain to the minute," he added virtuously. "I was reluctant to make a loose statement."

"And how far is Asphrodiske?"

"Allow me to examine the map in the almanac."

Glyneth, perhaps overly cautious, removed the key from its socket, then extended it to Visbhume.

Visbhume pointed a crooked knob-knuckled forefinger. "We would seem to be at this point, near this depicted river, which is the Haroo; and I believe I observe the flow ahead, on the left hand. The town Pude marks the beginning of settled territory. Here is the Road of Round Stones; it runs past the Dark Woods and across the Plain of Lilies and so to Asphrodiske, here at this symbol. After Pude the distance still is thirty or forty leagues, and the time draws short. I fear that our sleep has been too sound and our travel too meager."

"And what if we missed the time?"

"A wait at the axis would seem to be in order."

"But if we returned to the hut where we started, we could go through there the sooner; is that not correct?"

"So it is! You are a particularly clever girl: almost as clever as you are appealing to the eye."

Glyneth compressed her lips. "Please keep your compliments to yourself; the implications make me sick to my stomach. When would the pulse again be favorable at the hut, if so it became necessary?"

"When the moon reached the same place in the sky. Notice these notations: they refer to the azimuth of the black moon."

Glyneth went forward and reported to Kul what she had learned.

"Very well," said Kul. "We will sleep less soundly and travel more briskly."

Two or three leagues further along the way, a road slanted down from the north, where a small village of gray houses could be seen. It came around a forested knoll and led off into the east. Kul urged the wole upon the road, but the creature preferred to run on the blue turf, which provided a kinder footing. This road, according to Visbhume, might well lead all the way to Asphrodiske. He pointed at the map. "First we cross the River Haroo, here by the town Pude, then Asphrodiske lies onward, across the Plain of Lilies."

Down from the slopes of neatly tiered mountains flowed the River Haroo, to pass across the way to Asphrodiske. The road led to a stone bridge of five arches and away to the east, beside the village which Visbhume had named 'Pude'.

Glyneth asked Visbhume: "Who are the people of the village? Did they come into being here?"

"They are folk from Earth, who across the ages have inadvertently dropped through sink-holes into Tanjecterly. A certain number have been placed here for one reason or another by magicians like Twitten, and they too must bide on Tanjecterly."

"That would seem a bitter fate," said Glyneth. "How cruel to be torn away from those who love you! Do you not agree, Visbhume?"

Visbhume put on a lofty smile. "Sometimes stern little reprimands become necessary, especially when one deals with wilful maidens, who refuse to share the bounty of their treasure."

Kul turned his head and stared at Visbhume, whose smile instantly faded.

Along the road came a wagon, carrying a dozen peasants. They turned to stare in wonder and awe as the wole went by. Their attention seemed primarily fixed upon Kul, and several jumped down from the wagon to take up staves as if to defend themselves from attack.

"That is an odd attitude," said Glyneth. "We offered them no threat. Are they timid or merely hostile to strangers?"

Visbhume gave a fluting chuckle. "They are fearful for good reason. Feroces live in the mountains and no doubt have earned themselves a dubious reputation. I foresee problems. It might be wise to dismiss Kul from our company."

Glyneth called to Kul. "Come into the pergola, on the low bench and draw the curtain, so that the village folk will not be alarmed."

Kul somewhat reluctantly slid into the lower bench of the pergola, and drew the curtains. Visbhume, watching carefully, came forward and stood in Kul's previous place. He looked back at Glyneth: "In case questions are asked, I will say that we are pilgrims visiting the monuments of Asphrodiske."

"Be sure that is all you say," came Kul's voice from behind the curtains.

Glyneth, now uneasy, looked in the wallet and brought out a Tormentor Bulb, which she placed in her own pouch.

The wole ran smartly across the bridge and down the principal street of the village. Visbhume seemed extraordinarily alert, and looked back and forth, from side to side. He touched a pad on the wole's crest and the creature sensibly slowed its pace. Kul rasped: "What are you doing? Keep moving at speed!"

"I do not wish to arouse adverse comment," said Visbhume. "It is best to pass through settled areas at a seemly and sober pace, so that they will not think us irresponsible hoodlums."

From a tall structure of dressed stone stepped three men wearing tight black trousers, voluminous tunics of green leather and elaborate wide-brimmed hats. The foremost held up his hand. "Halt!"

Visbhume brought the wole to a stand-still. "Whom is it our privilege to address?"

"I am the Honourable Fulgis, Constable and Magistrate for the village Pude. And you?"

"Innocent pilgrims bound for Asphrodiske, that we may see the sights."

"All very well, but have you paid toll for the use of the bridge?"

"Not yet, sir. What is the fee?"

"For such a medley as I see before me, ten good dibbets, of sound tolk."

"Very good! I was afraid that you might ask for a tassel from the rug, each of which is worth twenty dibbets."

"I meant to include in the toll such a tassel."

"What?" Visbhume jumped to the ground. "Is not this slightly excessive?"

"Would you prefer to return over the bridge and swim your way across the river?"

"No. Glyneth, pass me down my wallet, that I may pay Sir Fulgis his due."

Glyneth wordlessly passed down the wallet. Visbhume now took Fulgis aside and spoke earnestly into his ear. Kul spoke to Glyneth in a husky whisper: "He is betraying us! Start the wole to running!"

"I do not know how!"

Visbhume returned and taking the wole led it into a walled courtyard. Glyneth called sharply: "What are you doing?"

"There are certain formalities which I fear we must endure. Kul may be discovered. If he becomes violent, he will be dealt with harshly. You, my dear, may step down from the pergola."

Kul jumped from the pergola, seized the wole's horns and caused it to canter from the courtyard. Warriors ran forward and hurled nooses; Kul was pulled from the wole and lay dazed for an instant; during this time he was bound hand and foot with many turns of rope, then dragged off to a barred cell in the side of the courtyard.

The constable spoke to Visbhume: "Well done! Such a feroce might well have done damage!"

"It is a clever beast," said Visbhume. "I suggest that you kill it instantly, and make an end to its threat."

"We must wait for the Lord Mayor, who may well call in Zaxa and provide us some sport."

"And who is Zaxa?" asked Visbhume indulgently.

"He is defender of the law and executioner. He hunts feroce in the Glone Mountains and it is his delight to derogate their prideful savagery."

"Zaxa will do famously with Kul. Now we must be on our way, since time is short for us. From my esteem, I give you personally two rich tassels, worth many dibbets. Glyneth, we will proceed. It is a pleasure to be rid of that cantankerous beast."

IV

THE WOLE PACED SMARTLY EASTWARD beside the Road of Round Stones, with Visbhume riding in state high on the top bench of the pergola and Glyneth huddled miserably below. Visbhume, with the wallet once more under his command, made a suspicious inspection to ensure that Glyneth had sequestered none of his properties to her own use. Satisfied that all was as it should be, he brought out the almanac and, discovering a mistake in his computations, made a flurry of new measurements, but discovered nothing to alarm him.

At last reassured, he brought out his fiddle, extended the bow to its almost excessive length, tuned to a call of "Twiddle-dee-doodle-di-diddle-dee-dee!" then played a rousing selection of ear-tickling tunes: tantivets and merrydowns, fine bucking jigs and cracking quicksteps, rollicks, lilts and fare-thee-wells. His elbows swung first high then low, while his feet pounded the floor of the pergola in full justice to the meter. Peasants standing by the side of the road looked in wonder to see the great eight-legged wole running at speed, with Visbhume playing fine music and Glyneth sitting glumly below, and when the peasants returned to their farmsteads, they had much to tell of the strange sights they had seen and the excellent music they had heard.

Visbhume suddenly remembered a new aspect to the calculations, which he had not heretofore considered. He put aside fiddle and bow and made his corrections, to such good effect that, halfway along the road to Asphrodiske, he decided that the black moon afforded him somewhat more than adequate time for all his purposes, which brought him a great exhilaration of spirit.

The road now had entered the fringes of the Dark Woods. Visbhume steered the wole to the side and off across a little meadow of blue grass to the shade of three dark blue trees, where he halted and threw down the anchor. With stately demeanor he descended to the sward, set out the miniature cottage and caused it to expand. Finally he turned to Glyneth, still on the low bench of the pergola. "My dear, you may alight."

"I prefer to stay here."

Visbhume spoke crisply, with an overtone of menace in his tone: "Glyneth, step down from the wole, if you please. We have important matters to discuss."

Glyneth jumped down from the wole, ignoring Visbhume's hand. With a cool smile, Visbhume signaled Glyneth to the doorway of the cottage. She entered and seated herself, while Visbhume closed the door and shot the bolt.

"Are you hungry?" asked Visbhume.

"No." As soon as she had spoken Glyneth realized that she had made a mistake. Any procedure which used time was to her advantage.

"Do you thirst?"

Glyneth gave a noncommittal shrug and Visbhume brought wine from the cupboard and poured full two goblets. "My dear, we are at last genuinely and intimately alone! Is that not a thrilling thought? I have yearned long for this moment, meanwhile ignoring insults and indignities as befits a knight of chivalry. Such matters—pah! They are the twitchings and squealings of small minds; noblesse allows me to put them aside, as a gallant ship rides over the spatter and spray of the envious waves! Drink now! Let this good vintage bring warmth to your veins! Drink, Glyneth, drink! . . . . What? You shun the wine; you push aside the goblet? Truly, I am not pleased! Rather than sparkling eyes and excited mouth I find a squint, a hunching, a dyspeptic pinch of nostril, a grim behavior. This is a time for gayety! I am somewhat puzzled by your posture. You crouch and watch me sidelong as if I were a rat eating the breakfast cheese. On your feet, then! Let us act in the manner of dainty lovers! Be so kind as to loose your garments and let them slide, and so to display your lovely supple limbs!"

Glyneth shook her head. "I will do nothing like this."

Visbhume smiled. "Really? What a pity that I lack a full measure of time so that I might match you at every turn! But time is of the essence; the affair must be effected in a makeshift manner, and first, for reasons which will become clear to you, I must know what I brought you here to learn. Quickly now, that we devote the greater time to our pleasure!"

Temporizing, Glyneth asked: "What did you wish to know?"

"Ha hah! Can you not guess?"

"Not really. I am puzzled."

"Then I will tell you exactly! After all, why should you not be told? Surely you will never use the knowledge to my disadvantage! Am I correct in this?"

"Yes."

"Of course I am correct! Listen then! King Casmir heard a prediction regarding the first-born son of Princess Suldrun. There is mystery in connection with Suldrun's child. Princess Madouc is a changeling, but what of the boy the fairies took? There was a boy who left Thripsey Shee and who became your companion. His name is Dhrun, but he would seem much too old to be Suldrun's child. Who then is Dhrun's mother? Where is that boy whom the fairies took and gave back Madouc in return? This boy would now be five or six years old. By the prediction he will sit on Evandig before Casmir, or some such affair, and Casmir is anxious to locate him."

"So that he may put the child to death?"

Visbhume smiled and shrugged. "Such is the way of kings. And now you can understand the import of my curiosity. Do you so understand?"

"Yes!"

"Excellent! Then, in all kindness, I ask that you tell me what you know of the matter, and I therefore put this easy and harmless question to you: who is Dhrun's mother?"

"Dhrun never knew his mother," said Glyneth. "He was nurtured by fairies and spent a most curious childhood. Once he told me the name of Madouc's mother; she had consorted with men and her name was Twisk."

"Words, words, words!" cried Visbhume fretfully. "They are not responsive to my question! Once more: who is or was Dhrun's mother?"

Glyneth shook her head. "Even if I knew, I would tell you nothing, since it might aid King Casmir, our enemy."

Visbhume spoke sharply: "You try my patience! But I have a remedy!" He brought a little green glass bottle from his wallet. "This, as you will recall, is the true and veritable Essence of Amour. One drop brings yearnings to every nook of the female soul and encourages prodigies of sexual valor in the male. Suppose that I forced you to ingest not just a single drop, but two or even three? In your urgent zeal you would tell me what I wanted to know in a trice, nor would you be at all loath to step from your garments."

Tears rolled down Glyneth's cheeks. What a sorry end for her life! Visbhume clearly intended either to kill her outright, or, at best, to abandon her on Tanjecterly.

Visbhume came up to her with his bottle. "Come then, vixen; open the pretty little mouth. One drop shall I give you; one drop will suffice, and if not, then we shall try another."

V

IN HIS CELL AT THE TOWN PUDE, Kul rubbed the ropes binding his arms against a sharp edge of the door-frame, and rasped them through. He untied the ropes from his legs, broke open the door to the cell with a single lurch and burst out into the courtyard. A pair of guards jumped up to intercept him and were sent sprawling; Kul took his sword from the gatehouse; he ran out into the street and eastward along the road.

Fulgis the constable organized a party of pursuit, including the redoubtable Zaxa, a hybrid creature half-man and half-hespid batrache, with arms like baulks of timber, a heavy gray hide proof against spear, arrow, claw or fang. Zaxa rode a small pacing wole, and carried his fabulous sword Zil, while the others of the party rode steeds of other descriptions.

The posse set off in hot pursuit and presently overtook Kul, who ran into the Deep Woods. The pursuers coursed behind, shouting and hallooing, and exchanging repartee. Kul dropped from a tree into their midst, destroyed eight warriors and ran off. The pursuers came after, more cautiously, consulting among themselves and exchanging terse instructions, with Zaxa in the lead. Kul slid around to their rear and attacking once more, wrought further carnage. By the time Zaxa arrived on the scene, Kul was gone once more, only to leap from the shadows, seize the constable Fulgis and break his head against a tree trunk, but Zaxa at last confronted him.

Zaxa bellowed: "Feroce, you are clever, you are fierce, but now you must pay for your murders, and the cost shall be high!"

Kul responded: "Zaxa, allow me to make a suggestion: you go your way and I will go mine. In this case, neither shall take harm from the other. It is a plan which redounds to the profit of both. Can you perceive the wisdom of my proposal?"

Zaxa stood back blinking as he pondered the concept. At last he spoke: "No doubt there is something in what you say. But I rode this far distance with the express and stated purpose of lopping away your head with my fine sword Zil, and it seems somehow bootless to turn about now and ride emptyhanded back to Pude. The townsfolk would ask: 'Zaxa, did you not ride from town pell-mell that you might destroy the murderous feroce?' And I could but answer: 'True! That was my purpose!' Then they would say: 'Ah, the clever brute evaded your search!' To this I would be forced to answer: 'Quite to the contrary! We met and spoke a few civil words to each other, then I came home.' The townsfolk might say nothing aloud, but I feel that I would lose esteem around the neighborhood. Therefore, even at the risk of discomfort, I find myself obliged to kill you."

"What if you die first?"

Zaxa bellowed and beat his great chest. "Once I lay hands on you, the issue is closed. Prepare to learn the full extent of the infinite hereafter."

The two joined battle. In the end, panting, bloody, and with one arm mangled, Kul stood above the corpse of Zaxa. He gazed around the forest glade, but the surviving villagers, seeing how the battle went, had departed. Kul looked down at the great gray carcass and almost could feel a pang of pity.

Kul took up Zaxa's magnificent sword Zil, staggered to Zaxa's mount, climbed to the seat, and set off in search of Visbhume and Glyneth.

Only a mile down the road Kul spied the anchored wole and the house. Keeping to cover he approached, dismounted and went to the door. From within he heard a sudden crash of broken glass.

Kul burst the door wide and stood in the doorway. Visbhume, engaged in tearing Glyneth's clothes from her body, looked up in a panic. A bottle of green glass lay broken in the fireplace where Glyneth had seized and thrown it. Kul hurled Visbhume against the wall with such force that Visbhume fell senseless to the floor.

Glyneth ran sobbing to Kul. "What have they done to you? Oh, your poor arm! My dear poor wonderful Kul, you are hurt!"

"But not too badly," said Kul. "I am alive, and Zaxa is learning the length and breadth of the infinities."

"Sit in the chair, and let us see what can be done for you."

VI

ONCE AGAIN THE WOLE RAN EASTWARD toward Asphrodiske, beside the Road of Round Stones. In a clothes-press at the back of the cottage Glyneth had found garments to replace those which Visbhume had torn: peasant trousers of striped gray, black and white bast and a blouse of coarse blue linen. She had done her best to ease Kul's wounds, mending his cuts and slashes and contriving a sling to support his arm until the fractured bone might mend. Zaxa had sunk his fangs into Kul's shoulder, injecting a poisonous saliva, and the wound had mortified. "Take the knife," said Kul. "Cut. Let the blood flow. Then dust on the powder."

Glyneth, gray-faced, took a deep breath, and holding her hand steady, slashed deep into the wound, releasing a gush of noxious matter and then a flow of healthy red blood. Kul groaned in relief and stroked Glyneth's hair, then sighed once again and looked away. "At times I see strange visions," said Kul. "But it was not intended that I should dream, especially impossible dreams."

"Impossible dreams come into my head too, sometimes," said Glyneth. "They confuse me and even frighten me. Still, how can I help but love you, who are so brave and kind and gentle?"

Kul gave a mirthless laugh. "So I was intended to be." He turned away and gave his attention to Visbhume. "I would kill you at this moment, except that we still need your guidance. How goes the direction of the moon?"

Visbhume painfully rose to his feet. "What if I guide you correctly?"

"You will be allowed to live."

Visbhume showed the caricature of an airy and confident smile. "I will accept that condition. The black moon is close on the quaver. You have loitered overlong."

"Then let us be away."

Visbhume made as if to take up his wallet, but Glyneth ordered him to stand back. She reduced the cottage, packed it away. The three climbed aboard the wole and once again rode toward the pink star, now almost in contact with the black moon.

As before, Glyneth rode the high seat in the pergola, Kul crouched by the wole's horns and Visbhume sat at the hind-quarters, looking to the side with eyes as liquid and large as those of a lemur.

Glyneth rode in a welter of a dozen emotions, and any one of them, so she felt, might bring her heartbreak. Despite the salves and powders, Kul was not the Kul of old; perhaps, thought Glyneth, he had lost too much blood, for now his skin had taken on a pallor and the crispness had gone from his movements. She sighed, thinking of her return to Earth. Already Tanjecterly had become the reality and Earth the fanciful land behind the clouds.

League after league fell astern to the thrust of the wole's running legs, and now the road led across the Plain of Lilies. In the distance appeared a line of low hills, a town of gray houses and, somewhat to the north, a low flat dome of gleaming gray-silver metal.

Visbhume came to stand by the pergola. He spoke to Glyneth: "My dear, I will need the almanac, that I may find the great axis."

Glyneth removed the key from its socket and handed the almanac to Visbhume, who read the text with attention, then studied a small detail map.

"Aha!" said Visbhume. "Fare to the side of the dome; we should see a platform, and thereon an iron post."

Glyneth pointed. "I see the platform! I see the post!"

"Then forward in haste! The black moon has sounded the pulse, and here the time is short, without pause or rest."

At best speed the wole coursed across the countryside and arrived at the side of the dome. "That is an old temple, which may well be deserted now," said Visbhume. "On to the platform. Glyneth, the key!"

"Not yet," said Glyneth. "And in any event I will use the key."

Visbhume made an annoyed chattering sound. "That is not as I planned; it is impractical!"

"Nevertheless, you shall not pass until both Kul and I are safely through the portal."

"Bah!" whispered Visbhume. "Then up to the platform, and halt! . . . Glyneth, alight! Kul, down from your perch! To the post!"

Glyneth went to the steps leading up to the platform. Kul wearily stepped down to the ground and followed. Visbhume pulled the pipes from his pocket and played a shrill discordant arpeggio. The wole bellowed in rage and lowering its head charged down upon Kul. Visbhume came dancing with knees high, blowing tones at angry discord. Kul tried to jerk aside, but the spring was gone from his legs. The wole hooked him with its horns, and tossed him high.

Glyneth ran crying back down to the limp form. She looked up at Visbhume in horror and hatred. "You have betrayed us once again!"

"No more than you! Look at me! I am Visbhume! You call endearments to this creature who is half a beast, and only partly a man; it is unnatural! Yet you scorn me, the proud and noble Visbhume!"

Glyneth ignored him. "Kul lives! Help me with him!"

"Never! Are you mad? Now quickly! He lives; shall I call the wole to trample him?"

Glyneth looked up in horror. "No!"

"Tell me: who is Dhrun's mother? Tell me!"

Kul whispered: "Tell him nothing."

"No," said Glyneth. "I will tell him; it can make no great difference. Suldrun was Dhrun's mother and Aillas his father."

"How is that possible, with Dhrun now twelve years old?"

"A year in the fairy shee is like ten years of life elsewhere."

Visbhume gave a crow of exultation. "That is the knowledge I have been seeking!" He snatched the key from Glyneth's hands, and jumped back as if dancing to some surging music heard by himself alone. He made a flamboyant flourish. "Truly, Glyneth, what a little fool you are! If you had spoken long ago, we would have been saved both toil and pain, from which I profit not at all! Little does Casmir care! He will only commend me for the results and call me efficient.

"Now then: will you come to Earth in a submissive manner, and there do my bidding?"

Glyneth fought to keep her voice under control. "I can not leave Kul!" She turned her head so as not to look at Visbhume. "Take us both safely to Earth, and I will do your bidding."

Visbhume judiciously held high his finger. "No! Kul must stay! He has treated me with contumacy; he must be punished. Come, Glyneth!"

"I will not leave without him."

"So be it! Remain here and cherish this beast you love with so peculiar a passion! Give me now my wallet!"

"I will not give over the wallet."

"Then I will blow a blast on my pipes."

"And I will throw a Tormentor bulb at you. I should have done so before!"

Visbhume uttered a curse, but dared delay no longer. "I am áway for Earth, where I will enjoy honours and wealth; goodbye!"

Visbhume leapt up to the platform, struck with his key, and disappeared from view.

Glyneth knelt beside Kul, who lay with eyes closed. Glyneth stroked his forehead. "Kul, can you hear me?"

"I can hear you."

"I am here with you. Can you manage to climb upon the wole? We will take you to a quiet place in the forest and you shall rest until you are well."

Kul opened his eyes. "The wole is an uncertain creature. It has done me a great harm."

"Only at the bidding of Visbhume's pipes. Otherwise it seems an orderly creature, and it runs well."

"That is true. Well then, let me see if I can climb on its back."

"I will help you."

Attracted by the activity, folk from the town had started to gather and some of them began to jeer Glyneth's attempts to help Kul. Glyneth paid the crowd no heed, and finally Kul half-climbed, half-fell aboard the wole. Now the crowd moved in close and surrounded the wole and started to pluck tassels from the rug. Glyneth brought a Tormentor-bulb from the wallet and tossed it into the crowd, which immediately dispersed amid cries of pain, and the wole was free to go its way.

An hour later Glyneth took the wole veering across a meadow and behind a copse, where she dropped anchor and set up the house. Kul for a period lay in a daze, and Glyneth watched him anxiously. Was her imagination playing her tricks, or were odd changes occurring within Kul, causing his expression to move and change and at times even blur?

Kul opened his eyes to find Glyneth watching him. He spoke in a soft drained voice. "I have had strange dreams. When I try to remember, my head swims." He made a fretful movement and started to raise himself, but Glyneth pushed him back. "Lie quietly, Kul! Rest, and never mind the dreams!"

Kul closed his eyes and spoke in his vague soft voice: "Murgen spoke to me. He said that I must guard you and bring you back safe to the hut. It is proper that I love you, because that is my reason for being alive. But you must not waste your emotion on me. I am half-beast, and one of the voices I hear is the voice of the feroce. Another voice is reckless and cruel, and it urges me to unspeakable deeds. The third voice is the strongest and when it speaks the others are still."

Glyneth said: "I too have thought long and deeply. All you say is true. I am awed by your strength and grateful for your protection, but I love another part of you: your kindness and bravery, and these were not taught you by Murgen. They come from somewhere else."

"Murgen's orders ring in my mind: I am to guard you and bring you safe to the hut, and since we have no better place to go, that shall be our destination."

"Back the way we came?"

"Back the way we came."

"Whenever you are strong enough to travel: then we will go."

Chapter 17

I

Two days before the final Goblin Fair of the season, Melancthe arrived at that inn near Twitten's Corners known as 'The Laughing Sun and The Crying Moon'. She engaged her customary apartments, then at once went off to the meadow, where she hoped to find Zuck and remind him of their contract in connection with the flowers.

Zuck had only just arrived and, with the aid of a nondescript boy, unloaded his goods and appurtenances from a pony cart. At the sight of Melancthe, he politely nodded and touched the brim of his cap with his first two fingers and proceeded with his work; apparently the provision of flowers for Melancthe had not yet occupied his attention.

Melancthe made a sibilant sound of annoyance and confronted Zuck where he worked at his shelves. "Have you forgotten our agreement?"

Zuck paused in his work and gave her a blank side-glance. His face cleared. "Ah, yes! Of course! You are the lady who so anxiously wanted flowers!"

"Quite so, Zuck; have you forgotten so soon?"

"Of course not! But many small details throng my mind and detract from my attention. Just a moment."

Zuck gave the boy instructions, then took Melancthe to a nearby bench. "You must understand that in our business we often deal with persons who talk largely but put little gold upon the counter. As I recall, you wished another flower or two, to grace your lovely hair."

"I want all the flowers, be they one, two, ten or a hundred."

Zuck nodded slowly and looked off across the meadow. "At last we understand each other! Such flowers command large prices; I already have a list of customers as impatient as you, and I have yet to consult my supplier in regard to the produce of his secret garden."

"Your other customers must look elsewhere, and you will be adequately paid, never fear!"

"In that case you must apply to my booth tomorrow at this time, when I hope to have definite news from the gardener."

Melancthe could extract no further information from Zuck, and most especially he refused to identify the mysterious gardener who nurtured such remarkable blooms, and at last Melancthe returned to the inn, fretful and dissatisfied but unable to implement her wishes.

As soon as she was out of sight, Zuck thoughtfully returned to his work. After a bit he called to the boy, who on closer inspection seemed to be either full falloy, or falloy with traces of goblin and humankind. His stature was that of human youth, with a supple easy quality to his movements; otherwise he showed a silver skin, pale green-gold hair and enormous eyes with dark silver pupils in the shape of seven-pointed stars. He was a pretty lad, calm, slow and even somewhat naïve. Zuck had found him a willing worker and paid him well, so that, in general, affairs went well between the two. Zuck now called the boy's name: "Yossip! Where are you?"

"Here, sir, resting under the cart."

"Come here, if you please; I have an errand for you."

Yossip came around to the front of the booth. "What is this errand?"

"No great matter. This summer you came to work one day with a fine black flower, which, as I recall, you left on the counter, and which I later gave away to one of my customers."

"Ah yes," said Yossip. "A flower from my secret garden."

Zuck ignored the remark. "I am of a mind to put out some trifling decoration, to distinguish our booth and mark it from the ruck. To this end, a few flowers might be just the thing. Where did you obtain the black blossom?"

"Out in the forest, along Giliom's Lane, at a place I like to consider my secret bower. This summer I found only a single bloom, though I noticed several buds."

"A few flowers may be enough. After all, we are not flower-merchants or herbalists! How far is the garden? Direct me and I will cut exactly to my needs."

Yossip hesitated. "I remember neither landmarks nor exact distances. I myself will find the place with difficulty. Still, if you want the flowers, instruct me, and I will bring them here."

"A good idea," said Zuck. "Take the pony cart, so that you may make haste. Ride out Giliom's Lane this very moment; cut neither buds nor seed-pods, only those flowers which have come into full bloom. In this manner we will not injure the growth."

"Just so," said Yossip. "I will need a sharp knife to cut the stems and a bite of bread and cheese to stay me along the way, which, as I recall, is two or three or even four miles down the lane."

"Go then, and do not loiter!"

As soon as Yossip had departed, Zuck closed the booth. He borrowed a mount from an acquaintance at a nearby booth and set off after Yossip. He rode with stealth and caution, pacing himself by the squeak and clatter of the pony cart. When the lane turned, Zuck hastened forward, to peer along its way ahead, and then ride swiftly to the next turning, so remaining close behind Yossip but always out of sight.

The sound of the cart suddenly ceased. Zuck dismounted, tied the horse and advanced on foot. The cart had halted in the middle of the lane and Yossip was nowhere to be seen.

"Well done!" said Zuck to himself. "Here is the site of the mysterious garden! It is all I need to know!" Now — to return to the booth in haste, and Yossip would never know that his secret had been broached.

Zuck's curiosity prompted him to steal forward, for a better indication as to the location and size of the flower bed. Step by wary step he came down the road, running at last on tip-toe, darting glances to right and left.

Yossip stepped from the shadows carrying a small bouquet of four flowers. He seemed not at all surprised to find Zuck on hand.

"I came in haste," said Zuck. "I decided to use bunting and multi-colored streamers for my decoration, rather than despoil the flower bed; therefore I thought to inform you at once of my new plans."

"That was kind of you," said Yossip. He seemed to have difficulty speaking; he warbled and lisped. "But what of these flowers I have already cut?"

"Bring them along; better yet, give them into my care. Are there others in bud?"

"Very few."

Zuck looked frowningly slantwise at Yossip. "Why are you speaking with so odd a voice?"

Yossip grinned, showing silver teeth. "As I worked, I disturbed the soil and discovered this wonderful gem." He took a lambent green sphere from his mouth. "For convenience I carry it thus."

"Amazing!" said Zuck. "Allow me to examine it."

"No, Zuck! By stealth you learned the secret of my garden. By nature, I am easy, even ingenuous; but on this occasion I must pass a judgment, and your deceit must be punished by death." So saying, Yossip stabbed Zuck first in the neck with the knife he had used to cut flowers, then in the heart. Then, to halt Zuck's twitching, he thrust the knife hard into Zuck's right ear, all the way to the hilt. "Now then, Zuck! We have properly put an end to your skulkishness. I will say no more of the matter."

Yossip rolled the corpse into the ditch, and returned to the meadow, leading the horse Zuck had ridden behind the cart.

Yossip returned the horse to its owner, who asked in wonder: "And where is good Zuck, who rode off so briskly?"

"He has gone to examine a new line of merchandise," said Yossip. "I must meanwhile take care of the booth."

"That is a great responsibility for an inexperienced stripling like yourself! If you find any difficulties, or if you suspect that you are being cheated, call me and I will set matters right!"

"Thank you, sir! I am much relieved."

The time was still two hours short of sundown. Yossip opened the booth, arranged the flowers in vases and, after some hesitation, placed the green pearl on display, in a dish on one of the back shelves. "It is a wondrous gem," he told himself. "Still, what use is it to me? I am not one for earrings nor other adornments. Well, we shall see. The gem must bring a good price or I will not sell."

In the morning Melancthe appeared early and looked here and there. She noticed the flowers and gave a glad cry. "Where is the good Zuck?"

"He is searching out new merchandise," said Yossip. "The booth is in my care."

"At least he has found flowers for me! Bring them forward; they are mine alone and must never be sold elsewhere!"

"As you wish, lady."

Melancthe took possession of the flowers. They were indeed of startling distinction, with colours that seemed to shudder with the force of their nature. Each was different; each projected a unique personality. The first: pungent orange, mingled with vermilion, plum-red and black. The second: sea-green with purple glowing under a luster of beetle-back blue. The third: black glossy-harsh with spikes of strident ocher-yellow, and a scarlet tuft at the center. The fourth: a dozen concentric rings of small petals, in turn white, red and blue.

Melancthe asked no price. She tossed down four golden crowns. "When will you have more of these blooms?"

Yossip at once saw how the wind blew. Zuck had been deceitful by an order of magnitude larger than Yossip had imagined. Still, whether for good or for bad, he could not be punished a second time. Yossip reflected. "Tomorrow, lady, I may have more flowers."

"Remember, they must be reserved for me alone! I am fascinated by their bizarre complication!"

Yossip said smoothly: "To ensure yourself full ownership, I advise that you pay over at this moment a sufficiency of gold coins; otherwise someone may be quicker than you tomorrow morning."

Melancthe contemptuously flung down five more crowns of yellow gold, and the transaction was thereby validated.

Dusk fell over the meadow. Lamps hung in the trees and a variety of folk who preferred night to day came to stroll among the booths and to chaffer for articles which aroused their interest.

At the inn Melancthe dined modestly upon a chicken wing and a turnip cooked with honey and butter. She sat with her flowers set out in four vases, that she might admire each in turn, or all together, as she chose.

A saturnine dark-haired gentleman in splendid garments, distinguished by a neat mustache, a small beard, and keen features, approached her table. He bowed, doffed his hat, and without further ceremony seated himself.

Melancthe, recognizing Tamurello, made no comment. He inspected the flowers with curiosity. "Most fascinating, and, I would think, unique! Where do such extraordinary blossoms grow?"

"As to that, I cannot be sure," said Melancthe. "I buy them from a booth at the fair. Smell them, one after the other. Each is different; each purports with its odor an entire cascade of meaning, and meanings of meanings; each is a whole pageant of subtle and nameless aromas."

Tamurello smelled each bloom in turn, and then each once again. He looked at them with lips pursed. "The odors are exquisite. I am reminded of something to which I cannot now put a name. . . . The thought hangs in a far corner of my mind and refuses to stir. A maddening sensation!"

"You will recognize it presently," said Melancthe. "Why are you here, where you come so rarely?"

"I am here by curiosity," said Tamurello. "Only a few moments ago there was a tremble at Twitten's Post. It might mean much, or it might mean little, but such a tremble is always worth the investigation. . . . Aha! Look then, who has just entered the inn! It is Visbhume, and I must confer with him at once."

Visbhume stood by the counter, looking this way and that for Hockshank, who at this moment was busy elsewhere.

Tamurello went to stand beside him. "Visbhume, what do you do here?"

Visbhume peered at the black-bearded grandee who addressed him so familiarly. "Sir, you have the advantage of me."

"I am Tamurello, in a guise I often use while going abroad."

"Of course! Now I recognize you, by the clarity of your gaze! Tamurello, it is a pleasure to see you!"

"Thank you. What brings you here at this season?"

Visbhume puffed out his cheeks and gave his forefinger a wag. "Now then, who can explain the foibles of a vagabond? One day here, the next day there! Sometimes the way is rude, sometimes it is rough, and sometimes one must tramp onward through the rain and the dark compelled only by the gleam of one's own far star! But for now, I wish only for Hockshank, that he may find me a comfortable chamber for the night."

"Your wants will not be satisfied, or so I fear. The inn is full."

Visbhume's face fell. "In that case I must find a tuft of hay in the barn."

"Unnecessary! Step outside a moment."

Somewhat reluctantly Visbhume followed Tamurello out the door and into the road. Tamurello looked up into the sky. He pointed aloft to where the moonlight shone on a floating manse of three towers, a terrace and a surrounding balustrade.

"That is where I shall take my rest this night," said Tamurello. "But before I say more, I am curious as to why you are here when you were on last accounts hard at work in the service of King Casmir, upon my recommendation."

"True, true! With your usual acuity you understand the exact state of affairs! I believe that I will now take a bite of supper. If you will excuse me—"

"In a moment," said Tamurello. "Tell me, how went your business with Casmir?"

"Tolerably well."

"He is pleased with your information?"

"In truth, I have not yet reported to him. The knowledge I have gained is so footling that I may not even trouble to do so."

"What, in fact, did you learn?"

"Sir, I feel that I should best retain these few trivialities for Casmir's ears."

"Forsooth, Visbhume! Surely you have no secrets from me?"

"All of us have our little areas of privacy," said Visbhume primly.

"In some areas and at some times and with certain persons," stated Tamurello. "Not at Twitten's Corners by moonlight, in converse with Tamurello."

Visbhume made nervous flourishes of the hand. "Well then, if you insist, you shall know." And Visbhume added heartily: "After all, who referred me to Casmir but my good friend Tamurello?"

"Exactly so."

"I learned this much. Casmir is troubled by a prediction in regard to Suldrun's first-born son."

"I know of this prediction, by Persilian the Mirror. I know of Casmir's concern."

"The fact is simple yet most poignant! Suldrun's first-born son was sired by Aillas, King of Troicinet. The son's name is Dhrun, and in one year at the fairy shee he attained the age of nine Earthly years."

"Interesting!" said Tamurello. "And how did you come by this information?"

"I worked with vast toil and cunning. I took Glyneth to the world Tanjecterly, and there I would easily have had the knowledge had not Shimrod sent down a great monster to harass me. But I am nothing if not indomitable; I gained my information, I killed the beast, and I came up from Tanjecterly with my information."

"And the Princess Glyneth?"

"She remains in Tanjecterly, where she cannot tell tales."

"A wise precaution there! You are right! Knowledge of this sort is best kept secret, and reserved to the fewest possible number of minds. Indeed, Visbhume, one mind is enough, for knowledge of this sort."

Visbhume drew back a step. "Two minds are quite as secure."

"I fear not. Visbhume—"

"Hold!" cried Visbhume. "Have you forgotten my loyalty? My relentless efficiency? My aptitude for performing impossible services?"

Tamurello considered. "These arguments carry genuine weight! You are both loquacious and cogent, and so you have earned your life. Henceforth, however . . ." Tamurello made a gesture and uttered a phrase. Visbhume's garments slumped to the ground. From the dark tumble crawled a black and green snake. It hissed once at Tamurello and darted away into the forest.

Tamurello stood quiet in the road, listening to the sounds from within the inn: the mutter of voices, the clink of glass and earthenware, Hockshank's occasional call to his serving boy.

Tamurello's thoughts went for a moment to Melancthe. Her flowers, for a fact, were intriguing; he would explore them further in the morning. As for the attractions of Melancthe's person, his moods were ambiguous and to a certain degree defensive. He had been the lover of her brother; now she showed him a cool half-smiling detachment, in which Tamurello often thought to sense the flavor of contempt.

Tamurello listened a final moment to the sounds from the inn, glanced toward the forest, where he knew a black and green snake watched him with passionate eyes. Tamurello chuckled for the sheer logic of the situation, then held his arms wide, fluttered his fingers and was wafted high through the moonlight to his floating manse.

Five minutes later Shimrod appeared in the road. Like Tamurello he paused a moment to listen, then, hearing nothing but sounds from within, he entered the inn.

II

SHIMROD WENT TO THE COUNTER, and Hockshank leaned forward to attend his wants. "Again, Sir Shimrod, I am filled to capacity; still I notice that the beautiful Dame Melancthe again visits the fair and already has bought a fine bouquet which is the envy of everyone. Perhaps she might again share her accommodations with a dear and trusted friend."

"Or even with a total stranger, should the mood be on her. Well, we shall see. Tonight I came prepared and in fact I have no need for her hospitality. Still, who knows how the evening will go? In the name of gallantry, I will at least pay my respects and possibly take a cup of wine with her."

"Have you dined?" asked Hockshank. "Tonight the civet of hare is tasty, and my woodcocks are beyond reproach. Hear how they sizzle on the spit!"

"You have tempted me," said Shimrod. "I will test one of the woodcocks, along with half a crusty loaf."

Shimrod joined Melancthe at her table. She said: "Only minutes ago Tamurello sat in that very chair and admired these same flowers. Is this the reason for your presence?"

"The flowers, no. Tamurello, perhaps. Murgen sent me to investigate a tremble of Twitten's Post."

"Twitten's Post is all the rage," said Melancthe. "Tamurello came at the same tremble."

Shimrod looked around the room. "His guise must be unusual; I see no one here who might be Tamurello, unless it is yonder youth with the copper ringlets and the green jade eardrops."

"Tonight Tamurello is an austere grandee, but he is not here. He noticed his crony, Visbhume, and took him outside, and neither has returned."

Shimrod strove to keep his voice casual. "How long ago was this?"

"Minutes only." Melancthe held up one of her flowers. "Is this not glorious? It quivers with the very essence of its being; it tells a provocation for something I cannot even surmise! See how the colours glow against each other! The odor is intoxicating!"

"Yes, perhaps so." Shimrod jumped to his feet. "I will be back in a few moments."

Shimrod left the inn and went out into the road. He looked right and left; no one was in sight. He cocked his head to listen, but only sounds from within the inn came to his ear. He walked quietly to Twitten's Corners; he looked north, east, south and west; the four roads stretched away from the crossing, empty and pale in the moonlight, with trees standing somber to the side.

Shimrod returned toward the inn. To the side of the road, half in the ditch, he noticed a tumble of clothes. Shimrod approached slowly. He knelt and so discovered a tall gray book with a golden rod engaged in the web.

Shimrod took the book to the light streaming from the windows of the inn and read the title. He reached into his pocket and withdrew a small silver bell, which he tapped with his fingernail.

A voice spoke. "I am here."

"I am standing beside the inn at Twitten's Corners. Just before I arrived Visbhume came into the inn. If the post trembled, he was the cause. Tamurello met him and took him outside. I fear that Visbhume is gone: either dead or dissipated. He left behind his garments and his 'Twitten's Almanac', which now I hold in my possession."

"And Tamurello?"

Shimrod, raising his eyes, saw Tamurello's manse silhouetted across the moon. "He has brought a floating castle; I see it now in the sky."

"I will come, but early in the morning. Meanwhile, take full precautions! Do nothing at Melancthe's behest, no matter how innocent! Tamurello's mood is reckless; he suffered at Khambaste and now he learns that he has gained nothing. He is ready to perform any act, be it desperate or irrevocable, or merely tragic. Be wary."

Shimrod returned inside the inn. Melancthe, for whatever reason, had departed.

Shimrod consumed his supper and for a period sat watching the folk of the forest at their revels. At last he went outside, and going to a nearby clearing put down a miniature cottage much like the one Visbhume had carried in his wallet.

"House, grow large!" said Shimrod.

He went to stand on the porch.

"House, stand tall!"

The house grew cabriolet legs at the corners, each terminating in claws grasping a ball, so that the house stood at a secure height of sixty feet above the clearing.

The night passed and dawn came to the Forest of Tantrevalles. As the sun raised above the trees, Shimrod came out on his porch. "Down, house!" called Shimrod, and then: "House, grow small!"

Tamurello's manse still floated in the sky. Shimrod went into the inn and made his breakfast.

Melancthe came quietly into the room, demure as a young shepherdess of Arcady in her knee-length white frock and sandals. She paid Shimrod no heed, and went to sit in an inconspicuous corner, which suited Shimrod very well.

Melancthe wasted little time at her breakfast. Departing the inn, she went to the meadow where the fair was already in full progress.

Shimrod followed casually behind her. As she entered the meadow he joined her side. "What do you look for today?"

"I have a whole bouquet of flowers on order," Melancthe told him. "These blooms are now my fascination; I dote upon them!"

Shimrod laughed. "Is it not strange that they work so strong an influence upon you? Do you not fear falling under an enchantment?"

Melancthe gave him a startled side-glance. "What enchantment could it be, save the force of sheer beauty? They are my dearest loves! Their colours sing to me; their perfumes bring me dreams!"

"Pleasant dreams, I hope? Some of the odors are remarkably rank."

Melancthe showed him one of her rare smiles. "The dreams are various. Some are most surprising. Some, I suspect, might exceed the limits of your imagination."

"No doubt whatever! I am denied such ecstasies by my mean and paltry soul." Shimrod looked around the meadow. "Where is this merchant of dreams?"

Melancthe pointed. "Just there! I see Yossip, but where are my lovely flowers? No doubt he has put them aside for me."

Melancthe ran to the booth. "Yossip, good morning to you, and where is my bouquet?"

Yossip shook his head mournfully. "Lady, in this case the truth is more simple, more elemental and more convincing than any lie. I will tell you the full and exact truth. This morning when I went to cut flowers, I came upon a grievous sight! Each plant had fallen and died, as if ravaged by the blight! There are no more plants! There are no more flowers!"

Melancthe stood rigid. "How is it possible?" she whispered. "Must it always be thus? That when I have found something sweet and dear it is taken from me? Yossip, how can you be so cruel? All night long I have pined for these flowers!"

Yossip gave a shrug. "Truly, lady, the fault is not mine, and therefore the coins you paid over to me should not be returned."

Shimrod said: "Yossip, allow me to cite the first principle of business ethics. If you give nothing of value, then you may not expect payment, regardless of all else. I speak only as a disinterested spectator."

Yossip cried out: "I cannot give up so much good gold! My plants have been destroyed; I deserve pity, not new strokes of misfortune! Let the lady select elsewhere from among my treasures! I hold nothing back! Here is an absolute prize: a black pebble dredged from the bottom of the River Styx! And observe this touching scene of a child caressing his mother, done in a mosaic of birds' eyes in gum. I stock a good selection of amulets all of great power, and this magic bronze comb invigorates the hair, repels infestations and cures scabies. These are all valuable articles!"

"I want none of them," said Melancthe crossly. "Still — let me look at that green gem you have on display."

Yossip hissed between his teeth, and reluctantly brought down the shallow box in which reposed the green pearl. "I am not so sure that I wish to part with this exquisite object."

"Come then! You yourself declared that nothing was held back! These gentlemen will testify to your word!" She indicated Shimrod and two or three others who had paused to watch the altercation.

"Again, as a disinterested spectator, I must corroborate Melancthe's statement," said Shimrod. He spoke in an abstracted voice, in search of a memory which for the moment evaded him. Somewhere he had encountered news of a green pearl, but the context evaded him. The green pearl, so he recalled, had been some sort of evil token.

"I as well!" declared a florid young peasant with yellow hair caught under the dark green cap of a woodcutter. "I know nothing of the case but I will avouch the hearing of my two good ears."

"So then!" said Melancthe in triumph. "Bring the box closer so that I may see the pearl."

Yossip angrily brought down the box and held it so that Melancthe was afforded barely a glimpse at the pearl. In a surly voice Yossip told her: "This gem is worth ten times the gold you paid me; I cannot let it go on the cheap!"

Melancthe leaned and craned her neck that she might see more readily into the box. "It is extraordinary!" she breathed, her flowers now forgotten. She reached to take up the gem, but Yossip jerked back the box.

"Come now!" demanded Melancthe. "Is this proper conduct for a huckster? To proffer, to allow a glimpse, then to snatch away the merchandise as if the customer were a robber? Where is your master, Zuck? He will not be pleased with such conduct!"

Yossip winced and grimaced in confusion. "Never mind about Zuck; he has given me full discretion."

"Then show me the pearl, or I will call for the steward and these two gentlemen shall be my witnesses!"

"Bah!" grumbled Yossip. "Such intimidation is only a step removed from robbery itself. Can you blame me for not trusting you with the gem?"

"Either the gem or my gold coins!"

"The gem is worth far more! First let us agree to that!"

"Perhaps a trifle more."

Reluctantly Yossip allowed Melancthe the box. She stared down entranced. "The colour envelopes me with its fervor! How much more do you ask?"

Yossip had still not recovered his equanimity. "Truth to tell, I have not yet determined its value. This jewel might readily grace the King of Araby's crown!"

Melancthe turned to Shimrod, with arch mischief in her face. "Shimrod, what is your opinion of the jewel?"

"It is handsome, if somewhat baleful," said Shimrod. "Somewhere I have heard rumors of a similar jewel, perhaps in a fabulous legend; I cannot remember the occasion. I recall nothing good to be said for the pearl. It was worn by a bloodthirsty pirate."

"Shimrod! Dear cautious, good, mild-mannered Shimrod! Does the legend so perturb you, when you have hardly glanced at the pearl itself?" She extended him the box. "At least give me your estimate of its value."

"I am hardly an expert!"

"In such matters everyone is an expert, since he knows what he would pay for it."

"I would give nothing."

"For once behave like an ordinary man! Take it up and feel its heft! Study the surface for flaws; gauge the subtlety of its sea-green fire."

Shimrod took the box and looked down sidelong. "It shows no obvious flaws. The colour has an envious malignant overtone."

Melancthe was still dissatisfied. "Why are you so diffident? Look at it from all sides! I want only your best and truest judgment."

Shimrod reluctantly reached to take the pearl, but his elbow was seized by the florid young peasant with yellow hair. "Shimrod, a word with you aside about this pearl."

Shimrod placed the box back on the counter; the two went a little apart and the young peasant spoke in an edged voice: "Did I not warn you against Melancthe's behests? Do not touch the pearl! It is a node of pure depravity, nothing more."

"Of course! Now I remember! Tristano told us a tale of such a pearl! But Melancthe can know nothing of this!"

"Perhaps a voice talks into her inner ear. . . . Tamurello is coming into the meadow; I do not want to be recognized. Tax him strongly for news of Visbhume! Under no circumstances touch the pearl!" The peasant mingled with the crowd.

Subdued and crestfallen, Shimrod went back to Melancthe. He muttered into her ear: "The fellow has some knowledge of pearls and tells me that this object is not a true pearl, since true pearls are never green. I now remember the rumor. Do not touch this false pearl as you value your soul; it is worse than worthless; it is a whorl of depravity."

Melancthe cried out in a low voice: "I have never been so affected before! It seems to sing to me, in a haunting music!"

"Still, If you have never believed me before, believe me now! Despite all your treacheries, I would not have you come to harm."

From his post behind the booth Yossip stated grandly: "I have calculated the worth of this glorious jewel: one hundred gold crowns exactly!"

Shimrod spoke harshly: "The Lady Melancthe does not want the thing at any price. Return her coins at once."

Melancthe stood limp and silent with mouth drooping; when Yossip, glaring sidelong at Shimrod, paid out the five gold coins, she dropped them into her wallet without giving them a glance.

Tamurello, in the same guise as of the night before, halted and gave Shimrod a polite salute. "I am surprised to find you so far from Trilda! Have you lost all interest in my affairs?"

"Other matters occasionally intrude upon my attention," said Shimrod. "At the moment I want a few words with Visbhume. You saw him last night; where is he now?"

Tamurello smilingly shook his head. "He went his way, I went mine; I know nothing of his present locality."

"Why not alter the habits of a lifetime and speak with candor?" asked Shimrod. "Truth, after all, need not be only the tactic of last resort."

"Ah, Shimrod! I am concerned by your negative opinion! In regard to Visbhume, I have nothing to hide. I spoke to him last night, then we parted company. I can offer no insights as to his plans."

"What did he tell you?"

"Hm hah! I fear that we verge close upon the question of confidentiality! Still, I will tell what I know. He reported that he had only just arrived from Tanjecterly, which is one of Twitten's 'Dekadiade', as perhaps you know."

"Something to this effect has reached me. Did he mention the Princess Glyneth? What were his reports of her?"

"In this regard he was somewhat evasive, and I infer that she came to an unhappy end. Tanjecterly is a cruel domain."

"He was not specific in this regard?"

"Not altogether. In fact, his intent was to tell me as little as possible."

"While in your presence did he discard all his clothing, for reasons totally beyond my conjecture?"

"What a startling idea!" declared Tamurello, in mild reproach. "The images which you place before my mind's eye are deplorable!"

"Most odd! Last night I came upon his garments in a heap at the side of the road."

Tamurello gave his head a bland shake. "Often, in cases of this sort, the simple explanation is ignored or overlooked. Perhaps he merely exchanged his soiled and travel-worn garments for others more presentable."

"Would he discard his valuable copy of Twitten's Almanac along with the soiled clothes?"

Tamurello, caught offguard, arched his sardonic eyebrows high and stroked his neat black beard. "One can only suspect him of absentmindedness, or vagary. But of course I cannot presume knowledge of Visbhume's quirks. Now, please excuse me."

Tamurello turned to Melancthe. "And what have you found of interest?"

"Here is where I found my flowers, but now the plants are dead, and I will never know their charm again."

"A pity." Glancing into the booth, Tamurello caught sight of the green pearl. He became instantly rigid, then advanced step by slow step, to bend his head down over the box.

"It is a green glory, a nonpareil!" declared Yossip in excitement. "The price? A trifling hundred gold coins!"

Tamurello paid no heed. He reached out his hand; his fingers fluttered down upon the pearl. From the shadows at the end of the counter a green and black snake lunged forth. It seized the pearl in its mouth and gulped it down in a trice, then slid back across the counter, down to the ground and away into the forest.

Tamurello gave a choked cry and ran around the booth, in time to see the snake slide into a hole between the roots of a gnarled old oak.

Tamurello clenched his hands, cried out a spell of six syllables and transformed himself into a long gray weasel which darted into the hole after the snake.

From below ground came faint squeaks and hisses: then silence.

A minute passed. Up from the hole came the weasel carrying the green pearl in its mouth. For an instant it glared red-eyed across the meadow, then jerked into motion and started to bound away.

A florid young peasant with flaxen hair moved even more quickly. He clapped a glass jar over the weasel and fixed tight the lid, compressing the weasel down upon its haunches, where it sat, the green pearl firmly in its mouth, the long nose pushed down on its belly, and its hind legs thrust up past its ears.

The peasant put the jar on the counter of Yossip's booth, and as the group watched, the weasel dissolved into a green transparency, like a skeleton in aspic, with the pearl glowing green at its center.

III

THE GRAY CRUMBLE OF THE ASPHRODISKE SKYLINE became lost in the haze astern, as the wole ran to the west: away from the black moon, back across the Plain of Lilies. Overhead the yellow sun and the green sun circled each other with a languid incessant inevitability, which Glyneth thought might ultimately disturb a person of erratic disposition, and which, if the truth be known, she herself found unpleasant, now that she had time to brood.

With Visbhume's departure, the tension along taut nerves had suddenly loosened, and the stimulation of Visbhume's mercurial, if odd, personality was gone, leaving a flat tired aftermath.

At the first halt Glyneth insisted that Kul rest and renew his strength. Kul, however, quickly became moody, and refused to lie quiet in the manner which Glyneth considered proper. "I feel trapped in this little house!" he growled. "When I lie still, staring up at the thatch, I feel like a corpse with his eyes open. I hear voices shouting as if from far distances; as I lie idle the voices come wild and angry, and grow louder!"

"Still, you must recuperate," Glyneth declared. "Therefore, rest is needful; nothing else will serve, since I dare not use Visbhume's tonics on you at random."

"I want none of Visbhume's stuffs," muttered Kul. "I feel better when we travel west; that is the command given into my mind, and I feel easy only when I obey."

"Very well then," said Glyneth. "We shall travel, but you must sit quietly and let me nurse you. I do not know what I would do if you sickened and died."

"Yes, that would be most tragic," Kul agreed. He sat up from the couch. "Let us be on our way. I feel better already!"

Once again the wole ran westward. Kul's spirits improved and he began to show traces of his old vitality.

The Plain of Lilies fell behind, and the Dark Woods, and presently the town Pude appeared in the distance. Kul took up Zaxa's two-handed sword Zil and went to stand in front of the pergola, legs apart and the point of the sword between his feet. On the high bench Glyneth arranged the blow-tube and the fire-mites, and made sure that the Tormentor bulbs were ready to hand.

Entering Pude, the wole cantered down the center of the main street, while folk peered down through the windows of their tall crabbed houses. No one came out to challenge their passage, and they crossed the bridge without a thought for the payment of toll.

With the River Haroo safely to the rear, Glyneth gave a nervous laugh. "We are not popular in Pude. The children did not bring us flowers and there was no trace of a celebration. Even the dogs refused to bark and the mayor hid under his bed."

Kul looked back with a grim smile. "To my great relief, since I too would like to hide and skulk. If the children struck me with a single flower petal I would fall flat; I lean on this sword to hold myself erect; I doubt if I could lift it to strike a blow if Visbhume's neck itself were the target."

"Why stand there then? Sit down and rest! Think strong and hopeful thoughts and soon you will be as healthy as ever!"

Kul limped back to the low bench. "We shall see."

Ahead lay the trackless Tang-Tang Steppe, and Glyneth began to fear that they might deviate from their course and so lose their way. The only dependable landmark was the pink star in the east, but to keep this star directly astern was a difficult task, and the two continually searched for landmarks along the way. They passed through the region of vast trees; as before the half-human tree-dwellers issued hysterical threats and made offensive signs. Kul steered the wole so as to veer around the trees and took refuge in the pergola. "I wish to provoke no one, not even these miserable creatures."

"Poor Kul!" said Glyneth. "But do not fret; soon you will grow strong again, and you will no longer take such frights. Meanwhile you may rely on me, since I have Visbhume's wallet ready to hand."

Kul made a growling noise in his throat. "It has not quite come to that yet. Though, for a fact, I am of little value."

Glyneth indignantly contradicted him. "Of course you are of value, especially to me! We shall go slowly and give you time to rest."

"Not so! Have you watched the black moon? It is moving around the sky! When we get to the hut, my work is done, and then I can rest."

Glyneth sighed. Such talk oppressed her. If she survived, she would never forget these strange journeys across the world Tanjecterly, and perhaps the dreadful events would lose their force, while Kul's companionship, the rests at the pleasant little cottage and the wonderful landscapes of Tanjecterly would assert their charm, to which for the time being she was numb. . . . Could it be possible that she would leave Tanjecterly with regret? Assuming, of course, that she were to leave. . . . Glyneth sighed again and gave her attention to the country-side.

Travel, then rest, and travel again, and each cycle brought new events. On one occasion the wole barely evaded a stampede of eight-legged ruminants, the size of large boars, dappled red and white with long tusks and tails ending in spiked knobs. Squealing, screaming, emitting a vile odor, the column of beasts a quarter-mile wide rushed past, from north to south, and finally disappeared.

Another time they passed by an encampment of swarthy human nomads, dressed in gaudy garments of black, yellow and red. Instantly scores of children ran out to beg, and the sight of Kul deterred them not at all. Glyneth had nothing to give them and they tore tassels from the wole's rug until Glyneth caused the wole to accelerate its pace and leave the encampment behind.

At this point Glyneth began to suspect that they had strayed from the most direct route across the steppe, and her suspicions were confirmed by the sight of two knolls, each crowned by a fortified castle, and, beyond, a crag of rock surmounted by a castle, even larger and more dire. As the wole ran past, a pair of enormous knights, each taller and more massive than Kul, rode down from the first two castles. One knight wore splendid purple armour with a crest of green plumes, while the other wore blue armour and orange plumes. They halted their steeds in front of the wole, and held up their arms in apparently amicable salute.

The purple knight asked: "Good gentlefolk, we extend our greetings and ask as to how and in what style you name yourselves?"

Glyneth responded from the top seat of the pergola. "I am the Princess Glyneth of Troicinet, and this is my paladin Sir Kul."

The blue knight said: "The place 'Troicinet' is unknown to us. Sir Kul, if I may say so, somewhat resembles a syaspic feroce, though his face, manner, and nobility of bearing, suggest the status you have ascribed to him."

"You show discernment," said Glyneth. "Sir Kul is under an enchant-ment and must use his present guise for a certain period."

"Aha!" declared the purple knight. "You have explained much."

The blue knight said: "We also note that Sir Kul stands with hands enclasping a great sword of uncommon fabric. It is much like the sword Zil, carried by the murderer Zaxa of Pude Town."

"True. Zaxa at one time wielded this sword, but he gave offense, and Sir Kul took both his life and his sword. It was a tedious exercise since Zaxa roared a great deal during his dying."

The two knights examined Kul askance. They conferred together, then the blue knight, moving to the side, blew a great blast on his horn.

The purple knight meanwhile came to address Glyneth and Kul: "In view of your victory over Zaxa, we implore you to kill his father, Sir Lulie, as well. Lulie is stronger by far than Zaxa and we feel no shame in admitting our own fear of him. Lulie is guilty of a thousand horrid deeds, with never so much as a wince of remorse, much less an apology."

Glyneth said hastily: "We deplore such misdeeds, but now we have no time to take action; in fact, we are already late for very important business."

"Is that truly the case?" asked the purple knight. "Then it seems that my brother was premature in sounding the challenge."

"Absolutely! We are now departing and you must explain to Sir Lulie as best you can. Kul, stir the wole to his best speed."

"Too late," called the purple knight. "I notice Sir Lulie riding down from his castle at this very moment."

With a sinking heart Glyneth watched the approach of Sir Lulie. He sat in a massive throne-like chair on a wole, and carried a lance forty feet long. He wore half-armour: a cuirass, greaves and a casque in the mold of a demon's head, with a crest of three black plumes.

Sir Lulie halted his steed at a distance of a hundred feet. He called out: "Who blew so brashly his horn, to disturb my rest? I am quite put out of sorts."

The blue knight spoke: "The horn was blown to announce the presence of invincible Sir Kul, who has already killed your son Zaxa and now wants to see the colour of your liver."

"That is a cruel ambition!" cried Lulie. "Sir Kul, why do you pursue such violent aims?"

"It seems to be my destiny," muttered Kul. "In this case, however, you are a bereaved father and I relent. Go back to your castle with your grief, and we will proceed. Our best wishes to all; goodbye."

The purple knight cried out: "Sir Kul, evidently you spoke in jest when you described Sir Lulie as 'the dog of a dog' and 'a coward whose deeds stink even worse than Sir Lulie himself!'"

Sir Lulie said: "I am not a sensitive person, but these remarks carry a sting."

Kul said: "Sir Lulie, your quarrel lies with yonder two knights, not me. Please excuse us from further conversation, as we are anxious to go our way."

"Still, you have killed my son Zaxa, and you carry his sword. If nothing else, this deed calls for retribution."

"I killed him when he attacked me. If you attack me, I will find some way to kill you."

"Ha ha! I interpret that remark as a challenge."

"It is not intended to be so. Please allow us to continue."

"Not until all accounts are settled. Climb from your perch. We will fight afoot, and you shall swing Zaxa's sword against his father, if you dare."

Kul turned to Glyneth. "Do not stay for me. Fare west, Glyneth, at all speed, and may good luck go with you."

Kul jumped down from the wole, carrying not Zaxa's unwieldy weapon but his own short heavy sword. He advanced toward Sir Lulie with that lurching, forward-leaning gait characteristic to him.

Lulie drew his sword from the scabbard, and flourished it high. "Devil-beast, behold my sword Kahanthus! Your time has come!"

On the top seat of the pergola Glyneth inserted a fire-mite into the tube, aimed carefully and blew. The pellet, spreading and beating its wings, flew through the eye-hole in Lulie's casque and struck with an explosion of white fire. Lulie gave voice to a wild ululation and, dropping his sword, clawed at his helmet. Kul cut down on Lulie's elbow, so that the fore-arm dangled loose at the joint. Lulie kicked, more by reflex than intent, and sent Kul hurtling through the air, and when he struck the ground he lay still. Lulie pulled away his casque and blinked here and there through his one remaining eye; he saw Kul and lunged down to choke him. Kul raised his sword and the point penetrated Lulie's neck under the chin and thrust up into the brain. Lulie slumped down upon Kul and the spike protruding from his cuirass stabbed Kul high in the chest.

Straining greatly, Glyneth rolled Lulie's corpse to the side. To staunch the red blood spurting from Kul's wound, she wadded a kerchief into the puncture, then ran to find Visbhume's wallet. She brought out the cake of wax and applied it in desperate haste. With the wound in Kul's chest finally staunched, Glyneth found to her dismay that blood welled from the wound in his back where the point of the spike had emerged.

The wounds in Kul's chest and back at last ceased to flow, but for a period Kul knelt with hanging head, coughing and spitting red foam from his lungs. At last he turned Glyneth a ghastly grin. "Once more I am well! Back to the wole; the black moon rolls!"

Kul rose swaying to his feet; with Glyneth's help he managed to clamber into the pergola, where he slumped heavily upon the bench.

The purple knight and the blue knight had long since departed, and now Glyneth saw them riding up the road to Sir Lulie's castle, whether to claim Sir Lulie's treasures or to liberate his captives she could not guess.

Now Glyneth steeled herself and, gritting her teeth, she pulled Kul's sword from the corpse, and, after wiping it clean on Sir Lulie's garments, she carried it to the wole.

Sir Lulie's sword, Kahanthus, lay on the turf: a blade of pale blue metal and a handle fitted with plaques of carved ebony and terminating in a glowing red ruby cabochon. The sword was heavy; with an effort Glyneth lifted it to the wole's back. Glyneth climbed aboard and once again the wole coursed into the west.

Kul slumped back with his eyes closed, his face pallid, his breath shallow and rasping from the blood still caught in his throat. Glyneth tried to make him comfortable, and sat close beside him, watching the flicker of expressions crossing his face. They became gradually more marked and more definite, and Glyneth began to feel eery chills at what she imagined she saw. At last she touched the gaunt cheek. "Kul! Wake up! You are dreaming bad dreams!"

Kul stirred. He groaned and drew himself up into a sitting position. Glyneth anxiously searched his face; to her relief she saw only the Kul whom she loved and trusted.

Glyneth asked: "Do you remember your dreams?"

After a moment Kul said: "They are gone now. I do not want to remember them."

"Perhaps we should stop to rest, until you feel stronger."

"I need no rest. We must travel as far and as fast as we can."

The wole ran on: league after league, across the blue grass. To the south a few two-legged wolves appeared from time to time, to appraise the wole and consult wisely among themselves, then to bound away through the trees.

Travel, rest, travel: across the Tang-Tang Steppe, a landscape whose aspect at last began to seem familiar. They passed the tall manse of the robber knight, whom Visbhume had tricked with his mirror; on this occasion no one came forth from the manse. Over the western horizon appeared the shadowy loom of mountains, and presently the River Mys swept down from the north to flow parallel to their course. The two-legged wolves, which had kept warily apart, became joined by a new troop whose elders, gesturing toward the wole, seemed to counsel bolder tactics. The band gradually closed in to run on either side of the wole, and also at the rear. One darted close and tried to gnaw at one of the wole's legs; the wole kicked the creature forward and trampled it without losing the rhythm of its stride.

Wearily Kul rose to his feet and took up his sword, and for a space the wolves drew back. Then, deciding that Kul posed no instant menace, they returned to bound close alongside, while two jumped up on the rug behind the pergola. Glyneth was ready with the tube and blew a fire-mite at the closest. It struck the creature's chest in a flash of blue and orange flame; the creature howled loud, and tumbled from the wole, to bounce here and there in wild convulsions. Glyneth aimed the tube at the second wolf, but it sagely hopped to the ground and ran skipping to the side.

After a few minutes the wolves loped off to the south and gathering in a circle discussed tactics, with much nodding of long-nosed faces and snapping in and out of thin black tongues. Meanwhile, Kul urged the wole to its best speed, and ahead, where the mountains began to swell up from beside the river, stood the hut.

The wolves loped once again to the attack. In accordance with their plan, they came up on both sides of the wole and jumped up to throw themselves on Kul. He chopped with his sword, hacking at reaching sucker-arms and heads, and cleared the space to the right, only to find the wolves surging upon his back from the left. Glyneth sent down fire-mite after fire-mite, until over the top of the pergola came a hairy arm to seize her around the neck, and a grinning long-nosed face looked closely into hers. She gasped and tore herself free and blew a fire-mite into the black mouth, and the creature departed, now concerned only with its own woeful destiny.

The hut was only a hundred yards distant, but the wolves had pulled Kul from the wole, which came to a confused and trembling halt while the wolves crowded in upon Kul. Finally, they carried him down and seethed over him in a yelping furry mass.

Kul found strength; he heaved himself erect, to stand with sucker arms clamped all over his body. Cursing and kicking, he tore himself free, then, lunging with his sword on high, seemed for a moment the Kul of old. But the wolves had tasted his blood and would not be denied. With snaps and yells they flung themselves upon Kul; he hacked and slashed, but his strokes were drained of force. He called to Glyneth: "Set up your house; secure yourself! I am done."

Glyneth looked frantically from side to side, then jumped to the ground and prepared to do Kul's bidding.

In the doorway of the hut appeared a tall man with dust-blond hair. Glyneth looked up incredulously and her knees went limp with joy. "Shimrod!"

"The portal is open, but not for long. Come."

"You must save Kul!"

Shimrod stepped out on the plain. He held up his hand; from his fingers came darts of black fire, which, striking the wolves, shrivelled them to wisps of gray ash. A few fled shrieking to the east; the black darts followed them and struck them down one by one, and all were gone.

Glyneth ran to Kul and tried to support his swaying form. "Kul! We are saved! Shimrod has come!"

Kul looked around with dull eyes. He croaked: "Shimrod, I have done your bidding, to my best ability."

"Kul, you have done well."

"In truth, I am already dead; now I will lie down and become still." Kul sank to his knees.

Glyneth cried out: "Kul, do not die! Shimrod will make you strong again!"

Kul spoke huskily: "Dear Glyneth, go back to Earth. I cannot come with you. I am a motley thing, held together with red blood, and now all my blood is gone. Glyneth, goodbye."

Glyneth raved: "Kul, only a few moments more! Do not die! I love you dearly and I cannot leave you here! Kul? Can you speak?"

Shimrod took her arm and raised her to her feet. "Glyneth, it is time to go. You can not help Kul; he is about to return to his matrices and it is better that you come with me. Kul's body is dead but his love for you is very much alive. Come."

IV

SHIMROD LED GLYNETH TO THE HUT. She halted. "On the wole are two great swords; please, Shimrod, bring them with us."

Shimrod led her to the door. "Go through the gate. I will go for the swords. But do not go out; wait for me in the hut."

Numbly Glyneth stepped through the door and entered the hut. For an instant she looked back over her shoulder toward Kul. After a single glimpse she turned her head away.

Something was different. She breathed deeply. This was the air of Earth; it carried the beloved odor of her own foliage and her own soil.

Shimrod came into the hut, staggering under the weight of the two swords. He laid them upon the table and, turning to Glyneth, took her hands. "You loved Kul, and properly so; had you not I would think you heartless and unnatural, which is foolishness since I know your loving nature too well. Kul was a magical being, constructed from two patterns: the syaspic feroce and a barbarian pirate from a far moon, named Kul the Killer. These two patterns, superimposed, made a terrible creature, relentless and indomitable. To give it life and a soul, with love and loyalty for you, we gave it the blood of someone who loves you. Indeed, he gave almost all his blood and also the whole strength of his soul. Kul is dead but these are alive."

Glyneth, crying and smiling at the same time, asked: "And who was this person who loves me? Am I to know? Or must I guess?"

"I doubt if you need to guess."

Glyneth looked at him sidelong. "You love me and Dhrun loves me, but I think that you are speaking of Aillas. . . . Is he outside?"

"No. I gave him no hint that the quaver was open. If you were not at the hut or if you had come to harm, he would only be tortured all over again. Kul did not fail and Murgen did not fail; and you are here. Now I will bring Aillas here by magic. You may come out when I call you."

Shimrod departed the hut. Glyneth went to the table and looked down upon the swords Zil and Kahanthus, and her mind went back to Tanjecterly and the long way to Asphrodiske. For a moment she wondered as to Visbhume.

A minute passed. From outside she heard voices, and started to go out, then, remembering Shimrod's instructions, waited.

Shimrod called: "Glyneth! Are you there? Or have you gone back to Tanjecterly?"

Glyneth went to the door and into the dappled sunlight of the forest. Beside a carriage Aillas waited for her.

Shimrod carried the swords to the carriage and said: "I will await you at Watershade; do not loiter along the way!" He went off through the forest and was gone.

Aillas came forward and took Glyneth in his arms. "My beloved Glyneth, I will never let you leave me again."

After a moment he released her and looked carefully into her face. Glyneth, smiling, asked: "Why do you look at me so?"

"Because under my very eyes you have become the most beautiful and appealing of all maidens alive."

"Truly, Aillas? Despite my soiled clothes and dirty face?"

"Truly."

Glyneth laughed. "Sometimes I despaired of attracting your attention."

"No fear of that now. In fact I am afflicted with all the tremors and doubts of the uncertain lover. I am anxious to learn of your adventures. How did your paladin Kul serve you?"

"He served me so well that I came to love him too! I should say, I came to love that part of Kul which was you. I saw glimpses of the feroce and of Kul the Killer and both frightened me; and then always you seemed to appear and set things right."

Aillas said ruefully: "I seem to have done much which I do not remember. . . . Well, no matter. Kul brought you back to me, so I must not be jealous. Here is our carriage. Let us be away to Watershade, and the happiest banquets the old stones have ever known."

Epilog

THE GREEN PEARL is locked in a bottle and Tamurello's guise, the skeleton of a crouching weasel in green aspic, is probably the least comfortable of any he has yet known. . . . The Forest of Tantrevalles shades a deep dank soil; somewhere under this mold lies the carcass of a snake which in better times used the name Visbhume; he no longer tippety-taps and moves and jerks to the rhythms of a propulsive inner music; and sometimes one wonders in cases like this: here is the dead thing; where has the music gone?

Tamurello and Visbhume are extraordinary folk, beyond a doubt, and both have come to grief. Still, the Elder Isles abound with remarkable folk, whose ambitions often transcend the advisable and sometimes even the possible.

As an example the Ska renegade Torqual might be cited. He has survived his wounds and now mends his strength in his inaccessible castle. Here he thinks bitter thoughts and forms gloomy plots, and he has vowed revenge upon the young Troice warrior who worked such grievous mischief upon him.

Queen Sollace of Lyonesse fervently hopes to build a cathedral. Father Umphred assures her that if King Casmir were converted to Christianity, he might be more sympathetic to the cathedral. Queen Sollace agrees, but how to convert King Casmir? Perhaps with the aid of some holy relic. Several centuries before, Joseph of Arimathea brought the Holy Grail down to the Elder Isles from Glastonbury Abbey; for Queen Sollace's purposes the Holy Grail would serve very well, and Father Umphred enthusiastically agrees.

King Casmir is still perturbed by the prediction of Persilian the Magic Mirror and still lacks knowledge as to the identity of Suldrun's first-born son.

The Princess Madouc of Lyonesse occupies an unenviable position. King Casmir knows her to be a changeling, with none of his blood flowing in her veins. Still, she may serve him some useful purpose when she reaches marriageable age. Madouc, by the very nature of things, is a strange little creature, with even less patience than the tragic Princess Suldrun for the conventions of the court at Haidion; and the third in the set of chronicles of the Elder Isles is:

Lyonesse III: *Madouc*

Glossary I

THE ELDER ISLES during the course of ten thousand years had known incursions, migrations, armed invasion, as well as the coming and going of traders to their commercial depots, at Ys, Avallon, Domreis and Bulmer Skeme: all founded by foreign traders.

From every direction came the newcomers: pre-glacial folk with identities lost to history; what indigenes they discovered can only be a matter of speculation. Later came Kornutians, Bithynians, a remarkable folk known as the Golden Khaz, and presently contingents of Escquahar (precursors elsewhere to the Basques, the Berbers of Morocco, the Guanches of the Canary Islands, and the Blue Men of Mauretania).

Then later, and sometimes in a succession of waves: Pelasgians, blond Sarsele from Tingitana, Danaans and Galicians from Spain, Greeks from Hellas, Sicily and Low Gaul; a few shiploads of Lydians turned away from Tuscany; Celts from all directions under a host of names; and in due course Romans from Aquitania, who toyed with the idea of conquest but presently departed, taking with them the Christian doxology. A few Goths and Armoricans settled along the shores of Wysrod, while new bands of Celts from Britain and Ireland took advantage of weak Daut rulers to establish the Kingdom of Godelia. Finally, from Norway by way of Ireland* came the Ska, who settled on Skaghane and other of the Outer Isles, from which they moved into North Ulfland.

---

*See Glossary II, this book. Also see *LYONESSE I: Suldren's Garden*, Glossary III.

Glossary II

THE HISTORY OF THE SKA was an epic in itself. Originally the indigenous inhabitants of Norway since before the ice-age, they were expelled by invading Aryan Ur-Goths and driven south to Ireland where they entered Irish history as the Nemedians.

The Ur-goths, now supreme in Scandinavia, adopted Ska folk-ways and in due course sent hordes back into Europe: Ostrogoths, Visigoths, Vandals, Gepids, Lombards, Angles, Saxons, and other German tribes. Those who remained in Scandinavia called themselves 'Vikings' and using boats built after the Ska designs, ranged the Atlantic, the Mediterranean and the navigable rivers of Europe.

The Ska, defeated in Ireland by the Fomorians, again were compelled to migrate. They sailed south from Ireland to Skaghane, westernmost of the Elder Isles, where they found an environment much to their liking.

At a Grand Moot, they bound themselves by three great vows, which are basic to any understanding of the complex and contradictory Ska character:

First: Never again would the Ska be driven from their homeland.

Second: The Ska were at war with all the world's peoples: so it had been demonstrated; so it was.

Third: The blood of the Ska race ran pure. Interbreeding with Otherling sub-folk was a crime as abominable as treachery, cowardice or murder.

Glossary III

AILLAS HAD BEEN THE LOVER of Casmir's daughter, Suldrun, and the father of their son, Dhrun, who had been taken by the fairies of Thripsey Shee and replaced with the half-fairy changeling who became the Princess Madouc of Lyonesse.

Happily for King Casmir's peace of mind, he knew nothing of these facts and so was mightily perplexed by the prophecy uttered by the magic mirror Persilian, to the effect that Suldrun's first-born son before his death would sit on the throne Evandig and also in honour and authority at the Board of Notables, the ancient 'Cairbra an Meadhan' — this table in fact, the model for the Round Table of King Arthur of Cornwall, still two generations in the future.

The world's greatest science fiction authors now available in Panther Books

Brian W Aldiss

Helliconia Spring	£2.50	☐
Helliconia Summer	£2.50	☐
New Arrivals, Old Encounters	£1.95	☐
Frankenstein Unbound	£1.25	☐
Moreau's Other Island	£1.95	☐
Last Orders	£1.95	☐
Galaxies Like Grains of Sand	£1.95	☐
The Dark Light Years	£1.95	☐
Barefoot in the Head	£1.25	☐
Space, Time and Nathaniel	£1.25	☐
Starswarm	£1.25	☐
Hothouse	£1.95	☐
Cryptozoic	£1.95	☐
Earthworks	£1.95	☐
Brothers of the Head	£1.25	☐
Moment of Eclipse	£1.25	☐
Greybeard	£1.95	☐
Enemies of the System	£1.95	☐

General Fiction

The Malacia Tapestry	£1.95	☐

Introduction by Brian Aldiss

Let's Go to Golgotha	95p	☐

Brian Aldiss with Harry Harrison (Editors)

Farewell Fantastic Venus!	75p	☐

To order direct from the publisher just tick the titles you want
and fill in the order form. **SF781**

The world's greatest science fiction authors now available in Panther Books

Piers Anthony
'Cluster' series

Vicinity Cluster	£1.95	☐
Chaining the Lady	£1.95	☐
Kirlian Quest	£1.95	☐
Viscous Circle	£1.95	☐
Thousandstar	£1.95	☐

'Tarot' series

God of Tarot	£1.50	☐
Vision of Tarot	£1.50	☐
Faith of Tarot	£1.50	☐

'Split Infinity' series

Split Infinity	£2.50	☐
Blue Adept	£1.95	☐
Juxtaposition	£2.50	☐

'Bio of a Space Tyrant' series

Refugee	£1.95	☐

'Incarnations of Immortality' series

On a Pale Horse	£2.50	☐

Other Titles

Phthor	85p	☐
Chthon	£1.50	☐

Fritz Leiber
'Swords' series

The Swords of Lankhmar	85p	☐

Other Titles

A Spectre is Haunting Texas	£1.25	☐
Ship of Shadows	£1.50	☐

To order direct from the publisher just tick the titles you want and fill in the order form.

SF681

Isaac Asimov, grand master of science fiction
now available in Panther Books

The 'Foundation' Series

Foundation	£1.95	☐
Foundation and Empire	£1.95	☐
Second Foundation	£1.95	☐
Foundation's Edge	£1.95	☐

Other Titles

The Science Fictional Solar System (editor)	£1.50	☐
Opus: The Best of Isaac Asimov	£2.50	☐
The Bicentennial Man	£1.50	☐
Buy Jupiter!	£1.95	☐
The Gods Themselves	£1.50	☐
The Early Asimov (Volume 1)	£1.50	☐
The Early Asimov (Volume 2)	£1.50	☐
The Early Asimov (Volume 3)	£1.50	☐
Earth is Room Enough	£1.95	☐
The Stars Like Dust	£1.50	☐
The Martian Way	£1.50	☐
The Currents of Space	£1.25	☐
Nightfall One	£1.25	☐
Nightfall Two	£1.25	☐
The End of Eternity	£1.25	☐
I, Robot	£1.95	☐
The Rest of the Robots	£1.95	☐
The Complete Robot	£2.95	☐
Asimov's Mysteries	£1.25	☐
The Caves of Steel	£1.95	☐
The Naked Sun	£1.95	☐
The Robots of Dawn	£2.50	☐
Nebula Award Stories 8 (editor)	95p	☐
The Left Hand of the Electron (non-fiction)	75p	☐
The Stars in their Courses (non-fiction)	£1.50	☐

To order direct from the publisher just tick the titles you want
and fill in the order form.   **SF181**

The world's greatest science fiction authors
now available in Panther Books

Philip José Farmer
The Riverworld Saga

Other Titles

To order direct from the publisher just tick the titles you want
and fill in the order form. **SF281**

The world's greatest science fiction authors
now available in Panther Books

Robert Silverberg

Earth's Other Shadow	£1.50	☐
The World Inside	£1.50	☐
Tower of Glass	£1.50	☐
Recalled to Life	£1.50	☐
Invaders from Earth	£1.50	☐
Master of Life and Death	£1.50	☐

J G Ballard

The Crystal World	£2.50	☐
The Drought	£2.50	☐
Hello America	£1.50	☐
The Disaster Area	£2.50	☐
Crash	£2.50	☐
Low-Flying Aircraft	£2.50	☐
The Atrocity Exhibition	£1.50	☐
The Venus Hunters	£2.50	☐
The Day of Forever	£2.50	☐
The Unlimited Dream Company	£2.50	☐
Concrete Island	£2.50	☐

Philip Mann

The Eye of the Queen	£1.95	☐

To order direct from the publisher just tick the titles you want
and fill in the order form.   **SF581**

All these books are available at your local bookshop or newsagent, or can be ordered direct from the publisher..

To order direct from the publisher just tick the titles you want and fill in the form below.

Name_____

Address _____

Send to:
Panther Cash Sales
PO Box 11, Falmouth, Cornwall TR10 9EN.

Please enclose remittance to the value of the cover price plus:

UK 45p for the first book, 20p for the second book plus 14p per copy for each additional book ordered to a maximum charge of £1.63.

BFPO and Eire 45p for the first book, 20p for the second book plus 14p per copy for the next 7 books, thereafter 8p per book.

Overseas 75p for the first book and 21p for each additional book.

Panther Books reserve the right to show new retail prices on covers, which may differ from those previously advertised in the text or elsewhere.